GRAYSON'S KNIFE

GRAYSON'S KNIFE

KNIFE

Russell H. Aborn

ISBN 13: 9781709656392

DEDICATION

To Susan
And my parents

ACKNOWLEDGEMENT

Many thanks to Dennis Lehane and Tom Bernardo for their support during the early days of writing this and for their friendship over the years.

My business partner and good friend Jill Clifford covered for me in work and encouraged me to keep at it.

My wife, Susan M. Aborn, kept after me to finish and wouldn't let me quit when the going got tough.

"And that is the terrible myth of organized society, that everything that's done through the established system is legal—and that word has a powerful psychological impact. And therefore, society can turn its conscience off, and look to other things at other times."

William Kuntsler
February 1970

CHAPTER ONE

Michael Grayson, plagued by yet another hangover, is mocked by the memory of his latest vow of abstinence. He winces periodically, as random bolts of pain section his brain, like lightning in a thundercloud.

He says, "I was still sleeping when you woke me up."

Hugh Grayson says, "That's the way it works. You have to be asleep if you're going to wake up. Plus, you were drooling on my couch."

"Aren't you getting a new one, or something? Where are you looking?"

"Sure, let's talk furniture. Way to change the subject," Hugh says.

"There is no subject. I told you yesterday, no. Count me out."

It's a murky, pre-dawn March morning and the Grayson brothers sit in Hugh's brand new 1973 Ford Galaxy 500 parked at the sea wall on the shore of Quincy Bay at Wollaston Beach.

"Look," Hugh Grayson says. "You owe me, you know it, and I know it and this is what I'm asking."

Hugh holds a large take-out coffee in his left hand, as does Michael, who is known to everybody but family and his ex-fiancé, as Grayson. He alternates small sips of coffee with great drafts of orange juice from the half gallon carton in his right hand.

Hugh says, "These are students, at the pharmacy college, so they're not like real drug dealers, with loads of firepower and so on. I need you to drive and for you and Donny be the muscle, to discourage them. You'd have a third duty to keep Donny from acting up. But, if you're stiffing me, I guess I can have Charlie drive. He should be able to handle Donny, too. Charlie goes, what, 125 pounds?"

"Charlie is going to drive? Have you ever seen his car? We call it the golf ball; it's got a million little dents."

Hugh waves his hand dismissively. "Don't worry about it, if you're not going. It's not your problem."

"I thought it was going to be a walk in the park?"

"Just an abundance of caution. Belt and suspenders."

Quincy Bay hides out in the gloaming, quiet, shallow and well protected, and on clear days it has the aspect of a large lake. The scattered islands and protective peninsulas that make up this part of Boston Harbor shelter the beach, and today there is no wind to break up the light gray curtain of fog that hangs from the grayer clouds to a point just above the dark gray water.

Grayson swallows some OJ, even though the acid in the juice isn't helping his stomach any.

"Why are you doing this?" he says.

"I need money, quickly," Hugh says. "I owe Gumby."

"You borrowed from Gumby? To pay gambling debts? What the fuck?" Grayson says. "I suppose you went to China Blue last night?"

Hugh says, "No, the Dragon. I landed on a very bad run of cards, right away. And, because I didn't have enough money to wait it out, I got trimmed before my luck had a chance to come back."

Hugh loosens his necktie a little. His suitcoat is hanging in the back seat. He has a sales conference in two hours.

Grayson says, "That makes zero sense."

"Because you don't know anything about it. My error was not having enough cash to hang in until my luck came back."

Hugh believes in luck the way Job believed in God.

"I've got money saved," Grayson says. "How much do you need?"

"I'm not borrowing from you."

"No. But you'll take money from a loan shark, knowing when you can't pay it back, he'll cut your ears off and give them to his dog for chew toys."

"Twenty thousand, give or take. Do you have that much laying around?" Hugh says.

Grayson is shocked.

"If so," Hugh says, "Great, hand it over. Because I wish Gumby would only cut my ears off. He's a pain fiend. That's the part of the business he likes most.

"So why would you go to him?"

Grayson's head is swimming, stunned by the amount of money Hugh owes Gumby.

"Why? You could almost buy a house for that money. What'd you do with it? That's like a year's pay. For me."

"This and that, you know. And I didn't borrow it all at once."

"So, you had to make a series of stupid decisions."

Hugh does a 'so what' shrug. "In any event, it's done. I choose to focus on the future."

"You have a nice sales job, an expense account, a brand-new company vehicle," Grayson says, sweeping a hand around the car. "What the heck?"

Hugh says nothing, maybe letting the big, scary number do the work.

Twenty thousand dollars. Not to mention Gumby.

Hugh points out through the windshield where the beach is hiding.

"Or if Gumby's really mad, he'll have his guys bury me up to my neck in The Muck at low tide."

Because the beach is so well sheltered, the rising tide does not arrive in waves, but instead the water slides in on its belly, like a reptile. One of the side effects of the beach being sheltered is The Muck, and its' signature, rotten egg smell, which is, in many ways, the smell of their childhood.

"Well, if you're not going to help me there's no point in talking anymore. Hop out."

Hugh sounds resigned, like he's giving up.

Grayson, too, is done. It's getting harder to say no.

"Sorry." He grabs the door handle, just as Hugh grabs his shoulder.

Hugh says, "Listen, let me give you a few more facts. They're not kids, they're our age. Just listen. They're selling pharmaceutical grade drugs, drugs that they've stolen from the VA in Jamaica Plain, where they have these low wage, on-the-job, work-study type gigs. What they've learned so far is how to order extra narcotics from the suppliers, sneak them out of the hospital and have the VA pay for it."

"Stealing medicine from hospitalized veterans in JP? That's nice."

"Donny said yes, and he's a vet, and it obviously won't impact those guys, but Donny has no sense of proportion when things get rough, so I need you to keep him in check."

Donny Gates, their first cousin, is 6'5" and weighs 280, about the same size as a newborn killer whale. Starting at age 14, he began lifting weights daily and for a while he practiced a menacing smile in the bathroom mirror, and all credit to him, he got crackerjack results. When that empty eyed smile beams from his big face atop that giant body, he looks like a head from Easter Island. That smile could cause Dirty Harry or Mean Joe Greene to lose bladder control.

Hugh says, "And it has to be Saturday night because of all the St. Patrick's Day parties. There will be a bunch of them all around that college area. The Fenway, Allston, Beacon St, Comm Ave, there will be parties everywhere. A girl in their building is having a party, so that's where we'll go. So, the pharm boys snatched extra supplies to sell to the party goers. The pharmers are somewhat cautious about who they sell to, but they also know if their screening is too tight, they won't move much product. They rely on their friends to refer customers. So, all you have to do is let Donny do his thing with the girl throwing the party, get her to call upstairs, then you guys go and knock and say you're from the party downstairs. Charlie will be front and center at the keyhole up at the pharm boy's door, looking as harmless and friendly as only he can."

"Where are you going to be? At the movies?"

"Hanging out on the fifth-floor stairwell, waiting for you to get them to open the door."

"I'm too busy," Grayson says.

"Well get un-busy. You owe me. And Gumby is going to fuck me up if I don't get him his money by next Friday. Besides, these pharmacy guys are total feebs." Hugh waves his hand dismissively.

"So, it's okay to have Donny bounce them off the floor so you can take their money. And the drugs, too, I bet."

"We take only the money. If we take the drugs and sell them, then we're drug dealers, too, and as bad as them. You know I can't go for that." Hugh says. He looks at Grayson, as if hoping for applause.

Grayson says, "You're a fine man and a great American."

"Plus, this other guy is taking the drugs."

"What other guy? Who's the other guy? You never said there's another guy."

"You can't expect to know everything, if you haven't committed. This guy has done stuff like this before and will help us. We're meeting tomorrow night to go over everything in detail. All I want you to do is manage Donny, and be another big body to discourage them from even trying to resist, and also to drive."

Grayson shakes his head a little bit, and quickly regrets it.

"No more gambling, right? You're going to quit," Grayson says.

"Yeah. You quit drinking and I'll quit gambling and Ma will live to be a hundred, Paul will turn out to be still alive in Vietnam, and we'll all live happily ever after. Right after we do this."

"Who's the guy who's helping?"

"If you're in you'll meet him Friday. His name is Bird. He's a badass," Hugh says.

"No guns, right?"

"I don't know. I'm not telling Bird what to do. But, if he does, he won't use it except to scare people. He's already been acquitted of manslaughter, so he's not looking for trouble."

Grayson keeps his face forward. "If you want a winning bet, bet this is going to end up going sideways."

"All the more reason to help. Protect me. From myself," Hugh says, and forces a phony laugh. "And, I need Donny, for two reasons, but as we know, he can be unpredictable. One, in case multiple parties need punching, and two, because it's a chick who's throwing the party."

When not projecting menace, Donny is a big hit with the ladies. He looks like the Superman in the funny books, and women vibrate like tuning forks when he comes into a room. He loves the women and the women love him right back.

Grayson says, "How the hell do you know all this?"

"I got the idea a couple of weeks ago. You remember that story I showed you from the newspaper?" Hugh says.

"No."

"Here, this one."

Hugh pulls down a newspaper clipping from the visor. Grayson reads about an apartment on Bay State Rd. in Kenmore Square that had been invaded. Neighbors had heard loud noises and called the police. When the Boston cops arrived some young men in the apartment appeared to have been beaten up and their place had obviously been tossed. The boy's faces were flushed, swollen and bloodied, one had a broken nose and another was icing a large knot on his head. The neighbors griped to the police that based on the amount and kind of traffic at the apartment, they long suspected drugs were being sold inside. The young men said no, unh-unh, no way. Asked why they were disheveled to such a degree, they claimed they'd merely been rough housing. The Boston police force is comprised largely of WWII vets, men now middle-aged. They had seen real trouble close-up in their youth, so they know real trouble, and this isn't it. Their official motto is, "To serve and protect," but their working motto was, "Don't bother me with your stupid shit.' The cops likely pretended to believe the kids so they could head back to the station and get off work on-time.

A reporter from the newspaper must have heard the call on a police band radio. He showed up and tried to get the kids talking, but only managed to interview the neighbors. On another, busier night, the story might have gone unreported.

Grayson says, "These pharmacy kids might have seen this story, too. What if they have protection?"

"These kids are feebs, rich snots, from like Hingham or Marblehead. They hope to be pharmacists, for Pete's sake. They do have a neighbor who's supposed to provide security, but he's some burnout, an older guy, he's like twenty-six or seven, but it's only one guy. Like I said, Bird might be armed and anyway, Donny's like having three guys."

"How do you know all this? Did you put this together?"

Hugh says, "It's a long story that doesn't matter. The drug kids are paying the girl having the party a commission if she sends buyers up."

"They might have guns. What then?"

"Not likely."

"If you get shot that will kill Ma."

"This is not going to be a big deal. We're not robbing Brink's. These fancy pants will roll over like trained seals," Hugh says.

"What about the older guy? The burn-out neighbor. He could be a mental case."

"With all of us going, we'll be equipped to deal with whatever comes our way."

Grayson says, "You will never be out of the hole. Not until you stop gambling."

"Wisdom from The Shitface Kid."

"Yeah, that's right. The Shitface Kid. The guy you need for this idiotic plan. I'm a fuck up, and you're counting on me. That makes you worse. Listen, let me lend it to you."

"I don't want to borrow money," Hugh says.

"You're in this mess from borrowing money! From a sadist masquerading as a loan shark."

"I mean borrow *more* money"

"All right. I'll *give* you all the money I saved. I don't need it anymore."

"Are you talking about the money you and Catherine saved to get married? For a house? The money you've been saving since high school? No thanks."

Grayson says, "Don't worry. No more wedding. That's over with. She's not even talking to me. For the rest of my life, she says."

11

"Again? From New Year's Eve? Or is that one fixed and you're working on the second breakup of 1973?"

"New Year's."

"Wow," says Hugh. "That's a long breakup for you two." He puts a hand on his brother's shoulder. "Keep your money. She'll change her mind. She has before, right? Come over to my place Friday night and just listen. Donny's coming, you can meet Bird. Then if you don't like the plan, don't come with us. But hear us out. I do need your help."

Brother Hugh has him boxed in. If he doesn't help Hugh, and something goes wrong, Grayson will blame himself. Plus, if Donny's agreed to go, the potential looms large for things to get out of hand, and Grayson does have a knack for keeping Donny focused. If they get away with it, whatever this "it" is, there would be another "it" soon enough, because at the heart of Hugh's gambling was neither winning nor losing money, it was all about the rush. He started gambling when he could no longer play football.

"It's not really about the money, is it? It's about the adrenaline buzz, right?"

"Is that your diagnosis, Doctor Freud?" Hugh smiles, but he doesn't deny it. "Let's go. We have to get to work."

CHAPTER TWO

G rayson slides his time card under the clock
face in the last half of the final second before it would have snapped past his start time at
Triple T Trucking.

"Did you make it?" Rosario the dispatcher says,
grinning.

Grayson looked at the card to be sure the time
stamp confirmed he had indeed made it, and it
read: 7:00 AM March 15, 1973.

"Why do you have to cut it so close?" Rosie says.

Rosie leans back against the counter at a pre-
cipitous angle, his fingers loosely intertwined at his
belt buckle and his legs crossed at the ankles. This
pose of amused nonchalance is made poignant by

the great likelihood that within the hour some minor setback, a load that isn't ready or a truck that won't start, would have him unhinged.

Grayson says, "To keep you in suspense."

Grayson is still slow witted after only three hours of fitful sleep, looks at his card again and says, "Hey, be nice. Today's my birthday."

"BFD," Rosie says.

"Birthday-fun-day?"

"Is that why you look like hell? Again?" Rosie says. He takes some paperwork from the counter and straightens up. Another driver, Normand Frechette, an old Fall River Frenchman, comes out of the men's room, drying his hands on a paper towel.

"I'm twenty-two."

"Jeez. You look older than twenty-two. Don't he, Normand?"

Normand shrugs. Grayson sighs and looks up at the nicotine-stained panels on the dropped ceiling of the break room, his eye caught by the rapid flicker of a fluorescent tube in the recessed bank of lights.

"Alright, already," Rosie says. "Let's get to work."

Through the glass door Grayson sees brother Hugh heading in to the conference room with the other salesmen, all of them clutching yellow pads on the off chance their boss says something that makes any sense, which they'll write down to commemorate the date.

Rosie hands Grayson a freight bill tucked into a typed-out driver's manifest. The freight bill is for the delivery of a trailer load of shirts to the new Jordan Marsh warehouse in North Quincy. Rosie then hands a manifest to Normand.

"Procter and Gamble," Rosie says to Normand.

"What's this?" Grayson says. "Jordan's? Give this to Normand. Give me the soap. I like the exercise." He turns to Normand. "Normand, I had this load before, it's those tee shirts, from New Bedford. It's all on pallets. You just have to cut the shrink wrap, then stand on the dock and make believe you're counting. It's ice cream, man."

Old Normand is about five-six, and so thin he's damn near two dimensional. A P&G load weighs 45,000 pounds, and every 50-pound box of it has to be stripped off of the conveyer, and stacked, right up to the roof of the trailer. Normand is older than Grayson's father, who has already been forced into retirement by the company because he was too old and worn out to keep up with the work.

Normand is not shy with his opinions, but he is economical in speech since he has to deal with the challenge of a profound stutter. In the warm up to speak he begins snapping his chops together like an alligator going after a team of ducks.

Whimsy gone, Rosie glares at Grayson while Normand clacks his teeth together.

Grayson shrugs. "It's just I hate standing around. I like being busy."

"You know what?" Rosie says. "Guess what? Who cares?"

Rosie claims to start each day afresh, with a positive attitude, and advises his drivers to do likewise, but it is clear his daily frustrations accrete. He yanks off his clip-on necktie and undoes the collar button on his short sleeve white shirt. If he didn't do it now, he's certain to have the tie off before he takes on the big 8:30 AM crew, fifty-two bumptious Teamsters.

Rosie says, "I don't make decisions based on what makes you happy, my boy. You're not the center of the universe."

Normand ceases his exertions, puts his hands on his hips and smiles.

Grayson says, "Yeah, sure, like you know where it is."

Rosie scrunches up his face, making his disdain evident.

"You don't know," Grayson says. "It might be me."

"Yeah?" Rosie says. "If you go in the toilet to take a wiz, does the center move with you? Or does it stay here in the driver's room?"

"No, the whole universe kind of shifts." He gestures with arms wide, as if making a slight turn on a giant steering wheel hovering chest high. "But not that much in universe terms. The shitter ain't too far away."

Normand laughs and points at Grayson. Normand's mouth is agape; he snaps it shut a few times, then moves on to Plan B, and begins to nod with vigor. He reaches up and puts his hand on Grayson's shoulder and they wait until his nodding head pumps the words up and out into the air.

"We know!" Normand shouts. "The shitter is you!" He smiles, all the way back to the bottom of his ears, and then walks off a dozen steps, stops, turns, and poses a moment. On Normand's home turf of Fall River this act symbolizes getting in the last word. A long moment passes, and he apparently feels that it has been established he has gotten in the last word, so he comes back.

"I don't want this Jordan's load," Grayson says. "Stand there like a drip all day. Is that P&G a full load, Normand?"

Normand takes his glasses out of the vinyl case clipped to his shirt pocket. The brown case is imprinted with the Teamster coat of arms, a spoked wheel with two horses above it, Thunder and Lightning, facing in opposite directions. He flicks open the arms of the black framed glasses, puts them on in a deliberate manner, then unfolds his delivery manifest to its full length and lifts and drops and lifts his chin several times looking it over, like a town crier about to issue a proclamation.

Meanwhile, Rosie seethes. After several seconds, he beats Normand to the punch.

"Enough! Shut up, Normand." Rosie points at Grayson. "Who's the boss here? Huh? Me, that's who. So, take the load and go, mister. If you don't, I will take your refusal as a resignation."

"Wow," Grayson says. "Don't have a conniption."

"You're just dropping the trailer at Jordan Marsh," Rosie says. "Grab the empty there and bring it back. I need you to peddle downtown today. Mike G. McCarthy booked off. So, move it." It's Boston, and there are multiple Mike McCarthy's' in most workplaces so they are forced to go to middle initials for specificity.

Grayson could have squawked about union rules and bid jobs, but didn't, since now it seemed like Rosie assigned the easier job to Normand. Peddling freight in a straight truck is a young man's work. Grayson actually likes banging a P&D run around in the city, not all the time, but occasionally, because when you drove a straight job on a P&D run you work hard and fight the clock all day, trying to make all your deliveries and pickups.

It is like a day-long two-minute drill in football, and the time flies by. Hustling a straight truck around in downtown Boston and the Back Bay on a near-spring day is a good way to see a lot of pretty college girls going to class, or sharply dressed women going to work.

He and Normand walk down the ramp and out into the terminal yard as Normand tussles with his speech apparatus.

"Why did you squawk?" he says, at long last.

Grayson says, "To see how quick his necktie would come undone."

He does the drop and hook at Jordan's, returns to the terminal and gets the paperwork for the downtown peddle. He walks out to the dock and looks into the back of his load. He sees four shrink wrapped pallets about midway up in the truck. On the way back out, he stops at his car to retrieve his shades, an extra deck of smokes and a paperback. He also roots around in the trunk, looking for his utility knife, to cut the shrink wrap on the pallets. He makes sure the blade is fully retracted before he puts it in his pocket. One of the guys he works with did not check the blade on his box cutter and as a result, he slit a hole in his pants pocket, and cut his leg to boot.

Grayson hustles around the city the rest of the morning, making deliveries in a Mack cab-over diesel straight truck. The cab-over is a terrific piece of machinery for working the city. The face of the truck is flat with the top half all glass. The road is about two feet in front of the driver's nose, and the front wheels are right below him. The wheels can be turned almost side-ways and the truck can get into and out of spots that conventional trucks can't. One drawback is it gets hot in the cab and with the windows down, it is also loud; the diesel engine mixes a clatter with a roar and a whistling undertone.

Sometime before noon, the Mack is stopped at a red light in the far-right lane on Arlington St. near the entrance of the Mass Pike. Grayson picks up his clipboard and is looking at the receipt for his last delivery when out of the corner of his eye he sees a motley band of young guys crossing the street by the high school on the corner. He puts the board down, happy he padlocked the back door of the truck. He looks a little closer at the boys who are by now loosely occupying the middle of the street. These guys, not content to just cut class, are making a raucous escape, raising a racket, loud voices, big showy gestures, playing to the captive audience in the vehicles bunched up at the stoplight.

The leading edge of the crew is in front of the truck now, and one large, fattish boy emboldened by his cohorts, and, from the look of his rosy cheeks, way overexcited, comes up to the center of the windshield and looks at Grayson.

"Hey, buddy, that's a nice bulldog," the red-faced shithead says, pointing to the chrome hood ornament Mack attaches to every truck. "I think I'll take it home."

With that, the big boy climbs on the front bumper and yanks at the bulldog, while being cheered on by his fellow birdbrains. Grayson slips the transmission into neutral, smiles and stomps on the gas pedal. The big diesel roars, and simultaneously, the fat kid launches himself off the front bumper and lands flat on his back in the road, while his pals jump straight up, and their legs churn the air like cartoon characters. The would-be bulldog snatcher is ass down on the asphalt and wicked quick for a fat kid; he rolls over in a blurry whirl until he reaches the safety of the gutter.

"Nice reflexes, Pugsley," Grayson yells through the open window.

The doughy desperado is on the sidewalk now with his boys, and they are all pushing one another and laughing, pretending to faint and otherwise enjoying having the hell scared out of them. All but the large red-faced boy, who is clearly irate, and gives Grayson the finger, then slaps the crook of his arm, and follows that with flicking his fingers across the bottom of his chin. He is leaving no insult undemonstrated. Grayson blows him a kiss, waves and roars away.

About quarter to twelve he is in the Back Bay. As he wheels the straight job around the corner from Berkeley to Newbury St., the two-way radio got his attention.

The straight jobs were all equipped with two-way radio so Rosie could pester the drivers with "hurry up" all day. The radio could be entertaining, too. Rosie would shout a driver's truck number over the air and get a response, but one driver couldn't hear what another driver had said, all you could hear was Rosie's end of the conversation. It often sounds like a Bob Newhart telephone skit. Management and sales cars also came equipped with two-way radios, too, but they were set up to hear both sides of the conversation between driver and dispatch.

"Go ahead, six-six-three," Rosie bawls.

A sound like cloth being ripped came over the air.

"Six-six-three," Rosie shouts. "Are you crazy? Tell him no! Wait? We don't wait!"

Rosie is still irate when he called Grayson's truck number.

"Six-oh-nine!"

Grayson reaches up and presses the transmit button without saying anything.

"Whatta you got left?" His ire is easily trans-
ferred from one man to the next.

Grayson picks up the hand set. "Just Kakas
Furs on Newbury Street. I'll be empty in fifteen
minutes." Grayson will actually be empty in ten
minutes.

Rosie says, "Make it ten, and call me."

If Grayson had said ten minutes, Rosie would
have told him to make it five. Rosie thought he was
a great motivator.

Grayson kept the growl low on the way up
Newbury Street, and slides into the loading zone
space at the curb. He grabs the red plunger and
pulls it out, which cuts the fuel and shuts down the
diesel, pulls the switch to lock the brake, slides the
delivery receipt off his clipboard, jumps out and
heads into the fur store.

Grayson's apartment was on Newbury Ave in
North Quincy, and here he is on Newbury St. in the
Back Bay of Boston. The difference between the
Newbury in Back Bay, and the Newbury in North
Quincy is the difference between Paris, France and
Paris, Maine. Grayson enjoys a glance at the gals,
and this street is a fine place for it. He is careful
not to ogle, what with three sisters and a number
of nieces coming up, he behaves toward women as
he'd like others to behave toward the women in his
family. But, man, some of these women take your

breath away. From time to time, he'd be lugging cartons in or out of someplace and look up to find some sophisticated lady eyeballing him, and he figured what she saw when she looked at him was some L'il Abner-type yokel; a sweaty dipshit in a faded flannel shirt, dungarees and beat up work boots.

He walks up to the front door, sees a well-dressed woman of a certain age on the other side of the big display window. Her chin is raised, her eyes are closed, her face still, as it is warmed by sunbeams that traveled from 93 million miles away, maybe for just this reason. Grayson hesitates before he goes in the store. This woman is enjoying the sun, one of life's small pleasures. Unfortunately, Rosie cares about nothing but deliveries, pickups and the Red Sox, and if Grayson doesn't bust up this moment of Zen, he'll be in the shit.

Grayson is announced by the trill of chimes on the door, and it takes the woman a long second to turn. She stands with her hands folded in front of her pelvis, and her knees and ankles together. She is positioned beside a mannequin wearing a mink coat. Behind her, tightly racked furs line the walls, packed in like the cans in the soup aisle at Stop & Shop. On tables set around the store sat hats, stoles, gloves and who knew what else?

The woman seems to struggle, pulling herself from the sublime to the commercial. She looks over at Grayson and then out the window to the truck.

"Yes?" she asks.

"Hi. I have a delivery for you, from Moore Business Forms. Collect." He held out the delivery receipt for her. She cranes her neck to look at the DR without touching it, as if touching it would convey ownership.

"For me?" she says.

"For Kakas Furs," he says.

"It's pronounced *kay-kus*," she says, snippy.

"Good. It sounds a lot better when you say it that way."

"Who ordered them?"

"I don't know." He shrugs amiably. "I'll bring them in the backroom, while you get me a check for $18."

"Just to bring them in?" the woman asks.

"No, no. For the overall delivery charges."

"May I see that again?" He holds the delivery receipt out, and she looks it over fervently, as if hoping to see this is all just one big, horrible mistake.

"Here," he says, handing her the DR. "It's okay. You can touch it. Look at it all you want while I bring them in, okay?"

"Why did you bring them here?" she asks.

"Well, my guess is someone here ordered them. It's not like we picked your name out of a hat. This store is a business, and these are business forms. They go hand in hand, right?"

She gives him a cold smile, as if she imagines kneeing him in the groin. "What if we didn't order them?"

"Does that happen a lot? People come in giving you stuff, nobody knows why? That how you wound up with all these fur coats and everything?"

She wrinkles her face and says in a tight-lipped whisper. "Don't get smart, Buster."

"Look, I'm just a working stiff trying to do my job, lady."

"And don't pull that beleaguered proletarian act with me. My father was a longshoreman, and I grew up on Bunker Hill St."

Grayson smiles. "Well, then be nice or I'll tell them you're a Townie."

She turns so her back is to the mirrored wall.

"Listen pal ---" she says.

Grayson smiles brightly, and shakes his finger. "If Mr. Kakas hears that he's got a Charlestown gal hanging around the minks he'll think you're just here to plot a caper."

Her laugh surprises her, but she catches it, kills it and shakes her head.

"Bring them in, wise guy. I'll have to go upstairs to get you a check."

"Muchas gracias," he says, bowing slightly.

At the back of the straight job he stacks five cartons of paper forms on his two-wheel hand truck and gigs them in, through the middle of the store and into the back room. There an armed security guard sits on a raised platform looking out at the store, hidden behind what the customer would only see as a big mirror positioned high on the back wall. The uniformed young man is also watching a row of closed-circuit TVs, with shots from six different camera angles, both indoors and out.

Grayson salutes the guard, who replies with a nod, "Sss-happenin, man."

"You tell me," Grayson says. "You got the fancy TVs."

"I see you out there grinning at Lauren," the guard says.

"A man can grin, can't he?"

"Not for long, brother. She tell you to put them here? They usually go upstairs."

Grayson shook his head. "No, no, not these. These don't go upstairs, they're special order or some shit. She said, specifically, she said, 'and don't let that idiot back there tell you otherwise.' She mean you?"

The guard looks hurt, and shrugs. "I'm the only one here."

Grayson laughs. "No, she didn't say that. I'm just kidding you."

The guard frowns. "Hey, man, you shouldn't go about fomenting trouble for people."

"Yeah, you're right. Sorry."

Grayson pulls the two-wheeler out from under the cartons and left them standing five high. He goes back through the store and out the front door to the street.

As he is going out, a young woman wearing a short skirt and black nylons is coming in and he holds the door open. She's a knock out; mid-twenties, long, light brown, almost blonde hair, perfect features, high cheek bones and brightly lit, sandy brown eyes. She smiles at him like they both know the same secret. The woman is wearing a three-quarter length, brown leather coat over a black V-neck sweater and a white turtleneck. Her clothes look expensive and exotic, and Grayson has no idea why they do; maybe it's because she's wearing them going into a fur store. Her scent drifts by and touches off a desperate longing that makes him want to crumple to the sidewalk. It is the same perfume that Catherine uses, but for a time, he can't retrieve the name; then it came: Shalimar.

"Merci," she says with a smile.

He smiles back and tips an imaginary cap.

He shakes off the bad moment and moves down the sidewalk to the Mack, rolls the rear door part way up and slides the two-wheeler in face down, and locks the empty truck. He hustles back up to the store to get the check.

Lauren is absent and the young woman is at a display table poking around some fur hats. She picks one up and puts it on, looks at herself in a mirror on the table. The image would have made a great ad for the Sunday magazine in the newspaper. She admires her image from all angles, and it's clear she is pleased. She turns to Grayson, who begins to look at some sort of long piece of fur on a different table. He picks it up and grimaces when he sees that the fur had a fox head at one end and a tail at the other. He drops the stole and wipes his hands on his pant legs.

"Have you seen a clerk?" she asks. She spoke with a French accent and it sounds as if she asked for a cleric, rather than a clerk.

"She should be right back."

The young woman smiles and gazes at him as if she expects him to say more.

Grayson breaks the awkward silence. "Big sale on the mink hats?"

"Oh, no, I just need one," she says, and holds up the hat. "I'm leaving for Chile soon." She pronounces it *chee-lay*. "Winter is coming in the southern hemisphere." The French accent is stronger now. She cocks her head. "And it's always cold in the Andes."

"Wow. Are you a mountain climber or an ar-chaeologist or something?"

"No. Yes, or something." She shakes her head and smiles. "The weather business."

"Cool."

Lauren The Townie comes down the steps on the fly but slows to a regal pace as she spots the French woman spinning the hat on her forefinger. The security guard must have alerted the upstairs office that they have a live one downstairs petting a hat and talking to the truck driver.

"She forgot my check," Grayson mutters.

The French woman hands the hat to Lauren and Lauren says, "Six hundred dollars, plus tax." The amount causes Grayson's eyebrows to rocket up to a point just below his hairline.

The younger woman pulls a wallet from her coat pocket without saying a word. She slips out some bills as they walk over to the sales counter.

"Are you kidding me?" Grayson says under his breath.

The French woman will walk out in under five minutes with a purchase that would have cost Grayson about two week's take-home pay. He's pondering that when a thin, slicked down, ferrety fellow buttoned into a shiny suit appears in front of him. The man holds up a hand-written check.

"I have your money," he says.

"Thanks, but it ain't mine. It's for The Man," Grayson says, while taking the check. "You know The Man, right?" He writes "paid check" on the delivery receipt, and hands it back. "Sign that for me, will you, buddy?"

The young woman walks toward the exit. She turns, looks at Grayson and smiles. Out she went, and he relaxes. He's been tense without knowing it.

"Where should I sign it?" the man asks.

Grayson, gloomy, gets snappish. "How about where it says 'sign here'?"

In the breast pocket of the man's jacket a silk handkerchief flourished. He produces a Bic pen from an inside pocket and signs the receipt with bold strokes, as if in defiance of George III. He replaces the pen, returns the receipt in an officious manner and shoots his cuffs.

"Is that it, or what?" the guy asks. He may have a suit and a haircut from Newbury St, but he still has a Revere attitude and accent.

"Yes, that is it, I'm afraid," Grayson says. He pulls the back copy off the receipt and hands it to the guy along with the used carbon paper. "We used to have President Nixon call you to say congratulations right after you got a delivery, like he does with the astronauts and Super Bowl champs, but now, he's too busy with the Watergate mess, so that is indeed it, as you say."

The fur store fop seems at a loss.

"Look," Grayson says. "I already put the cartons in back, my friend."

"They go upstairs," the man says, as if every child born of woman knew this.

"You know what?" Grayson says, looking at the signature on the receipt. "Warren, is it? Warren, you want them upstairs, hop to it, brother. It's a tailgate delivery, means I didn't even have to bring them inside, but I'm a big softie."

Warren appears to be terribly disappointed.

"I will show myself out," Grayson says, and leaves.

For his lunch hour he has his battered paperback of *It Happened in Boston,* written by some guy he'd never heard of. It was a weird book, strange and dark, and he would almost feel drunk while reading it and had a hard time shaking it off when he finished reading. He'd stop at a corner store and buy a PayDay and a Pepsi, find a place to park, and read for an hour.

He's about to climb in the truck cab when a car stops beside him and the driver double taps the horn. Grayson turns to see his brother Hugh, in the company Galaxy.

Grayson opens the passenger side door and looks in.

"Hey," Hugh says. "Are you going on your lunch break?"

"Probably. You buying?"

"Sure. It's your birthday," Hugh says.

Grayson climbs up into the truck and clips the delivery receipt to the board and picks up the microphone to hail Rosie.

"Yeah, I'm empty on Newbury Street," Grayson says. He hears his voice echo over the company's two-way radio in Hugh's car.

"Take your dinner and call me after. I got a list of pickups a mile long," Rosie shouts.

It seems to be Rosie's hope that this would make Grayson wolf down his lunch and return to duty early. Rosie's fantasy life appears to revolve around the drivers all taking very short lunch breaks, not using the full hour required by the union contract, and jumping back into the fray to rescue Rosie from his own ineptitude. Grayson clicks the mic button, shorthand to acknowledge his understanding, pulls the key out, looks at the Timex hanging from a clip on the heater. He jumps down and gets into his brother's car.

Hugh says, "You looked surprised when I said it was your birthday. Did you forget?"

"No. Just kind of surprised you remembered."

"Will Catherine call you, you think, birthday and all?" Hugh says.

"I've seen her once since the last week of January."

"Keep your chin up, kid. Life can change in a second."

"Yeah, okay, thanks, Socrates."

They drive up Newbury St. to Mass Ave to Boylston on their way to the closest Burger King, which is over near Fenway Park. One thing that never has to be discussed, once they decide to eat, is where they would eat. There may be a discussion about which Burger King is the nearest, but that is the extent of it.

"I sold a new customer in Hartford," Hugh says. "I got a call and a verbal commitment from them this morning."

"Who?" Grayson asks.

"Colt."

"Colt .45 malt liquor?"

"You wish it," Hugh says, chuckling. "No, the gun maker."

Hugh flashes his friendly smile. He's picked up all the tricks of the successful, young sales executive, and dresses the part in his pin striped suit, starched, white button-down shirt and silk rep tie. With a smile and the duds, he looked like he'd been born in the manger of the Brooks Brothers Christmas display.

"A lot of freight?" Grayson says.

"It's only short term, for now. If we do a good job we could get in on a regular basis. But, it's a foot in the door. We're helping them out, moving five government loads they can't cover with their regular carriers."

As always, Hugh is tense while driving; he grips the steering wheel like he was trying to break the car's will. He had his license at seventeen but was never a confident motorist after being T-boned by a crazy man in a pickup truck trying to kill himself and his terrified wife. Hugh, miraculously unhurt, didn't drive at all for over a year. However, staying put was anathema to him so he is forced to deal with his fear on a daily basis.

"Why are they busy now, with the war over?" Grayson asks.

"The government had all these M16 rifles made, and paid for, before the war was over, so they have to store them in the National Guard armories. They'll fill the local armories first, which means five loads for Triple T, but we have to move them in one day. They're running a bunch of loads all around the country. They're going into storage, and will probably be destroyed someday, but being the government, they delayed the release date until everything was good and screwed up."

"Congrats," Grayson says. "Are you starting to get more into this job?"

"It's something to do, for now," Hugh says. "Gives me a cover story."

"Because you're really Batman?"

"This Monday I have a big meeting with the security guys from Colt and our people. Then we have to move the loads within a week. Your boss will be there."

"Rosie?"

"No! Rosie?" Hugh snorts. "The Senior VP of Operations, Stephen Richardi himself, is coming up from Jersey."

"He's not my boss. I've never even seen him."

"That doesn't mean he's not your boss," Hugh says. "He calls the tune that everyone dances to, so he's your boss."

They're sitting in a booth at Burger King, eating, when Hugh looks at him with a squint.

"You check out the security set up in Kakas?"

"Yeah, sure," Grayson says.

Hugh says, "Hey, I told you why I took this job."

"Don't start."

This talk makes Grayson nervous. They grew up in the same house, slept in the same room for sixteen years, but his older brother is different after his accident.

"I don't want to hear it," Grayson says.

Hugh smiles behind his cheeseburger. "Don't be a baby."

Grayson, changing the subject, says. "I did see a woman buy a six-hundred-dollar mink hat in less time than it took for you to buy cheeseburgers and fries. And with about as much thought."

On the other side of the window glass, the sun hangs just off center in the cloudless March sky and exposes everything with a sharpness, a clarity that is disorienting after winter months of seeing the world in cataract drab. After a long winter in the old city, the salt-stained cars shudder at the stoplight, their rotted rocker panels shedding rust flakes while college kids pass by in the crosswalk. The students are colorful in their pricey peasant wear, and so stereotypical they seem like extras in a movie.

"What did she look like?" Hugh asks.

"She was the kind of gorgeous that hurts in the pit of your stomach."

"Did you put a move on her?" Hugh says.

"Yeah, I offered her a spin around the city in a Mack truck."

"You can't mope around about Catherine forever. Move on, man."

"This woman paid four times more for a bonnet than I paid for my first car." Grayson fishes a French fry from the big bag, then looks in and paws around in it. "You have an extra salt?"

Hugh slides over a couple of packs.

"Does that bug you?" Hugh asks. "People buying fur, while other people can't get enough to eat?"

Grayson thinks about it as he extracts his sleeve of fries from the big bag, dumps them back in, puts the empty sleeve on the table and pours the salt into the bag.

"Yeah, I guess it does. I don't know," he says, shaking the bag. "There might be someone out on the sidewalk, looking at us in here, saying, 'How can those guys eat *two* cheeseburgers, and a *large* fry, when people go hungry?" He shakes his head. "I don't know. Maybe she just gave a million bucks to the Jimmy Fund."

"Imagine no possessions," Hugh sang, his voice no worse than John Lennon's.

"Screw him and Yoko," Grayson says. "He has about fifty million bucks and the gall to sing that. Why doesn't he give it all away, except for like five million, and see if they can scrape by on it."

"The big shots just have the ideas for the rest of us," Hugh says. He takes a sip of his soft drink. "They don't live by them."

Grayson's attention is taken away from his brother when he sees the mink hat girl walk through the door at Burger King.

"Holy mackerel," Grayson says. "There's the chick who bought the hat!"

Hugh glances over his shoulder, smiles, and says, "Wow. What a coincidence."

The woman walks straight over to their booth and puts her hand on Hugh's shoulder and looks at Grayson, smiling. He sits stunned, silent.

Hugh says, "Remember Mrs. Nihill, the older lady, lived down the hall from me? She died a few months ago?"

"On Christmas Eve," the young woman says.

Grayson nods, even though he has no idea who or what they are talking about.

"This is her granddaughter, Amy."

"Oh," Grayson says. He stands and offers his hand. "I'm sorry for your loss."

"Amy, my brother Mike."

"Didn't he tell you? We've met, in a way," she says.

Hugh slides over and she sits beside him, while Grayson sits opposite.

She keeps the high-beam smile at full strength, showing teeth gleaming white, as perfect as Chiclets. Those teeth would bring a dentist to his knees.

"I've been dying to meet you," she says. "I've heard so much about you."

"Me?" He looks over at Hugh. "What's going on?"

For an instant, Grayson thinks Hugh is going to announce that he's eloped with this woman, even though Hugh is seeing Corinne, the latest in a string of stunners dating back to his early teens. In addition to her knockout looks, Corinne has the added attraction, for Hugh, of being thoroughly bananas. Has Corinne been jilted?

Amy says, "Corinne wanted me to meet you, back in early January."

"Corinne told her Catherine gave you the broom New Year's Eve," Hugh says.

"Meet me? What for?"

Amy smiles and cocks her head. "Corinne said you were smart, handsome and eligible. Why wouldn't I want to meet you?"

"Are you a friend of Corinne?"

"New friend, yes. We met in the lobby at the apartment building, when? November? And later on, when I met Hugh, I said to Corinne, 'Gee whiz, he's so big and handsome. Where can I get my hands on one of those?'" She keeps on smiling. "She also said you had a great sense of humor."

That seems out of character for Corinne. Grayson has known her since junior high and, in his experience, she is almost entirely humorless. The only time he has ever heard her laugh was about ten years ago, when his cousin Donny fell out of the balcony at the Strand.

Grayson looks at his brother. "Where is Corinne?"

Hugh says, "She's down with her aunt in Florida for a couple of weeks. She's going to drive the aunt back home April first."

At a loss for words, Grayson says the only thing he could think of to say.

"You sounded French in the store."

She smiles and her eyes light up. "That was just for fun, pretending to be someone else."

Hugh says, "You went in just to check him out, and end up buying a six-hundred-dollar hat? Can you return it?"

"Oh, I can always use a nice hat." She smiles in a mischievous way; as if being wealthy is embarrassing and naughty, but also fucking great.

"She's wicked rich," Hugh says, looking at his brother.

"I'm not, my mother is." She puts on a fake pout. "I live on an allowance."

"Amy's getting her masters at B.U.," Hugh says.

"I did my undergrad at Brandeis, but I wanted to study with Howard Zinn in grad school. I'm so fortunate, I got Howard as my advisor."

Back on his feet, but wobbly, Grayson says, "He advise you to buy the mink hat?"

She forces a smile, perhaps disappointed that he isn't impressed by her hobnobbing with Howard.

She sits close to Hugh, implying an intimacy which arouses some jealousy in Grayson. He doesn't know if it's because he's without Catherine, or because he's drawn to Amy; or maybe it is just sibling rivalry rearing up again?

She says, "Hugh told me that you're a Teamster. Do you have a strong trade union consciousness?"

"What do you mean?"

She says, "Do you feel strongly about worker's rights, labor's struggle for a fair wage, dignity, and so on?"

He shrugs. "No, not really."

Hugh says, "The Old Man is a big Hoffa supporter, from back in the early days."

"Which is why he hated Bobby Kennedy," Grayson says.

"I'm very pro-worker," she says. "Unionism is a noble cause. So many people are no more than slaves, working for peanuts, at jobs designed to break their spirit, jobs with no chance to make a better life for their kids."

Grayson pauses before speaking.

He says, "Management only cares about making money for the owner, because he pays their salary. I don't expect them to care about me. I just want my check to clear every week."

He doesn't want to offend her, so he proceeds carefully. She nods, leans across the table, her face closer, her eyes focus on him, watching like she is Jane Goodall and he is an interesting chimp.

"But," Grayson says. "They're right up front with it. Produce or you're gone. The union doesn't care either, but since I pay them monthly dues, they make believe they do." He looks at Hugh. "Did you tell her how the union threw The Old Man overboard so the business agent's nephew could get a job?"

Hugh shrugs, and looks away.

Grayson turns back to Amy.

"My father was a driver. He got too old to keep up the pace the company wants. They fired him and it stuck because the union didn't fight it. The fix was in. The same week, a new driver was hired and put on the seniority list, and it turned out the twerp was our business agent's nephew. Betrayal can only come from the inside, so only the union could betray my father, and it did."

"The old must make way for the young," she says. "It is a natural law. The union movement's overarching requirement is to make their values clear and set their priorities."

"Do you belong to a union?" Grayson asks.

"No, not right now," she says. "But I'm down with the movement." She looks around the Burger King. "Where is the waiter? I could use a martini." She looks sideways at Grayson, waiting for him to laugh, and he obliges her.

It should have been easy to be pissed off at her, a rich kid, telling him how things work in a union, but he wasn't. The casual way she spent six hundred bucks is daunting to a working stiff, but he's dazzled by her smile; it feels like an invitation to a place he's never been. She also has an edge, like she could be fun but dangerous. Certainly, she is not better looking than Catherine, but their looks are different. Catherine glows, Amy throws heat. Amy is sexy, sultry, distant. Hot is the perfect word.

"So, you haven't walked a picket line or participated in an outreach program?" she says.

"What do you mean by outreach? Like, 'Stay in school, kids. Brush your teeth twice a day,' type of thing?"

Amy says, "When I was at Brandeis doing my undergrad, there was an outreach program to the prisons. Each week, I'd drive to Walpole and tutor the prisoners, in reading, or math. One of my students was the president of a motorcycle club, Stan Belzer. He won early release by virtue of his efforts at rehabilitation. Thanks to our program." She flashes a wide smile. "Isn't that marvelous?"

"Yeah. That's great," Grayson says.

"We're still in touch. He's good to know."

"You know? The Dark Lords motorcycle club?" Hugh asks.

Grayson nods.

She considers him as she lights up and flourishes a small brown cigarillo, called a Swisher Sweet. She drags on her smoke without inhaling it into her lungs and blows it out with a puffing sound. She flicks the filter end of the cigarillo awkwardly, as if for the first time and she'd never seen it done before. All in all, she handles the cigarillo like it's a prop.

She starts up again, "Despite all the consciousness raising we've done, it's nowhere near enough. It's time to take more direct action. We tried to bring fairness to the workers. We played by the rules and within the system, and we failed. We see now it's not possible, so we are about to begin an armed struggle, our aim is to bring about justice by toppling the despotic government."

"What? Like in Nicaragua or somewhere?" Grayson says.

She grins. "No, no. The U.S. of A."

Hugh has his head down, facing the mound of fries he's dumped on the thin waxy paper he unraveled to get to his cheeseburger. He examines the pile and extracts each French fry as if it were a game of pickup sticks.

"Wow," Grayson says. "I'm not ambitious, but I admire it in others."

It's not unusual for some of his generation to discuss revolution, but it was difficult for him to take them seriously. The "revolutionaries" he knows, were by and large, at the better colleges and still living off their parents. But Amy is really into it, her face is all lit up, as if she were about to tell a great story.

"You look skeptical," she says.

"With regard to your success, I have to say, I am, yes."

Grayson had gone to Boston State for half a year, and at the state schools, there are very few students that want the government overthrown, at least not until they graduate and find work. This other cohort, the student/revolutionaries, were usually close to flunking out and so throwing a riot, encouraging anarchy and leaving bodies in the street seems a better option than having to go get a fucking job.

The people Grayson knows who work for a living never talk about a worker's revolution; they usually talk about their kids, wives, husbands, sports, or maybe fishing. Once most guys had a decent job, one that paid enough to house and feed the family, cover the bills, save a couple of bucks, buy a carton of smokes and a case of beer every week, that is pretty much all they want out of work. Everyone knew the boss was a donkey; nobody expects the boss to be anything but a donkey. Of course, the company sucks. So what? Work usually sucks, too. That's why they had to pay you to do it, and why they called it work. You considered yourself lucky if you didn't hate the job. Life was not about what you did for a living, it was about who you lived for, as he'd recently discovered too late.

A young guy wearing a Burger King two-toned smock that was cut like a Nehru Jacket, is mopping his way to their booth. He stops and reaches over to another table, takes a green, flat, metal ashtray from it and puts it in front of Amy, and then continues mopping his way up the aisle. She didn't seem to notice him, drops her cigarillo on his clean floor and steps on it.

"Did you play football, too?" she says. "Were you a line man like Hugh?"

"No," Hugh looks up from the fries. "No, no, hell no, he wasn't a lineman and neither was I. He was a quarterback. I was a middle *linebacker*. Big difference. We saw line*men* as cattle. A middle linebacker is like a quarterback, but on defense. A linebacker disrupts and destroys. You might say a linebacker 'smashes the system.'" He smiles and raises his eyebrows. "He was a quarterback, and I was the opposite. The anti-quarterback."

"Quarterbacks throw the football at the other people, right?" Amy asks.

"Not me," Grayson says. "As a quarterback, I sat home watching *The Three Stooges* on Channel 38."

Amy puts on a puzzled look.

"He got hurt in a car accident the summer before his senior year in high school, and couldn't play anymore," Hugh says. "But, yeah, a quarterback throws the ball. He's the boss of the offense. He runs the play."

Grayson lights a smoke and pulls the ashtray over.

She says, "In any case, the point I wanted to make is that the game is rigged but our generation is going to change things. Things are changing, you say, but I say, not fast enough."

"I didn't say---"

"You can make a stand, get involved in the *quote* actions and passions *unquote* of your time."

When she said 'actions and passions, she'd held up both hands and made some kind of two fingered scratching movement in the air that Grayson has never seen before.

"What's that, with the fingers?" Grayson asks.

"It means I'm quoting someone."

"It looks weird," Grayson says. He hopes the gesture doesn't catch on.

Hugh says, "Amy, can you hop up, I have to find a phone and call the office for messages."

She gets up and Hugh walks by the teenager mopping the floor, and to a bank of phones at the sidewalk.

Grayson watches him leave.

She says, "Corinne said you were handsome and funny. I'm not looking for Mr. Right, I'm looking for someone who is fun to be with. I like a good time, smoke some weed, get naked and see what's up. Hugh called and said you were free to date and were working in Boston today. He said we could meet up and figure out where you were and

I could get a peek at you. I came up with the idea of following you into Kakas."

"I'm happy to meet you, but Catherine and I are just in a rough spot. We're trying to work things out. Anyway, I'm not political, not at all. I don't pay attention to that stuff. I hardly even know who's running the show down in DC."

"The Evil One," she says, with a happy grin.

"I was exaggerating, for effect. I know its Nixon."

"Him, too," she says.

"I was just trying to make a point."

"Oh, well," she says. "So politically we're incompatible, and you're hoping to get back with your girlfriend. We could always just fuck."

He feels his face heat up.

"You're blushing? My word. It's 1973. Don't be a prude. It's bourgeois."

"I'm hardly a prude," he says, sounding like a dink.

"Why not just fuck," she holds up a hand. "Sorry, I don't want your head to pop, why don't you *ball* me until you get Kathy back?"

"Catherine." He pauses. "What do you want with me? A woman like you could be going out with some rich playboy, like Derek Sanderson, or Joe Namath."

"They don't look like Che, you do. Che turns me on."

"Che? Che Mullins, from down the Wonder Bowl?" Grayson says.

"You make jokes when you're nervous," she says. "Che was handsome, too, very sexy. And, his passion for the people was inspiring. He was a physician, brilliant, deep and complex, capable of holding two contradictory ideas, the mark of real intelligence. Che said, 'The true revolutionary is guided by great feelings of love.' And, 'A revolutionary must become a cold killing machine, motivated by hate.' "

"Oh, *that* Che. On the tee shirt, with the beret," Grayson says.

"Wouldn't you have loved to meet him?"

"Yeah, he sounds like a hot shit. His advisor should tell him lose the beret, wear a bowtie instead. The intellectuals go ape for bowties."

"He's been dead since 1967," she says. "Executed by fascist thugs in Bolivia."

Hugh comes back and Amy slides over on the seat. He swept the litter from where he'd been sitting to where he sits now. Preoccupied, he balls up the crinkly paper wrappers the burgers came in and stuffs them into the paper sack. He balls that up then jams the sack into his soda cup, on top of the remaining ice before snapping the plastic lid back on the cup.

She says, "Aren't you infuriated by the way the bastards send off the poor and working-class males to be killed in wars that benefit the fat cats? It's no coincidence that those men most likely to challenge the system are the same men sent out to die."

Hugh says, "Like Paul, killed for the oil in Vietnam."

She says, "Hugh told me about your brother. How terrible."

Grayson, sitting by the sun heated window glass, is suddenly cold.

"No, don't, man. Don't," Grayson says. It's one thing to play around, bullshitting about the world, being a smart-ass, trying to get a laugh from a good-looking woman, but leave Paul alone.

"That's just one of the ways the poor are exploited by the rich," she says.

"That's undeniable. The poor are always getting exploited," Hugh says, "One way or another. We exploit each other when there are no rich people around to do it for us."

Grayson stands up. "I have to go back to work."

"Sit down for five more minutes," Hugh says.

"Are you trying to get me fired?" Grayson asks.

"What do you live by?" she asks. "Anything? What do you believe?"

"I believe a Pall Mall and a can of Schlitz is a perfect breakfast."

Amy says, "Do you remember the 'God is Dead' issue in Time magazine from a few years ago? The cover was shown in *Rosemary's Baby*?"

Hugh looks at his brother and smiles, before turning to Amy.

"Oh, yeah," Hugh says. "My mother saw that issue in the dentist's waiting room and yelled at him for having it out where people could see it."

She smiles.

Hugh points at his brother. "He went straight up to the drug store and bought one."

"They wanted to sell magazines, and the provocation worked," she says. "It always does. Only we don't provoke to sell magazines."

"Good Friday, 1966," Grayson says. "It said, 'Is God Dead?' Not 'God *is* dead.'"

"That's not how I remember it. In any case," Amy says, "The old God *is* dead. We need to replace the old God with a new god."

Hugh examines his fingernails.

"One of our new gods is spectacle," Amy says. "We need to capture the attention of the masses, to get them to take part in a worldwide worker's revolution. Do you remember the Roxbury police station that got bombed in the summer of 1970? How about the break-in at the Newburyport Armory?"

Listening to her is disorienting. What does she want? She has some kind of energy; her eyes sparkle and are full of life. She is having fun. Snatches of a song from one of The Old Man's Sinatra albums plays in his head: Witchcraft. It struck him that she'd be likely to get away with just about anything.

"You did those things?" Grayson says.

"I'd have to be pretty stupid to admit it, and I'm not stupid. But, if we did, we're not the only ones. The Times reported there were over 2,500 bomb explosions in the U.S. in an 18-month period in 1971 and 1972. Fact. Look it up."

Hugh says, "I didn't realize that."

"Look it up. We've been busy," she says, with a twinkle in her eye.

Grayson gestures to Hugh. "Up. Let's go. Amy, it was nice to meet you."

Her smile gone, she says, "The next time you come by to see Hugh, be sure to hit my buzzer."

CHAPTER THREE

The brothers are in Hugh's car, on the way back to Grayson's truck on Newbury Street.

"What the hell is going on?" Grayson asks. "Who is that?"

"She wanted to meet you. Just this morning you said Catherine's gone and she won't be coming back."

"Mind your own business. Besides, you two seemed pretty cozy."

Hugh says, "You think? Maybe a little." He puts on a face that says he's considering Grayson's opinion. "We're simpatico. I admire people like her for their passion for equality. She's into the whole brotherhood of man thing."

Grayson says, "And blowing shit up. Be careful she's not one of these rich kids, getting her kicks until her mother tells her it's time to quit it and marry an investment banker. Meanwhile, regular slobs get hurt, because she's out looking for cheap thrills. You better keep away from her."

Hugh says, "Me? You heard her, she's all yours."

"Okay, I'll say it again. Mind your own business."

"It would be cool, though, to be part of something big," Hugh says. "Changing the world? That would be an adventure."

"I can't even change myself. You know how many times I've tried to quit smoking? Told myself I'm going to jog twenty-five miles a week?" he says, leaving aside his multiple, unsuccessful attempts to manage or quit drinking.

Hugh says, "Man! What do you want from your life? You want to be The Old Man? Drive a truck every day, wind up in AA, living on Social and a lousy $400 a month pension? Maybe you're looking to carry on his legacy. I'm not."

"I should be like who, Al Capone? Fidel Castro? Abby Hoffman?"

"I'm not going to live like everyone else," Hugh says. "I refuse to be the goofball who works all day for an idiot boss, goes home to a fat wife and screaming kids, shovels some meatloaf down his neck, watches the Sox game with a six pack, goes to bed and gets up the next day and does it all over again. That's what you want?"

Grayson can't answer that honestly, because he doesn't know. Or he knew that what he wanted today was going to change when he woke up tomorrow and change again by the time he got into bed tomorrow night. He wanted to be Blackbeard The Pirate *and* St. Francis of Assisi. Some days he wanted to be Al Capone, and some days Elliott Ness. Grayson thinks the primary difference between him and his two-year old nephew was that one of them was toilet trained and the other wasn't.

"I don't think that far ahead," Grayson says.

"Bull. You don't have a plan for your life?"

"My plan is to get up in the morning and see what happens," Grayson says.

"No, answer me. I'm serious."

"My plan is to keep my nose clean, at least as long as Ma's still alive."

"You don't have a dream?" Hugh says.

"That's different than a plan."

"What's your dream?" Hugh says.

"Drop dead. If I had one, I wouldn't tell you. So you can twist it all around and make fun of me? No thanks."

"No, I want to know," Hugh says. "Why would I laugh at it?"

Grayson ignores him. Catherine had spent six years planning a dream life for them. It was a life he wanted most of the time and wanted to want all the time. Now she is gone, and now he did want it all the time. After a while they would say it to each other, back and forth, like it was the lyrics to a favorite song, or The Pledge of Allegiance or the roster of the 1967 Red Sox. He turns to look at his brother.

"Marry Catherine," Grayson says.

"That's all?"

That wasn't all, there was a lot more. They would have a house full of happy kids, and live down in Marshfield, near the beach. Grayson would make a beeline home from work, have a lively dinner with his family, then go watch the kid's Little League games, or dance recital or school play. Summer Saturdays, he'd mow the lawn while they played in the yard, and at the end of the day he would read bedtime stories to them. For his part, he wanted to make love to Catherine every night, and fall asleep with her there. Wake up, go to work feeling good and do it all over again. Grayson loved each aspect of their story and his last contribution to the dream was that on Sunday mornings he would cook bacon and eggs for everyone. But the dream began with Catherine; she made him promise he'd rent a cottage down the Cape for their honeymoon, and they'd go back to it on their two-week vacation with the kids, to the *exact same cottage*, each and every year. Now he wanted it all, too, he was certain he did. He didn't know if he was capable of it, though. There were too many yawning holes in him. Eventually she felt the same way.

"That's everything," Grayson says.

"Why don't you have it already?"

"I didn't know that was what I wanted until I found out I couldn't have it," Grayson says.

"You should have cut down on your drinking, at least. With or without her."

He looks over at Grayson, who says nothing.

"Okay," Hugh says. "So what's the rest of it?"

"Emma told me she's seeing some guy from Braintree," Grayson says.

"You think it's serious?"

"I don't know."

"Keep your chin up, kid," Hugh says.

"If we're giving out advice, you better be careful. Hanging out with crazy people."

"Crazy *rich* people. Anyway, she's an idealist."

"An idealist who tries to kill cops. That's the new kind, I guess."

"Not new at all," Hugh says.

CHAPTER FOUR

Sally-At-The-Window hands Grayson his time card, which he slides under the face of the clock where it takes a snap.

One of the other women in the office is saying something from behind the glass and Sally says, "Oh, yes. You got a message to call someone. I wrote it down at my desk. Catherine?"

"Really? She called today?" Sally nods. He hands the card back to her for her to initial the overtime and walks to the pay phone in the break-room, then realizes he doesn't want to call from a phone where guys will be walking by, maybe yelling and swearing, she might think he's in a bar-room, so he barges out the door and across to the employee parking lot. He salutes a couple of the boys who are shooting the shit, hops in his 1967 GTO and rolls away.

Does she want to say 'Happy Birthday' he wonders? He won't call her, because she could say that and then hang up. He'll have a better shot at changing her mind if he's there in person. He hopes.

He imagines her giving him one more chance and it brings a smile to his face.

"Wouldn't that be a nice birthday gift?" he says.

But the smile flies out the window when he's sucker punched by a realization.

"Oh, no."

Maybe it isn't about his birthday at all, maybe she is going to tell him she is serious about this Braintree guy, whoever he is.

He has dismantled his life, torn it apart, and for what? He wants to get out and smash his head against the curb.

Instead he composes himself and continues his drive to Catherine's brick duplex, to get the word, whatever it is. He climbs the steps to the front door as if heading to the gallows.

He rings and Mrs. Chrisolm appears in the doorway and smiles at him through the storm door and pushes it open.

"Hi, sweetheart," she says. "It's seems so funny that you ring the bell now. You don't have to, you know."

She backs up to let him in. Mrs. Chrisolm is a battle tested veteran of life, scarred, widowed, but not hardened by an alcoholic husband, "Wilfred-God-Rest-His-Soul," and four daughters, three of them married.

Grayson says, "Why, good evening, Mrs. Cleaver. My, don't you look nice. Enchanting, if I may say so."

"You can skip the Eddie Haskell stuff, Michael Grayson. I'm glad to see you. I told Catherine she was crazy to break up with you. But who listens to me?"

He follows her down the hallway which smells of chemicals, maybe bug spray.

"This is just a bump in the road to happily ever after," Grayson says. "I'm thinking she wants to holler at me a little bit more, and then we'll be all set. She say anything to you?"

She cocks her head as if she can't hear him. "Oh, yes. She says today is your birthday. Happy Birthday!"

"Thanks. I'm getting old."

"How is your mother, the poor thing?" Mrs. Chrisolm says.

"She's hanging right in. She's tough."

"Give her a hug for me."

She pulls him to herself, gives a squeeze and pats him on the back. The smell of chemicals is coming from her hair.

"Thanks, I will." He looks at her hair. "Your hair looks nice. Did you go to the hair-do saloon today?"

"Yes, I had a permanent." She chuckles. "It's salon, not saloon."

"Oh," he says. "You have a date tonight?"

"A date! Lord Jesus, no. Way better. I'm celebrating the announcement of my seventh grandchild," she says.

"What?"

"Yes, Maura called and she and John Webster are expecting their third. I hope I get a boy this time. Six granddaughters is a lot. Are a lot." She waves a hand. "Is a lot. The nuns at St. Pat's would kill me."

"That's great. Tell Maura and John Webster I said congrats. Cee in her bedroom?"

"No, she's ironing, down in the rumpus room. Go down. Tell your mother I'm praying for her."

He opens a door near the kitchen and fishes around under the winter coats for the light switch at the top of the cellar stairs and flicks it on. No light. He starts down, then turns and goes back to the kitchen where Mrs. Chrisolm had put on long-sleeved, yellow rubber gloves before starting in on the dishes in the sink.

"You want me to put a bulb in the cellar light? I can reach."

"We're out of bulbs. I have to pick some up at Purity Supreme," she says.

"Want me to take one from the living room lamp until you do?"

"Well, if you feel you need it," she says, visibly uncomfortable. "Just, please. Take your shoes off before you go in. I hate to see people walk on the rug."

He pulls off his shoes in the hallway and walks over the white shag to an end table. Mrs. Chrisolm stands in the doorway, arms folded, and keeping an eagle eye on him, in case he goes insane and thinks it would be okay to sit on the couch while he screws a bulb out of a lamp.

"The room looks great," he says.

He looks around, at the console TV, with the built-in AM/FM radio and record player, the mirrored wall and the satiny wallpaper. A durable clear plastic cover encased the upholstered living room set. She loved him, he knew, but not enough to leave him alone with the couch or the rug. No occasion in memory had risen to a level that warranted a full-scale usage of the living room. Certainly no one under the age of thirty has been allowed in unattended since she'd had this room, and part of the cellar, done over with some of her late husband's insurance money.

At the top of the cellar stairs, he puts the bulb in and then heads down to the basement, passing by the oil burner and tank, and knocked on the door to the rumpus room before he opens it and sticks his head into the room.

"You down here raising a rumpus, Miss Chrisolm?"

"Yes. If you call ironing my uniform and watching TV a rumpus."

Herman Munster is clopping around on the screen of an old TV that has rabbit ears on top.

"Finally," he says. "I got you turned on to The Munsters."

He steps into the room, closes the door and stands on the other side of the ironing board. The knotty pine paneled room smells of hot metal, steam and spray starch.

"Not really. This only gets one channel now," she says.

He'd first seen her on opening day of kindergarten and he'd tried to see her at least once every day since. Seeing her that first time had thrilled him and had ignited strange and strong feelings that he didn't know what to do with. This beautiful woman was the same little freckle-faced girl who had kissed his cheek, pinched his arm and ran away. He had chased her to this house that day and then ran back home and got his bike and rode back and forth on her street, "no hands," until he'd crashed into a parked car and put a wobble in his wheel. That year his mother had often packed his favorite snack of green grapes, but this bewildering feeling he had for Catherine Chrisolm was so strong he could not resist chucking the grapes at her. Her face is thinner now, the freckles are almost gone, and her hair has darkened but her sandy green eyes are as they always were, and when she ran away now it was on the best legs he'd ever seen.

"What's up?" he says. "You ready to admit your mistake and come back to me? Well, forget it. You'll wait a long time before that happens." He pretends to look at a watch he isn't wearing. "Okay, that's long enough." He holds out his arms. "Baby, you're the greatest."

She looks at him briefly and back to her blouse. "Thanks."

"So, let's get married. Strike now, while the iron is hot. Get it?"

She continues ironing and doesn't look at him. "I'm pregnant."

His head snaps back, and he takes an involuntary step to keep under it. "Oh, wow." She doesn't look up. "Jeez." He moves closer to her, bends down and tries to look up at her face. "You okay?"

She nods but doesn't look at him.

"Okay," he says. "Well then."

He moves toward her, but she stops him with a look.

"Don't," she says.

He goes over to the broken-down upholstered recliner that sits by the bulkhead stairs, still awaiting removal years after it had been taken out of service. He turns the chair to face Catherine and sits on the front edge of the cushion. If he sat all the way back on this chair it would flip over and send him ass over teakettle, as it had done many, many, *many* times to an always surprised Mr. Wilfred Chrisolm. Each time it happened, he picked it up, and climbed back in, refusing to throw it out or fix it.

"So, okay. Here's what we do," Grayson says.

"Why don't you ask me if it's yours?"

He winces, just as she looks up.

"Don't say that. Christ. It's not the Braintree guy?" he says.

She readjusts the uniform on the ironing board and steers the iron along a seam.

"If it was his, why would you call me?" he asks. "You wouldn't. So, let's trot up to Sacred Heart and get Father What's-His-Name to say his mumbo jumbo to us."

She looks up from her blouse, but not at him. "My father drank until it killed him, and my mother was a mental case until well after he died. What did my sisters do? They ran out and married guys just like him."

She presses a button on the iron and it hisses steam.

"I guess they missed the drama," she says. "But I've had my fill already, enough for me anyway. I want a good life. Not like the princess in a fairy tale good, but good, you know?"

He nods, looking at the floor.

"Maura wanted to be a veterinarian," she says, "Jan was going to be a nurse, and Sherry wanted to cure cancer. And I wanted to marry you, and you'd have a quiet, regular job, like an accountant, or something in an office."

She looks away from him.

"We would get married, and we would be happy," she says.

He knows the prayer, but she is saying a slightly different version of it; the tenor has shifted from a promise to nostalgia.

"You'd get home at the same time every night," she says.

"We'll go to our kids Little League games," he says.

"We'd live away from here, in our own home, way down in Marshfield," she says. "With a big yard."

"With Big Wheels and doll carriages in the driveway," he says.

"Our four kids would be sweet to each other, do things together," she says.

"We'll have a big mutt that goes everywhere with them."

"My kids are going to have a father who comes straight home from work every night."

"And reads them bedtime stories," he says.

"They will *not* worry they might find him dead drunk on the sidewalk when they go off to school."

"I'll cook breakfast on Sunday morning," he says.

"We'd go on a two-week vacation in Falmouth, at the same cottage, every year," she says, her voice cracking. "Every, every, every year, like Ellen King's family did."

He is silent. Hoping. She stops talking, and ironing, but is still looking at her uniform. On the television, Herman Munster runs through a brick wall leaving a perfect silhouette of his big, goofy self.

"No," Grayson says, "I hear you, Cee, I want all of that, too. That sounds great, like a terrific life, for us and our kids."

"I can't do that married to you. I've known that, really since high school, but I thought I could change you."

"Of course, you can," he says. "Do that, I mean."

"You'd come home drunk, or not at all. Even when you want to come home, you won't be able to. That's what happens."

"No, I wouldn't," Grayson says. "But be careful you don't ask for something to be perfect. You know? It's bad luck."

And now the tough chick from North Quincy turns up to defend the wistful girl.

"Yes," she says, "I should leave some good things for heaven. Like the two weeks in Falmouth."

"Okay, so what are you going to do? Are you taunting me? Or are you telling me you're marrying this Braintree guy? What?"

"Go," she says. "I have to get to work. One of the girls didn't show up."

"Did you even tell him?"

"Tell him what, exactly?" she says.

"That you're having a baby? Have you told anyone?"

"Go, I said."

"You are going to have the baby, right?" Grayson says. "Right?"

She grabs the can of spray starch and wings it at his head. He pulls back to avoid it and the chair starts falling over backwards, and he with it. The chair follows an arc back, then tilts to the side and crashes. It happens in slow motion and he's surprised that he can hear the can rattling as it bounces off the walls. The chair lands but he continues on, rolling once on the floor before jumping to his feet.

"Hah!" he says. "Missed me!" He pretends to dust off his pants.

"Too bad. Go. Just go."

She means it and he looks down and shakes his head.

"What do you want from me?" he says. "Huh? What? You call me and I come over. You tell me you're pregnant, I say, great, marry me, and next thing I know, you peg a can at me."

"Thanks for coming, now leave."

"You came back to me that night, for a reason," he says.

"Because I had heard about your mother. I wanted to comfort you. I should have left you alone. I'm sorry."

"Wrong. Because I'm the guy you're going to spend your life with. Why not just accept it? It's fate."

"Yeah? That's what you think? Well, screw you, and fate."

CHAPTER FIVE

B ack at his apartment, Grayson takes a shower, puts on his sweatpants and a tee shirt, drinks a bottle of Pepsi, and heads to the couch. He is tired, ashamed, dispirited and dying for a drink. He can't sleep in his own bed; he'd been battling insomnia for weeks and weeks now. He can fall asleep readily everywhere else, which was how he wound up on his brother's couch after the 2AM last call.

Lying on the couch all he can think about is how he can fix everything he's screwed up. He wants her and the baby without question but is troubled when he wonders if he's capable of being a good father and husband. He thinks of himself as an idiot and the only reason everybody he knows doesn't think that is because he knows himself better than they know him. He shuts his mind off by turning on the TV.

Now, somehow, Grayson is only awake enough to know he isn't awake. There is light on the outside of wherever he is. There is a voice speaking. He tries to push through to consciousness. He is swimming up but it takes a great effort. He gives up, floats back down, feels sick, and has to try to go up again. It's hard work. He hears the voice again. He opens an eye for a second and sees it's the TV.

"*And over in jolly old England this weekend, Queen Elizabeth will ceremoniously open the new London Bridge. We hope a jolly old time is had by all. Next! Jolly old Len Berman with all the sports.*"

Now a heavy hand grabs Grayson's forehead and moves it side to side. He has to work his whole face to get his eyes open. When he does, he finds himself stretched out on the couch, facing the TV. On the tube, in a kitchen someplace, someplace that is flooded with early morning sunshine, impeccably dressed Happy Dad sits at a breakfast table with Happy Little Jane and her Happy Brother Dick in their spotless home. But then, Happy Mom set a small plastic tub of something on the table, and the Happy Family looks at it closely, and their happiness is no more.

Here in their gloomy living room, roommate Ron Kerr looms above Grayson, blotting out the light.

"Grayson," Kerr says. "Wake up." Grayson sees what looks like a clean, empty dinner plate, but, in fact, it is Kerr's face.

"Hey, Curly," Grayson says. He sits up and rubs his eyes.

"Why are you sleeping on the couch?"

"I'm going out."

"Maybe I'm wrong, I doubt it," Curly says. "But I remember that we, all of us, collectively, took a vote then made a rule about not sleeping on the couch. Am I crazy or did that occur?"

"Both. Sorry. It was unplanned. It just happened. Unintentionally. Sorry. I have to go out."

He rushes around, getting ready to go out and he makes a lot of noise, opening and closing dresser drawers, gargling, slamming the medicine cabinet door, and then the bathroom door. He's slapping his big bare feet along the hallway floor, when the door to Ron Kerr's bedroom opens.

"Grayson!" Curly shouts in a stage whisper.

"Hey," Grayson says. "What's up? Why are you whispering?"

Curly has a shoe brush in one hand and a shoe on the other. He uses the shoe to point to Dave

Barry's closed bedroom door, and then beckons Grayson into his room.

The bedroom is well ordered, the bed is made up and it looks like a place where an actual human being slept. Curly's Cheech and Chong poster is gone, and so is the pile of dirty clothes that could have hidden a VW bug. Also, Curly is shining his shoes. These clues reveal that Kerr is going through another "adult" phase, where he is trying to behave as he thinks a responsible adult male would behave.

Curly closes his door and displays his serious face.

"Dave is sleeping. He's in bed with his ears," he says. "Again."

"Shit. I thought he was still out. I'll be quiet."

"I told him, he should get his tonsils and adenoids removed."

Dr. Curly puts the brush down and picks up the other shoe, puts both shoes on his dresser and fits a pair of plastic shoe trees into them.

"Oh, right," Grayson says. "You got the job, huh?" Early in the week Curly had mentioned an interview he had lined up for a job as assistant manager at the Mug and Muffin. His oldest brother Dwight manages it, and their mother owns it.

"What? Oh, yeah, I did." He turns to the closet. "Look at this special hanger I got just for neckties." He holds up a complicated metal object. He looks at it as he twists it around. "I guess you just hang the clip over one of the little bars here."

"Nifty. Hey, great news on the job. Good luck, Ron. I'll see you around."

Grayson will call him Ron, maybe even Ronald, until Curly passes through this phase. Before long, his brother would fire him, and Curly would be back chugging Bali Hai mixed with gin, smoking dope on Wollaston Beach and rolling around on the mud flats at low tide.

"Where did you go last night, Grayson? Out with the fellows?"

Ronald Kerr asks this with an air of maturity so Grayson is certain he is not interested in the answer. The question is merely the fulcrum needed to seesaw back to whatever he, Ronald Kerr, wants to express.

"Nowhere, really. You?" Grayson says.

"I went up the South Shore Plaza with Nancy Anne to look for another suit. I already got a pisser one at The Bargain Center. A three-piece suit, you know, with a vest." He pauses, waiting for the next question.

"How much that run you?" Grayson asks.

"A three-piece suit." Kerr pauses to build the tension. "For seven bucks!"

"All right. Nice work, man." Grayson smiles and nods with approval.

Grayson finishes getting ready, goes down the stairs quietly and out to Newbury Ave. He trots across the street to the GTO, gets in, fires it up; while he listens to the engine rumble, he torches a smoke, inhales deeply and drives away.

Grayson backs in to a parking spot next to Catherine's LeMans in the lot at The Harvest and shut the engine down. She had parked nose in, so the two cars headed in opposite directions, and their driver's sides were faced off.

Week nights, the waitresses got through around 11PM and usually ate together in the kitchen before they left.

He'd been waiting about half an hour when she comes out through the kitchen door, talking to Suzanne Darwin. They both stop walking but continue to talk and look back toward the kitchen as if they are concerned about being overheard. As the women talk Grayson tries to imagine his life without her and he can't. He can only summon a still image of himself looking like a hammy, silent film actor slumped over the table in what looks like Ralph Kramden's kitchen. He wants to talk to her about the baby, about everything being all right in their future, starting now. He's lost his best friend, right at the time she needs him most. How can he talk about losing his best friend to his best friend? It wouldn't work. Until recently, his life had seemed to be a long line of little screw ups, but now, this is a life changer. If she'd gotten pregnant while they were together, so to speak, it was an easy fix: Get married now, rather than later. He has to hope things will change

"Snap the fuck out of it," he says aloud to the otherwise empty car.

Suzanne says something to Catherine, and she shakes her head. Suzanne touches her on the upper arm and cants her head to one side. Catherine gives her a quick hug and they back away from each other, still talking. On her way over to the LeMans, Catherine spots him, which put a hitch in her step, but she recovers and merely ignores him.

When she'd broken up with him, this last time, he felt gut-kicked, though he had seen worrisome clouds on the horizon; there had been signs. She began talking about it being past time to grow up. Repeatedly.

He loves her, at least he thinks he does, because he really doesn't know what that means. All he really knows is that he misses her to the point that it hurts; when he sees her, it feels like he's being hollowed out by a rusty fishing knife. He'd kept himself going by hoping that she would take him back. Again. Now that she was pregnant, he'd seen the fear and the anger, but also determination in her face. She was a terror when she set her mind on something.

She has her keys in one hand, her pocketbook in the other and a sweater laid over her forearm. She unlocks her car door and throws the pocketbook and sweater in, closes the door and leans back against it.

She raises her eyebrows in a question.

"I'm going to an AA meeting," he says. "Probably tomorrow."

She nods.

"That's all you have to say about it? Nothing?" Grayson asks.

"You don't want to hear what I have to say."

"Yes, I do. I do. Say it."

"Okay, why tomorrow? Why not tonight? Why not a week ago? Or five years ago?"

"Because it's too late to go tonight, or last week, or five years ago."

"It's too late?"

"Besides, tonight, tomorrow night, what's the difference?"

"I'm afraid the answer is none," she says. "It makes no difference, not now."

"You know what I meant. The difference is only a day. Not a lifetime."

"If you put things off long enough, a day can be a lifetime."

"So, if I had gone tonight, are you telling me tomorrow we would've gone out to buy a doll carriage and a Big Wheels and a house in Marshfield?"

"No," she says. "Not now. It doesn't matter."

"I love you, you know," he says.

"I know you think you do."

"Tell me you don't love me," he says.

"It doesn't matter."

"Love doesn't matter?"

"Not by itself, no. You need more. I need more."

"Look, let's get married and move far away from here, like California, to some city with 'beach' in the name. I need to get away from all these people and their problems, they're making me nuts. I'll be a new man out there."

"Stop it," she says.

"Tell me," he says. "Tell me what to do to make you happy and I'll do it."

"Leave me alone. Leave me alone, for good. I'm almost twenty-two years old and way too old, and way too tired, for all this. And it's too late."

She gets in her car and pulls away, leaving him behind.

As he is driving back to his apartment Grayson thinks about the different things she could have meant when she said it was too late. Then he tries to stop thinking about what she might have meant.

When he gets back to the apartment, he calls work and tells them he's booking off, that he won't be in tomorrow.

CHAPTER SIX

Friday morning, after three hours sleep, Grayson woke up, this time in his own bed. He celebrates by sitting on it and smoking a cigarette. Maybe a run will help. He goes to the bathroom, washes his face, brushes his teeth, and wets down his cowlick. In his room he puts on his sweat pants, sneakers and a black sweat shirt and trudges down the stairs. He runs slowly, warming up, then heads out toward Squantum. He runs faster, along the causeway, up Dorchester Street and out by Squaw Rock, and over the Long Island Bridge to the entrance of the chronic disease hospital, where he turns around and comes back.

Last night's dream revisits him, and despite the details being fuzzier, it again manages to fill him with the same withering, sour grief.

In the dream, he'd learned she did love some-one who wasn't him, and this someone had no name. The enervating dream, and his recollection of it now while awake, was worse than the reality: It wasn't only a dream, she really was seeing an-other man, but the reality of it didn't hurt in the same way as the shivering emptiness he felt in the dream, and that feeling, now refreshed, drains him. All of which seems really fucked up. How could it be that dreaming of losing her was worse than actually losing her?

He runs up a steep hill in Squantum and across the hill, down Crabtree Rd and back to the cause-way, the only way into this part of North Quincy. He gets to the boulevard and Wollaston Beach, turns left to run along the sidewalk on the water side. When he gets to his parent's street he slows to a walk, catching his breath as he walks up to the house.

He is surprised to find his father sitting on the enclosed porch. He's wearing his work pants and a white tee shirt and sitting in one of those brightly colored beach chairs that is a tangle of woven plastic straps wrapped around aluminum tubes. Beside him on a TV tray sits a cup of coffee, an ashtray and a pack of Luckies with a book of matches on top.

Grayson comes up on the porch and drops him-self into a high-backed wicker chair, a throne-like thing that reminds him of half a clam shell. The cushion on the chair still smelled from thirteen years of Rex, the mutt puppy born next door, and kidnapped at six weeks old by Grayson's then ten-year old sister, Susan.

"What, are you taking the day off?" his father asks. "You must be one of the Rockefellers."

"Yeah, I'm Ray-Ray Rockefeller."

His father laughs. "I didn't know there was a Ray-Ray Rockefeller."

"Oh, sure. There's a Ray-Ray and a Ray-Ray, Junior. But they call him Junie. You're up early for a retired guy."

"Unemployed, you mean."

"No," Grayson says. "You have a pension."

"I'm kidding. Retired is right."

Even though Daniel Grayson had always had a taste for the booze, he never missed a day of work for any kind of sickness, rum or otherwise, and he never drank on the job. He drank heavily a couple of nights a week but since he went to work every day nobody thought much about it. Daniel always worked hard when he was on the clock, but not for the company, not for the Teamsters union, or for God, or the USA. He worked for his family. No one had ever taught him this, but he knew how to do it. What he didn't know was how not to do it.

"I've been up early since I was five years old," Daniel says. "Ancient habit. What's going on with you?"

"I wanted to talk to you about a couple of things," Grayson says.

"Now's a good time," Daniel says. "The visiting nurse is here, bathing your mother and getting her dressed. She's wonderful with her."

"Can I bum a smoke, Dad?"

The Old Man held out the pack and the matches.

"How far did you run?"

"What time is it," Grayson asks.

"Quarter after eight," his father says.

"Maybe eight miles, a little more, a little less. About an eight-minute mile."

"Jeez. Imagine if you didn't smoke, the kinda shape you'd be in."

After Paul was declared MIA, his father's drinking problem became a drinking catastrophe and he fell into the drink like the leading edge of a melting glacier, and then bobbed in it for two years. His character demanded that he go to work every day. Some nights he drank until the bar closed. Some mornings he'd show up at work still half drunk, so the way Grayson saw it, his father's good character did him in. It took losing his job to yank him back from the brink of losing his wife, too.

"I have some money I want you to take," Grayson says.

"For what?"

"So Ma can get a massage every day, from a professional who does house calls, for starters. She's stiff from being in that chair. Make the living room a bedroom, put in a first-floor bathroom, big, with a special shower. Get a ramp into the house at the side door, so you two can go outside whenever you want."

"Boy, those are all good ideas. We can start the massages today, even. But the other stuff." He shakes his head. "There's no time."

"I don't mean you build it. We'll have it done, by contractors."

"You know what I mean," his father says.

"How do you know? The doctors don't know, but you do?" Grayson says.

"They said two or three months, and that was weeks ago."

"That's my point. They don't know. No one does," Grayson says.

"No one ever does, that's right. What do you want me to say? You're a bright kid, you know what's going on. I don't have the luxury of making believe it's not."

"So much for all the positive thinking you talk about," Grayson says.

His father shakes his head and looks down. "The first AA meeting I went to, I sat there shaking, looking around, and I saw two of those little, blue cloth banners they hang around the rooms. They look like the Boy Scouts made them. One banner says, '*Hang on*,' and on the other side of the room, another one says, '*Let go*.' How do you do both?"

"You can't," Grayson says.

"You can, and you have to. But the timing is hard to learn. You can learn what to hang onto, what to let go of, and when. That's something you need to know about living."

"I'm talking about helping Ma here." Grayson jumps to his feet. "You're giving me your David Carradine, Kung Fu, 'take the pebbles from my hand, grasshopper', AA bullshit."

Daniel Grayson points up at his son. "Don't get smart with me, mister. I can still knock you on your can. What the hell do grasshoppers have to do with anything I just said?"

"Jesus Christ," Grayson says. He throws his arms up. "Look, I shouldn't have said that. I'm sorry."

"Okay. Forget it." Daniel points at the wicker throne. "Relax, will you. Relax."

"No. I gotta go."

"You're not going to say hello to your mother?"

"Later. Tell her I'll see her later. I have to run."

"You've been running. You ran here."

"I can't. Not now. I have to finish."

He pulls the screen door open, goes down the porch stairs, turns and goes back up. He stands on the top step and speaks through the screen.

"Dad, your AA sponsor? Do you know where he is right now?"

"John Minahan? He's at work. He owns a garage on Beale St. Why?"

"Go talk to him about the whole live and let live procedure. Because you need to get off my back."

His father got up slowly and came over to the screen door, as Grayson backs down one step, so he can see him more clearly.

His father put his hands in the pockets of his blue work pants.

"What was the other thing you wanted to talk about?" Daniel asks.

"I forget."

CHAPTER SEVEN

His roommates aren't home. He ate a bowl of cereal at the table while he reads the paper, and later, falls asleep on the couch. He wakes about noon, and stares at the ceiling. He is waiting for something, what, he doesn't know, but it doesn't matter because whatever it is it has to be better than this.

The phone rings and he picks it up.

Hugh says, "I need a hand today and Rosie says you're off. Are you sick, busy or what?"

"What do you need?"

"I think I told you I bought a couch and it's being delivered between three and five this afternoon. So, if you can be there to check it over and then sign for it, I'd be much obliged. Get Manny from maintenance to let you in the lobby door. I should be home between four-thirty and five-thirty, so we can grab dinner before the guys come over for the meeting. There's a key under the mat."

"Got it."

Around quarter of three, Grayson sets out on foot for the ten-minute walk to his brother's apartment. His right leg still gives him a bad time if he works it too much or if he doesn't work it at all. He cut through the thinned woods to the parking lot at Hugh's place. Hugh lives on the second floor in an eighty-unit, ten story apartment building that had a name; The Tradewinds. The building is about half a mile from the Neponset Bridge and the expressway into Boston. Hugh had waited for a second-floor unit to become available. He insisted on the second floor because he wouldn't have to use the elevator, and it was somewhat difficult to break in to a second-floor unit from the outside, but it was easy to escape from it, should that become necessary. He has never said that aloud, Grayson didn't need it to be said to know.

In the parking lot a woman is leaning into the passenger seat of a yellow 1970 Corvette soft top convertible. She stands up and turns around and he is not surprised to see that she's gorgeous, as you didn't see many homely chicks wheeling a

Vette. He is, however, quite surprised to realize it's Amy Nihill. How did the expensive, flashy wheels go over with her political crew? She looks different somehow, even hotter than she did on Thursday, maybe because of the Vette, or maybe it was the case of St. Pauli Girl beer she had in her grip.

Grayson trots over and takes the beer from her.

"Thanks," she says.

"My pleasure." He hefts the case of bottled beer onto his shoulder. "I've heard of this beer but never saw it. It's not available around here, is it?"

"Not just yet, but soon. Lawrence, my mother's current husband, is in the liquor business. He's an 'importer of spirits.'"

She bent in to the passenger side again and came out with a clanking brown paper bag in her arms. She slams the car door closed with her foot.

"Nice ride," he says.

"It's a kick," she says. "Of course, I have to take my VW bug to school and a lot of other places. I can't have anyone questioning my values."

He follows her into the lobby. She punches a code into the key pad by the glass door and in response the door lock makes a loud snapping noise. Inside, they go up the stairs to the second floor, accompanied by the jolly tinkle of the bottles in the box. She looks back at him, but he is quick, and when he sees her head start to turn, he drops his chin so she wouldn't catch him admiring her ass. What an ass it is, and what a fine pair of pants she wore. Made of some kind of shiny, silky looking material, they fit her really well, and hung just right in some places and clung wonderfully in others and highlighted just the right amount of jiggle here and there.

She says, "Would you like to come over and have a girl?"

"What?"

"A St. Pauli Girl. That's part of the marketing campaign. They want the drunks, I mean the customers, to ask, 'Can I have a girl?' They hope it will provide a risqué aspect to the product, enhancing sales."

"The buxom blonde on the label should cover it."

"So, do you want to come over and have a girl?"

"No thanks," he says.

"Oh?" she says, cocking her head. "I'm surprised. Most guys would."

"I'm giving Hugh a hand, signing for his new couch."

She shrugs. "Come in and wait. I'll leave my door open so we can hear the delivery men."

He stops by Hugh's door, puts the beer down and lifts the mat. No key. He reaches to the top of the sill and runs his hand across. Then he tries the handle to see if it is unlocked. Meanwhile, Amy keys her door open and stands there.

"Great. The key isn't here."

She says, "Come in. Put the beer down. You can look out every few minutes."

He hefts the beer up, saying, "Even if they come, I can't get in."

In her apartment he sets the case on a small table beside the half wall in the designated kitchen area. It is a one bedroom, one bath apartment, laid out exactly like Hugh's. It feels weird because Hugh's decor in the living area consists of a couch and a TV, while this one was clearly decorated by an older, much older, woman. There were two puffed up upholstered wing chairs that looked too big for the room, and a huge plump sofa placed with the back against the half wall of the kitchen, and every flat surface staged knick knacks, or pictures taken long ago. Here and there were weird dolls; weird because all dolls are weird and spooky. His older sisters loved to tease him still, by reminding him that when he was a toddler he'd cry when they brought their dolls out to play. He starts toward the door.

"Okay, then," he says. "If you see Hugh when he gets home tell him I was here and couldn't find the key."

"Relax, big fella. You can wait here." She takes his hand and leads him to the sofa.

"Sit. Do you want a drink? I'm going to have a beer."

"No thanks." He sat in a way to avoid eye contact with the dolls. "You don't strike me as a beer drinker."

"Every so often. I took a case because some friends are coming over."

"Tonight?"

"One night, next week. But, I saw Lawrence, and my mother, this afternoon. Always a joy."

"You don't like him?"

She takes an opener from a kitchen drawer, pulls out a bottle, snaps off the cap and stood there holding the bottle.

She says, "I like Lawrence more than her. She'll apologize for the weather. 'Oh, honey, I'm so sorry it rained on your birthday.'"

Grayson chuckles, figuring she saw that as a loveable foible of Mom's.

Amy says, "But if she steps on your foot, she'll say, 'Well, what was it doing on the floor?'"

His chuckle is stoppered when he realizes she sees that not as loveable but, it seems, as a hanging offense. How sharper than a serpent's tooth, indeed.

Here and there were a few framed photos of a plain girl with sad, swampy eyes. In one she was squeezed between two adults, one male and one female, both of whom may have been mistakenly thinking they were showing happy smiles but looked more like they were in mid-shriek.

She gestured to the room at large and says, "I'm only staying here until I've finished grad school, so I can't be bothered redecorating. It's a convenient location, and I got sick of all the silliness that goes on in the student neighborhoods. So, when Nana died, I packed up my clothes and came here." She looks around, in a way that seemed wistful. He figures it is a way for her to hold on to her grandmother, too.

"She was a sweetheart," Amy says. "I miss her terribly. She was my paternal grandmother. My father disappeared before I was born, so she was the only relative from that side."

Before they were called swamp Yankees, the early settlers from England were called Puritans, and The Old Man descended from a long line of them. If you showed an emotion, you were being "dramatic." On Grayson's mother's side, they were full blooded Irish, all the way down, clannish and volatile. So, he believed it was his nature to be uncomfortable with any emotion, except anger. He noted the apartment looked like The Museum of Lace Doilies. They seemed to be everywhere but the floors and the ceilings.

"Boy," he says. "Nana sure liked doilies."

She laughs. "And those little painted ceramic figurines. They're supposed to be cherubs, I think." She sweeps her extended arm around the room. "She placed them all over the apartment. I think they're creepy."

She reaches down and hands him the beer, he took it, automatically, before he realizes what it is. She turns to go into the kitchen.

"Wait a second, no, I don't want a beer." He hops up, follows her out and puts it on the table.

"Oh, that's right." She reaches out and picks it up. "Do you want a joint? I've got some very nice Colombian."

He thinks about it: He rarely smokes dope. The few times a year he did smoke, it just made him mellow. He doesn't have a problem with pot. He quit drinking and smoking pot isn't drinking. Maybe smoking pot could be a solution to the drinking issue.

"Yeah, that sounds good," he says.

"Sit. I'll get it."

He sits back down on the couch and she came out of the bedroom shaking a small re-sealable plastic bag.

She says, "My papers are on the shelf above you. No sit, I'll get them."

She puts a hand on his left shoulder for balance and reaches with the other arm to take a pack of rolling papers off the shelf, pressing her flat belly against the right side of his head. It is done with an intimacy that seems to be comfortable for her but is both thrilling and discomforting for him.

She sits beside him and soon they fire it and smoke up, passing the joint back and forth. One reason he isn't a keen pot smoker is that he found the rituals, and holding the smoke and the burning lungs, unpleasant. But, worst was the smug self-regard, and the 'Aren't we hip,' bullshit was really tiresome. He is happy that she isn't doing the whole observing-herself-being-cool like so many pot heads did. Plus, he identifies pot with hippies, and he certainly isn't a hippie. By this time, the pot has worked and he is numb. Beside him, she seems dreamy.

"Good stuff, huh," she says.

"Stunning."

"Watch," she says. "Look at this." She gets to her knees on the couch and reaches up to the shelf again, leaning against him. She sits back down and now there is no space between them.

She hands him a ceramic cherub and says, "Look at this. Imagine if you had to paint this? With tiny little brushes? I ask you, isn't it weird? The little boy in the cloth cap, standing in some kind of basket, his hand shading his eyes."

"He's a lookout in a crow's nest," he says.

"He's a lookout in a crow's nest?" she says. "What's he looking for? The white whale?"

"Yes. Could be Ishmael," he says. "And I only escaped---'"

"'Alone to tell the tale,'"she says.

That wasn't exactly right, he knew, but they were close. He hands back the figurine. "I don't want to break it. It looks fragile."

She stretches again to put Ishmael back, and this time he finds he's turned his face to her belly.

"Good dope. Very good dope," she says. "Nice. I'm going to have a glass of wine. I have a gorgeous red."

He says, "Oh, are you like a wine...person? What do they call them? A wine something?"

"Are you thinking of an enthusiast, or a snob?" she says. "Or, like, a wine bibber?"

He laughs. Bibber! What a great word.

"What's funny?" she says.

"Wine bibbers," he says.

"I told you," she says. "Excellent dope."

"Absolutely," he says.

"That reminds me. Did you ever try absinthe?" she asks.

"Yeth," he says. "Just kidding. No. It's not legal, is it?"

"It is, I mean, no, it's not, but I just happen to have some, again, courtesy of Lawrence," she says. "My mother calls him 'Lawrence of Inebria'. You have to try it."

"I don't want to drink any booze," he says.

"I think it's more like a hallucinogen than booze."

"Oh, well," he says. "That should be all right."

She came back with a bottle and stops to read it. "Yes, I guess it is a kind of booze. It's 148 proof," she says.

"I've never had it."

So, how could he quit it? He'd never tried it, for Pete's sake. But he is definitely off the beer and whiskey.

She says, "I know it really fucks you up."

"Make mine a double."

He second and third guesses his decision to sample the absinthe during the tedious and ostentatious preparation, which involves a sugar cube, a peculiar spoon, fire, ice water, and slow stirring. When it is ready to drink, it looks awful, a shade of kid snot green.

He says, "That sugar cube isn't dosed with acid, is it?"

She says, "No, but I do have some windowpane, if you want that."

He shakes his head, takes a sip of the drink and tastes licorice. The taste is unexpected and disconcerting. He stops just short of a shudder and childish grimace.

"Is this made out of melted licorice?"

"Anisette seeds, plus fennel and wormwood."

"Oh yeah, seeds, flannel and wormwood, that sounds delicious," he says. "None for you?"

"I'm going to get that glass of wine." She gets to her feet and floats away.

He says, "You're going to bib some wine," and cackles, then tosses off the drink, taking it like medicine.

She comes back with her half-filled wine glass. "You drank that right down. You're supposed to sip it."

He doesn't want to tell her he drank it down fast because it's awful. That didn't make sense to some people.

She says, "What do you think? Would you like another?"

"Not right now. I'm, uh, phew. That really does taste like licorice."

"You can't handle your licorice?" she says.

He closes his eyes and smiles as a glow starts in his belly and radiates out, and he shivers to a sound made by a small gong somewhere in Tibet.

Peace, through unrestrained animal spirits. Time to stop grieving.

"If I don't live, I will die," he says.

He must not have said it because she says, "Have you ever tried Tullamore Dew?"

He shakes his head a couple times, stopping when he feels like his brain is going to slide out of his ear.

"It's a very nice Irish whiskey."

His grandfather Spike used to say, 'Might as well be hung for a sheep as a lamb.' Grayson never got the exact reference, but understood the sentiment to mean, if you're going to screw up, screw up good. No sense breaking a promise only slightly. He could always stop again tomorrow.

"Sounds good. Should I go see where Hugh is?" He thinks about standing. "In a minute."

She came back and hands him a water glass with a healthy dose in it.

"Now sip this," she says. "Don't gulp it down."

He sips, frequently. "That is nice."

She sits beside him, taking a peck at her wine now and again, and then she put the wineglass on the coffee table. She angles toward him, lifts her legs to the couch so her knees touched his thigh, put her hand there, and slid it back and forth slowly.

She says, "I may be a tough Movement woman and all that, but my feelings were hurt the other day. I felt rejected."

"Oh no," he says, feeling terrible that he'd made her feel bad. "No, no. It isn't you. I still have hope Catherine will take me back."

"That's fine, I don't want to marry you. I just want to have some fun. Corinne said you were a great guy."

"I'm surprised. She doesn't like me."

"She told me you were fun. That's what I need. I'm involved with big things, heavy shit, you know? I can't fraternize with the guys in my group. Marxists talk all day about equality, but as soon as you fuck one, they expect you to cook for them and wash the dishes, and they will never take you seriously again."

He takes a sip from his glass. "I'd really like a cigarette, if that's okay?"

She removes her hand from his leg. "Me, too."

He puts his empty glass on the coffee table and takes his smokes from his shirt pocket. He shakes a couple out and hands one to her.

"I like to smoke when I drink," she says. She takes a lighter from the table and lights both cigarettes.

He says, "I should go and check on Hugh's couch. See if they're there. The truck drivers." He holds up the cigarette and looks at it. Smoking, standing up and walking to the door involve too many things all at once, way too many things. "After this."

She takes his hand and began to rub his thumb with hers. Soon, their thumbs were pressing pad to pad, and writhing around each other. Thumb wrestling is really getting him amped up, way past horny. This is ridiculous, what could be goofier, and yet he increases the tempo. Wow, he'll have to remember this.

She gets to her knees on the couch again, leans in, takes his bottom lip in her teeth and rubs her tongue on his lip. She puts one hand behind his head and runs her hand through his hair, let go of his thumb and with that hand caresses his thigh. Then she moves her hand higher, and takes a loose hold of what she found.

She stops kissing but doesn't pull away.

"Oh. You're not going anywhere. This," she squeezes and releases it, "is a lie detector."

Despite his best intentions, he validates her theory by shifting position to allow her better access.

She puts her hand on the side of his face and turns his head toward her and kisses him. Her lips are open and her breath smells of sweet wine, and her tongue is darting, small, warm and slick. She kisses him, and his lie detector expands to the point where he feels like his scalp is stretching. She nips at his earlobes and the hand he was going to use to gently push her away instead goes around and cups a cheek of her ass, her super-duper ass. Her hand fumbles with his belt, she makes a hissing noise, and he shifts so she can get at him, and he can use his other hand, too. He changes position so now they knelt face to face on the couch, and he drops his free hand between her legs for a second, before he is driven to get closer, to get inside; she reads his mind and arches back so he can put his hand inside those fantastic pants to where she's wet, she gasps, struggles to get his belt undone. She is not as facile as he would like, so he shifts to a seated position with a quickness, uses the toes on each foot to pull his shoes off, stands up so fast he is lucky not to faint, hooks his thumbs on his belt and falls back on the couch as his pants and boxers go down at the same time, and then lends her a hand, sliding off her silky pants, leaving her in some flimsy red panties. He picks her up and fastens her on his lap and as fantastic as she looks in her pants, she looks way, way better without them and she fucks even better than she looks.

CHAPTER EIGHT

He came to on the couch in Amy's place and she is nowhere to be found. He finds a note on the table.

I have study group. I had a great time and I would love to see you again. And again, and again………

He looks at Nana's clock and sees it's almost seven. He crosses the hall and slams his knuckles against his brother's door several times before it opened.

"Where the hell were you?" Hugh says. "You said three o'clock you'd be here."

"I was here. There was no key under the mat."

"What?" Hugh bends and pulls up a corner of the mat to reveal a key. "What do you call that?"

"You just put that there," Grayson says

"In any event, I was here at four, just as they were pulling in. Luckily, I left work early."

"Let me in, if you're going to, but spare me your tale of woe."

Hugh backs away. Grayson nods, and lurches into the apartment.

Inside the one-bedroom apartment Hugh has a minimum of furniture; the new sofa, a small kitchen table, a clock radio on the counter and a table top black and white TV. All in all, the place has the ambiance of a budget motel room.

He made it to the couch, "Oh, it's a beauty," and fell back on it, landing on it like a man defenestrated.

Hugh says, "I told Charlie I'd pick him up after work. I gotta go."

"You're going all the way in to Oliver's?"

"No," he says. "At the Red Line. Back in 10 minutes."

Charlie is the day bartender at a bar across the street from Fenway Park. He looks way younger than twenty-two, and anytime a cop comes into the bar and gets a look at Charlie, the cop asks for his ID. His youthful appearance is mainly due to him being the size of an eleven-year old boy.

"There you are," says Donny. His jumbo-sized cousin comes out of the bathroom cinching up his belt.

"Go back and wash your hands," Grayson shouts.

"I did already! Mind your own business."

"You washed your hands? What, with your pants around your ankles, you washed your hands? I doubt it."

"Hugh go to get Charlie? Hey! Where have you been?" Donny says. "I came over to help you move the couches out and in."

"They just had to be signed for. No moving out and in."

"I went looking for you when you weren't here. Where were you?"

"Nowhere," Grayson says.

"I looked everywhere," Donny says.

"Yeah, well, I wasn't there. I was nowhere and I'm now here."

"Good. P.S., you look like shit."

"Flattery will get you nowhere," Grayson says.

"So, what's the matter with you?" Donny says.

"Nothing," Grayson says. "I told you I'm fine."

"Oh, I get it. You're still on the wagon. Well, praise the Lord and pass the macaroni salad." Donny squints at him. "No, you're not. You have been drinking! What a liar."

"While you're arguing with yourself, I'm gonna use the bathroom. Is it safe?"

Donny ignores him.

Grayson washes his face in cold water and rinses his mouth. He's not hungover, not too bad anyway, so he must not have drunk to excess. Progress.

When Grayson comes back to the living room, Donny starts in again. "I went to your place when I was looking for you. You should keep that door locked. You're a sap. Someone could come in and steal all your valuables."

"Like my Picassos and shit?"

"The TV?"

"It's Curley's. Everything is, except my bed."

"Never mind then. Maybe I'll go back later for the TV. Anything else good?"

"If you had any brains, you'd say no to Hugh, too," Grayson says. "He won't do it without you, and if you guys do it, it's bound to go bad."

Donny finds a piece of open space and drops gracefully to the floor into a meditation position.

Donny says, "All the more reason for you to go. If it goes bad, he'll need help more than if it goes well. Anyway, this guy Hugh brought in is an experienced strong-arm robber."

"The clown who was charged with manslaughter?"

"Yes," Donny says. "I mean no. The guy who's the boss of the motorcycle gang was inside for vehicular homicide, so he's sending over this guy, who, I don't know, what his crime was, this other guy. It got complicated and had nothing to do with me or anything I'm interested in so I zoned out until he started talking about some chick named Amy. Hugh says you knew her. She good looking?"

"Yeah, she is. She's also trouble looking for a place to happen."

"She's a teacher in prison?" Donny says. "Weird job, for a good-looking babe."

"No, it's just as part of her college course, or something."

"Hmm," Donny says. "The biker coming is supposed to be a bad hombre. Strikes fear into the hearts of men."

"These are college kids dealing the drugs," Grayson says. "They might not be smart enough to be afraid."

"Well, in that case, we may have to slap these brave bozos around in order to take their money and drugs."

"I thought we were just after the money?" Grayson says.

"Yeah. That's right. The bikers are taking the drugs."

They hear a key going into a lock and Hugh steps inside the apartment and closes the door.

"Where's Charlie," Donny says.

"I don't know, he didn't show up. Maybe he'll call."

"Who is this biker coming here," Grayson says. "Is he mentally ill, like every other biker in a gang."

"What are you talking about, mentally ill," Donny says.

"People who don't wash themselves or their clothes for weeks at a time are mentally ill."

Hugh pauses a moment. "They are a different breed, that's for sure. But I met him already and get a good vibe from him."

"Just tell him he didn't make the cut," Grayson says.

"You don't tell these kinds of people any-thing, especially like, 'You know the job we were going to cut you in on? Never mind. Thanks anyway.'"

"What? They're treacherous?" Grayson says.

"Right," Hugh says.

"And we're going to hang out with these treach-erous bikers?"

"But you're saying you know these people, Hugh?" Donny says. "You can vouch for this guy and the chick, right? So, we don't need to worry, is what I'm hearing from you."

Donny looks at Grayson and shrugs while mak-ing a 'Why not?' face; No big deal.

"How much security are you really expecting to be in the drug dealer's apartment?" Grayson asks. "I'm waiting for you to tell us instead of three goofy college kids and a burnout, there'll be a squad of Green Berets."

The buzzer sounds, Hugh hits a button, continues talking.

"I've been told there are never more than four guys there. So, we'll have them outnumbered."

There is a knock on the door. Hugh opens it and a bearded man walks in, hesitates and then comes into the room warily, like a dog sneaking up on a skunk.

You guys are real punctual," the man says. "I like that in an outlaw."

"This is Bird," Hugh says, "Bird, this is my brother Mike and my cousin Donny. They're good boys. Donny is an ex-Marine."

"No such thing," Bird says, with a horrible smile.

"You were in The Crotch?" Donny asks.

Bird held up a hand. "No. I'm not saying I'm a Marine. I just know the deal."

Bird wore an oversized Army field jacket with a peace symbol on the breast pocket, bib overalls and engineer boots. He was a strange mix of styles; a top-heavy Irishman sporting an early Beatles haircut and a skuzzy beard. In the spaces between the thin whiskers and extra-large freckles, his face was the same color as a raw chicken. His legs were long and very thin, giving the impression his pant legs would snap like a flag in a gusty wind. He has some manner of tattoo that starts on the top of his right hand and appears to continue up his forearm. His image changed with each subsequent viewing. At first, Bird looks like a good-sized man in his mid-twenties, but when Grayson considers him more closely, he realizes he is older than that, maybe mid-thirties. When Grayson looks some more, he sees that if Bird shaved the beard, dumped the Ringo Starr haircut and took off the Army Jacket, he'd disappear: He is all disguise.

Bird turns his head and looks in the direction of Grayson, but not at him, as if Bird senses he is being examined and only wants to be seen in profile. His nostrils flare, his lips slide back and now Bird points his face at Grayson and gives him a good look at his stubby, yellow teeth. This may have been another example of a smile; if so, it was one not even a mother could love.

"Why don't you take a picture?" he says, and he turns away again.

"Yikes," Grayson says. "Bird, don't be giving me them scary looks, okay? You got me terrified." Grayson looks at his brother. "This guy looks like he's dressed up to play a role or something. I think he may be a cop."

"Lose this nitwit," Bird says. "Or count me out."

"Stan Belzer is the president of The Dark Lords," Hugh says. "He's known Bird since their diaper days and he sent Bird over, so he's not a cop."

Grayson says, "Oh, that's right. And Stan's the guy dumb enough to do time. Now I feel better."

Bird moves toward Grayson, and Hugh steps between them with his hands up in a "halt" sign. "Let's all settle down, please. Bird, he's okay, he's just a little jumpy, and tends to get nasty when he's nervous. He's an excellent driver, and can be very physical, if need be. We have a nice score on the horizon. Let's not fight amongst ourselves and foul up this terrific opportunity."

"If he calls Stan stupid again... Let's just say there will be Hell to pay."

"Jesus, God help us," Grayson says. "These guys believe their own bullshit."

Hugh hangs a white board on the wall and begins drawing squares and rectangles, and then populates them with red X's and black O's and layers on some swooping arrows, while narrating who does what.

Grayson says, "I understand everything except for which ones are we, the exes? And, is this a pass or a running play."

Hugh turns toward Bird. "You have a piece, right?"

Bird snorts. "You want me to shoot him? I'll do it, just say the word."

"What do you carry, Bird?" Donny asks. He's trying to calm the waters, addressing Bird as a trusted colleague.

The phone rings and Hugh heads into the kitchen and picks up.

Bird says, "Depends on the action. For this, I'll use my snubby .38."

"You like it?" Donny asks.

Bird reaches into his Jacket pocket and pulls out a revolver, and hands it to Donny. He hefts it, points it at the wall, sights along the barrel.

"It's okay," Bird says. "The recoil is a bitch, but it's compact. It's easy to get the rounds. It's heavy for a carry piece, though."

"Does it shoot where you point it?" Donny asks. "Mine kicks right. If I have to use it, I'm liable to shoot someone by mistake."

"That's no good," Bird says. "This is dead on. We sell a lot of them, and I carry an extra one in my saddle bag. Brand new. A .38 Colt Special, two-and-a-half-inch barrel. I can even provide a box of rounds. All yours for $100."

"Deal," Donny says. He hands the revolver back to Bird.

"Hey, hey," Grayson says. "You already have a gun, you told me?"

"I need a bigger one. Mine's only a .22."

Bird looks at Hugh. "Where is this other guy you said? Charlie. Does he need a piece, too?"

"No," Hugh says. "That was him on the phone. He got jammed up at work. He's coming over here tomorrow night for his run through." He turns to the others. "Pick him up here tomorrow night, around seven."

"Does he need a piece" Bird asks.

"He and my brother don't do guns."

"What good are they?" Bird says.

"My brother will drive, he's an excellent wheel man and really knows his way around. Charlie will make the first buy," Hugh says. "He's small, looks harmless and friendly, kind of like a baby duck. The girl having the party will definitely like him."

"Wait a minute," Grayson says. "He's tending bar about a five-minute walk from this place, right?"

"It's not that big a deal. He already says he's leaving Oliver's. He got a new job down the Cape, at a place called Dick's, or something."

"Is it in Providencetown? Sounds like a queer bar," Bird says, and laughs a little too much.

"Provincetown," Donny says.

"You say it your way, I say it mine."

Grayson looks at Hugh, "I mean what if she's already seen him at the bar?"

"Those are details. Big picture."

"Man, you're picky," Bird says.

Donny says, "So, Hugh? So, whoever she likes best, me or Charlie, one of us gets her to call upstairs to the pharmacy students and tell them she's sending him up, right?"

"Why would she do that?" Grayson asks. "Because you're so charming and debonair?"

"No," Hugh says. "She gets a cut on everyone she sends their way."

"This is weird, somehow, and way more convoluted than I like," Grayson says.

Hugh says, "Well, then, go home. Jesus, you're a pain in the neck. You're out, you're in, what the heck? Go!"

"No, don't," Donny says. He turns toward Hugh. "I don't want to go in with only Charlie. He doesn't just look harmless, he is harmless. At least with Grayson, I know someone else has my back."

"Okay, okay," Grayson says. "I'll stay."

"And shut the fuck up, while you're at it," Hugh says.

"Allow me to finish, as I want to be sure I fully comprehend," Donny says.

Donny Gates, when angry or frightened, is profane. In situations where he gleaned that a show of intelligence would be of utility, he tended to use, or employ, words, often very, very numerous in number, which were correct, perhaps, but loosely fitted, and/or oversized, in any event, just not right in the context. What's more, he rambled on and on and on and on.

He says, "So she telephones upstairs. Then Charlie appears in the peephole at the door and we're with him, me and this shithead," he says, pointing at Grayson. "We then purchase some narcotics from them."

"You could say we procure them," Grayson says.

"At which point, you and Bird emerge in behind us, and if any of them, meaning the four drug kids, get any big ideas about acting out, we drop the customer disguise and dent their derbies. But if all goes smooth, you and Bird flee with the money and the narcotics, and we stay on and plead with these kids not to call the cops because we can't afford to get arrested. When we've mollified them, we take off?"

"Mollified? What does that mean?" Bird says. "I never heard that word in my whole life."

"Soothed, or calmed down," Donny says.

"So, just fucking say, 'calmed down,'" Bird says.

"Let me mention, if they act up, no guns," Grayson says. "No need. If there are only four of them, we can handle that."

"Of course," Hugh says. "When we come in, we'll shake them up good, and when the kids have been subdued and we scoop the cash and drugs, we bolt."

"I hope these guys are incredibly stupid," Grayson says. "Seems like the plan hinges on that."

"Okay," Hugh says. "Do you really think they're going to call the station house and report a robbery?"

"I don't know," Grayson says. "First off, we need some way to really put them off balance, slow them down, and make sure no one goes for a gun. Second, we need to make it seem like calling the cops is the worst thing they can possibly do."

"Okay. But I still say they're not going to call the cops. They'd mess themselves up."

Grayson says, "We need to insure they don't call."

"Look," Hugh says. "They aren't calling anyone and they won't be coming after us. They're not the Mafia."

Grayson didn't say anything. He looks away toward the small TV.

"What are you thinking," Hugh asks.

"What we should do," Grayson says. He doesn't say anything for a beat.

Then, "When you and Bird come in, we become rogue cops, four of us, except for Charlie. He is an innocent who is there because of shit luck. Then we tie them up, we say, some shit, like, 'the courts can't stop drug dealers, so we rip them off and put them out of business.' We take everything, money, drugs, and tell them they better stay out of the drug business. If they start up again, we will know and we will come back, and next time we'll not only take their stuff, we'll break things, like arms and legs. If they call 911, it will be us that dispatch sends, and it will get a lot worse than broken arms and legs. Have Charlie stay, and talk them out of calling the real cops. He says 'I didn't know those guys were cops.' But he can't get lugged because he has an open drug case in court already. That way if someone knows him from the bar, he's covered."

"See?" Hugh says to Bird. "I told you he was smart."

"Who cares what they think?" Bird says.

"No," Hugh says. "That's good."

Donny looks at Grayson with what seems like prideful love.

"This," Donny says. "This is exactly why I don't kill you every single day."

Grayson shook his head. "It doesn't take much to impress you guys."

CHAPTER NINE

On Saturday morning Grayson stops at the curb, the nose of the car just short of the pitch-covered telephone pole. He crosses the street to a small, brown bungalow with a porch enclosed by jalousie windows. A strip of sidewalk and a stripe of grass separate the house from the street. If an eighteen-year-old lad who stood over six feet tall tripped in the gutter and fell forward, his head would bounce off the bottom cement step, and suffer quite a gash. The morning after the night Grayson had demonstrated that, his father had thrown him out.

Hugh is coming out the front door and Grayson waits on the sidewalk.

Hugh says, "Be on time tonight. We have to run Charlie through the new plan."

Grayson took the front steps two at a time, opens the door and goes in.

The Old Man is in the kitchen, sitting in his chair at the same spot at the same table they'd had since Grayson was a small boy. He is reading one of his goofy AA books and now he puts it face down on the table, so the title was readable, unless you were to studiously ignore it.

"Mike. How've you been?" His father stands and offers his hand.

"Hey, Dad. You say that like you haven't seen me in years. I was just here a couple of days ago."

"Yeah? Seems longer."

"What's new?" Grayson asks.

"Nothing," he says. "How's work?"

"Ah, you know," Grayson says.

"Yup. You still white knuckling the booze?"

"I call it exercising my will power. How's Ma?"

"Go up and see. She's awake, Hugh and I just put her in the chair."

Upstairs in the front bedroom, his mother is propped up in her wheelchair, by the window, looking out at the street. As a result of the stroke, or the shock, as his aunts called it, her left hand has curled into a claw, and her left arm is as rigid as the left side of her face is slack. The muscles on the entire left side of her upper body are taut and tightening a little more every day from lack of use. While her brain is unable to deliver any useful signals to that side, that side is doing a bang-up job sending pain signals up to her brain. Grayson's father and three sisters massage her as best they could, but it's hard on her and they didn't have the expertise to know when enough is enough.

"Hi, Ma."

He kisses her forehead and put his chin on the top of her head. His eyes stung, and he squeezes the bridge of his nose until it hurt enough to stop the tears. He kisses her cheek, and sat on the side of the bed, hunched forward, with his elbows on his knees, as they both look out the window to the street.

"Michael?" Her voice sounds like she'd swallowed shards of glass, and the way she says his name broke his heart. "Is it time for *Soul Train*?"

Grayson looks down at his feet. "Almost."

"I saw you out the window, talking to Hugh, before he drove off," she says. "It looked like you were having a nice talk. I'm glad. You need to get along with your brother. Promise me."

"Okay, Ma. I will."

"Catherine came to see me," she says.

"Yeah?" Grayson says.

"She wanted to know how you were doing."

"Did you put the fix in with her, Ma? Slip her a few bucks to talk to me?"

She smiles and flicks her right hand in a dismissal. "Tell her you'll go to AA to stop drinking. That's all she needs."

"I quit, she knows that, but it didn't seem to help."

"She and I see it the same way. Her father quit a million times but never really stopped until he died, and that's almost the same way it was for your father, except he went to AA."

"What's the difference?" he says.

"Stop that," she says. "Oh cripes, there's Joe. Is he going to water the grass? In March. He's as soft as a grape."

Across the street a retired welder named Joe McCarthy came from the back side of his house with a hose nozzle in his hand with the hose trailing behind. He stops short and nearly falls on his back when the hose caught on something that can't be seen. He plants his feet and yanks on the hose without result, then disappears around the side again.

It's a bright, unseasonably warm March morning and all stages of life pass by on the street below. Mothers push strollers carrying big headed toddlers; preteen boys ride Stingray bikes, tossing footballs back and forth and hollering at each other, on their way to play tackle in the sand on Wollaston Beach; old cars with teenaged drivers roll by, windows down, volume up, sharing the thump with one and all, like it or not. Sixteen-year-old Rosalind from the house next to Joe's backs her father's Chevy out of the driveway an inch at a time. When she finally straightens it out on the street, her father is on the passenger side. His posture and the visible side of his face would lead you to believe someone has a gun to the back of his head.

"Rosalind got her learner's permit?"

"Yes, she only had to take the written a couple of times, God love her."

Joe McCarthy has solved his hose problem and is now out in the front yard rinsing his storm windows. He's also turning and aiming the hose on the louder teen drivers, hitting their cars with a stream of cold water as they race by. One Camaro screeches to a stop, then backs up to McCarthy's front yard. The driver slams the transmission into park, and he and the passenger throw open their doors. Grayson jumps up, opens the window, ready to tell the guys in the car to back off when he sees Vinny Santoro, a thirty-year old neighbor and father of three girls under ten, trot over to McCarthy.

Up in the bedroom, Ma says, "Oh, oh."

"Those guys better get back in their car," Grayson says. "Vinny'll slap them silly."

Down on the street, Vinny holds his hands up in the 'stop' position.

"Hey fellas," he says. "That was an accident. He didn't mean anything."

The young guys hurl curses from the car toward Joe McCarthy, deriding him for his advanced age, lack of hair, and baggy pants as McCarthy looks at them innocently and sprays the cellar windows at the base of his granite block foundation. The boys continue to issue invective, until, at some point, it violates Vinny's sense of what is proportionate. Vinny takes the hose from the old guy and points it at the driver and walks toward the car, shooting water at the driver and into the front seat of the Camaro.

"But now, this, this is definitely not an accident," Vinny says, advancing. "Keep going, you frigging clowns."

The doors close and the car speeds off. Joe McCarthy raises his right fist and shakes it mightily at the departing villains, a flamboyant gesture he'd probably seen in a silent movie when he was a young man.

"God help us," Ma says. "That McCarthy is a crazy old bastard."

Grayson laughs, and Ma, though not exactly sure what is funny, laughs too, for the simple pleasure of it, delighted to have half an excuse to do so.

Grayson looks at the clock radio on her nightstand. "*Soul Train* is starting, Ma."

"Oh, good."

He rolls her wheelchair in to the girl's room, which is now furnished and arranged to allow easy access. The room where Emma, Jen and Susan had slept, fought, made up and helped each other with home permanents, was now an upstairs den with a TV, one recliner chair and a pullout sofa, should someone want to sleep over. Next to it was his old bedroom, which he'd shared with Paul and Hugh, and is now occupied by his father. Grayson had helped The Old Man dismantle the marriage bed and moved it into the room still called the boy's room when his wife required the hospital bed that raised and lowered in sections. Now his father's double bed, one side pressed against the wall, occupies the space where the boy's bunk bed had been.

Grayson pulls out the knob on the TV, and the new set sprang to life. He turns his head to look at her.

"I can't believe you got The Old Man to splurge on a color set," he says.

"I told him it was high time he spent some money on me." She was looking at the screen, as if she couldn't quite see it clearly. "What's this?"

One of the networks has interrupted their regular Saturday morning lineup of cartoons and kid shows to broadcast a shot of veteran newsman

Harry Reasoner holding up a sheet of paper and talking. Harry is elbowed out of the way by a live shot of a rolling staircase being pushed up to a military airplane. Harry is saying something about "Travis Air Force Base in California" and the "Last of the POWs come home."

Grayson reaches to turn the channel but is stopped.

"No," she says. "Leave it."

They watch while the stairs are adjusted under the open airplane door. Soon, an Air Force pilot hobbles down the stairway. A knot of people wait on the tarmac but waiting proves too much for an adolescent girl. She bursts away from the crowd and runs toward the pilot with outstretched arms, a look of joy on her face that could be seen from the dark side of the moon. The girl is followed across the blacktop by her teen-aged brother, a younger sister, and a pre-teen boy. The mother is the last to arrive and is crying as she winds up on the outside of the group hug.

Ma says, "Your father told me some of these men were handed Dear John letters when they got on the plane to come home. Heartbreaking."

"Every last man there got a Dear John letter," Grayson says, "from everyone back here."

"I thought it would never end," Ma says. "It was longer than your father's war."

Grayson nods.

"All the boys who will never come home," she says.

She didn't mention Paul; she didn't have to.

"Ma, you ready for *Soul Train*? It's started."

Grayson gets up and snaps one dial over to the UHF frequency and then slides another dial to Channel 38.

Soul Train host Don Cornelius is trying to coax a few words out of a couple of wildly dressed young guys who appear to be in shock, maybe because they are talking to *Soul Train* host Don Cornelius. One of the young men throws worried glances at the camera as if concerned the camera might actually be a rocket launcher.

Grayson stretches out on the couch with his hands folded on his stomach and during commercial breaks tells her he had recently visited two of his three sisters, he is putting together a softball team, might grow a mustache, and wishes he could buy a puppy, all of which is just fine. What he says doesn't matter, what she needs is the comfort of his voice.

Grayson sits up straight and pays attention when Don Cornelius introduces, "The Mighty Al Green."

Don Cornelius disappears, replaced by the performers on the stage, and the kids in front of it, seen from up high and far away. The band kicks in with a flourish of horns and the kids begin to move. As the music revs up, the picture on the screen switches to a shot from the left-hand side of the stage, where in the corner of the screen, a black woman stands behind two giant conga drums, smacking the tops with cupped hands, steadily. She has a big kerchief draped over her head, worn like a woman at Mass in the 1950's. Though it doesn't cover her facial features, the kerchief obscures them somehow. She is wearing a black suede track suit with a silver chain running down the length of her leg. She set the beat but soon only Al Green is on the screen.

Al Green is wearing a vest and bright yellow pants, and he has one arm in a sling, and carries long-stemmed roses in his injured hand. He sings "Here I Am," easily, and sounds as good, or maybe better than, his recording of it.

"I have trouble understanding his words," Ma says. "But I feel his passion."

"Oh, yeah. The band is great, too. I wish they'd show the woman on the conga drums again. She looks like she was chiseled out of stone, like a mysterious goddess, or something. I don't know."

"Mysterious? Do you mean pretty?" Ma says.

"Yes, but not just that. I don't know how to say it. I wish they'd show her again so I can figure it out."

But there are mostly shots of Al Green. At times he dances in a conscious but not self-conscious way. Grayson looks carefully at close ups of Al's eyes and face for signs of booze or dope, but there are none he can see. Seated at the drum kit behind Al Green is an intense, skinny, cock-eyed black guy with a short haircut and a thin face. His eyes are, at all times, locked on Al Green, and the drummer beat the skins in the same pattern, again and again and again, as he stares, one eye is filled with love, and the other eye murder.

But Al Green dances like he knew he could never die, not really, and there are moments when Al Green is being moved, almost ecstatically, but then he would come back to himself and resume what Grayson could only think of as an unselfconscious performance. It is electrifying to see someone dance like this because Grayson couldn't even imagine letting go like that, whether drunk, sober, alone, and never mind in company.

"Wow," Grayson says.

"He is really good," Ma says.

The kids dancing in the front of the stage look like they were on the edge of letting go, too. There are far more kids with eyes closed, and they are moving more idiosyncratically than Grayson has ever seen. It is difficult not to be spirited away by Al Green, the music, the beat and what Grayson can only think of as the drama of what is happening on the screen.

"*Here I am, baby, Lord, have mercy, come and take me,*" Al begs. He begs one more time, and then he demands. "*Come and take me!*"

"Oh," Ma says.

As the band plays Al Green dances, whoops and capers back and forth. He begins to hand out roses to the kids in front of the low stage. Occasionally Al Green closes his eyes and becomes the beat, but only for a moment, as if to go longer has too great a cost. Neither Grayson nor his mother speak.

"*Good God,*" Al Green sings, "*Do you love me, love me, love me. Good God! Do ya love me!*" He dances back and forth across the stage. A few shouts, then he slows down the band with his raised hand.

"You may not know what I mean this evening," Al Green says, in preacher speak. "But everybody aboard the soul train, just git aboard the soul train this evening, you don't need no money, you don't need no ticket."

"He sounds like he's praying," Ma says.

Grayson shakes his head. "Who knows?"

Then he sees that is what his mother believes. "Yeah, I think he is."

The camera pans the stage and Grayson sees the conga player. She is there and has the beat going, but she looks unaffected by it all, as cool as New Year's Eve in Iceland.

The horns wail, the man on the drums kept up a steady unchanging beat and from the corner of the stage Al Green waves and steps off. The *Soul Train* logo comes on and a limp whistle sounds.

"Yow," Grayson says.

"My, oh my," his mother says. "What a great number. I thought I was going to get up and dance."

"He is dynamite. I have that record, but Al Green doing it live is wild."

"Speaking of praying," Ma says. "I've been praying that you'll agree to do a few things for me."

"Of course, I will. What is it?"

"I guess it's really one thing, with three parts."

"It sounds complicated," Grayson says. "Do I need a pen?"

"Stop now, I'm serious."

"I'm listening."

"I want you to go to AA, make up with Catherine, and stop blaming yourself for what happened to Hugh. It was an accident."

"I'm trying, Ma. Mostly."

"Meaning?" Ma says. "You have to do all three to get any one of them fixed permanently. One or two out of three won't work."

"Football meant everything to him," Grayson says. "And I took it away from him."

"You're his brother, you wouldn't hurt him on purpose," Ma says. "Did you mean to do it?"

"I know. You've said that," Grayson says. "I try not to think about it. Not anymore."

"He doesn't blame you," she says.

How was it that his mother did not know her sons? How is it that a woman can give life to a boy, bear that boy, feed him from her flesh, keep him within the sound of her voice until he's grown, and yet not know him? Or did only she truly know her sons, and know them better than they knew each other and themselves?

"You said you'd do it," Ma says. "Will you promise?"

"Yes," he says.

"Promise."

"Promise," he says.

"I see your face," she says. "I mean before I die."

"Ma. Stop that." He stood up.

"Sit down. I am going to die, and it's all right. I can't say I'm 'ready,' but I know I will be when the time comes. But I want to see you do these things first."

"Good. Wait until I do." He rubs the palms of his hands together. "That's a nice loophole for both of us."

"Be careful you don't hang yourself in that loophole," Ma says. She'd always had a sharp tongue when pushed, and still did. "Do I have to get mad at you?"

"No, Ma. I'm sorry. I'll take care of it. Be a little patient."

They adjourn to their metaphorical corners and watch *Soul Train* for a while longer, but The Mighty Al Green wore her out and she falls asleep in the chair. In daylight she could drop off quickly and easily; she'd sleep on and off now until late evening. Most nights she'd lie awake in the dark, listening to Larry Glick on the radio.

Grayson hears the steps squeak and a few seconds later his father comes into the room. The Old Man sits in an armchair and they talk quietly about Yaz and the Red Sox. If Grayson wants to avoid the AA jive he has to stay on his toes. When the conversation begins to slow, Grayson moves rapidly to other topics, safe topics, like politics, war and religion. The Old Man can spot the smallest opening and race through it, turning an innocent remark about the weather into a tale of winos in winter. Many are the trolls pulled from under a bridge and into a meeting by a hazy memory of free doughnuts, but not all who are called by the pastry are chosen by the higher power to live clean, dry lives, and those that are give thanks to the program, the program, the program.

His mother is snoring softly in her chair.

"She's been asking me if I think you're going to come around soon," his father says.

"Yeah, I'll stop by again, soon." Grayson looks at the clock radio and gets up. "I got to run. I'll be back in the next few days, okay?"

"Yeah," his foiled father says, a note of resignation in his voice. "Okay."

As he is leaving the room, his mother says, "Michael?"

"Yeah, Ma?" He goes over and kisses her good-bye.

"I had a dream that Al Green was praying for you."

"Well, God knows I can use it," he says.

He kisses her again and then flies down the stairs, light footed now, loving both his parents with a crazy love; he was happy as hell to be leaving, even as he already missed them. No longer the giant figures of his childhood, they'd gotten smaller as he'd gotten bigger and seeing them is like visiting his old grammar school and stooping to use the water fountain he once had to drink from on tiptoes. Watching them age faster and faster each year is painful, although he loves them all the more. He wants to save them from old age, sickness and death, and if he can't, he can't sit there and watch. He isn't man enough. He feels terrible about not spending more time with them, and knows one day he'll feel much worse, but, right now, this is about all of the love he can stand.

CHAPTER TEN

Just before 6PM Saturday evening, Grayson wheels the GTO into the parking lot at The Harvest Restaurant. The early evening sky is dimly lit, but even in mid-March there is a shade of deep blue high in the western end of the sky as the planet rolled on toward the longest day. He did a quick spin in the lot, looking for Catherine's old LeMans. She works every Saturday night.

The waitresses who came in before noon went home at six, run ragged during the 'Feed the kids for a dollar," special that ran from 3PM until 5:30 PM. Catherine had worked that shift but there was no money in it, so she preferred nights. The kid's meal cost a dollar and for that they got a hot dog, a carton of milk and unlimited amounts of macaroni & cheese and rolls. Parents in their twenties and thirties came with their kids, most of who were under ten. Most of the families who ate at The Harvest were just now getting to where they could afford to splurge once a month or so for dinner out. This allowed them to dine out and not have to pay a baby sitter. The kids were often dressed up, and they struggled to behave, but a sibling skirmish would inevitably break out at one table, and swiftly spread across the restaurant. Catherine said once the peace has been broken, the disorder spread table to table unbelievably fast and seemed as well coordinated as a prison riot. Happily, no one ever got shanked, but many bread rolls were fired across a table. She found the kid's fine dining experience to be great fun, but the tips were meager in comparison to the effort.

In the early evening, she waited on old couples who liked to avoid the family scuffles. She said they, meaning the old folks, were sweet and most of them wore their hats all through dinner. They ordered Manhattans, left them unfinished, took almost the whole meal home in a doggie bag, and proudly dispensed tips. Shambling out, the old men would often alert her that they left cash laying there on the table, cash that some klepto might grab, if she didn't get to it quick.

He knows one thing for certain: The baby she carries is his. She'd dumped him January first, and based on his crude calculations, if she is finding out now that she was pregnant, she has to have gotten pregnant in late January, specifically January 23rd. She had come to him on the night of his mother's stroke, and took him to bed, and besides, there was no way the Braintree dentist was going to…advance so far in just a few weeks.

As Grayson circles again in the parking lot, he sees another one of the waitresses, trotting toward the kitchen door.

"Suzanne," Grayson calls.

Suzanne Darwin was a great looking Braintree girl who had married a guy Grayson knew from around the bars in North Quincy. Suzanne was a lot better woman than Ape deserved, but Grayson thought you could say that about most women and their men.

"Hey, Handsome," Suzanne says. She walks over to the open passenger side window. "Did you come to take me away from all this?"

"Now, now. What would Mr. Darwin say?"

"How would you like to be married to a guy called Ape?" Suzanne says.

"I wouldn't. When is Catherine due?"

"Two minutes ago. If she's not here, we're both late."

She slaps her hand a couple of times on the metallic strip on the window slot so her wedding ring makes a clinking noise, turns and disappears through the screen door to the kitchen.

Grayson backs the car into a space from which he could see Adams St. He only waits a couple of minutes before he sees her faded green 1966 LeMans streak into the parking lot and around the other side of the restaurant. He drives over as Catherine is gathering her things from the car. Her face falls when she sees him.

"What? What?" she says. "Please, not now. I'm already late."

She fools him by going toward the lobby entrance, in the opposite direction. Grayson rolls down the window, puts the transmission in reverse and backs up alongside of her as she walks. Her body is framed by the passenger side window, only visible to him from her hips to her breasts. He throws his arm over the seat and looks behind the car, turning his head every so often in her direction. He could only see her midsection. His heart aches.

"I'll quit drinking," he says. "Immediately."

"For me?" she says.

"Yes. And the baby."

"Wrong answer. You would just quit until we're married. Then you'd nip and nip and nip until you're back at it full blast," she says.

"Nope. I'll quit for good."

"How much have you had today?" she says.

"Oh, come on. Why would I start quitting until you agree to terms?"

"Very funny. How many chances are you going to need? Fifty? Five hundred? A thousand?" she says.

"What if I go to AA?"

"Big whoop. My father had a shoebox full of thirty-day medals from them. He was always quitting. For us."

"What if I pledge that my kid will never see her father drink," he asks.

He stops the car as they reach the lobby doors.

She bends down and looks in at him. "I'm way ahead of you."

She turns and walks inside.

CHAPTER ELEVEN

Donny holds the glass lobby door open as Grayson leans on the black button beside Hugh's name on the brass wall plate anyway, knowing the buzzer annoys Hugh.

"What are you doing?" Donny says. "You know he hates the buzzer."

Grayson shrugs.

"Real mature," Donny says.

They trudge up the stairs, down the carpeted hall and Donny pushes Hugh's door open, and they walk in.

"He's taking a shower," Donny says.

Where's Charlie?" Grayson says, looking around.

"He had to go to a wake. He's getting a ride over."

Hugh comes out his bedroom dressed in a starched white shirt and a dark blue pair of chinos, perfectly ironed. He slips his feet into a pair of black, shiny shoes.

Hugh says, "We're going to review things as soon as Charlie gets here."

Hugh holds up a jar of instant coffee, but they shake him off, and he makes a cup for himself while the other two wait on the couch. Coffee made, he sits at his table, leans back in the kitchen chair, spreads his fingers and runs his hands back through his wet hair several times, fast, like he is trying to comb the spiders out.

'Where is Charlie?" Grayson asks.

"He's coming," Hugh says. "We need a final review of the plan, and to make sure everybody is in tip-top shape."

"Why did you bring this biker, this wild card in? We don't know him," Grayson says.

Hugh shrugs. "One, it has to be now because of the St. Patrick Day bash, two, you kept saying no. Three, Donny says he'd probably be going to New York for the weekend. I couldn't go in with just Charlie. So, I asked Amy for help."

"Yeah, but I said I was only going to see those new World Trade Center buildings. I can do that anytime." He looks at Grayson. "I was taking Michelle down for the weekend, show her a good time."

"Which Michelle?" Grayson asks.

"Big Teeth Michelle."

Hugh looks at Grayson. "You'd said no. I told Amy I might need to find some outside muscle since my guys were doing the fade on me. She talked to her ex-student, the bike club president from Walpole, and he sent his best guy over. He has experience in this type of work and he said yes. So, he's in."

"Now, where's Amy?" Donny asks.

"You'll meet her. Soon."

"She's a revolutionary," Grayson says.

"A revolutionary what?" Donny asks.

"Toaster oven. Idiot. You know, a Commie."

"Get out of here," Donny says. He turns to Hugh. "What's he talking about?"

"Hey, wait a minute," Hugh says, pointing at Grayson. "I thought you and her were bosom buddies now. I heard you got ripped on absinthe over there."

"I'll tell you what I'm talking about," Grayson says to Donny. "She's a fucking nut. She has to stay indoors in the fall when the squirrels are out gathering food."

"No, she's not. She's political," Hugh says. "She's hardly alone. You may have noticed, there's a lot going on in this country, and the world. Donny, just wait until you meet her, decide for yourself."

"She's dangerous. For us, not her," Grayson says. "This Bird? Is he crazy, too? He sure looks it."

"Crazy like a fox," Hugh says. The buzzer sounds and Hugh hits the button and Charlie shows up, and they do another review.

Grayson needs a drink. He hopes this activity will take his mind off drinking, and maybe even Catherine. He can use a break.

CHAPTER TWELVE

Grayson is behind the wheel, Donny is in the back seat of the GTO, and Charlie is riding shotgun as they head away from Donny's place where they'd stopped to get some speed to sharpen their wits, and Donny put on a bowling team shirt.

Charlie says, "I wasn't going to say anything, but you put on a bowling shirt with the name Maurice on it. Who is Maurice and why do you have his shirt?"

"I don't know the man personally. I bought this at the Goodwill store. It's a good disguise, don't you think? People will say, 'One of those guys was named Maurice.'"

Grayson is silent and inattentive while the other two are talking through clenched teeth and almost audibly humming, like overworked high-tension wires.

"I think we went too heavy on the bennies," Donny says. "The pills must have held a bigger dose than I was told."

"You always administer too much, anyway," Charlie says. "I like to be sharp, but I never overdo it. You, on the other hand--"

"Oh?" Donny says. "You don't? How come you're chewing your shirt collar?"

"That's not the pills, I always do that," Charlie says.

They fall into an argument over Charlie's claim to be compulsive shirt collar chewer.

Meanwhile, Grayson who had taken only one pill, drifts away and back.

Would I be doing this shit if I had a kid? What did she mean that their child would never see him drink? Was she moving away from here, like Franny Walton did when she got pregnant? Or was she thinking of putting the baby out for adoption? Abortion? Maybe she thought it was better that she had an abortion? How the fuck could it be better? Maybe she had asked him to come over so she could read his reaction when she told him she was pregnant. He must have failed the test.

He thought of himself as a stand-up guy. He broke promises to himself all the time; but it was also true he almost always came through on a promise to somebody else. What he committed to do for others almost always got done. Or was that just a line of bullshit he'd sold to himself?

Maybe she thought he unconsciously wants her to have an abortion? Maybe she picked up that vibe. Maybe she knows him better than he knows himself. She'd known him since he was five years old. Or maybe she just knew he wasn't up to the job of being a decent father, and she thought their child would be better off not having a life.

"Mr. Charlie," Donny says. "Let me ask you this. You're a guy who likes words, like in the Reader's Digest and all. Where does the word 'car' come from? What, did old Robert T. Ford look at the Model T and just say, "Let's call this mother a 'car.'"

The gist of the babble on the TV, radio talk shows and in the paper was that what she chose to do with regard to her pregnancy is none of his business; it had nothing to do with him; but how could this be true?

He loves her and she is carrying a child they'd made together.

"Robert T. Ford?" Charlie says. He laughs and then looks over at Grayson to see if he is going to join in. "Hey, man. Wake up."

"What?" Grayson says.

"Yeah, I meant Henry T. Ford," Donny says. His face was in the rear-view mirror and he smiles toward Charlie, and taps him with a light punch on the arm.

"Henry T. Ford must have made up the word, I guess. Where else would it come from? It's not Latin or anything," Charlie says.

"What word?" Grayson asks.

"The word 'car,' for cripes sake," Donny says.

They are quiet as they roll down the Dorchester side of the Neponset Bridge.

Grayson moves his left hand to the open vent window and flicks out cigarette ash.

"I think car is short for carriage," he says. "I saw an old sign one time on the floor in a warehouse that says 'Columbia Motor Carriage Company.' I figure motor carriage got shortened to motor car and then just car. But it's only a theory."

"And it is a dandy," Charlie says. He waited for a response of some kind from Grayson. "What's the matter with you? Something got you down in the dumps?"

"He's still hung-over, no doubt. You need more go-get-um, boy?" Donny shouts.

"No, I'm alright. Maybe a little nervous."

"Because Mr. Charlie here is right, you don't sound too chipper," Donny says.

"Are you lethargic, sir?" Charlie says.

"No, I'm Catholic," Grayson says.

"There he is," Donny says. "There's old Grayson. Nothing to worry about, Charlie."

"Let's go kill some time in the Combat Zone. Go to a strip joint," Charlie says. "We're way too early anyhow."

The plan calls for them to hit the party at midnight and the drug merchants just after 1AM. The thinking is most of the sales would have taken place, everyone at the party would be wasted, the pharmacy boys would likely have begun sampling their own wares and the money would be gathered in one easy-to-rob spot, rather than in the pockets of the party-goers from all around the area.

"No strip joints," Donny says.

"What are you, goody-two-shoes?" Charlie says.

"No. They suck. Going to a strip club is like going to a cook out, seeing the food, smelling it and not being able to eat. It's aggravating."

"Wow," Charlie says. "You're a chauvinist pig."

"I suppose," Donny says.

Grayson suggests that they turn around and stop in at The Pony Room at Neponset Circle to have a couple of belts and allow time to pass in a civilized manner.

They climb the stairs to the second floor, the only bar above ground level that any of them has ever been in. It is dark and subdued, the lights wore red shades, the floor is a red rug and the bar was painted with a black lacquer and lined with red leather stools. Here in the devil's waiting room, the customers are smart enough to mind their own business.

They sit at a small table near the front window and the waitress comes to take their orders.

After a couple of shooters apiece, all three shift to beer. They look out the window at the cars traveling over the Neponset River Bridge.

"Hey, look at that chick," Donny says, pulling Charlie's arm.

Charlie turns to see. "What chick, the waitress?" he says. "Oh, the bartender? Yeah, she's hot. Waitress is old. What's she, almost forty?"

"Jane Fonda's almost forty," Donny says. "The traitor."

"She was wicked hot in Klute," Charlie says.

"Oh, man, she was," Donny says. "She was wicked hot. And the space movie a few years ago? Wow."

Donny looks at the bartender again, and his head lifts as the movement on the shiny TV screen anchored up in the corner captures his attention. The local news is on, and for a while they watch Tom Ellis imitate Ted Baxter, then the weather comes on after a commercial.

"We're in March and the weatherman is saying warm," Charlie says, "Warm is good, but I like hot better."

Donny turns back.

"I like hot better, too. Hot, like Tina Turner," he says. "Hey, is your sister still living over here in

Port Norfolk?" He points to the other side of the wide road.

Port Norfolk is an isolated neighborhood of Neponset, which itself was part of Dorchester. Port Norfolk had an end of the world feel to it, since it was sliced off from the rest of Boston by the Southeast Expressway, and almost scraped into the mouth of the Neponset River.

"She's married, pal," Charlie says. "Don't you be thinking about my sister. You have only one thing on your mind at all times. Don't be thinking about her."

"I just asked if she's still living over here?"

"Yes, but she's moving. Some biker gang moved in, across the street from them," Charlie says. "Typical biker antics, choppers roaring around at all hours, bearded fat guys passed out on the street, drunk fights, chucking beer bottles at passing cars. They didn't want their kids around it. They're staying at my mother's, while they find another place. Gave their 30-day notice to the landlord."

"That's got to be Bird's gang, The Dark Lords," Grayson says.

"The cops weren't helpful?" Donny asks.

"Cops won't even come. They're scared shitless of the bikers," Charlie says.

Back in the car, Grayson wheels the GTO over to the street where Charlie's sister Cheryl lived, or used to live. They are curious to see if, in fact, it was The Dark Lords who'd run off Cheryl.

They'd gone by the house but couldn't really stop to look because there are a number of bikers outside, in the yard. They did spot a piece of plywood nailed to a tree which has written on it, *The Dark Lords.*

"Look how nice the penmanship is on that sign," Charlie says, shaking his head. "That is weird."

The Lords themselves were in the midst of a bottle fight, whipping empty beer bottles at each other, relaxing with a bit of horseplay. One would hide behind a raggedy ass white van parked in the bare yard, then step out and fire a bottle tomahawk style. Another would charge his position and chase him around the van like in the cartoons. A smoldering, badly stained mattress was leaning against a porch railing, and in the side yard the guts of a 1956 Chevy Bel Air are strewn about before it, as if the car has vomited.

Grayson picks up speed as he passes the sagging house, and heads for the expressway.

"Pigs," Charlie says. "I'm glad my sister got away from those creeps."

"Hey," Donny says. Grayson feels his car seat tilt back as Donny pulls himself forward and sticks his big head into the front seat area between Grayson and Charlie. "Hey! Turn that radio up. Hendrix!"

Not willing to wait a half second for the front seat occupants to process and act on his demand, he reaches across for the radio knob. Grayson has to lean away to avoid being jammed against the steering wheel by Donny's elbow.

"For crying out loud," Grayson says.

The volume at max, Donny began to scream along with '*All Along the Watchtower*,' his face filling the rear-view mirror.

"Sit back and shut up," Grayson says. He turned the radio down. "Or I turn it off."

"Okay, Dad," Donny says. Charlie laughs, but Grayson doesn't think it's funny.

"Turn it up, I can hardly hear it now," Donny says. Grayson does and Donny fell back and sings along.

As the song comes toward the end, Donny pulls himself forward again, so their faces were in a row. "And the wind begins to howl!"

Soon they hit the bunched-up traffic near Andrews Square. It usually slowed down a mile or so before the tunnel, where the cars coming from the south and the cars coming from the west off of the Mass Pike and merge at the mouth of the tunnel, amidst a flurry of rude gestures and shouted curses.

"Traffic jams at night. What a city," Charlie says.

"Yeah, she's old," Grayson says. He sits up straight and looked to the left, across the top of the one story pre-fab buildings in the new flower market on Albany St, and at the crumbling, dusky brick structures that lined the other side of Albany. "Been around a long time."

"Too long," Charlie says. "It's a frigging mess. No wonder everyone's leaving."

"Maybe it's because everyone's leaving," Grayson says.

"That's what the BRA is for," Charlie says, referring to the Boston Redevelopment Authority. "Death and rebirth, man. That's the whole story in a nutshell."

"Yeah," Donny says. "Sweep away the old. Tear it down, haul it off, throw up something new. Speaking of which, let's go by the new Hancock building."

"The Plywood Palace," Charlie says.

Grayson says, "No way. Those windows that fall out weigh fifteen hundred pounds each. One falls out you'd get crushed and minced simultaneously. I'm going Storrow Drive."

"Well," Donny says. "I didn't say, 'Let's go there and stand on the sidewalk until we get chopped to bits,' did I?"

Fifteen minutes later Grayson is driving around the Fenway neighborhood looking for a parking space around the corner from the Peterborough Street address they have, something within running distance.

"Not easy parking," Charlie says.

"The Sox open the season in a few weeks," Donny says. "It'll be worse."

Charlie taps Grayson's arm. "You're really quiet again. You all right?"

Grayson nods. "I'm fine."

"Lucky you. Now we're here, I'm afraid I'm going to piss my pants in there."

"I have something that will make you feel like King Kong," Donny says.

"I've got something," Charlie says. "I can wait 'til we get up there."

CHAPTER THIRTEEN

He finds a place to park down the block on Kilmarnock St. They get out, look up at the windows of the turn of the century apartment buildings, four and five stories high, brick or stone and crammed together so tight you couldn't get a knife blade between any two. They walk around the corner to Peterborough Street, and pass a VW bus parked under a street light. The original paint job is now a faded blue and the backdrop for a hand painted peace sign, a Black Power fist and other homemade touches like swirls, loopy lines, and a representation of a famous cartoon dog.

"Lotta hippie wagons around," Donny says.

"I see one," Grayson says.

"That's right," Charlie says. "Way too many." Donny laughs, and pats Charlie on the back.

In some ways, this area is not a part of Boston. It is more like a far-flung suburb of New Jersey or New York. Locals often felt they were in hostile territory here or in another of Boston's several student ghettos. For most of the year the streets and apartment buildings of this Fenway neighborhood teem with students from the local schools. The Fenway neighborhood is within walking distance of Wentworth, Boston State, Harvard Med School, Emmanuel, Simmons, B.U., Northeastern and Mass. College of Pharmacy. This part of Boston is occupied by people who laugh at your accent, right in front of you, but only once, and paid $1.50 to sit in the bleachers at Fenway Park and root for the Yankees. The newly educated who seemed to think that the ability to talk *really, really, really fast* meant that what they say is righteous.

Grayson, Charlie and Donny have family roots in the southern Boston neighborhoods. Dorchester, Roxbury and South Boston are the sections of the city where they and their parents were born. It is where their parents grew up, married and started a family. But in the 1950's and early 60's many of the young families headed by the men who'd made it home from the war, moved kin and kit to the nearby suburbs of Quincy, Braintree, or

Weymouth. The reasons why they moved varied; a big yard, or child safe streets. For some, though not many, it was because they believed there were no "coloreds" in the suburbs. But the usual reason for about nineteen out of twenty of them was that a working man could now afford his own home, a single-family home, no less, if he was willing to sweat the mortgage. Coming up with the monthly payment would not be easy, but that was all right. A school teacher could make the payments on his own home in Weymouth, if he was willing to paint houses in the summer or drive an ice cream truck. A Teamster who put in a couple of hours of OT a day could have his own 200 square feet of soft suburban grass, not that city grass, that grew through a crack in the asphalt and had the texture of sandpaper. A shipyard worker who tended bar a couple of nights a week could say goodbye to the second-floor apartment in a triple-decker.

So, their offspring, these young men, born in this city, feel estranged from it. And yet, they believe that they know it better and love it more than those who came later or those who stayed. Who knows a love better than he who has regrets that he left?

"Listen," Charlie says. "Don't get into a beef with anyone. Not tonight."

"Then tell the hippies to be nice," Donny says.

Grayson often wondered why when they were back in the place where they were born, they were argumentative. In the blue-collar bars they were flaming liberals, in the student ghettos, raging conservatives. Maybe it was like an ex-lover trying to start a brawl with his replacement. Or maybe if they didn't know you, they'd go to any lengths to piss you off. Or maybe they are just jerks who like to annoy everyone.

They all hate Nixon and the rest of the Republicans but they also despise the Democrats who started the war, got 55,000 American kids killed and then ran away from it and now call it Nixon's War. Now, as opposed to a short while ago, when people talk about government and politics on TV or write columns in the newspapers, the talk of "the Left" and "the Right," instead of Democrats and Republicans. So, in the new vernacular, the bombast and boosterism of the Right embarrassed them and the certainty and self-righteousness of the Left sickened them.

"I do not like hippies, not even a little bit," Donny says.

"Nobody does," Charlie says. "Because they're all assholes."

Donny nods. "Amen, brother."

"I'd still fuck a good-looking hippie chick, though," Charlie says.

"Goes without saying," Donny says.

"Men of strong convictions," Grayson says.

"My father thinks they're still called beat-niks," Charlie says. "He sees them on TV, he says," and here Charlie growls in an older man's voice, "'Beatnik bastards are always protesting some stu-pid shit like starchy food in the cafeteria. Too much macaroni and cheese. Close down the campus. They're always squawking over something goofy.'"

When Grayson, Donny, Charlie and their friends are in their own haunts and certain they can't be heard by outsiders, they argued amongst themselves about things. Charlie says the anti-war hippie Left was comprised of a bunch of spoiled college kids with rich parents. Donny believed the anti-war geek's main goal was self-promotion. They have a sick need to be seen cavorting in the mass media. They are mostly freaks and hysterics, self-important, silly dinks. It pisses Grayson off that ten percent of his generation is made up of these drips, but the mass media makes it seem as if the ten percent is the majority. To the world, the mangy losers shown lurching around and gyrating in *Woodstock* in muddy assed bellbottoms are the icons of the generation; to their working class con-temporaries they are posers; posers with posters of Che; they are sheep, dreaming they are rebels, unaware that should the revolt they wished for suc-ceed, they would be counted among the rich, and escorted to a perch on the lip of a ditch, and given a personal demonstration of the one shot solution to a potential counter revolution.

"We're close," Grayson says.

He points up at a double winged stucco apartment building, where someone has opened a window and stuck a stereo speaker in it, facing out.

"Sylvester Stewart is coming out that second floor window."

"What?" Charlie asks. He looked up, then heard the music, too. "Oh, Sly."

"*It's a family affair,*" Donny croaks, in a piss poor imitation of Sly and The Family Stone.

Donny executes a couple of James Brown spins, and a few dance moves he had mastered and felt compelled to perform whenever he heard the blues or soul music, or merely came across a black entertainer's name. Grayson and Charlie ignore him, as Donny whirls on the sidewalk in his oversized blue bowling team shirt, with the "Kandlepin Killers" logo on the back and the name *Maurice* stitched over the pocket.

Charlie nods his head toward the wide brownstone, with five floors and probably about forty units.

"Yeah, this is the one we're looking for," Charlie says.

They go up the block granite steps to a vestibule and get inside to eyeball a bank of buzzer buttons beside the apartment numbers. Scattered around the floor of the vestibule are take-out menus, flyers for stereo equipment, and sections of the free weekly tabloid newspaper. The air stinks of pot, piss, puke, wet paper, and warm pizza box.

Shortly after Donny presses the right button a female voice crashes over the tinny speaker and says something that ends in a question mark.

Donny presses a hand over his mouth and speaks in a badly muffled but decidedly mellow, exaggerated hippie drawl. "Hey, man. We're here for the party." He punctuates his words with an idiotic cackle.

A loud noise snaps and buzzes, and seems to fill the vestibule with static electricity. Charlie jumps and shouts for Jesus. Donny laughs, and pulls the now unlocked glass door open.

"Man, you could electrocute a cow with that buzzer," Charlie says.

Grayson resists the urge to make a remark, knowing they are all nervous now, and will be until it all was long over.

As they start up the wide interior staircase in the middle of the big foyer, the apartment door closest to the vestibule opened and an elderly woman leans out and looks around. The old gal looks like she'd just gotten out of bed. She inhabits a large housecoat and has her hair up in bobby pins.

"You people better hurry up and have your fun," she says, "because I'm calling the police. You tell that fat Judith that the noise is unbearable! I'm not going to put up with it."

"We are the police, mam," Donny says. Frowning, he takes out his wallet, holds it up for a second and then put it back in his pocket. "We're here to quiet them down."

"Thank God," she says. "I'm going to have her evicted. I've lived in this building for forty years and I've never been afraid like this, even when The Strangler was going around killing everyone. These dope fiends."

"Shhh," Donny says. "Don't worry, it'll be fine. We're here now. We'll get them to settle down, or there will be hell to pay."

"I hope you have to beat them up!" the old woman says, eyes afire.

"Yes, mam," Donny says. He nods. "We do, too." Then he smiles, showing her a set of gleaming choppers.

"I shouldn't have to live like this," the woman cries out. She sobs and slams the door. The despair in her voice takes all the fun out of their Dragnet skit.

Grayson shakes his head. "She's right. She shouldn't have to live like this, with these jerks and their antics."

"Yeah," Donny says. "Let's go beat the shit out of them and steal their money. And their drugs."

They climb up the stairs, now pissed off at the partiers.

At the top of the steps, Grayson wishes there were more. A lot more. Steps he could keep going up and up and up and never get to where he is going.

The door to 32 is closed but seems to pulse and throb in its frame from the noise beating against it. This is the place.

Donny knocks on the door, and a fraction of a second later, knocks again, much harder.

"Oh, oh," Charlie says. "The bennies got him amped way up."

"Yeah. Simmer down," Grayson says. "You're so nervous you're making me jumpy."

"Fuck off," Donny says. "You simmer down."

A pretty young woman, who would have been described as voluptuous in Victorian era pornography, opens the door.

"Wow," Donny says. "You must be Judith. Nobody said you were a fox."

"What?" Judith asks, with a smile.

Donny looks her up and down, but says nothing more.

"My friend told us you're having a party," Charlie says.

She smiles again. "Oh, you're Jack's friends?"

They don't know Jack, but play it out as if they do.

"Exactly right. Is he here?" Grayson asks.

"No, he couldn't make it," she says.

"Oh, too bad," Grayson says. "Jack's the best."

"He said you might come. What's your name again?"

"I'm Barry LaBreck," Charlie says. "These two sad sacks aren't with me."

"Oh, heck. Don't listen to him," Donny says. "He's whacked out on beans."

The woman turns to Charlie.

"Well, that's cool, Barry," she says. She pronounced the name as 'Beery.'

She looks up at Donny. "Jack didn't tell me his friend was so handsome."

Charlie looks over at Grayson, smiles indulgently and shakes his head. Here it is again, the expression says. She thinks this enormous screwball is handsome? It is absurd, and yet they've heard it more than a few times from different females of various ages.

"I haven't seen Jack the last couple of weeks," Judith says. She registers their blank faces. "At B.U.? I'm in one of his poly-sci classes."

"Right," Donny says. "He mentioned that."

Judith nods and leads them inside, then excuses herself, turns left, pushes open a swinging door to give them a forty-five-degree angle peek into the kitchen. They had hoped to see the occupants, as part of their mission is to mingle and determine if there is any rogue muscle on site. Spot any tough guys who may want to give chase if the plan went awry. Some aggressive types who might get angry that their supplier has been ripped off. Judith heads into the kitchen and shuts the door leaving them none the wiser.

The air in the apartment is thick, spiced by cigarette and dope smoke plus beer and the tang of sweet, kiddie wine, sharp with its robust alcohol content. From the record player in another room comes the melancholy voice of John Lennon singing, *No Reply*. Sly has been played and now laid underneath an old Beatles album.

They head toward the music but are halted by a young man built like an upright piano, who is blocking the double doorway to the living room. The large lad has bushy black eyebrows and a head shaved close enough to clear him for a seat on the electric chair. He was a little over six feet tall, but he was wide, and bigger than Donny through the upper body. The guy was showing off his muscles in a tight black tee shirt. He nods toward another room, and makes a loud announcement in a honking New Jersey accent:

"Three bucks entitles you to help yourselves to your choice of Schlitz, Dawson Ale and Carling

Black Label, which are placed in coolers sited strategically around the common areas. Drink all you want. But there is one rule. Stay out of the kitchen, that's a private party."

Grayson figures they were chopping cocaine in the privacy of the kitchen. People at a party would thump up a vein and bang heroin with less reticence than they would light a Viceroy, but they got secretive around coke, especially good coke. The hippies love everyone, man, but not enough to give anyone a free taste. Love has its limits. Did the pharmacy college boys sell coke in addition to pills stolen from the VA? If the pharmacy student/ drug dealers upstairs had a steady source of medical grade coke, they were probably baling their cash with metal straps, crating it and using a fork lift to move it around.

"We're common folk," Charlie says. "You'll find us in the common areas, guvnor." Perhaps inspired by the Beatles music, he was attempting some kind of mangled cockney accent. "No suh, we'll not go into the kitchen. We know our place."

Grayson chafes; someone from New Jersey forbidding him to go anywhere in Boston, private property or not, is annoying. Unhappily, annoying is not enough; what Grayson needs, in order break out of this funk is either booze or outrage. Beside him, Donny apparently didn't hear the guy in the black tee-shirt; he stood there grinning, likely thinking about Judith. She is a lot of gal.

The big boy may take Donny's vacant look as a signal of submission, because Billy leans into Donny's personal space and looks at the name stitched over the pocket of Donny's bowling shirt.

"Okay, Maurice, three bucks each to me. I'm Billy. The Bouncer."

This Billy the Bouncer has a tone in his voice that Grayson doesn't like. Grayson tilts his head, and looks Billy the Bouncer up and down.

"I don't think you'd bounce. I bet you'd splatter," Grayson says, standing beside Donny.

Billy seems to think about that, as Donny snaps awake.

Donny steps in front of Grayson, blocking Billy's view of him, and speaks quietly to his cousin.

"What am I hearing in your voice?" Donny asks. "Do not start anything. You're here to keep me in line, not vice versa." He turns again to face Billy.

"Billy!" Donny shouts with brio. "What a kidder this kid is, say, you're a big boy Bill. You must play football?"

"Yeah," Billy says. "B. U., nose guard."

Behind Billy's back John Lennon loudly brays the opening line of, *"I'm a Loser,"*

Donny gives Billy a ten, and Billy fishes through some bills looking for a one.

Donny turns and grabs Grayson by the arm. "Don't say anything."

Grayson feels his arm go numb and yanks it free before it atrophies.

"Please," Donny says.

An exuberant Judith bounces out of the kitchen, comes over and grabs Donny by the hand and tugs him into the living room, and the other two follow.

Alcohol, amphetamine, and anger are not working as hoped, and Grayson, neither drunk nor high, just badly wired, has a copper taste in his mouth. Nothing is working right tonight.

Donny breaks away and dances Judith into a corner, smiling what he calls his suave smile, and for some reason, he's pointing at his feet.

Grayson and Charlie mill around looking for the cooler with the one potable beer of the three named. The ratty furniture is filled to overflowing and many of the guests are sitting on the floor, so they have to be careful not to trip over their fellow bon vivants. Those of the female persuasion are drinking wine from waxy, paper cups while some of the males manifest their *machismo* by downing their fruity Strawberry Hill straight from the bottle.

They see a cooler and sidle over to it. While Charlie, a bartender by trade, digs the beer out of the ice, Grayson catches a snatch of the conversation going on behind him.

A guy's voice says, "Bunny says you were tripping last night. How was it?"

A girl's voice says, "Not good. A real bummer. I could say it was because of my neuroses, but then what? Fuck that."

Charlie came back with four beers. He hands two to Grayson and they work their escape from the crush of knee-high people, retreating to the long hallway that was the spine of the apartment.

"Most of these chicks are hoodsies," Charlie says.

"Yeah, college girls used to be the older women. Now they're the hoodsies. Oh, well," Grayson says.

"Yeah, doesn't matter anyway," Charlie says. "I'm laying low."

"Endings are tough. I should know."

"That's true," Charlie says. "Listen, I'm starting to get bummed. Let's engage in some small talk."

"You bet. How about them Red Sox?"

"Who cares?" Charlie says.

"That's not how you do it," Grayson says, shaking his head. "Try this. What did you do last night?"

Charlie brightens and says, "Me and Yow got high and watched an old movie. It was hilarious. That James Dean rebel flick, where he's supposed to be a teenager. He cries all the time and gets hysterical at the drop of a hat. The one part when he puts his hands over his ears and screeches, 'You're tearing me apart,' we fell on the floor we laughed so hard. Some funny shit."

"You don't need to be high to laugh at that movie."

Billy the Bouncer comes over with two more of the beers they'd selected and hands them one each.

"Do you guys think you're tough?" Billy asks, looking at Grayson. "You and your pal Maurice?"

"I don't," Grayson says. He jerks a thumb toward Donny. "He doesn't boast, but he's tough. Highly tough."

"By the way, Mr. Billy," Charlie says. "My friend's name is *Mah-reees*. Not *More-iss*. The mispronunciation of his name can sometimes upset him."

"And not only is Maurice tough," Grayson says. "He's wicked mean."

Charlie says, "But, this guy right here, he's actually a good guy." He lifts a hand and lays it up on Grayson shoulder. "He just hides it well. Like, he may almost kill you, but when he cools off, he'll feel bad. Drive you to the emergency room. Put you in a wheel chair, wish you luck, tousle your hair. Well, not you, you have a baldie, but you get my drift."

"I can take care of myself," Billy says. "And I'm right here, too, if he'd like to take a swing at me."

"No, not me," Grayson says. "That big guy, Maurice? He might. If he looks at you, I'd recommend that you just drop to the ground and play dead. Trick him. That's your best bet. If he comes over and swats at you with a paw don't fight back, you'll just be prolonging your agony."

"You guys are real funny," Billy says.

"See here, Billy," Charlie says. "I offer this in the spirit of brotherhood." He points to Donny. "That organism over there is even meaner than he is big, and he was meaner at six years old than you and all your friends will be at thirty."

"You don't even know me," Billy says.

"No, I don't," Charlie says. "But what I do know is this, that those who have eyes to see know that yonder stands certain death."

Billy turns to look at Donny, who, it appears, is imitating a chicken crossing the road while Judith laughs and claps her hands. When Billy turns back all cockiness has disappeared from his face.

"He looks like he has something mentally wrong with his head," Billy says.

"Oohhh, yeah," Charlie says.

"Well, I won't fight retarded people, or mental nuts, whatever he is," Billy says. He walks away shaking his head.

"Wow," Grayson says. "What's with you baiting that big doofus."

"I don't know," Charlie says. "Raw nerves and a solid supply of speed and I'm a real chatterbox. I'm shaking like a wino jailed over a three-day weekend. Let's get the fuck out of here."

"You serious?" Grayson says, thinking about it.

"Yeah, fuck them, and their stupid ass plan," Charlie says.

"We can't do that. Leave my brother hanging. Not now."

Charlie takes a couple of deep breaths.

"Maybe I just need more bang," Charlie says.

He pulls a wad of paper from his pants pocket, and unfolds it. He holds out his quivery hand, palm up, offering the pills to Grayson, who shakes his head.

"What are those?"

"Purple hearts," Charlie says. "They really buck me up when I'm feeling bad, sad, or mad."

Charlie slaps the pills up to his mouth and washes them down with beer.

They lean against the wall drinking beer and watching Donny work on Judith. Then she takes him by the mitt and leads him out of the room and further into the apartment.

"Unbelievable," Charlie says. "Fifteen minutes, and they're in the bedroom. And he looks like a fuckin' T-Rex to me."

They drink beer and talk until Donny comes into the room and summons them with a toss of his head.

"Judy says up on five, apartment 52."

"Where is our buxom hostess?" Charlie asks. "Did she call them?"

"Yeah, from the phone in the bedroom," Donny says. "She's resting." He waggled his eyebrows like Groucho Marx.

"Probably exhausted from trying to escape," Grayson says to Charlie.

Charlie smiles.

"What time is it?" Grayson asks.

"Quarter 'til," Donny says.

"'Quarter 'til what? Eleven, midnight?" Grayson says.

"One," Donny says. "We're supposed to go in at one."

"Shit, it's actually gonna happen. Here we go," Charlie says. He has a look on his face like a spy who accidentally bites through his emergency cyanide capsule.

They leave the apartment and walk quietly down to the back stairway. They push through a door and out to the landing. Charlie and Grayson wait on the third while Donny goes down to the basement to let Hugh and Bird in the emergency exit. Charlie is breathing hard and sweating.

Grayson starts up the stairs. "Let's wait on the next landing."

They go to the next landing and wait against the wall for the others. Grayson feels a change in the air pressure when the exit door from the basement floor opens and closes quietly below. Soon the shushing of rubber soled shoes on cement steps conjures the other three.

Donny falls in behind Hugh and Bird and at the landing he crowds the others.

"Back down, Moose," Bird says. "How we supposed to get the door open?"

Donny steams. "Hey, Birdbrain we're not going in here. It's on five."

Hugh whispers, "Are we ready? Good. But one last time, here's how I want it to go. Charlie, remember the plan, just go up and knock on the door. You guys stay to the side so they only see Charlie through the peep hole. Bird and I will come up to five, but we'll stay on the landing until you're in. When you go in, leave the apartment door open a crack. When they give you the dope, say 'Bingo.' Then Bird and I will come in like the cavalry and we'll scare the shit out of them. Donny pull your gun when we announce we're cops."

"Here it is," Bird says, and hands Donny the gun. Bird looks at the gun in Donny's hand and says, "No that one's mine." He reaches into a pocket and pulls out an identical gun. "This one is yours."

Hugh says, "Twenty minutes from now, we'll be yukking it up in our cars, heading home."

"Don't forget the drugs. I want the drugs," Bird says.

Charlie nods for no discernable reason. He is clearly nervous but he would function. Charlie climbs up the stairs like they lead to the gallows, with Donny and Grayson right behind him.

They go out the door and into the fifth-floor hallway, and down to apartment 52. Charlie knocks with a single knuckle, and in a moment the door opens and they hear hipster jazz. Above a playful flute they hear what sounds like a black guy bitching someone out. The music bops out to the hall and then they hear talking. A kid sticks his head out, tells them they have to wait a minute and closes the door again. He's carrying on a tense dialog with someone else in the apartment who is out of earshot.

The kid yells at someone in the apartment, and can be heard out in the hallway.

"I said I would, so I will. Don't sweat it. Sheesh."

"Hear that?" Donny asks. "It sounds like there's an unhappy brother in there."

"The kid screaming?"

"No, they're playing the TV or the radio, something."

"That's *The Revolution Will Not Be Televised*," Grayson says.

"That a TV show?"

"A song," Grayson says.

"That's not singing. He's talking."

"I get tired hanging with you, man. It drains the life out of me." Grayson lights a cigarette and huffs it.

Charlie waits fretfully while Donny does push-ups off the wall, until Grayson tells him to cut the shit. Grayson slides over to the door to the back stairs, looks down the stair well and sees Hugh and Bird crouched and whispering. They look like two guys pitching pennies behind the corner store.

A minute later, the apartment door opens and another young guy steps out with a zonked smile and pulls a sandwich bag full of pills out of his pocket to wag at the trio.

"Forty bucks," the happy customer says. "For fifty pills!"

"Beautiful," Grayson says. "What a deal."

The kid nods a few times with everything from the waist up, then turns and walks away in a stroll that mimics the guy in the *Keep on Truckin* cartoon by Robert Crumb.

Charlie raps on the door, it opens and a tall, skinny kid with long blonde hair, wearing a head-band and a dashiki stood there. He held the door open only just enough to insert his gawky frame.

"Hey, are you Eric? Good. Eric, Judith down-stairs says you were selling snacks." Charlie says."

"Are these guys with you?"

Charlie says, "Yeah, I guess. They were at the party, too. Judith gave us your contact info at the same time, so we came up at the same time."

Eric opens the door and waves them in. "It's been a busy evening, we're almost out of some merchandise. We're very low on gange, if that's what you're looking for."

"Magic beans will do," Donny says. Then quickly adds, "I shouldn't speak for this little guy here, but me and my pal, we know we want pills. About this guy, I don't know. I don't even know his name. What's your name---"

"Hey, what are you reading," Grayson says, interrupting jabbering Donny, who is going way overboard in explaining how much he doesn't even know Charlie, for crying out loud.

Eric has his finger inserted in the middle of a paperback book to hold his place. Grayson figures he's dutifully doing his homework when not engaged in the illegal sale of stolen narcotics.

"*The Great Gatsby*," Eric says.

"What's that about, a magician?" Donny asks. Grayson wants to laugh but doesn't, because he's not sure if his cousin is making a joke.

Eric appears confused, then says, "No, not really."

He leads them down the hallway inside the apartment. Grayson turns the door knob and shuts the door, but slides the button down on the lock so the lock doesn't click.

Donny walks in back of Eric, thus cutting off any chance Eric might have to see back down the hall behind him.

Donny says, "We're looking for a regular supplier we can have confidence in."

Eric says, "We offer quality pharmaceuticals, as well as organic, home-grown marijuana."

As they stood there someone in the far room lowered the volume on Gil Scott Heron.

"No, man," Grayson says. "Turn it up."

Eric says, "I love that song, too."

Donny says, "Yeah, but it sucks to dance to. Back to biz. A double saw for forty reds?"

Seeing the kid draw a blank, Grayson pitches in. "Twenty dollars."

"No. We're getting forty for fifty."

"I heard twenty for forty."

"No," Eric says.

"Well," Donny says. "If that's what you're getting, we have to pay it."

"Let me get you what you're looking for," Eric says.

"Cool," Grayson says. "As long as we don't get what we deserve."

Eric cackles. "Yeah!" Then he says, "What do you mean?"

"Hey, that was a great song, the not-being-on-TV thing," Donny says. "Play it again."

"We're down with the revolution," Eric says.

"Right on," Grayson says. He pumps his fist in the air.

The kid walks down the hall and into a room at the end.

"What a shithead," Donny whispers.

"This is the age we live in," Grayson says. "Rich, white suburban kids, who probably never had dirty hands are 'down' with the revolution."

They hear a whiny voice coming from the other room.

"Shhh," Grayson says.

He moves toward the room and listens.

"I didn't hear you *ask* them if they were cops, Eric?" the voice says.

"That's so stupid anyway. Like they'd tell me if they were cops."

He comes back out into the hall with red pills in a plastic sandwich bag.

Grayson gives Eric forty bucks and then takes the bag.

"Bingo!" Donny screams, his voice booming in the narrow hallway. Eric jumps back, hard, slamming into the wall behind him.

Behind them the apartment door flies open and Bird, gripping a pistol in one hand, races past them, stopping at the end of the hall. Hugh closes the door into the apartment and follows Bird.

"Police! Nobody move." Bird speaks in a strong, controlled voice.

Hugh points a gun at Eric.

"Hands up, face the wall. Now!" he says.

Eric is likely unused to being spoken to in such fashion. No please, no thank you, but, whatever the reason, he just stands there with his mouth open.

Donny steps in front of Eric's horrified face and grabs a mitt full of Eric's dashiki and pins him against the wall. Donny's ready to launch into some cop verbiage, but Eric's eyes roll back and he slides down the wall to the floor. Donny holds on to the shirt as Eric slides, and he lands him gently.

Down the hall, Bird is barking orders.

"Police!" Bird says. "On the floor. Now!"

His voice is urgent but modulated.

Bird steps into the back room, and Hugh remains in the doorway with his gun raised.

In the hall, Donny pulls a length of rubber coated wire from his back pocket, goes over to the unconscious Eric and rolls him face down and cinches Eric's arms behind his back. Then he goes down the hall, nearer to the other two.

Down the hall, Bird's voice is louder. "Face down, on the floor. Now!"

Hugh says, "Okay." He speaks with less heat and lower volume than Bird, but loud enough so they can hear him in the hallway. "Stare at the floor. That's how to do it."

"Where are your weapons?" Bird says.

Donny goes down to the room where the action is and Grayson grabs Eric by the desert boots and drags him down the hall closer to the room. He stops and presses the prone Eric against the wall, like he was caulking a seam, and then he hurries down and stands outside the room, looking into it. In the room, Hugh, Bird and Donny are each standing over one of the three men on the floor.

On the hall floor Eric begins to come to and when he does turns his face away from the wall. Grayson and Charlie both turn to look at Eric.

"Oh, shit. Are you a cop, too?" Eric says to Grayson.

"Yes," Grayson says. He crouches facing Eric. "Be still and stay quiet."

Eric groans. "Oh, wow. Who narc-ed us out?" He looks up at Charlie. "You're not...oh, no, you're cop, too?"

Charlie shakes his head. If he's pretending to be scared, he's an amazing actor.

"No. We used this sap as our Trojan horse," Grayson says. "He's just a clapped-out junkie, like the rest of you, aren't you, son?"

Charlie nods and drops his chin to his chest.

"I'm not a junkie," Eric says. "I'm a college student. Take these off, please. What are they wires? They really hurt."

"Down at the station," Grayson says.

Donny comes out into the hall and looks at Eric. "What's with all the gabbing out here? Keep this bozo quiet."

Then there is a flash of light and a crack sounds from the other room; the crack bounces like a super ball between the hall walls. It might have been the sound of two bricks being slapped together like cymbals, but it isn't. It is a bang, one that sounds like the end of the world. Grayson is flash frozen for a fraction of time that seems like forever, and also like it would last way longer than forever. He is snapped out of it by a sharp cry from Hugh.

"What!" Grayson says. He and Donny push down to the back room. Donny gets there first, but stops dead in the doorway, and Grayson runs into his back, then pushes him aside and steps into the room. Hugh is standing there, unharmed.

"What'd you shoot him for?" Hugh says, looking at Bird.

"He was moving toward that bag," Bird says. "He could have been going for a gun."

"So what?" Donny says. "Clout him on the head."

On the back of one of the prone guys, a dark stain spreads, turning his blue tee shirt shiny. Bird with the gun still in his grip stands looking down at the man on the floor. Grayson knows Bird is going to shoot again.

"What the fuck?" Hugh says. He's down on one knee beside the guy who's been shot and puts a hand on his shoulder.

"Hey, buddy?" Hugh says. "Can you hear me?"

The guy's face is slack and his breaths are ragged. He looks to be about the same age as the rest of them, maybe a few years older. The thumb on the guy's left hand is twitching, tapping a soft, involuntary beat.

Another guy on the floor in the room wails. "You shot Jimmy? He wasn't doing anything."

Hugh gets up to face Bird, and Grayson sees Bird tilt the gun slightly in his brother's direction. Donny has his revolver out and moves quickly.

"That was loud," Donny says. "Let's get the stuff and go."

Bird bends and picks up a green trash bag. "There's a bunch of pill jars in here, but no cash." He looks at the guys on the floor. "Where's the cash?"

No answer.

"Where's the money?" Bird says.

"In the couch," says the other kid on the floor. He begins a rapid muttering, like he is praying quiet, fast, seriously.

"What's going on?" Eric shouts from the hall. "Are you guys all right?"

Aside from the bleeding man, there are two others, face down on the floor in front of the sofa with their arms stretched out like they are pretending to fly like Superman.

"He was going for a gun," Bird says. He appears as calm as if he was watching all this on TV.

"Is there a gun in the bag?" Hugh asks.

"Coulda been."

"No. No. Fuck no, you asshole," the mouthy guy says. "We don't have any guns. My father is going to sue the shit out of the Boston police. He's—"

The kid is cut off in mid threat when Bird kicks him on the side of the head. The praying kid is suddenly silent, too.

"Shut up," Hugh says. "Don't make it worse."

"Hey, what's going on in there?" Eric says from the hall floor.

Bird snaps at Grayson. "Shut that clown up."

Donny and Hugh are closer to the couch than Bird is, and he gestures to them.

"Go through the couch. Get the cash."

They turn and start fishing the couch, like Bird is the boss or something.

Grayson is across the room from Bird; from there he could see the prone men and the guy Bird had shot.

"Let's go, let's go, c'mon," Bird says. He steps over the man he shot and moves over the mouthy pharm boy. Bird's looking back at Hugh and Donny, then turns to Grayson.

Hugh straightens up from searching under the cushions, elbows Bird out of the way, and speaks to the other kid, the one who had been praying.

"Where's the rest of the money?" He taps the kid with the toe of his shoe.

"The couch. In back. Not the cushions. Is Jimmy okay? He doesn't even live here," the praying kid says.

Bird smirks. "Yeah, sure," he says.

"Shut up," Hugh says. "Nobody else has to get hurt. Just lay there and be quiet."

Grayson backs into the hall, blood pounding through his head.

"I don't get what's going on," Eric says. "Are you guys the cops?"

"Yeah, we're all undercover, except this little guy, and he's in the shit just like you," Grayson says, but his heart wasn't in it now.

"Who shot Jimmy?"

"Shut up," Grayson says. "Mind your own business, man."

Grayson went back to the doorway and watches Donny and Hugh each pick up an end of the couch to move it away from the wall. Then Hugh goes behind the sofa and drops out of sight. He tosses a roll of bills wrapped with rubber bands over the back of the couch onto the cushions.

"Help me," he says to Donny. "There are a bunch."

Now Donny disappears, too. Bird steps over to the kid he'd shot and points his gun at the back of the kid's head and pauses. If he shoots him again, Grayson knows Bird will execute the other kids, too.

Grayson says, "Don't."

Bird looks up and sneers, and then back at the kid on the floor. One of the kids on the floor is crying in a way Grayson has never heard before. The kid was actually making a sound like, 'wah wah.'

"Wait," Grayson says. "Don't."

Bird looks at Grayson with a horrible smile, and again points the gun at the bleeding guy's head.

If Bird kills this kid, he will kill all the others, too. Grayson takes two steps, drops his shoulder and drives it into Bird's mid-section. Grayson visualizes Bird bouncing off the wall and dropping the gun. But, unfortunately, instead of crashing into the wall, Bird crashes right through the fifth-floor window. The window had been cracked open, maybe to vent smoke, and Bird's back hit the crossbar on the double hung window, took out the glass and the old wood in the window snapped like kindling. Bird is through the glass and out of sight in nothing flat. He'd torn out the entire window, except for a few chunks of splintered wood stuck here and there in the frame.

Behind the sofa, Hugh pops up. "What the heck?" He looks around the room.

Beside Hugh, Donny, with his Marine training, only pokes up enough of his head to see what is happening. Satisfied he is not in urgent peril, he stands up, looks at the gaping hole in the shattered window and then at Grayson. "Where's Bird?"

Grayson looks at the window, then points.

"What did you do?" Hugh says, looking at Grayson.

"He was going to finish off this kid he already shot. I wanted to knock him over and make him drop his gun."

Donny moves to the window and looks out. "It worked. He dropped it."

Grayson starts over to look, too, but Donny holds him back. "You don't want to see."

Hugh goes to look, then shakes his head vigorously, as if to clear out cobwebs. "Oh, fuck." He gets the two green bags that hold the drugs, and throws some of the banded cash rolls into each bag, and heads for the hall.

Grayson is numb.

"Please call an ambulance for Jimmy," Eric says. He's been pushing himself down the hall with the tips of toes, because now his head is in the doorway into the room and he looks up from the floor. He was still belly down, with his hands wired his back. "Don't you guys have radios?"

"No," Donny says.

"All right, Eric," Hugh says, "Listen to me. Call an ambulance as soon as you can. But do not call the police. If you do so, because this is our sector, this Fenway area, dispatch will send us. Think about that. We will be the guys who answer your call and I promise you won't like what happens then."

"Jimmy, he's bleeding pretty bad," Eric says.

Hugh makes an arcing, global sweeping gesture. "And all this trouble you got in, let it be a lesson to you. Keep your nose clean. Get it?"

They move down the far end of the hall and speak in frantic whispers.

"What are we going to do?" Donny says.

"You and I gotta get Bird out of here. A fall like that, he's most likely dead, but we should check. If, by any chance he's still alive, we take him to the hospital and leave him there. We have to tell Amy that we tried to help him."

Donny looks out the window again. "Okay, but he looks really dead."

"Should we take his body then?"

"I was just trying to stop him from executing that kid. Really, it was an accident," Grayson says.

"We're going to have to do better than that," Hugh says. "His brother bikers are going to be pissed."

"Hey fuck them," Donny says. "The Lard Dorks. Shit happens."

Hugh grabs Charlie and pushes him into a bedroom, and Grayson follows. "Just tell these kids you're an unwitting patsy. Then book it. The cops will show up here in the next minute or maybe in an hour, who knows, but don't hang around. Okay, let's go."

He opens the door out to the hallway and looks side to side.

Charlie has been so quiet and still that Grayson had forgotten he was there. Grayson pulls silent Charlie down toward the front door, and speaks quietly. "Remember, tell Eric again you weren't with us, we just came upstairs at the same time. Say that, then beat it. I will be waiting at the car. Now go in there and pretend you're rattled."

"Pretend? I'm losing my mind," Charlie says.

"I'm with you there. Fucking Bird fucked up everything."

"You didn't help," Charlie says.

"Guilty."

Hugh is watching them from inside the front door to the apartment, and again he looks out into the hall.

"We're good. Go down the back stairs, but go out the front door," Hugh says.

They quietly cover the length of the outer hallway to the back stairwell and run down the cement stairs. At the bottom, Hugh says. "Hold up. Donny and I can't take the bags and move Bird, too. You take the bags."

"Okay."

"I'll try Amy and see if she can reach Belzer. If so, I'll say Bird wigged out and shot one of the pharm boys, and then another one shoved him out the window. I think if he gets these drugs he'll be fine."

"You may have to give him the money, too," Grayson says.

"Fuck that," Hugh and Donny say near simultaneously.

"All right, let's go see Bird," Hugh says. They run down the last flight and toward the door to the back alley.

Alone for now, Grayson exits out the front door and despite the heavy bags, he quick walks toward Kilmarnock St. and the car.

When he reaches the corner, he slows to a casual walk, under control. Grayson dumps the bags in the trunk, unlocks the car door, hops in and starts it up.

"Fucking Bird. Why did he shoot that guy?" Grayson says to the empty car. He's waiting for Charlie but Donny comes flying up from the back alley, opens the door and jumps in the front seat.

He looks at Donny, who stares straight ahead.

"Bird?" Grayson asks.

"Bird, Bird, Bird, the bird is the word," Donny says. "Here comes Charlie,"

Charlie is moving fast, considering the way he runs.

"He runs like fucking Jerry Lewis," Donny says.

"What's his, Bird's, condition?"

"Jelly like. We tried to move him but it was disgusting to touch him, he leaked from everywhere, so we split. Hugh had no blankets to wrap him or move him. We are unprepared for this circumstance."

"That bastard Bird was crazy, and not good crazy. Bad crazy," Grayson says. He turns again to Donny. "You all right?"

Donny doesn't answer, he just jumps out of the car and holds the door for Charlie to get in the back.

"Are you okay," Grayson asks. "Did you tell them what we said?"

"Am I okay? Fuck! What do you think? No," Charlie says. "I'm gonna lose it. This is bad. Bad, bad, bad."

As Grayson noses the GTO down Boylston Street toward downtown, Charlie looks out the window.

"Man-o-man," Charlie says, with a sob. "This is not going to have a happy ending. We are screwed."

"Not yet," Grayson says.

At the first red light they hit, Charlie pushes on Donny's seatback and tries to grab the door handle.

"What the fuck, man," Donny says.

"Where are you going?" Grayson says.

"I'm getting gone, gone, gone," Charlie says.

"I'll take you where you want to go. First, don't you want to go home and pack a bag or something?"

"I guess so. I have to get some clothes and my bag," Charlie says. "I need some money, too."

Donny says, "Won't it look bad if the cops come around and you've split?"

"What cops? Why would they come to me?" Charlie is sitting up and screaming in Donny's ear. "Where will they get my name?"

"I don't know, man. So, go, leave."

Grayson says, "Charlie, you should bail if you want to, but I think what he means is there is no immediate rush. If they do manage to piece it together it will take a while so you have a day or two, at least, to get your act together."

"Are you armed?" Charlie asks behind Donny.

"What? Why?" Donny says.

"Give me the gun, too. I need a gun."

They argued for a bit and then Grayson says, "Give him the gun." Donny handed the .38 over. "I bought that last night from Bird. You owe me $100. Hey, you're scared shitless of guns. The way you're shaking, you can't even hold it."

"Don't worry about it."

Grayson is taking as many backstreets as he can while they talked about where Charlie could go.

"Will you be taking your car?" Donny asks.

"I can't take a chance on my shitbox. If it breaks down on the highway, the cops will be in my face, and it can only get worse at that point."

"It's best if you don't tell us where you're going," Grayson says. "I also think you'd be better off not leaving from Boston. They might be watching the bus station, the train stations and Logan. Let me drive you to Providence. You can get a train or even a plane from there."

"In Providence? What kind of plane? A crop duster? No, thanks," Charlie says.

"It's not much of an airport, but they do have some flights," Donny says.

Charlie nodded. "No, I said. Dump me at the Greyhound station down on St. James Avenue. Last time I rode the dog I said it was the last time I'd ride the dog. Wrong again."

"So," Donny says, "Charlie's taking a bus to Timbuktu---"

"Hey!" Charlie says. "Fuck you and Timbuktu, I never said Timbuktu, you did."

Donny turns to the backseat. "Calm down, man," and turns back to Grayson. "What are you going to do?"

Grayson shrugs.

"Nothing personal but I have to get away from you fucking people," Charlie says.

"I understand," Grayson says. "I'm sorry about all this."

"Not your fault. You're just a dope like me. We should never have trusted Hugh. No offense, but your brother, I don't know about him, man. He's always in the middle of it."

They get to Charlie's place and Donny jumps out of the car and pulls the seatback forward so Charlie can get out.

Charlie pauses for a second and says to Grayson in a low voice.

"I put the .38 down the back of your seat. Keep it away from him," Charlie says.

"Call me," Grayson says. "I'll drive you in town to the bus station. Call me."

On the street, Donny tries to hug Charlie good-bye, but Charlie was too fast for him. He feinted left, went right, and took off down the street.

"See you later," Donny yells to Charlie's back. He watches him run off before climbing back in the car. "He really does run like Jerry Lewis."

He looks at Grayson, who is driving carefully. "Are you next? Dash off to parts unknown?"

Grayson says. "I can't leave. Not with my mother sick. Not without Catherine."

"And what am I supposed to do?" Donny asks. He looks out the window.

"Why can't you take off for a while?"

"I got nowhere to go, and no one to go with."

"Come on. You have more girlfriends than Warren Beatty," Grayson says. "Go to California for a long vacation."

Donny chuckles. "I wouldn't have to bring a girl there. They have lots."

"Good point. Do you have a passport?" Grayson asks.

"Yeah." He nods. "I could go to Australia. I was in the Marines with a kid who married an Aussie girl and is living there. Mark Golden. He says the chicks there are all knockouts, not an ugly one in the country, and they are always horny and ready to go. Hey, let's do it, you too. Golden says they sell these big, huge cans of beer down there, too. Something for both of us."

"That's it," Grayson says. "You go and maybe I'll go down there later."

"I saw a real old movie one night," Donny says. "Jimmy Durante played a sailor from Boston who went to Australia and ends up boxing a kangaroo. He got the shit kicked out of him."

"Jimmy Durante or the kangaroo?"

"Jimmy Durante. He looked like an asshole, trying to punch a kangaroo."

"It's worse that he got his ass kicked," Grayson says.

"Aah, I don't know how I could live somewhere they enjoy boxing with the kangaroos. Now I'm thinking, 'Why leave'?"

"The law says we're as guilty as Bird, since we were there, committing a felony."

"Tell me about it," Donny says.

"You're an adrenaline junkie like Hugh," Grayson says.

Donny says nothing, and keeps his face toward the window.

Then, "Hey, you remember the Civil Defense drills in elementary school, because of the nuclear threats. Hiding under the desk? Margie McCunliff sat in front of me, and when we'd go under, she'd pull her dress up and show me her business. I loved the drills. The Cuban Missile Crisis when we were in junior high? Made me really horny, man. I really hoped they'd make us go under our desks. I love the crazy shit. It's everyday life that's a killer."

"You were born for the times, then," Grayson says. "It's been one horror show after another. JFK, Martin Luther King, Bobby Kennedy. Vietnam, Chicago Seven, riots, student takeovers. Bombs. A guy I know says we're still in the 60's now because Nixon's still around. If you look at Kent State, the Munich Olympics, maybe he's right."

"I saw Oswald get shot to death, live," Donny says. "That was just exactly what I wanted to happen, someone to kill him, I kept wishing it and then it happened right in front of my eyes. Like magic. We were what, twelve?"

Grayson nods.

"For about two months after," Donny says, "I was trying to wish other things into happening like that. I wished my brother Joe would bring his Army gun home so I could shoot my father, so he wouldn't hit me anymore. Or he'd just disappear. That bastard, when he wasn't slapping me around, he had this look on his face, like he just found out the hard way there was bird shit on his potato salad. When I got big enough, I drove his head through the kitchen wall. While his head was stuck there, I kicked him in the ass a few times. Remember?"

"I remember your mother telling mine about it."

"I didn't see him for five years, until his wake," Donny says. "Your father told me, 'It was hard on your father to get beat up by his 14-year-old son.' He says my old man couldn't come back after that. I said I felt bad I did it, and Uncle Dan says, "No. Screw him. He deserved it.' So, I guess my wishing did make him disappear. Wishing and kicking."

"What I remember most from the 60's," Grayson says, "was Bobby Kennedy on the kitchen floor, man, that was…that was…terrible. It made me sick."

Donny says, "When the actual shooting was played back over and over again on TV, what I remember most was the yelling. Someone kept yelling, 'Get the gun, Rafer, get the gun!' I'll always remember that, 'Get the gun, Rafer!'"

They pull into Hugh's parking lot, where Donny had left his car.

"Man," Grayson says. "Do you realize the trouble we're in?"

"I don't want to talk about it," Donny says. "Give me those bags. I have to bring them inside to Hugh."

CHAPTER FOURTEEN

Grayson spends the rest of Saturday night, or actually the pre-dawn hours of Sunday morning, smoking cigarettes in the Newbury Ave apartment. He eats nothing and drinks only ice water. Around 4AM he takes a shower and goes to bed, expecting to lie awake. He's surprised when he wakes up at 5PM Sunday.

He shaves, brushes his teeth, takes another long, hot shower. He has something to eat at The Joy King, then goes back home to resume sitting around agonizing about what they have done. Or, what that bastard Bird had done, and what he had done to Bird. A line has been crossed, and Grayson has crossed it. While Bird might have pulled Grayson over that line, how it happened doesn't matter. The only thing that matters is that his life is way more screwed up than he'd ever thought possible, and now he wishes he'd fixed it while it was fixable. He sits in front of the TV until the national anthem plays and the test pattern comes on.

He gets changed into his work clothes and drives to the 24-hour Mister Donut at the Neponset Bridge. He buys a honey dipped donut and a small carton of milk. He sits in his car and eats part of a donut and drinks some milk, but it tastes like ashes in his mouth. He watches the seagulls stalk around the parking lot like a juvie gang. The birds make threatening feints at each other, while keeping an eye on him, ready to scramble, should he, the shaky fucker in the car with the doughnut, roll down the window. He tears the doughnut to pieces, cranks down the window partway and tosses the pieces out. He watches them fight over one piece and ignore all the others. The birds seem most interested in contesting each morsel rather than eating. As one piece disappears down a gullet, another is selected at random, and all the other birds scurry over to join in.

When the doughnut is gone, the birds are still there, together, but anyone would conclude, on the basis of body language, they don't much like each other.

Grayson goes into Mr. Donut again to call work and book back on. He gets a cup of coffee to go, brings it back to the car so he can drink it in peace.

He drives to work, parks in the lot, shuts the car off and discovers that he is exhausted and wants to go home. He wants to go home, crawl underneath his bed and sleep with the dust clumps.

Just a few miles away, there is a young man who was shot and might be dying or already dead. Why? Because they wanted kicks and cash and are willing to consort with an obviously depraved entity like Bird to get what they thought they wanted. Not to mention Bird was dead, too.

"Fucking Bird," he says. "Sorry, man. But why'd you shoot that guy?" He closes his eyes and lays his head on the steering wheel for a minute.

He gets out and makes his way to the driver's room, where Normand is sitting at one of the picnic tables reading the newspaper and drinking a cup of coffee from the machine. The machine coffee cost a dime and the cardboard cup the coffee came in had the picture of five different playing cards around the exterior of the cup. The five cards were random from cup to cup, and were intended to be read as a hand of poker. The marketing theory seemed to be that adult males would get excited by playing coffee cup poker and buy lots and lots of machine coffee. Grayson had never seen anyone look at or even mention the cards on the cup. When a guy bought the coffee, it was because the machine was there, he was, too and he had a dime and nothing better to do with it.

Normand looks up at Grayson coming in to the driver's room and rears his head in mock surprise. He closes the tabloid newspaper, and folds it while he clicks and clacks.

"You're here early. It's only quarter 'til!" Normand says, at last.

"Hey, Normand?" Rosie calls out from his perch on a high stool in the open office window. "He musta missed you something fierce over the weekend."

Grayson points to the newspaper. "Normand, can I look at that?"

Normand nods and slides it over.

Grayson unfolded it to show the front page, which was a picture of the St. Patrick's Day Parade in South Boston. He released a long breath, then nonchalantly thumbed through the rest of the paper. With each turn of the page he felt slightly better. Maybe what had happened Saturday night had not happened, not really, and it was all a gruesome dream. There was nothing in the paper about a shooting in the Fenway. Or a guy falling out a window. Maybe the guy who got shot had gotten up off the floor, and been helped down the stairs by his pals. Maybe the shot kid had only a flesh wound, and maybe Bird, who had only fallen five floors to an asphalt surface merely dinged his head and got knocked out and now he was walking around in one of those comical neck braces, with his head in a hilarious turban bandage. Maybe the kids were even now vowing to go straight and thanking the guys who'd robbed them for making them see the error of their ways. Yes, maybe that was it, and maybe JFK was alive and well and living as a painter in a Parisian garret.

On the back page of the paper he looked at a picture of some dejected Boston Bruin hockey players, skating head down toward the bench, as in the background, players from the other team exulted.

The headline read: *St. Patrick's Day Massacre.*

He slides the newspaper over to Normand, and he put the paper in the gym bag he toted around and periodically rooted in. He carried that frigging bag everywhere. What the hell was in that bag? He never took anything out of it, he would just put stuff in it. Occasionally, he'd unzip it and look down into it, then stick his arm in up to the elbow and Grayson would hear things rattling and scuffing about. But once something went in, it was gone for good.

Grayson had not slept last night, and while he is now exhausted, and traumatized, what made it all worse was that he'd stayed awake all night, maybe jiggy from lack of alcohol and sleep. He is a ghastly combination of physically ill and sick to his soul. He has to shut his head down in order to remain composed. For one brief moment, he wondered why he was even thinking about Normand and his fucking gym bag, but then he saw goddamned Normand digging through the gym bag and Grayson snorted and was staring at the wall when Rosie came out of the office and gave them their assignments.

"Are we all ready, boys?" Rosie says. "Let's go out and greet our beloved customers. The shop has your horse ready, Grayson."

Grayson took the papers for his assignment without looking at them, or speaking.

In the yard, he looked at his assigned job: P&G plant in Quincy. He had a 9AM appointment to pick up 45,000 lbs. of soap. He knew if he paid close attention to what he was doing in each moment, that he could distract himself from his scalding thoughts. Focus was one of the keys to ducking reality. The exercise would be good, he'd sweat like hell and clean out the booze.

He climbed up into his tractor, a red U Model Mack which he kept spotless. This was his assigned tractor, as opposed to the straight jobs, which were assigned to the routes they ran, rather than the man. He turned the key to the on position, and pushed in the black rubber nipple on the dash and kicked the diesel to life. At the top of the long side view mirror he saw dull gray smoke roll out of the stack.

At the P&G plant, two hours went by in a blur of second to second mindlessness, and physical exertion. Grayson was fast, and the conveyor was always loaded and pushing 50lb boxes of soap at you. The shipping manager liked Grayson, because Grayson got his load on and got out of the dock door so the next truck could come in. The P&G shipping manager called Grayson "John Henry" as a mark of respect for his work ethic. There was another Triple T load shown on the schedule board at 10AM. When the driver came inside, Grayson asks if he wanted to swap.

"Gordon, you take my load back, and I'll stay and load your ten o'clock, okay?"

"That sounds good to me, but what will shit-for-brains say?" Gordon asks.

"Rosie won't care. I fit over here, he knows that."

Grayson's blank mind was punctured from time to time by sharp images of the young guy bleeding on the floor, or of Bird pointing his gun at the kid on the floor, or of Bird going out the window so fast he didn't have time to yell. A visual of Catherine pegging the can of starch at him, and telling him to get lost was, in its way, the worst of the flashbacks. At 1PM Gordon was back with another empty and they swapped again and Grayson loaded the last Triple T trailer of the day.

When he was finished, Mr. Dromey, the shipping manager, came over.

"Are you tired yet, John Henry? Or are you just getting loose, getting the blood flowing? You handled one hundred thirty-five thousand pounds of soap today, you'll sleep tonight."

"I hope so," Grayson says.

Back at the terminal the work day was all over. He was straightening out his paperwork, when Rosie came over to the open window. He pulled down Grayson's time card and initialed it.

"Hey, good work today."

"Can you get my brother on the radio?"

"No," Rosie says. "He's done. He signed off already. He had a meeting this morning, bright and early, in Hartford. New account. Can't say any more about it. You'll find out later with everyone else. Let's just say your brother's going to be a big shot now."

Rosie turns and saunters through the big office, his back to Grayson. Rosie stops to speak with one of the younger women, Jill Clifford. She didn't look up, but she shook her head as if in disbelief. He laughs and strolls to the exit door. He put his hand on the doorknob, and turns back to the office, and casually leans against the door.

"Good night, all you ladies of the evening," Rosie says. He is anticipating a big laugh, and a grand exit but he got no response from the women, and then Rosie spots his nemesis, the night boss, coming into the office from the loading dock. At that point, Rosie executes a swift departure. Jill looks up at Grayson and summarizes the Rosie experience by mouthing the words, 'Nitwit.'

Grayson smiles and nods.

He turns in his paperwork, found his time card in front of him, and punches out and goes to the pay phone, drops a dime, calls the house, and his father answers.

"What's up?" Grayson asks.

"Emma and the kids are coming over. Stop by. Your brother, too."

"I don't know if I can," Grayson says.

"I'm going out to a meeting. Your mother was asking for you," Daniel Grayson says.

After he hung up, Grayson went over to the dispatch window and slid it open.

"Hey, Jill."

In the office, the young woman is putting her coat on. She froze with her arms in the air, and groans dramatically, trapped, before she could leave after a long day working in an environment that could be rough on young women. Having dealt with complaining customers and ornery drivers for a long ten hours, she is ready to flee.

"Book me off," he says. "I gotta book off again."

She reaches over in the corner for a green accounting journal, which is known as the Book-

Off-Book-On-Book. She flips through to tomorrow's date and then made a note.

"Grayson, 7AM, off," she says, as she writes. "Done. Make sure you call in and book on when you want to come back. Don't just show up. Call first."

"You think I don't know what I'm supposed to do?"

"Everyone knows what they're supposed to do, but very few do it," she says.

"If Rosie asks why I'm not in, tell him--"

She put her hand up in a stop signal.

"Nobody cares. The only thing that matters is you're in the book. You don't exist to the company until you call to book back on."

She slaps the book closed and tosses it back in the corner.

"Yeah, well, the reason is family matters," he says.

"That's what they all say," she says, and slides the window closed.

He'd missed work the day after Paul Grayson was officially declared dead by the United States, which was on Monday, January 22nd, the same day Nixon announced the war's end. Grayson's mother, already battling cancer, opened the front door that morning, early, to find two soldiers standing there. Everyone but Mary Grayson had accepted the fact that Paul, listed as MIA in 1970, was dead. But Mary Grayson would not, could not, accept that, and so as the war in Vietnam stumbled to a close, she became more convinced each day that they'd all soon be hearing good news. That day she learned he was confirmed dead, but his body, along with some other Americans had been thrown into a pit and incinerated by the VC.

That Monday was the same day she had her "shock," on the same day LBJ died, and the same day Foreman beat Frazier, and Howard Cosell shouted over the roaring crowd, "Down goes Frazier, down goes Frazier, down goes Frazier!"

There was also a big Supreme Court case that day, legalizing abortion, which a lot of people thought was good. He'd repeatedly heard he wasn't entitled to an opinion on it. He was male, he couldn't have a baby, so MYOFB. But now, now he had an opinion and his opinion is that it is wrong. That is his baby, too.

That Monday night, January 22, even though Grayson got back from the hospital late, Catherine had been waiting for him at the Newbury Ave apartment. She had come to comfort him, and when she hugged him, he broke down, crying for the first time since he'd met her, all those years ago. She tenderly kissed his face, and took him by the hand into his bedroom, closed the door quietly, and after a time, they made love, in total silence.

Now, as he rolled the GTO by her house, he knew she'd gotten pregnant on that date, the same day his mother had nearly died, the same day Paul was officially dead, the day the war ended. *One done, another begun,* was a saying that his father used, all too often, about many different things.

Now Grayson wanted to go in Catherine's home, take her hand, and say, "Everything will be all right because we belong together." How could he? How could he say anything will be all right? He could be arrested any time now, and for something very serious. If he doesn't get killed, he'll end up in prison, likely, for a long time.

He stops to pick up an afternoon newspaper. He pages through it, to find a story on page three about a Boston drug dealer who had been shot by an armed invader. Another man had been pushed, jumped or had fallen out of a fifth-floor window to his death from the same apartment where the man had been shot. Both men remained unnamed at this time, and the man who was shot was in critical condition at an undisclosed hospital. The identity of the suspected shooter was still unknown. No further details were available. Police say the investigation is ongoing. Grayson didn't trust the media to have the facts right. Every time he had firsthand knowledge of something that was reported on the news, the story was what his father called FUBAR-Fucked Up Beyond All Recognition.

He drives to Hugh's building, and in the parking lot, he boxed the compass, but didn't see Hugh's car, but went in to the lobby anyway and pressed the buzzer a few times, then sped off to see if he could sit still for ten minutes at the beach. The answer was no. He made it to five, though. He sat at the bottom of Vassal St. looking out across Quincy Bay. It was almost right here, maybe a hundred yards away, across from the bowling alley, at the sea wall between the yacht clubs, that he knew that he wanted to live his life with Catherine. They were twelve years old when she stood there and said, "I love the ocean. I don't own any of it, and it's all mine."

He'd always felt that same way, but he didn't know it, and couldn't articulate it, if he had known it, not then, but she did. He wanted to spend his whole life learning things like that from her. She told him what she was thinking, and that was all, but that was everything.

Now look.

Grayson parks at the curb outside his mother's house. Hugh is not here, either. The Old Man's car is gone and Emma's two tone 1964 Ford Ranch station wagon is parked at the curb in front of the house.

Grayson wonders why he is way more upset about the drug kid being in critical condition than Bird's being in a dead condition. Grayson hadn't

done that on purpose, plus Bird was going to execute the guy he'd already shot once, and then,
most likely the other three kids as well. So, fuck
Bird, and the horse he rode in on. Right?

Before he has a chance to cool out, two of
his nephews appeared in the open driver's side
window.

"Boo!" the five-year-old yells and his eight-year-
old cousin laughs.

"Howdy, boys," Grayson says. He shuts down
the engine and removes the key. "What's shaking?"

"I'm visiting," Alex says. He is the elder of the
two.

"Me, too!" Matthew says.

"What have you guys been up to?" Their faces
were dirt-smeared and they smelled like freshly
dug potatoes.

"We were building roads behind the garage for
our Hot Wheels," Alex says.

"How are the Sox doing in spring training,
Alex?" Grayson asks.

"They didn't play this afternoon," Alex says.
"Tomorrow they play the Twins."

Alex knew more about the Boston Red Sox
than the baseball beat man for the Quincy Patriot
Ledger.

"Hey, did you see the manager's picture in the
paper the other day, holding the snake?" Alex asks.
He turns to his younger cousin. "In Florida there

are about a million snakes. Eddie Kasko found a huge dead snake in left field. It was twelve feet long. I saw the picture."

"I hope he brings it to Fenway," Matthew says.

Their high spirits were usually contagious but Grayson is immune today, and the older boy may have picked up on the mood his uncle was in.

"Are you worried about this new designated hitter rule?" Alex asks. Grayson looks at the serious little faces.

"I have to say I don't like it," Grayson says.

"My teacher, Mrs. Dodd, says it won't last," Alex says.

"Uncle Mike, will you come to my games?" Matthew says. "I'm gonna be a pitcher. My Dad and also Pop are going. They'll be at Cavanaugh Field."

"Sure. When is it? Has the season started?"

"I don't think so," Alex says.

"I don't know," Matthew says. These were uninteresting details. He shrugs. "Ask my father or Pop. Maybe they know."

"Count on me, young man," Grayson says.

The boys hear something at the same time and turn their heads, look up the street and take off running. Grayson gets out of the GTO and looks up the street to see his nephews closing in on two other boys playing catch. Grayson walks up the front steps and into the house.

The TV is on in the living room, but there is no sign of anyone. He went up the stairs.

"Hello?" His sister's voice calls out from behind the closed bathroom door.

"Just me," Grayson says.

"Michael," his mother rasps. She's in there, too.

"Yeah, Ma. I'll wait in the girl's room."

Grayson goes into the girl's room and sits in the recliner.

A toilet flushes, water ran in the sink, the bathroom door opens and Emma pushed the wheelchair into the girl's room, and positions it beside the recliner.

Grayson stands and kisses his mother and sister.

"What a good surprise," Ma says.

"Okay, while you two visit," Emma says, "I'm going to make Dad some American chop suey and cook a chicken he can stick in the fridge."

"Mind the onions," Ma says. "He gets gassy."

"Was Hugh here?" he asks.

"Today? No," his sister says. "Our young executive is on the way up, I hear!" There was not an ironic fiber in Emma's being.

"God love him," Ma says.

Emma went off to cook up some gas-free food for The Old Man.

"How're you feeling?" Grayson asks.

"Catherine came to see me," Ma says.

"Again?"

"Oh," Ma says. "Did I already tell you?"

"Yeah, you mentioned it on Saturday."

"Did you talk to her?"

"A little bit, yeah."

"Anything new?" Ma says.

"No, not really. Where're Old Matt and the girls? Didn't they come over with Emma?"

"Matt took his mother up to the Square. Liz and Caroline went with him, I think to buy a record, or a magazine."

"It seems funny they're at that age already," Grayson says.

"Are you too young to remember Donny's father? He was Donald, too. Donald Joseph Gates. He was even more handsome than Donny is, but he was a son of a gun. He owned a record store at one time." She shook her head. "I don't know. I'm thinking about a lot of dead people lately, and I can't stop thinking about Paul, too. Mostly Paul, though. And my mother." She put her chin on her chest and wept silently. From the side she looked like a sleeping swan.

"I miss Paul," she says. "I miss my little boy. I miss all my little ones." She cries without passion; she cries in utter defeat. Grayson has never before seen her surrender so fully, not to anyone or anything.

"What about the grandkids?" Grayson says. "They're not gone."

"I haven't even died yet and I miss them already." She laughs and cries at the same time. "I'm always missing somebody, I guess."

"It's okay, Ma," he says.

"I was happy when you kids were little. I could keep you safe. Because you trusted me. You'd listen to me. When I think how happy I was it makes me sad."

"I still hear you. I listen."

She tugs out a handkerchief that is tucked in her dead left fist and wipes her eyes. Her upper body shudders as she tries to compose herself.

"No," she says. "You don't." She sighs. "When I'm gone, you will both just disappear. I see it. I see it."

"Who?" he says.

She shakes her head.

"Who do you mean?"

She looked at him with eyes walled in by tears. "The girls will be fine, they have their families, and each other. They'll look after your father, too."

"I know. Don't worry about him," Grayson says.

She takes a deep breath, exhales and closes her eyes.

"You and your brother have to stick together. Be good to each other. Stop this fussing you're always doing with each other."

"Ma. Ma. What are you talking about?"

"Hugh, Michael. Hugh. You lost one brother, and you boys will drift apart if you don't fix what's broken between you. Hugh needs you. Talk to your father's AA friend, John. Just talk to him. He got your father to accept help."

He looks down and nods. "Okay, I will."

"When? When will you talk to him?"

"Tomorrow."

"Don't say tomorrow," she says. "That's a trick to always say tomorrow. Say the day. When will you go to see him?"

"Tuesday."

She nods and neither of them speak, as if silence sealed the deal. She takes out her white handkerchief again and flutters it open, then wipes her eyes. They sit together, Grayson without the words to express what he felt.

"Good," she says. "Now. Go eat your supper."

"I'm not hungry."

"Go downstairs and tell your sister to make you something to eat. Turn on the TV before you go, it has to warm up. Put it on the Gunsmoke channel."

Grayson turned on the set, chunked the channel selector over and kissed his mother good-bye.

"See you soon."

Downstairs, Emma is listening to the radio as she cooks dinners for the future.

"I'm listening for news on the State Trooper," she says.

He shakes his head. "What happened to him?"

"He got shot on duty the other night."

"Oh, jeez. Dead?"

"No, but it doesn't sound good," she says. "Not the way they're talking."

Emma's sister-in-law, Matt's sister, is married to a state cop.

"He must have pulled over the wrong guy," Grayson says.

A shot cop would explain why the shot drug kid isn't big in the news. All the media attention is on the cop. Hell, maybe the kid is all right? In all the hullabaloo of a state cop getting shot the kid means nothing. Just thinking that fills him with relief. Hugh might know more.

"Did Hugh say where he was going?" he asks.

"No." She turns up the volume, in case the monosyllable didn't clue him in.

The announcer says, "In ten minutes we will be going live to State Police barracks in Framingham for a news conference. Trooper William James Hawthorne was shot in the line of duty earlier today and is in critical condition. More after we hear from our sponsors."

Emma turns it back down. "So much crazy stuff happening, it's awful. Did you have something to eat after work?"

He nods. "All set. She was crying."

"Her emotions are all over the place," Emma says. "She keeps asking me what's going on with Catherine."

"I saw her," Grayson says. "Catherine."

"Oh? Did she call you?"

"What's the story on the dentist? Do you know?" Grayson says.

"Matt and I bumped into them in the North End. They were coming in The European as we were leaving. He seems like a nice guy. He's cute."

"Cute like a puppy? He has floppy ears? Scratches his neck with his feet? Cute like that?"

She laughs. "No. Cute like curly hair, well built, compact, like a gymnast."

"Is he still in school, or out? He's already gripping and ripping?"

"*Now*, you want to know?" She shook her head. "He's a dental student at Tufts in town. His name is …. oh, what is it… Philip Carey, I think. His father and brother own the dental clinic in Braintree, down past the Plaza and Five Corners."

"Falling into Daddy's business. Must be nice."

"Actually, he says he was going to move to Southern California and open his own practice," she says.

"He knows he can't make it around here."

"Well, what did Catherine say? Anything good?" Emma says.

"She wants me to be someone else altogether, is what she wants. She says she loves me but wishes I would change. I love her, and I don't want her to ever change."

"You're both going to be disappointed," Emma says. "My guess is she wants you to not drink."

"She says that won't do it. It's too late."

"You'd give her up rather than try? You definitely have a problem."

"Oh, Jesus," Grayson says. "Now you, too? Is The Old Man feeding you lines? I'm a young guy who gets loaded once in a while. I just turned twenty-two! I'm mostly a social drinker. So, I have an occasional psychotic episode. Big deal."

"Mike, it's not funny. You have no idea what social drinking is. How could you? Watching Dad? Hanging down at that barroom?"

"I got to go."

"You can't run away, not forever.

"Listen, I know. I'm a screw up."

Emma grabs his chin with her hand and shook it. "Stop that. It's not true. Don't say it. You're still learning how to be a man."

"Paul was a man, and he was dead at my age," he says. "Do you know how many guys I know, guys younger than me, are dead in that war? And I'm moping around, wasting my life like an... fool."

"You should thank God they wouldn't take you. It's not your fault."

"I know, I know, but all those kids are dead and I'm pissing my life away. It's a damn disgrace."

"You're a late bloomer."

He laughs, and shakes his head.

"Just don't feel sorry for yourself," she says. "You know what's right. Do it."

"Sorry for myself? That's the last thing I am," he says. "I keep thinking how good I had it, and how I screwed it up so bad."

"You can still straighten everything out," she says.

"No, not now."

"Mike, everything will be fine. Just don't drink."

"I haven't been drinking, but--"

Emma says, "Not yet. Not this minute. But where are you going from here?"

"Who knows? To bed, most likely."

Grayson says good-bye and hugs Emma. Outside his nephews are playing catch in the middle of the street.

"We were playing Pickle with those kids," Alex says. "But they went in."

"Pickle? Oh, you mean Run Down," Grayson says. "Good. Hey, I have to go, fellas."

He starts the car, and Matthew hollers, "C-A-R," and the boys back up on the sidewalk. Grayson waves and drives away.

Alone, he is ashamed of himself again, now more than ever. On hearing that a cop had been shot, his first thought was that it was bad news for the cop, but good news for Grayson and the others. It would definitely take the heat off the shooting of a drug dealer. But it's pretty twisted, and shows him just how far gone he is.

CHAPTER FIFTEEN

Grayson trudges up the front stairs at Newbury Ave. He'd walked by David's parked car, but did not see Kerr's. The night air is getting more humid by the minute and clouds are gathering just above the tree.

He waves hello to Mrs. Rook who is looking out her first-floor window, and climbs the stairs to the apartment. It's quiet, the living room and kitchen empty, the doors to the three bedrooms closed.

There were two notes taped on Grayson's bedroom door. He peels them off the door, and read them.

Grayson-Charlie called. -DB

He crumples that one and reads the second.

Grayson – Your foolish fuck of a cousin was in here roaming around when I got back home. I threw him out. Did you give him a key? Also, someone ate some unauthorized Chinese leftovers and I believe it may of been him. See me please. – Ron Kerr

In the kitchen he opens the refrigerator and looks for the ice water. There is a masking tape line of separation that ran top to bottom in the refrigerator with Ronald Kerr's sundry food items crowded into the left half and David's cheese, cold cuts and salad stuff strewn around on the other side.

Ron Kerr apparently gotten his hands on a label maker and has punched RK into red strips of plastic and stuck them on all his food items, including six or seven white cartons of Chinese food pressed up against the back. Grayson wants to throw all of the RK stuff out the window into the swampy woods at the back of the house. Kerr is a cheap bastard who thought nothing about grubbing a beer off Grayson, but when it came to his old dried out fried rice, it was hands off, son. Grayson wouldn't eat leftover Chinese food under any condition, but Kerr marking it up was an affront. He stands with the refrigerator door open, glaring. The refrigerator belongs to Kerr; his mother bought it for him. His mother did things like that for him because she was a nice lady and she knew he was a half-wit. Grayson thought about dragging the frigging fridge out to the back porch and pushing the son of a bitch right off.

Instead he slams the door and goes back to the note Kerr had hung on the door. Grayson scratches out the '*of*' in the note and put in '*have.*' And then wrote, *Curly, go shit in your hat and pull it down over your ears. If you ever leave me a snotty note again, I will set fire to all your stuff including your Celtics memorabilia.*

Your Pal,

Grayson

xx oo

He slips the note under Kerr's bedroom door.

He takes a shower to cool down and has just stepped out when there's knock on the bathroom door.

"Hey, Grayson," Dave Barry says, "Donald is on the phone."

David Barry and Donald Gately had first met in kindergarten and still referred to each other by their formal first names.

"Ask him where he is. I'll call right back. Thanks, Dave."

Grayson dried off the best he could, but it is too humid in the bathroom after a shower. He puts on his flannel robe, steps down the hall and into his bedroom. He closes the door, and with the towel, mops himself off. He opens the one window in his bedroom which faced the marshy field that was thickly wooded with skinny trees. When it rained the field took a long time to drain and a festering smell would force him to close the window no matter how warm it was outside. It has not rained for a while, but it would tonight; the sodden air couldn't hang on much longer in this condition. Maybe he'd survive long enough to see it, because right now he's suffocating. He felt like he's wearing long johns that have been pulled from a sink full of hot water.

He puts on a pair of running shorts and a maroon tee shirt.

Dave is sitting at the kitchen table reading and spooning soup into his mouth.

"What is with the weather?" Grayson says. "It's the middle of March, for crying out loud."

"This warm weather can't get here too soon for me. I spend all winter waiting for it," Dave says. "Donald is at his apartment."

Grayson turns to the wall phone and dials Donny. He picks up after a couple of rings.

"What?" Grayson says.

"Are you going to be home?"

"Yup," Grayson says.

"I'll be over in a little while. Stay there."

Donny hangs up first.

Dave is up and washing his dishes in the sink. He stops and turns around, drying his hands.

Dave says, "I'm driving out to the Berkshires tonight for at least a few days. A girl from school has a family place." He takes out his wallet and gives Grayson two twenties. "Here's my third for the rent, in case I decide to stay out there longer. Give it to Curly for me, will you? I don't see him anymore."

"Lucky you. When did he tape the fridge up?"

"Who knows?" Dave says. "You know how he gets. He'll forget all about it in a couple of days. Don't tell him, but I ate the chicken wings."

Later, after Dave left the apartment toting a brown Stop & Shop bag with his clothes for the trip, Grayson's blatantly sprawled in a chair Ron Kerr had designated off-limits. Grayson half-watched *The Rookies,* waiting for Kerr to come home. The vinyl chair had been donated by Kerr's mother and he had insisted that no one sit in it, even when he wasn't home. The '*See me please*' in the note on the bedroom door pissed Grayson off no end, so he wouldn't move from the chair when Kerr came in. When he hears the downstairs front door slam, he hopes it's Kerr but when he felt the whole house begin to shimmy, he knew it was Donny. Grayson grabs his smokes and fires one up.

A few seconds later Donny burst in.

"Is David or Kerr here?" Donny says.

"No."

"Okay," Donny says. "It's a good thing that odd-ball Kerr isn't home. That guy is crazy. Next time he gets smart with me, I'll put him through the wall."

"I know how you feel. But it's probably best not to try it. He's skinny but he's as strong as an orang-utan," Grayson says. "You want some Chinese food?"

"I'm not hungry," Donny says.

"Have you talked to Hugh? Where is he?"

"I don't know. I called, no answer. Listen, have you seen the paper?"

Grayson says, "Which one?"

"The Ledger?" Donny asks. The Ledger is the local afternoon paper, primarily focused on the South Shore.

"It's in the Ledger?"

Donny held his fingers an inch apart and sat on the couch. "Small, tiny little square, page four. 'One dead, after falling out a window, student critical, shot at bash, police theorize drug crazed youths run amok.' The usual."

"Is Bird named in the story? Is Bird his last name?" Grayson says.

"No, he's not named. It just says six floors."

Bird could end up buried in a pauper's grave.

"Five floors. You said six."

Donny says, "The building sits at the top of a slope. In the front, the ground floor is the first floor, and in the back, the cellar is at ground level, it was like a bonus floor for Bird."

Grayson shakes his head. "I didn't know."

"Yeah, the one extra may have made a difference. Anyway, fuck him."

"I'm one hundred percent sure he was going to kill the kid he already shot, and most likely the others, too, so I see it as saving lives, I didn't mean for him to go out the window."

"That's the right attitude," Donny says.

Grayson says, "I just wanted to knock him into the wall so he'd drop his gun."

"Probably did when he started flapping his arms."

"The cops will find the gun and know he shot the kid, right?"

"No. I picked up the gun and put it in my pocket," Donny says.

"Why? Why would you do that? If you left it, the cops would say here's the guy who shot the kid, and here's the gun."

"Because my fingerprints may have been on it. Remember when he handed it to me? My prints may still be on it. I can't take that chance."

"Like Hugh says the pharm kids will tell the cops who shot the kid, anyhow. So, get rid of it. I don't know where. Just get rid of it."

Donny says, "Anyway, you hang tough. We need you to be alert at all times. No booze. Okay? You all right?"

"Far from it."

Donny says, "One, it was an accident, two, what if he was going to shoot you, your brother, or worst of all, me? So, fuck Bird, he was a loose cannon. Don't lose sleep over him."

"Easy to say," Grayson says. "I don't get how doing something you think is right can make you feel so bad. I guess because someone died?"

"All that, 'Thou shalt not kill' stuff they drilled in us as kids, man. It's hard to shake, even when you need to. And we really need to now."

"I know." It was then it occurred to Grayson that Donny meant that in a different way than Grayson did. "What do you mean?"

"Them Lard Dorks are going to be mightily pissed off. We may have to take it to them."

Grayson is shocked. Then he laughs. "You know, with all the other shit going on, I forgot all about them. They could come after us, too." He puts his face in his hands and laughs too hard and too long.

CHAPTER SIXTEEN

Grayson calls Charlie's apartment, and he picked up.

Grayson says, "Did you see the paper?"

"I did see it in the paper," Charlie says. "It's not as bad as I expected. I expected cops with bull-horns and floodlights outside by now."

"Donny says the guy was in critical condition. That sounds bad to me."

"As long as he doesn't die, I'm happy," Charlie says.

"How'd you get so mellow?" Grayson asks.

"Librium," Charlie says.

"Donny's here. Come over." He hangs up at Charlie's assent.

Donny stands in the kitchen, listening to Grayson's end of the discussion.

"Speaking of mellow, I went by Deet's house," Donny says. "I purchased something for anxiety. The greenies make it tough to sleep, and with the thinking we need to do, I need my rest, so I smoothed myself out. You want a couple?"

Grayson shakes his head. "Deet's wife hasn't finished him off yet?"

"No, she split, like a couple of months ago. Took her shotgun, the dog and the pickup, went home to Alabama. I never told you that?"

"No."

"I still call him Deet, but he has himself a new nickname. Skeet."

Roger Dietrich, or Deet, had been nuzzling his girlfriend on the couch in her second-floor apartment when he heard his wife call his name from outside. He peeked out to see her heading for the entry door with a shotgun in her hand. He opened the window and climbed out. He hung on to the sill, and was working up the courage to let go and drop to the ground when his wife stepped back out of the street entrance. She'd faked him out. She took aim, and when Deet let go of the sill, she blasted him in mid-air, riddling his butt with buckshot. As a result, Deet became Skeet.

"He's been behaving himself since then, too," Donny says. "Losing a big chunk of his ass made him self-conscious around the ladies. He can't even sit right anymore. Always tilted."

Donny stretches out on the floor and is quiet. Grayson is on the couch tossing a tennis ball in the air and catching it, repeatedly.

Sometime after 9PM, the downstairs hall door slams and a heavy, slow tread hit the stairs and came up. Grayson tenses, until he realizes it is only one man coming up. If it had been the cops, they'd have come in force.

There's a knock on the door.

"Hey, open up," Charlie says.

"It's open," Donny says.

Inside, Charlie says, "You aren't going to believe this,"

His voice is so fraught with tension, it sounds as if he's being strangled.

"If it's bad I will," Grayson says.

"I listened to the news on the radio," Charlie says. "You hear it?"

Donny stands up and rubs his face.

"No," Grayson says. "What did it say?"

"The guy that Bird shot?" Charlie says.

"He didn't die? Don't tell me that," Donny says.

"No. He's a state cop. An undercover state cop."

CHAPTER SEVENTEEN

Charlie's recap of the grim news is followed by much groaning and gnashing of teeth. When he starts relaying what exactly he'd heard on the radio, Charlie's legs begin shaking so much that he orders Grayson off the couch. Charlie feels his way around the coffee table to the couch, drops on it and mimes the image of forlorn; flat on his back, eyes closed, a forearm across his forehead.

"It's worse saying it out loud." His throat and mouth are so dry he's having a hard time getting his words out. "The State Police detectives, no doubt, already grilled those kids. You *know* they told them about the guys who set them up, the cops have talked to Judith, who told the cops about us. We'll have cops on us like stink on a monkey."

"Slow down," Donny says. "We're not in jail yet."

"Yeah! Yeah!" Charlie says. He sits up, his face red. "I'm getting out of town. No question. Bikers and the state police are hunting me down."

Donny says, "We need to be cool. Now's not the right time to panic."

"Make sure you let me know when it is time to panic," Charlie says. "I have to get my hands on some money."

Donny put his hands up in a 'Halt' position. "Let's take a break from talking for a few minutes, take deep breaths and see if that calms us down. Ready?"

"Cut the shit," Charlie says.

"I'm serious," Donny says, and looks at Grayson. "You got any Coke?"

"No. You're not going to hit the coke, are you?" Grayson says.

"Not that, the drinking kind." He heads into the kitchen.

Meanwhile, Charlie says, "I'm gonna barf."

"You know where the bathroom is. Go," Grayson says. Charlie trots down the hall and slams the bathroom door shut.

Donny comes back in the room with a tumbler of water, pulls a few capsules from his shirt pocket and throws them in his mouth and swallows the water.

Donny looks down the hall to get a position fix on Charlie. Then he comes over to loom above Grayson.

Donny says, "Shooting a cop is real bad trouble, man. We may have to do some damage control."

"Like what?"

"We may have to get rough with some people, like you did with Bird."

"That was---"

"Self-defense. I'm agreeing with you. This is also self-defense. Sure, sometimes I overreact. When I feel threatened, I'm often unable to control my impulses. That's what that school shrink told my mother."

Their high school gym teacher, Mr. Aaron Fuller, was, like many gym teachers, a bully. He had pegged a basketball at Donny, hitting him square on the face, and Donny, at fifteen and not yet full sized, responded by jamming the thirty-year-old teacher into a locker. Mr. Fuller was a large, muscular man, and he did not fit in the locker readily, but Donny, diligent when properly motivated, got him in eventually.

Grayson says, "Give me a chance to try and think before you wig out and make things worse."

Donny pulls the shade away from the window and peeks out.

Grayson says, "Under no circumstances are you to harm anyone."

Donny turns. "You were the one that did the harm. You and Bird."

"Promise."

"We need the scoop on the cop Bird shot," Donny says.

"The news says critical," Charlie says, standing in the doorway. "That's the scoop. Critical."

"Okay," Grayson says. "Critical means alive. Let's not fall apart yet."

CHAPTER EIGHTEEN

Charlie and Donny leave and about two minutes later Hugh is on the phone.

"Amy wants to talk to us," Hugh says. "Here. Now."

"Five minutes," Grayson says.

He gets to Hugh's and together they walk down the carpeted hall and knock on Amy's door. She pulls open the door, looking like a thirteen-year old boy's fantasy, standing there wearing a tight white sweater, a short leather skirt and a stern look.

Inside, she says, "Stan Belzer is beside himself. Bird is dead. What happened?"

"An accident," Hugh says. "He fell out the window."

"He fell? How? Was he stoned?"

"I bumped into him," Grayson says. "I didn't mean for him to go out the window."

"Listen," she says. She looks from face to face. "We're going to have to do better than that. I've got to tell Stan something. Or he could kill all of us."

"He might have been stoned," Grayson says. "Does he have a history we weren't told about? We're the ones should be pissed off. Sending that loon to work with us. He shot a guy who turned out to be a cop."

"He must have had a reason. Did he say why?"

"He was an idiot, that's why," Grayson says.

She says, "There has to be an explanation. Bird may have realized the man was a state cop. Maybe he recognized him... maybe he'd once been arrested by the man."

"Bird said the guy was reaching for the bag," Hugh says. "Bird thought there might have been a gun inside the bag. He panicked and shot him."

Grayson says "And he was ready to shoot him again."

"Oh?" she says. "Is that when he *fell* out the window?" She makes those annoying fucking finger quotes in the air again.

"Right around then," Grayson says.

"Well," she says. "We better figure out what we're going to tell Stan."

They go back and forth a few times and come up with a simple story in pretty short order. Hugh stands in front of them, recapping it.

"My brother and Charlie were in the hall, so they didn't see anything. Donny and I were behind the couch scooping the cash. We heard a commotion and stood up just in time to see Bird tussling with one of the kids. The kid shoved Bird, and as he was falling out, the kid started to run away, but despite being off balance, Bird managed to get a shot off as he struggled not to fall, but then, poor old Bird fell right out the window."

"He might buy it," Amy says. "I know it's bullshit but maybe I can sell it."

"Once again, we better hope the people we're dealing with are idiots," Grayson says.

CHAPTER NINETEEN

He blasts away from Hugh's apartment, and wants to drink so bad he almost starts crying. He can't think of a good reason why he shouldn't drink, but how is that possible? He didn't want to see or talk to anyone, so he went up past Quincy Square. He didn't want to be around anyone because they'd look right through him, see he was empty. He finds himself on the perimeter of Quincy Square, and heads south down Route 3A toward Hull and Nantasket Beach. On Washington St, there seems to be a bar every hundred yards. This is not the best street to be on for a guy who didn't want to drink.

"Oh hey," Grayson says aloud, alone in the car. "What the fuck? Why would I quit now? What is the fucking point?"

He wheels into a lot beside a dumpy joint just down the street from the Fore River Bridge. He feels relief just by walking through the front door. At the bar, his flesh tingles, he is breathing faster and he feels alive.

The bar maid, whose face is blurred and body has no definable form, just stands there and says nothing. She doesn't register as human, not because of her, but because Grayson's mind races. She is just a means to an end, there to deliver the goods, and he does not have to be charming in this hell hole.

"Double Seven with ice and a bottle of Miller."

It didn't take long, it took forever, a good fifteen seconds, to get the rye poured, the bottle cap snapped off, and his order set down in front of him. She seems to know a man starting a siege when she sees one, so she doen't press him for payment. If she runs a tab for him, there might be an opportunity to fleece him as the evening wears on.

He raises the Seven to his mouth, blocks the ice with his teeth and feels the cold whiskey flow, leaving in its wake a stream of warmth and light. He set down the glass, picks up the bottle of beer, drinks, and as the alcohol hits his blood, the world is left behind. Peace.

The bar maid forms up in front of him, and sets him up again without asking.

The first round brings light, and the second round takes it away. But, if he could stop now, if he could just stop, and go home, and be happy to be numb for just a little while. He could never predict the outcome once he started. There were times when four shots and two beers would render him legless, and other times when it works like he hoped it would, but always it took a while to find out which state was operative.

By and by he began to lose track of the fact... that...he was...something.

And when he reappears in his own life he is standing on the corner of Harrison Ave and Beach Street in Chinatown, pointed in the direction of the Combat Zone. He often finds himself, without knowing he'd been lost, popping in and out of the action like some time traveler on a sci-fi program, asking himself, who am I, how did I get here, and where am I going? He'd never gotten used to these blackouts but had no idea what to do about it. Now he lurched along the sidewalk for half a block before concluding he is without destination. Whatever mad plan had brought him here had stealthily deserted him somewhere along the line; it had washed away before he surfaced from the inky pool to find himself bathed in headlights and neon. Conventional wisdom is that guys went to the Combat Zone to get laid, but Grayson knew almost no one got laid in the Zone, and, if they did, it was never for free. They did drink while they hung out, and this is what makes it easy to get into a fight. Frustrated, boozed up, un-laid guys were irritable as hell. This is the real reason it is called The Combat Zone.

At the corner of Beach and Knapp he looked left, down the short street which ran to Kneeland, and the White Castle on the corner. While a hamburger would not help, it could not hurt, so he made his way down Knapp. Guys are rolling in and out of some bar a little way down. He tries to visualize a plumb line in front of him, and to walk along it, but he grows increasingly angry as he fails badly.

In a dark landing on his left a door flies open on an explosion of jocular noise, and surfing on a wave of merriment, five good sized young guys, sporting identical blue windbreakers came roistering out to the sidewalk, and knock into Grayson as if he were invisible. The collision provides Grayson a close up look at the UNH wildcat logo and the crossed hockey sticks below it. These guys are enjoying their Spring Break in the squalor of The Zone. The boys regroup, still without seeing him and start toward Beach Street.

"Hey!" Grayson says. "Say excuse me."

The boys stop talking and turned in various poses and look back at him. He sees that each of the five are as big or bigger than he was. Good.

At first, they appear to wonder if he is talking to them. Then one snorts and says, "Fuck you," drawing it out and saying it in exactly the wrong way. They turn and resume walking, hooting at each other as if they and only they were all that there was.

Rage reanimates like nothing else; silent, Grayson runs at them and leaps at their backs like Killer Kowalski. The three in the middle hit the asphalt like they'd fallen off a roof. Unfortunately, that still left two standing, and before Grayson can get to his feet, the two left up-right are raining down punches, spicing things up with a kick here and there. By the time Grayson struggles to a standing crouch, all five boys are taking shots at him and have gotten a nice rhythm going.

"One, two, cha cha cha," Grayson says.

In between the thumping noises, he hears a motorcycle approaching.

"All right! Knock it off," a voice hollers.

The punching ceases just before the ink pool floods in.

How long was he in the ink before the blinding white light appears? Who knows? But appear it did, and then it went out.

And when the light appears again, he hears a voice as if it came from behind the light.

"He's responsive," the voice says.

"That's great, doc," another voice says. "You wouldn't believe all the fuckin' forms I'd have to fill out if he died." He pronounces the word forms as, "foe-ums."

Grayson opens his eyes to see a droopy, florid face looking down at him from under a blue Boston Police cap. There is no accent as strong as a Boston cop's accent. He closes his eyes again, but not before the cop sees him.

"Good morning, you silly son of a bitch."

"He reeks of alcohol and his blood test shows he's intoxicated. Shouldn't you book him?" the first voice says.

"Not a bit of it. Shouldn't you observe him for several more hours?"

"I'd rather not keep him here. He may be agitated," the first voice says.

"Hey, look," the cop says. "I've had my fill of the agitated for tonight. My whole workday is awash with the agitated. The agitated, the criminal and the insane."

"I'm awake," Grayson says.

He looks to the other side and sees a small, sparkling clean fellow in medical scrubs. He is brainy-looking, fitted out with horned rim glasses and a preppy haircut.

"I'd rather you arrested him," the doctor says.

"We can't arrest him," the cop says. "As most of these frolicsome lads already know, we can no longer arrest for public drunkenness. It's strictly catch and release."

"I was beaten up," Grayson says.

"Like hell you were," the cop says. "I interviewed several credible eyewitnesses, college athletes in fact, who reported that you, drunk as a lord, took a bad spill and tumbled into a car bumper and then fell to the sidewalk, where you proceeded to pass out. If there's more to the story, I don't want to hear it."

"Sit up," the doctor says. "Can you?"

Grayson sits up. The doctor shines the pen light in his face again, then runs the usual tests for a concussion.

"I'll okay your release if you can get someone to keep an eye on you. Is there anyone you can call?"

Now, Grayson sits in a wheel chair in the Boston City Hospital emergency room waiting area. He imagines he is permanently confined to the chair, as his mother is; certainly, it would diminish his ability to fuck up his life. Some mornings on his way to work, he'd stop in an East Milton coffee shop to get a cup to go. Perched at the counter would be a line of lively, bantering, old men, up before the sun, out of the house, in the pink and as happy as five-year-old kids. He envied them; they were closing in on the finish line, and still able to smile. They had navigated the mine field that was life, and clearly had not screwed it up too bad, or they would not be there smiling.

In the ER waiting room he didn't want to look around and see what real threats to mortality his fellow humans are dealing with as the new day approaches. Instead he smokes cigarettes and stares at his feet, which are flat, still and lifeless on the wheelchair footrests.

The glass entry doors slide open and Donny appears in the breach. He scans the room from just inside the doors, sees Grayson, jerks his head, 'come on,' turns and goes back out.

Grayson stays in the wheel chair and rolls himself out to Albany St.

Out at the car, he sees Hugh in the front seat of Donny's station wagon so he gets in the back. Donny gets in, looks back at him and drops the transmission into drive and rolls away from the ER.

"Why are you here?" Grayson says. "I called Donny."

Hugh says, "What happened?"

"I'm not in the mood," Grayson says. He closes his eyes and leans his head back on the top of the seat. He hears a whisper of cloth, as something slams into his throat. His eyes snap open to see his brother's snarling face inches away from his own, as Hugh's forearm presses harder against Grayson's neck.

"Hey," Donny yells.

The car skids to a stop and Hugh coils back to his seat with the motion, as quickly as he'd attacked. He sits facing the windshield as if nothing had happened.

Grayson slams the heel of his foot into the back of his brother's seat.

"Hey, quit it," Donny says.

"Everything that's going on, and you get picked up?" Hugh says.

"I have to get my car," Grayson says.

"Where is it?" Donny says.

"Just drop me here," Grayson says.

Hugh says, "He doesn't know where it is."

Grayson lights a cigarette, and blows the smoke at the back of his brother's head.

"What's wrong with you?" Hugh says.

"What's wrong? We shot a cop in the commission of felony armed robbery, that's what's wrong with me. And then I killed a guy," Grayson says.

"Don't be dramatic," Hugh says. "What's really wrong is you're a drunk."

"You brought in a guy who shot a cop."

"So, you shoved him out the window," Hugh says. "That solves the problem?"

"What do we do now?" Donny says. "Fight ourselves? Or stick together and work on the problem?"

"He's right. I'm sure if we work on it together, we can find a way to fuck it up way worse," Grayson says.

CHAPTER TWENTY

Minihan Auto is a six-bay repair shop in a defunct gas station on the upper end of Beale Street, just past where it crosses Newport Ave.

Grayson parks the GTO off to the side in the small, crowded lot and goes over to the office. The hours are shown on the glass door, and he sees they won't open until 7:30, about forty minutes. He thinks about leaving and coming back but if he does leave he won't come back.

He sits on the front bumper of a junked 1964 Chrysler Barracuda. He has his head down and his elbows on his knees and is tracking the progress of a solitary ant that is either hurrying away from someplace or hurrying toward someplace else.

Grayson drops a glob of spit in front of the ant to see what the ant would make of it. The ant adjusts his momentum, bounces around the perimeter of the mound of spit and regains his speed. Grayson spits again, but his aim is off and the spit entombs the ant, but the little bastard is a gamer and he fought through and got back underway. The thing stops for a moment and is doing something with his antennae or arms, whatever they were. It looks like he is shaking his fists at the sky. Maybe the ant can't see him because his eyes are too small to see something so big. Then, perhaps motivated by a mental picture of a picnic still to come, the ant zips off.

"Enjoy the rest of your day, Mister Ant."

A wiry guy on the other side of sixty, wearing gray work pants and a black tee shirt and a canvas jacket had walked in from the street, and stopped a few feet shy of Grayson. The old guy has white hair shaved down to a fuzzy flat top at the very peak of a pear-shaped head. He has a shiny, flat face that curves away to the side and leads to scrunched up, pinned back ears. He balances the entire assembly at an angle that requires you to suppose he has a stiff neck. He looks like a lonely big toe poking out of a torn sock. He pulls a pair of wire rimmed glasses from his tee shirt and hooks the arms over his ears.

"Do you identify with the ant?" the man says. His breathing is labored.

"What?"

"Or the spitter? Me? In my time, I was both at once."

"That's way too deep for me."

The old guy pulls his keys out and jerks his head toward the door, inviting Grayson inside.

"Is John Minihan around?" Grayson asks.

"Right in front of you," he says. He sticks out his hand. "You are?"

"Dan Grayson's son."

"Michael. Nice to meet you."

Grayson smiles unhappily. "How do you know I'm not Hugh?"

"I deduced it."

Grayson bristles, and reaches in his pocket to grab his keys.

"Your father told me Hugh drives a company car." John M. smiles. "People don't come here to get company cars fixed."

Grayson looks at John M. and pegs him as another old drunk who thinks he's smart.

"That isn't a company issued 1967 GTO parked over there. It is the pride of Dee-troit that year. That Tempest body on the 67' was perfect. All in all, you got the best GTO made."

"Good to know," Grayson says.

"What can I do for you?"

John M. turns around, opens the door into the shop. He walks a couple of feet, pulls the string on a hanging troffer of fluorescent tubes that stutter and blink before filling one section of the room with a small but unforgiving hum that sounds like a bad guy bug getting the electric chair. The noise brought up an ugly light to go with the harsh hum. John M. then went to a door on the back wall, opens it and went inside. Grayson follows as John goes directly to a five-gallon coffee urn sitting on a counter and flips the switch.

Around the room he goes, pulling the string on more grim lights, revealing metal folding chairs set up in three rows of four beside a picnic table that is draped with an old flowery oilcloth covering that looked as if every smoker since Sir Walter Raleigh had a go at scorching it. Scattered about are red and yellow metal ashtrays, clearly subjected to hard but careless use, empty now except for crusts of ash that paint the air with stink.

Grayson says, "I promised I'd meet you. After that, I don't know."

"People come here to get their wagons repaired, usually, but sometimes someone will show up because he wants help to get off the booze."

"What's with all the chairs?"

"Some of the boys come in around noon and we have a meeting. Breaks up the work day," John says.

"You stand at the front and give a sermon?"

"No, we rotate, whoever chairs the meeting sits at the desk and speaks for five minutes or so, then whoever wants to talk, does. You want to come back for it?"

"No."

"You worried about one of your friends seeing you? Would anyone be shocked to learn that you drink too much?" John says.

"I'm worried they find out I'm not man enough to do anything about it myself."

"John Barleycorn has beaten better men than you and me, Sunny Jim. Beat them to death. You like team sports, right? This is a team sport."

"What happens if this doesn't work for me? What then?" Grayson says.

John nods. "Don't worry about that. You do this thing like it's laid out and it *will* work. I've never seen it fail, when pursued with heart."

John M. sits at the picnic table, and pulls over a tin ashtray crusted black and positioned it in front of himself.

"The smell from these things helps me remember why I want to quit."

Grayson leans against the wall and folds his arms.

"Isn't there some part confessing all the stuff I've done wrong? And facing the music?"

"Only when and if you are ready. For most, that's way down the line, too far off to worry about. Not yet. A day at a time. But, if you're doing something that's bothering you, you should stop."

"Because if you're talking about sin, I don't believe in God."

"That may be just wishful thinking on your part," John says.

"I guess if I go to meetings, my fun is done," Grayson says.

"Good-bye Rolling Stones, and hello Lawrence Welk," John says.

"That nails it," Grayson says.

"A great friend of mine says that Lawrence Welk bit, when he speaks at a meeting. It's how most of us felt coming in. But the evidence showed most of us weren't having much fun anymore."

"A lot of times, I was," Grayson says.

"I know I was all funned out. Or else, I wouldn't have been even talking about AA. If I was having fun, why would I need AA?"

"Because other people think I should quit."

"People who hate fun, right? Those fun hating bastards. But you can't do it for other people. You have to do it for you. Which is why I want a Camel so bad I'd fight you for it if you had one. My youngest daughter wants me to quit, my oldest wants me to die. Lung cancer killed their mother."

Grayson sighs. "Sorry to hear it."

"She was my-ex. Bounced me when I wouldn't quit drinking. I gave up her and my girls for booze. The only woman I ever loved. I love her still. I'm just grateful she would see me before she died. The day before she passed, she told me I broke her heart. I told her I was sorry, and I still loved her. She said, 'Better luck next time.'"

"When did you quit?"

"February 25th,1958."

"You missed all of the sixties," Grayson says.

"Not yet, I haven't. They're not over yet. Decades start late. The 60's didn't start until the Cuban Missile thing, and they won't be over until Nixon is gone."

"1976?" Grayson asks.

"I guess you don't watch the news," John says.

"If I was tough," Grayson says, "I could do it. But I'm not. I'm not strong enough, or tough. Whatever I need, I don't have it."

"There are different kinds of tough, different kinds of strength that apply here." He paused. "Listen, when you come to the Sagamore Bridge there, down the Cape, you see a Samaritan sign says, *"Depressed? Lonely? Call The Samaritans."* But if you drive down by the shipyard, to the Fore River Bridge, the sign there, in big, black letters, shouts, *"No Jumping!"* John M. laughed. "Maybe we should be glad it doesn't say, '*Hey Stupid! No Jumping!*' AA is like that. Different strokes for different people, or whatever the song says. Some need kindness, some need simple straight forward directions. Like, '*No Jumping!*'"

Grayson is not amused.

John M. looks out to the lot and says, "Okay, look, let me know when, or if, you want to go to a meeting."

He walks toward the door that led to the shop bays.

"All right, but," Grayson says. "Do I need to go with you? Can't I go by myself?"

John M. turns. "Sure, you can, but don't push your luck. The temptation is always to go out one last time. But a lot of men died because they took their time asking for a ride out to Dropkick Murphy's farm to dry out. But, listen, you do what you please."

"I'll get back to you."

"Okay if I don't hold my breath while I wait?" John says.

"I said I will, so I will," Grayson snaps. "I probably need to stop for a while. Until I can get my shit together. But I can't see myself panicking and deciding to quit forever, not at my age."

"See," John says. "If you do stop, your ability to gather your shit into a pile will definitely improve, if that's what you want. Your shit wrangling skills, so to speak, will get better. But, there is always way more shit to gather in a drunk's life. Your best bet is to reduce the amount of shit you have to deal with."

"So, I stop, and everything gets perfect?"

"No, not for me, it didn't. For you? I don't know. All I know is that when I was drunk I wanted to be sober, and when I was sober, I wanted to be drunk. An MDC cop found me passed out in the back seat of my car over at the Castle Island parking lot, Mike MacGillivray was his name. He said if I went to meetings and listened to the people talk, I wouldn't have to drink anymore. Even if I wanted to, I wouldn't have to. I was flabbergasted by the idea. What if it were true? So, I went and found out I have a disease."

"Okay, I'll be honest," Grayson says. "That's where the whole AA thing really gets irritating. That's a fucking cop out. A way to run away from your responsibility for all the shit you pulled."

"Did he run away from it?" John M. asks.

"Who?"

"Your father."

Grayson shrugs and shakes his head. "All I know is I don't have a disease."

"I do," John M. says. "It's the only disease that tells you that you don't have it."

Grayson rolls his eyes.

"There was an old time French writer, see," John M. says. "I don't know his name. He had a story about the devil, about the devil's best trick? You know it?"

Grayson shakes his head. "Oh, God. The devil?"

"The devil's best trick was convincing the world he didn't exist. The disease's best trick is convincing you that you don't have it. It insists that you don't have a disease. That's why they say it's cunning, baffling and powerful."

"So," Grayson says, "If you think you have this disease, you should sign up for AA. If you think you don't have it, then sign up faster. That's a surefire formula for growth."

"Look, I'd love to stand here and verbally joust with you all day, but duty calls. So, you're not an alky but you don't want to drink. Then just quit. People do it every day."

"I think I'll try that. I don't want to go to meetings. I'm pretty busy."

"I bet. Gathering one's shit can keep a fella occupied."

Grayson says, "Plus, no offense, but some of the stuff The Old Man says, it sounds goofy."

"You go to AA meetings and you will hear plenty of goofy stuff said about almost everything, definitely. But, you gotta pay attention because the goofy stuff is often followed by real wisdom." He shrugs. "Then more goofy stuff."

"I don't want wisdom. I wouldn't know what to do with it. I could go for a little peace."

"That's good. You can have either peace or wisdom, but not both. Listen, AA is not for everybody. It's for people who want it."

"I could always try it later, if I want," Grayson says.

"Sure, you can. We'll save you a seat. Just don't die in the meantime," John M. says.

Grayson twitches.

John M. puts his hand up. "Listen, I'm sorry I said that. I've got a problem with snappishness."

"You guys all sound like you're narrating your own life," Grayson says.

John M. pulls a card from the pocket of his tee shirt. "If you change your mind, give me a call."

Grayson looks at the plain white card.

John M.

Granite 2-7275

"You still use the old-fashioned exchange, huh?" Grayson says.

"I'm an old fashion guy. Call anytime, if you want to go to a meeting." He swept an arm back toward the garage. "Or, when you break down."

CHAPTER TWENTY-ONE

Grayson sticks an oversized, soft sponge in a bucket of hot, soapy water, and without wringing it out, slops it across the hood of the GTO.

Ron Kerr leans on the third-floor porch rail and yells down at him.

"Telephone."

Grayson climbs the three flights and opens the door to see Curly down at the end of the hall, holding the phone out to him.

"You are a real popular guy," Curly snarls. "Why don't you get a secretary?"

Grayson is still smarting from the note Curly left him, as well as the segmented refrigerator.

Grayson takes the phone from Curley, and says, "Why don't you get your label maker out and punch in "asshole" and stick it to your forehead."

"Wow," Curly says, now with a deep sadness. He shakes his head, disappointed by the level of hostility directed toward his personage. He inhales then expels a jet of air from his nose. "Bummer."

He stands there, way longer than appropriate, and keeps on with the gloomy puss, to manifest beyond a shadow of a doubt, his disappointment at Grayson's rudeness. Curley then walks away. He goes in his bedroom and closes the door, gently, to demonstrate his unflappable maturity.

"Yeah?" Grayson says into the phone.

"You giving Kerr crap?" Donny says. "Didn't you just tell me he was strong as a monkey?"

"That's right," Grayson says. "Meaning he could kick your ass, which doesn't mean he could kick mine."

Donny snorts. "Listen, I'll give it to you straight. I don't think Charley will hold up under pressure from the cops, or the bikers. He says he wants to get out of town. Right now, let's make that happen so he doesn't screw us up."

"I'll call him."

He does and there is no answer. He kills time, smoking on the front porch of the third-floor apartment. He can see pretty far from up here, but he didn't see anything.

Grayson is on the way to the bathroom when he hears Ron Kerr rustling around in his room. It'd be better to get this over with now.

He taps on Kerr's door.

"Hey, Curly? Are you in there, Curl? You got a sec?"

Kerr opens the door and stands there in a full set of black silk pajamas and a red smoking jacket with shiny black lapels. His hair is combed and still wet from the shower. He holds a lit pipe in his teeth and a can of Pepsi in his hand. He withdraws the pipe.

"What can I do for you?" Curly says, still a bit frosty.

"I'm sorry, bud, for getting shitty with you and everything, threatening your Celtic stuff."

Kerr relaxes, but not much. "Yeah, that wasn't cool, at all."

"I know. I'm sorry."

"That's my pride and---"

"Yeah, I know, Ron. I apologized, man. You want me to grovel, or what?"

Kerr sees he'd pushed as far as he is going to get without resuming the hostilities.

"Okay, Grayson. I appreciate it."

"I'm going up the Downs a little later. You need anything?"

"Like what?" Kerr asks.

"I don't know, man. That's why I asked you."

"No, I think I'm all set."

He walks from the apartment up to Norfolk Downs to his bank, hands the teller his passbook and asks for a cashier's check.

Back at the apartment, he sits at the kitchen table holding a pen and looking at a piece of clean lined paper he'd just ripped off the pad. He taps the top of the pen on the table for a minute, shrugs and puts pen to paper. Nothing. He lays his forearms on the table and his forehead on his forearms and wonders what he wants to say. Some time passes and he lifts his head and puts pen to paper. A few lines in, he writes:

I keep thinking about when we took the train to NYC the June we graduated. We went into that weird little restaurant and I ordered clam chowder and the strange looking waiter brought me soup with celery and tomatoes in it. I said I ordered chowder not vegetable soup and the waiter said I had to be from Boston and then he said, "Man, you are a stranger in a strange land. Maybe that's not what you wanted, but you got what you asked for. And I'm sorry but that is your problem if those are two different things."

He pauses to figure out what else he wants to say, then he bent over the paper and writes some more. He plans to drop it off, but if she sees an envelope from him, she might rip it up without opening it. If it came in the mail it would be more formal. When he finishes, he pulls an envelope from the kitchen drawer and addresses it. He looks for a stamp but can't find one. He knocks again on Kerr's bedroom door, and calls out.

"Hey, Ron. Do you have any postage stamps?"

Kerr opens the door, smiling.

"That's funny," he says. He holds up a Playboy magazine, showing Grayson the cover, where a blonde held a mocked-up postage stamp with the Playboy logo on it.

"Wow," Grayson says. "Wild."

"Tennessee Williams is the interview," Kerr says.

"That the guy who sings 'Sixteen Tons?'" Grayson thought that Curly would laugh.

Curly shrugs, "Maybe. I haven't got that far yet."

"So, no stamps?"

"No, but I'm going to the post office to get stamps for work. How many do you need?" Kerr asks.

"Just one."

"Leave the envelope on the table and I'll get a stamp and mail it right at the post office, too. They're eight cents each."

"Okay, thanks," Grayson says. "I'll put a dime on the envelope."

"I'll leave you the change," Ron Kerr says. He closes the door.

He calls Charlie's place: No answer. He tries several more times with the same result.

Thinking sleep may help him put off a drink, he goes into his room and stretches out on his bed. He is tired, beyond tired but he can't fall asleep. His mind bounces from one thing to another, but slowly, as if he has a hangover. He feels sick, sickened by despair. But he doesn't really know what despair is. Was he being dramatic? Part of the problem is he lacks the discernment to distinguish one emotional state from another, except for a very basic few. Whenever he'd hear people talk about emotions, not that it happened much, but when it did, he tried to change the subject. He was very sad about his mother getting cancer, sadder when she had the stroke, saddest when it became clear she wasn't going to get better. When he saw one of his sisters or their kids, he was glad. He was as sad as sad could be, it was as if he been crushed, when Paul had been reported MIA, because he knew instantly that his brother was dead. So, the *news* that Paul was really dead was not news at all, but it still hurt something awful, way worse than he expected. Grayson also knew when he was mad. But, with any emotion that could not be found in the pages of a Dick and Jane book, he is like a goldfish looking out from his glass bowl at a blueprint for a nuclear plant.

On New Year's Day, he'd woken up knowing Catherine was through with him, but he'd hoped it would blow over. When she was waiting for him at the apartment, which was the day his mother opened the door to the Marines and her world began ending, he thought Catherine had taken him back, but no. He waited. When she said she was pregnant he thought, at first, she'd agree to marry him if he was contrite, but somehow, he'd really let her down. Maybe he was supposed to grab her and drag her to the priest. Me Tarzan, you Jane. Who the fuck knows? Who the fuck knows? Who knows! If there are answers they are out of his reach.

At some point, he hears Ronald Kerr lurching around the apartment like a team of Clydesdales. How could a skinny guy make so much noise? He hears the door close as Kerr goes out.

He closes his eyes and falls asleep.

When he wakes up, it is late afternoon. Each minute that the cops didn't kick down his door and shoot him dead is gravy. He has to get out of the apartment. He asks himself why he needs that old bastard John Minihan just to go to a frigging AA meeting? Is there some secret password that he needs to know to get in, or what? Why doesn't he get up off his ass and go to a meeting himself? He's a big boy. He could see for himself, now, without someone yapping in his ear. Get it over with, go and tell them that the whole AA thing is a crock of shit, and it won't work for him.

"Get going, doofus," Grayson says.

He gets off the bed, looks around for his sneakers, because if this plays out like he expects, it won't take long to confirm the AA experience is for lames and he can make a quick, silent exit from the meeting, leaving the dead to talk to the dead.

The phone rings in the kitchen and he ignores it while he laces his sneakers. Would the cops call before they came over to arrest him? Not likely; they much prefer surprise.

Grayson groans, jumps to his feet and throws a flurry of punches at his invisible adversary, which, now, has the face of Hugh as it floats in front of him, but out of reach. He's lightheaded, so he stops punching and goes to the kitchen.

He fills a glass with tap water, goes back into his bedroom and opens his sock drawer, pulls out a sandwich bag half full of amphetamine capsules, the 'greenies.' Grayson doesn't like to take pills recreationally, only for practical reasons, because taking a pill to get high was too...bald. You can claim to be a social drinker; you might have to admit you really stunk at it, but still, you can claim that that is your intent. He's never heard anyone ever claim to be a social pill taker. But, boy, did he need something to lift him out of this funk.

He takes two with water, and wraps a third in a piece of torn off page from Time magazine, then because the two didn't seem like they'd be enough, he unwraps the third, downs it with water, then wraps two others in the paper and puts it in his pocket.

Anyone, who spends any time in the seedier bars, has heard the horror stories about AA. These tales are told in the same way that a gathering of ancient mariners spoke of monster sea serpents and rogue waves, and like those terrible yarns, often end with the words, "and was never seen again." So, Grayson knows there is a number in the phone book, and overpowering the instinct for self-preservation, he looks it up.

He walks carefully out the door, down the stairs, imagining a camera crew recording a documentary entitled *The Last of Grayson*. He gets in his car, zips down to the Merit Station and the bank of phone booths there. He gets in the booth, and closes the door, even though there is no around, then drops a dime and rats himself out.

"Can you tell me where there's a meeting tonight in South Boston?" he says. He wants to avoid Quincy meetings for fear someone will see him.

"Sure thing," says some chipper bastard. "There's one at the L St. Bath House at 7:30 in the rec room. That work?"

"Well, I'm a wreck so I guess it does," Grayson says.

The cheerful SOB began cooing some words that Grayson didn't have time to identify because he hung up so fast. He half expects to disappear down a hole in the floor of the booth, like Max in the opening credits of *Get Smart.*

CHAPTER TWENTY-TWO

Grayson racks the GTO on the residential side of the treed median, across from the L St. Bathhouse, which is more of a community center. The L St. Brownies is a club of mostly old men who were locally famous for taking a bollicky swim in Dorchester Bay, behind the building, every New Year's Day, regardless of weather.

He rolls the window down, smokes a cigarette and watches the foot traffic enter the building; all these noisy, rollicking, giddy geeks, greeting each other with hugs and handshakes. Inside, the joint is probably teeming with people who think they're happy. He'd like to give each drunk a kick in the nuts for running a scam. He doesn't belong there, and he can't fake it.

"Fuck that," he says. He slips the stick into first gear, and takes off like he knows where he's going.

He has no idea where to go or what to do, but moving offers comfort. His only lasting desire is to go, just go, go, no matter where he was. This is the one imperative: Go. Keep moving. Being somewhere else is like the future; you can head there, but you can never get there.

He pulls into the Stop & Shop lot at Neponset Circle and parks down the end, in front of the liquor store. He knew it was inevitable that he'd end up here. It is impossible to last all the way through life without drinking? No. Why pretend? Why postpone it? Give in, get it over with, everything's screwed anyway. He gets out, pulls the folded money from his pocket to see how much he has on him and the card John M. gave him falls to the ground. He looks down at the card lying there, and thinks about it. He leaves the card where it fell and the wind picks it up and it tumbles away. At the front door of the package store, he came to a quick halt on the rubber mat when the automatic door he'd expected to swing open at his footfall failed to do so. He pushes on the door, but it seems to be locked. He looks in the store and sees smiling customers and genial clerks busy with various stages of purchase. He looks at the hours of operation on the door and the store is supposed to be open until 11 PM. He knocks on the window, but nobody seems to hear him. Spooked, he wonders if he's a ghost? The thought scares him. He turns to go back to his car. On the way by the phone booth, he sees John M.'s card, lying there at the door of the booth. The wind has blown it his way. He hurries back to the Goat, disoriented and in fear. Have the greenies made him paranoid?

He fishes his pocket for the keys, and pulling them out, the key ring gets caught on a thread and the keys fall to the ground, like John M.'s card had fallen to the ground. He feels a strong wind blowing from behind him, pushing him toward the phone booth.

CHAPTER
TWENTY-THREE

John Minihan says the meeting is close enough to walk. So, they set off down Beale St., and cross Arlington where Grayson has parked the GTO at the hilltop beside the firehouse.

"Will my car be all right there?" Grayson says, mostly just to say something.

John M. looks. "Yeah, if you have the emergency brake on."

Down the hill they go, toward Beach St.

"I'm glad you changed your mind," John M. says. "You will be, too, although that might be hard to believe right now."

Grayson nods.

"I know how you feel. I'm sure there were guys who went to the electric chair more cheerfully than I went to my first AA meeting," John M. says. "I didn't really want to quit drinking. So, I know. I get it. But you have to trust me a little bit. I've been where you are. You've never been where I am. You'll be okay, if you let it work."

As they talk back and forth, Grayson notices John M. is verbose on the down side of the hills, and more economical word-wise on the flat stretches. Grayson's best chance to really plead his case was on the inclines where John is busy wheezing. The old guy is cagey, though, and slows noticeably and sometimes stops when he wants to make a point.

"I don't see how quitting helps anything," Grayson says. "I feel like if I don't drink, I'll crack up. I don't want to end up in Mattapan, sitting around in pajamas, making stuff out of gimp."

"Did your father crack up?"

"No. But he's no prize. He can still be an asshole."

John stops. "A son who thinks his father is an asshole is very common, and both parties can live with that. But when a father thinks his son is an asshole, both are grief stricken. I'm not saying that's what he thinks now, but you keep it up, and he will eventually."

It's never occurred to Grayson that his father might think of him in this way.

John may have seen he had dented Grayson's armor, because he changes topics.

"This is how I get my highs today," John M. says.

Grayson surfaces out of his gloom. "Walking?"

"Getting light headed, and not just from walking. A coughing fit, standing up quick, bending down to tie my shoes. Whoo!"

They go by Mass Fields grammar school, bearing down on some kind of Protestant church.

They descend a steep flight of stone stairs, go through a double set of swinging doors and onto a cement floor in a wide-open basement which is abuzz with the happy babble of people at a party. Or maybe this hall has been invaded and occupied by a second squad from the same army of smiling, cult-eyed Moonies that he'd earlier seen infiltrating the L St. Bathhouse.

John M. says he wants to introduce the skittish Grayson to this other young guy named Bob. They wait until Bob, whose back is to them, finishes drawing a cup of coffee from a big metal urn that sits on a shaky card table. Bob pulls a plastic spoon from a cup full of them and digs it into a bowl of sugar and shovels sugar into his coffee cup, and keeps doing it until, perhaps, the cup is too heavy. Then he stirs it, as he gazes about with a dreamy look on his face. The guy looks familiar, like the kid brother of someone Grayson knew in school.

"Bob," John M. says. "Let me introduce you to a friend."

"Hey, Grayson! Good to see you," Bob says.

He shakes Grayson's hand so vigorously that Bob slops his coffee over the top of the cup onto his other hand.

"I wondered if you fellas might know each other," John M. says.

"Igor?" Grayson says.

He barely recognizes him; Igor looks like Bob Hayes from sixth grade again, at ease, clean and tidy, as if his mother had gotten him ready for school.

"Yeah!" Bob says. "Boy, it's been a long time since I've been called Igor. Cripes, am I glad you made it. I'm really happy to see you."

"Yeah? Well, misery loves company," Grayson says.

Bob and John M. laugh heartily, like Ed McMahon laughs at Johnny.

"You're in the right place," Bob says. "This is a great meeting."

Bob turns away, picks up a pamphlet out of a wire rack on the table and hands it to Grayson.

"Here," he says. "Stick that in your pocket. It's a schedule of area meetings, where, what night they meet, and so on."

Grayson puts it in his back pocket, already wondering where he can throw it away. What if he gets killed in a car accident and someone finds that on him? Talk about embarrassing.

The low-ceilinged room is fluorescently lit and crowded with a hundred or so metal folding chairs which look like they've been lined up in rows by a team of German engineers. There are indeed Boy Scout banners with cryptic sayings hanging from wall nails, just like The Old Man said. *Expect a Miracle, But For The Grace of God,* and *We Can Do What I Couldn't.* Grayson again asks himself, what the hell am I doing here?

He is being herded along the wall, to the left of the chairs, toward the far end of the long room, which is much like the basement room in the grammar school where he and Bob had played Bombardment in an after-school recreation program. Bob could whip that rubber ball, man; that red ball *burned* like fire when you caught it against your belly, like it might blow a hole right through you.

But right now, Grayson is deeply concerned about the present; were they marching him toward that microphone up at the front? Is he supposed to weep and wail about bad luck, like on Queen For A Day?

"Why are we going up to the front?" Grayson asks.

"I can hear better," John M. says, "when I sit up front."

Bob nods at this wisdom, as if he admires it and is very impressed with John's sagacity.

The walls are smooth, painted cinder block, about six feet high. At the top of the wall, set in sideways, are casement windows that open inward. The windows are not the kind Grayson can crash through and make his way to freedom. They are too small. Maybe he could jump up, wriggle through and then claw his way to ground level, but by the time he got halfway out, even someone as old as John M. would have time to jump up, point and shout, 'Seize him!'

Soon he finds himself sitting on a metal folding chair in the third row, packaged between Bob on the aisle, and John M. on the other side. Underneath, the ceiling's a thick blanket of cigarette smoke.

"Wow," Grayson says. "These people like to smoke."

More Ed-style chortling.

Bob says, "There's a beginner's meeting here, before the regular meeting starts. You get thirty or so wired up beginners here, they can burn through a carton of smokes in sixty minutes, no sweat."

John M. thinks that is pretty funny, despite his own breathing issues.

Grayson says nothing more since it seems like anything he says leads to a trap where someone finds an excuse to talk about AA. Do any of these people have other interests? Plus, all this frivolity seems forced, like they are trying too hard. If you have to push it so much, it must be a shitty deal, after all.

By and by some goober gets up to the microphone and drones on, everyone went quiet for some reason and then the guy reads some more bullshit. It is all staticky and broken, like late night radio coming in from St. Louis.

Grayson looks around and wonders how he'd ended up in this crowd of old drunks. These people are the real article, while he's just a young guy who drinks too much from time to time, which is what happens to young guys, and that doesn't make him an alcoholic. Is he the only young guy here? He looks at Igor, who probably has a swelled head now with all these people going around calling him Bob. Grayson and Bob are the only young guys. There are a shitload of skinny, yellow haired old men hanging around the coffee urn. They all seem to be wearing white shirts and ancient, baggy suit pants which they'd probably swiped out of a Goodwill box. The sort of old guys who smoke Chesterfields, and live with their divorced, middle-aged daughters. Here and there are a few older women, always together in twos or threes, some of them avid knitters. But young men are badly underrepresented. But then he sees three young guys, sitting together and laughing. One of the guys is Buff Mulligan, Buck's twenty-year old brother, the last of the ten Mulligans boys fielded by their never-say-die parents. Buff isn't wearing his hooded black sweatshirt, the one that puts the finishing touch on his medieval zombie-leper look. If this gimmick straightened out Buff, turned him back into a human, then maybe Grayson should listen?

Grayson hears clapping and stops looking around and looks up to the front of the room where a trim man in early middle age starts speaking from the podium. The man's face is tanned and lined, as if from outdoor work, and his hair is a full white that matches his open necked shirt. The white hair is the sort that seems to happen to some guys early and overnight.

"Do you recognize him?" Bob whispers.

Grayson shakes his head.

"That's Mad Mike Ryan."

"The B.C. guy?"

Bob nods.

Mike Ryan is from East Milton and had been a great fullback for Boston College in the 50's, and knocked around the AFL in the early 60's. He was not the most talented player B. C. ever fielded, but it is widely held that he was the toughest.

Grayson listens.

"Finally," Mike Ryan says, "after years and years of me coming home drunk, the odd time when

I could find my way home at all, my wife gave me the broom. Guess what? I was surprised."

Laughter.

"You cannot be serious, I said to her. What about these kids, growing up without their father? Never mind that if I saw a bunch of kids playing on the street, I probably couldn't pick mine out. But I was offended she'd do such a thing. To me? I was a good provider, wasn't I? So, I came into the program hoping that my wife would reconsider."

Of course. Why the hell else would anyone be here? Grayson looks around and sees bobbing heads and smiling faces.

Grayson's gaze sweeps the room again, looking, with fading hope, to catch sight of someone whose very presence would free Grayson. He wants to find someone he could point to, mentally, and say, *'If that guy, who is a Dover St. wino, is here, and this other guy who beats his wife and kids, or even this pathetic fool who is known to shit his drawers and sit in it, then certainly I definitely do not belong here with them.'* He looks all around, but sees no sad sack savior. When he looks up at the casement windows again, he sees Bob's profile reflected in the dark glass, and beside Bob's reflection, he sees a sneakered foot attached to a jeaned leg that led to a knee that was pumping up and down fast enough to mix a gallon of paint. He recognizes the sneaker as his own.

"She's a good woman," Mad Mike Ryan is saying, "and I figured if she saw I was trying to quit she'd show me mercy. I wanted mercy. But my version of mercy didn't happen."

Then what, Grayson asks himself, is the fucking point?

Mad Mike says, "What's funny is, that about two years after I got in AA, I realized a few things. Things that don't add up when I think of them at the same time. One, if my wife had not divorced me, I would never have gotten sober. I only came here to take the heat off. My plan was to stay until she cooled off. Which was weird, because she wasn't mad, not anymore, now she pitied me, which was way worse. But she kept the divorce proceedings in motion so I kept coming to meetings, thinking she'd come around. She didn't come around, but I got sober. I would not have come here and gotten sober, if she'd taken me back. Two, getting sober is far and away the best thing that ever happened to me. Because it made me realize how blessed I had been, with my family, how much I love my kids, and my wife. Now, my kids, the oldest is twelve, the youngest, seven, we live in different houses, but I'm more conscious of them than I ever was. They are always on my mind, and in my heart. That's only because I don't have to go around thinking about booze all the time. When I do see my kids, they're happy to see me. They give their old man a hug and a kiss. I know they love me. Before, I just figured they didn't. Why would they?"

So, this is AA? Sitting around listening to depressing stories? This makes no sense.

Mike Ryan says, "My wife, my ex-wife, has moved on. She has a boyfriend. I wish I hated him because it would be easier, but I don't. I still love her so I'm happy for her, because she deserves a good guy and he is. Three, I wish my wife had not divorced me, even though I would not have gotten sober, and getting sober is the best thing that ever happened to me. Plus, if I was still drinking, I wouldn't have all this pain, like the pain of losing my family. I would be numb. Today I feel real love for my kids and my family, friends, you people and even a little for myself now and then, and it's something, really something. It's amazing. Being sober is the best thing that ever happened to me, but boy, sometimes it hurts so much I don't know how I can take it anymore. That's when my sponsor tells me, keep it in the day, don't worry about tomorrow. And then I say, but I'm not thinking about tomorrow, I'm torn up right now. He says, have faith. 'You're feeling love, and it will hurt for a while. Sometimes love is a knife that opens you up so the poison can get out, and when it does you start to heal and healing is painful.'"

Grayson almost frees a dry sob, even before he'd understood what Ryan said.

Ryan says, "And then I say to my sponsor, great! Wonderful! That's really swell. A lot of times, I don't know what the hell he's talking about but I don't drink anyway, just so I can keep coming to these meetings and maybe someday I'll know. Maybe. But for now, I have hope, mostly hope that he's not altogether full of shit."

The AA crowd responds with laughter and applause.

This is the good news?

"Hey, Bob," Grayson says. "Is there a men's room down here?"

Bob points to the back. "Take a right after the door."

Grayson goes through the door, and straight up the stone steps, two at a time, and runs down Beach St. like he is being chased, across Hancock to Beale St., up the hill, dodging the sadistic traffic as he crosses Newport, and jumps in the GTO parked at the top of the hill. He snaps the emergency brake off, points it down Arlington St, puts the clutch in and rolls out. He turns the key on, pops the clutch and jump starts the car as he hits the bottom of the hill. He is sick of reading signs, so he ignores the red Stop, blows across Brook St. without even looking, hoping to Christ that nothing is coming for him.

CHAPTER
TWENTY-FOUR

Grayson wants to occupy himself to avoid picking up something to drink, so he goes to Charlie's apartment and parks. Upstairs, he knocks and knocks but there is no answer. He's pulling away from the curb when Charlie hustles around the corner from Billings Rd., waves to someone in the pizza place and then cuts across Hancock, walking between two cars stopped for the light. He jogs across to the sidewalk and starts down the slight hill.

Grayson taps the horn and Charlie jumps, and whirls toward the noise. He sees Grayson and puts his hand over his heart and shakes his head.

He gets in the car saying, "You trying to give me a heart attack?"

"Sorry, bud. That's kind of why I'm here. You want to get out of town, right? What can I do to help?"

"Yes, I have decided to hit the road for parts unknown. Don't try to talk me out of it. I'm not set up to handle cops or people trying to kill me."

"That's what I figured and I want to help you."

"What about Hugh? Will he be okay with it?"

"No problem. To be honest they are a little concerned about you." Grayson speaks the last word and realizes his utterance is ill advised. In fact, really fucking stupid.

Charlie's face turns ashen. "Why? They worried about me talking? I would never talk. Never."

"Why would you say that?" Grayson says. "No one thinks that."

"Plus, there's something, I don't know, not right, about the way he pulled this together."

"Water under the bridge," Grayson says. "What do you need to split?"

"Money."

"I can give you money."

"Thanks anyway. I've got some upstairs. Maybe you could drive me in to Oliver's. It's pay day. Live park while I run in."

The area all around Fenway Park and Kenmore Square is always hopping at night, year-round, baseball or no. The Red Sox spring training season is well under way in Florida, and the regular season starts soon and the slightly warmer nights seem an encouragement to begin another soul crushing Boston baseball season. Students on break from the area's prestigious universities mix loudly with their peers from the humbler academies, most of them shouting and drinking in equal measure. The bars around Kenmore played live music by up and coming bands. The music bars served students, baseball fans, rockers, drunken louts and hooligans. On the streets, the louts mixed democratically with college kids. Now that the legal drinking age is eighteen, the area around the Square is a swarm of teenaged fun seekers. The guiding principle of many of these undergrads is that every night in Boston had the potential to regenerate into another Woodstock, minus the mud.

Grayson drives the pentagon formed by the city streets that surround Fenway Park, keeping his eyes peeled for cops and a parking spot.

"Park on the bridge," Charlie says. "They won't bother you if you're waiting in the car."

Grayson makes the loop around Kenmore station and is heading back toward Oliver's and the ball park when he spots an opening almost right on the bridge.

Charlie says, "That works. I'll be right back." He hops out and jaywalks across the bridge to the other side, heading toward the bar.

Grayson has never been in Oliver's, but he had been in the blue-collar barroom that preceded it. It had been a scrum before Sox games, and they'd serve anyone who could reach the bar and put money on it. The front door opens right onto the wide corner of Brookline and Lansdowne. The buildings on this section of Brookline Ave. had been torn down in the early 60's and an east-west corridor of land excavated here so that the brick backside of the bar building looms sharply above and beside the railroad tracks which run parallel to the Mass Pike. Where Oliver's ends, the Brookline Ave Bridge begins, and the Pike and railroad tracks run underneath the bridge. On both sides of the bridge an eight-foot high chain link fence has been erected to prevent playful kids from dropping boulders and such onto the speedy turnpike traffic or the passenger trains passing thirty feet below.

On the Oliver's side of the street Grayson can see clots of people milling around in front of the bar, watched over by the bouncers.

Grayson looks down at the car ashtray while grinding out his cigarette. In those two seconds a screech of tires startles him. He sees a dirty white

Chevy panel van with a blown muffler almost topple over as it rips off a crazy-fast U-turn in the wide intersection of Lansdowne and Brookline, and heads back to the bridge. The van slams to an abrupt stop on the up slope of the bridge, bobs when the passenger door flies open and a guy every bit as big as Donny jumps out onto the sidewalk. For a second, Charlie keeps walking toward the guy but finally he sees what's in front of him and he throws his hands into the air as if to surrender. The man spins Charlie halfway round and grabs him by the scruff of the neck and the ass of his pants.

Grayson is still, like prey, assuming it's the cops. But, as the big guy turns, Grayson can see he's wearing a ski mask. Grayson gets out of the car, held up by street traffic, gets ready to run across the bridge. The next thing Grayson sees, over the top of the van, is Charlie; he is being held aloft, prone, his puffy hair-do at one end and the soles of his little sneakers at the other. The big guy from the van is holding him overhead, facing him up to the night sky, like some kind of sacrifice. The horizontal Charlie disappears below the roof line of the van. Grayson sprints toward them, and sees Charlie again, as he is launched off the bridge and is arcing over the top of the eight-foot-high chain link fence that was supposed to prevent just such a thing. Grayson freezes in the roadway, trying to process what he's just seen. And now horns behind him begin sounding and the closest driver shouts out his window.

"Get out of the fucking street, you stupid bastard."

Grayson snaps to and runs around the stopped cars, intent on grabbing whoever it is that threw Charlie over, but before he gets there, the van bobs again, the door slams and it rips away from the curb and snaps a fast right on the barren section of Newbury St. that runs from Kenmore Square. It's gone from sight in under three seconds.

Around the bridge, what seems like a million girls start screaming; they sound like the train whistles in the old movies. Most of the crowd rushes away from the sidewalk and toward the center of the street, as if afraid they'd be tossed off next. Grayson gets to the fence and grabs the chain link, standing between two guys who have their faces pressed against the fence looking down at the Mass Pike and the railroad tracks. Grayson strains to see where Charlie landed.

He presses his face up to the fence beside an older guy, maybe thirty, with an enormous Fu Manchu. Like most hippies past their prime hippie years, he looks both very old and ageless.

"Far out. Too much, man. Too much."

Grayson grabs the hippie's arm and yells. "Where is he?"

"Too much, man." The man's eyes were all black pupil, from either shock or chemicals.

Grayson shakes him. "Did you see where he landed?"

"Not really. Somebody came out of the van and knocked me down. I got up just as the little guy got chucked over. That grabbed my eye, and blew my mind. Man, what do we do? Call the cops?"

The hippie starts gulping air, almost panting as if to ward off a fainting spell.

"Where is he?" Grayson says.

"Do you think he's dead?" the hippie says.

"Fuck no," the second guy says.

He seems rattled, but nowhere near as much as the hippie. He is younger, maybe late teens, with short, wiry blonde hair and Elvis sideburns. The kid's jaded face is colored by a sea of freckles; the face, combined with the hard-edged haircut, the shiny black pointy shoes, known locally as fence climbers, sharkskin pants and shiny black trench coat tells Grayson this kid is from Charlestown, or maybe Dorchester on the Roxbury line. He's standing a few feet further down the bridge, more toward Oliver's.

"I saw the whole fucking thing," the city kid says. "The little guy hit that bob wire on the fence."

The kid points toward five strings of barbed wire atop the rusty chain link fence that ran between the railroad tracks and the Mass Pike. The wire juts in toward the track at a 45-degree angle from the fence.

"His jacket got caught on the bob wire, and he was just hanging there a second, then he raised his arms over his head and slid, real slow like, right outta his jacket, and on to all them junk tires beside the fence. He hit them fucking tires and bounced up and landed on his feet, already running. He ran like a bastard that way." He pointed west, to the other side of the bridge. "It was like Tom and Jerry, man."

"What did the guy who threw him look like?" Grayson asks.

The kid's face registers shock and disgust. "I look like a rat to you? I saw nobody and nothing, pal." He looks both ways, put his hands in his trench coat pockets and hustles off toward Kenmore Square.

Grayson drains through the runny crowd and across the street to the western side of the bridge, grabs the fence and looks up along the tracks. No Charlie. On this part of the tracks, there is fencing on both sides until the tracks disappear under the Beacon Street overpass. Charlie might have squirted through a hole in the fence and gone up to the side streets off of Brookline Ave. Or maybe he'd find a place where he could hide, while he reaches the conclusion that his best bet now is to go straight to the cops and tell them everything he knew, which is not optimum at this time. Grayson stares some more, then takes off back to his car.

Now, out of nowhere there are cop cars rolling up on the bridge from both directions, sirens shrieking, and roof lights aboil. Grayson looks back at the chattering children, and the new people streaming from the other bars toward the sirens; the armed cops look big and surreal in the gaudy police lights, and more sirens close in as the Bad News Carnival continues to shriek its arrival.

Grayson fires up the engine and moves down Brookline Ave, makes a quick turn down Maitland Street, which ran off Brookline down toward the tracks. He navigates through a parking lot and comes out onto Beacon St., takes a right and a quick left, parking beside another section of tall fence that ran along the railroad tracks. He cuts the lights, shuts down the engine and gets out. He runs over to where a section of the high fence is attached to the fence pole, that being a sturdier place to climb over, but when he puts his foot in the fence it separates from the pole. He squeezes through the gash like it was a doggy door and crouches down beside a weedy bush. He closes his eyes for half a minute, adjusting to the darkness.

Who could have done this? Someone trying to quiet Charlie, someone very strong. Donny? He is prone to rash acts and paranoia.

Grayson sees dark figures far down on the tracks casting flashlight beams in the area underneath the bridge. Some of the beams ran up concrete shoulders girding the bridge as if the man they looked for may have clung to the side like a moth.

There are golf ball sized rocks on the ground all around the tracks, and Grayson hears them wheeze and clack as someone lurches toward him out of the dark. He sees the white tee shirt of now jacketless Charlie.

Charlie is looking backward, toward the bridge, but still moving forward, fast, coming closer to Grayson who holds his position behind the bush. How can he get Charlie's attention without scaring the bejesus out of him?

When Charlie gets closer, Grayson steps out and calls in a shouted whisper.

"Charlie!"

Without turning to look forward, Charlie bolts and runs straight into Grayson. The little guy bounces off him like a Superball. Grayson reaches down and pulls him up. In the faint light Grayson sees Charlie's face flash a rictus of panic, and he warms up with a small noise generally issued just prior to shrieking. Grayson realizes without thinking that he didn't have time to soothe Charlie into silence so he clips him under the chin with a sharp uppercut, and Charlie falls against the chain link fence and it rattles as he bounces forward before falling like a sack of sand. Charlie is now quiet, and quite portable.

Grayson carries Charlie over to the hole in the fence and sets him down. Then Grayson eases himself through the hole, reaches one arm back and drags Charlie through by the neck of his tee shirt. Beside the tee shirt, Charlie wore tracksuit pants and his Nike Flyte shoes. Grayson wriggles Charlie through the gash.

"Ow, ow, ow," Grayson says, voicing pain on Charlie's behalf.

He tosses him over his shoulder and runs to the car. Wrestling an unconscious guy into the back seat of a two door GTO would be an arduous process, so he keys the trunk open and carefully lays Charlie in it, slams it shut, and scrambles into the front seat of the car and rips away.

Charlie was ready to scream when he saw Grayson. He keeps in mind that Charlie's emotions are likely quite raw after being tossed off the bridge. That would do a number on anyone's poise. But, if it is Donny who threw him off the bridge, it would explain why Charlie tried to scream when he saw Grayson.

CHAPTER TWENTY-FIVE

Grayson pulls the GTO into the dark, truck filled market area that comprises the Boston meat district, which is located about two quick miles from the Fenway area.

The meat companies park their local delivery trucks and trailers in a weed choked, open, common lot in the center of the market. They leave space for the long-haul truckers to park. The truckers arrive at all hours of the day and night, coming in from the Midwest and Western states carrying loads of semi-butchered swinging beef or dead hogs hanging from hooks in refrigerated trailers. The drivers usually sleep until it's their turn to unload. They'd leave both the truck and reefer engines running, as they waited to drop dead animals into the maw of New England. Meanwhile the drivers dreamt in locked sleeper cabs, lulled by the white noise grumble and soothing vibration of their mobile wombs. When it's time to deliver, they'd open the trailer doors and the rank, refrigerated smell of blood, raw flesh and animal fat would drift out toward Mass Avenue and the back of the Old Mr. Boston distillery, where the stink of raw whiskey would meld with the smell of blood to form a memorable reek.

Grayson pulls in beside a section of long unused railroad track that sits between two dropped trailers, drives about thirty feet in and jumps out and opens the trunk. He wants to wake Charlie and put him in the front passenger seat. The poor guy has to be pretty rattled.

Charlie is still out cold. He slaps Charlie lightly on the cheek.

"Charlie? Charlie? You're okay now, Charlie. Everything's all right."

Grayson peers down into the dark trunk, trying to see if Charlie's light is back on. Charlie moans, then retches and Grayson flips him over quickly onto his stomach, so if he did vomit, he wouldn't choke to death.

Grayson reaches in and lifts him out, closes the trunk and leans Charlie against the back of the car.

Charlie begins to slide to the ground and Grayson catches him under the arms, lifts him and lays him down across the trunk. Grayson looks down into Charlie's face for a sign of consciousness, now with the sense that Charlie is faking being out.

"Wake up, Charlie. Come on, man, you're not afraid of me, are you? That's crazy."

Then Grayson hears shoes scraping behind him, and turns to see two big shadows, both wearing very large cowboy hats.

"Hey fellers," one hat drawls, "go somewheres else to perform your unnatural acts, now. You got decent folks trying to sleep—"

"Why, that's just a little feller he's got there laying on the trunk," the other hat says.

"Wrong. You got it wrong," Grayson says. "Go back to your trucks."

"Why? So you can mess around with that little boy in peace?"

"No. Of course not," Grayson says. "No. Shit! Hey, get the fuck outta here."

"Not gonna do it, buddy. Bert, git on the CB. Summon the 'thorities' out here."

"Beat it!" Grayson yells. "You shitkickin' fools."

He advances on the two cowboys and now sees they were a lot older than he'd first realized.

"Oh, yeah?" the other one says. "Come on, Sodomy Sam. Come on, an git it."

He pulls what looks like a sap from his back pocket and slaps the palm of his other hand with it. His sidekick backs up a little, and hung his hands close by his hips, like he's ready to draw a couple of six-shooters.

Grayson steps over to the old railroad bed and onto the multitude of stones lodged between the track ties. He picks up a rock about the size of a deck of cards, and throws it in between the two large shadows.

"You're going to have to leave sometime, bub," one of the cowboys says. "We can wait."

Grayson picks up two rocks and scales one and then the other. Judging from the howls, they'd both landed.

"Why you...." one cowboy hollers. Grayson always wondered what came after the 'Why you' in these situations, but before he could find out he pitches another rock, and from the thump, this one hit a big belly.

"The next ones are going for your heads," Grayson shouts.

Then he follows through and advances on the cowboys throwing one rock after another. The older men duck and throw their arms up to protect their heads, or maybe their hats, and then they turn and lurch away in two examples of gimpy running; foot speed and agility are unusual, if not unknown, among sedentary, middle-aged fat men. But the attempt to outrun rocks, at night, on frost heaved asphalt, broken up by areas of exposed cobblestone, urban trash, and railroad tracks while shod in cowboy boots, could be the final scene in a Three Stooges short.

Grayson recognizes that their cowboy hearts were in the right place, thinking they were saving a kid from harm, even if they had acted on a misapprehension of the facts.

"God love you," Grayson says.

He turns back to Charlie, but Charlie isn't there. Charlie is gone.

CHAPTER TWENTY-SIX

Grayson spends about two minutes looking around for Charlie. The cowboys, by now, have caught their breath and maybe used the CB radio to call the cops. Grayson holds the conviction that talking to the cops, which is always a bad idea, is especially bad right now. How would he explain why he had driven in between the trucks?

He zips away from the market and up Shetland St. into Roxbury. He makes his way up Norfolk Ave. to Humphrey St., to Dudley and through Uphams Corner, along residential streets he knew but couldn't name, then to Freeport and out to Morrissey Blvd, over the Neponset River and into North Quincy.

He drove by the bank, saw the time and turned on the radio to catch the news, delivered on the hour by WBZ.

"As we reported earlier this evening, Undercover State Police officer William James Hawthorne died late this afternoon as a result of being shot during an armed home invasion and robbery."

Grayson has a flash of panic, real panic, and imagines himself speeding up to ninety and ramming his car into the side of the Boston Gear building.

The young cop is dead, a guy who tried to do the right thing with his life. He died because of the chaos that entered his life in the form of Bird, Grayson and the rest.

He goes to a Chinese restaurant with a 2AM liquor license. He sits at the bar at The Joy King and drinks without a thought of what he is doing. It takes three drinks to remember he quit, and why he had quit. Rather than bringing relief, the drink is making him sick. There's no more relief to be had, but he kept turning back to it. It is nuts. He goes into the gents and sticks his fingers down his throat.

He washes up, leaves and drives around, wrestling with anger and fear. He heads over to Donny's place. Where has he been and what has he been up to? He drives up West Squantum St., stewing in fear, doubt and insecurity and is waiting to make the turn onto Harvard, now wallowing in depression when, at the last moment, he sees a white van making a right turn, coming from the opposite direction. It is already through the turn and all Grayson can see now is the back end. Is it the same van? Just a coincidence? Or, has the van just dropped Donny at home? Or, maybe they tried to kill him, too. Grayson shoots down Harvard Street to Donny's street, took a left and on the down slope of the hill, killed his engine and the headlights and rolls silently by Donny's second floor apartment. His station wagon is at the curb. He lives alone in his apartment, and in the living room window a blue-gray light shifts and changes.

Grayson parks down the street and walks back. He cuts through the neighbor's yard and hops over the fence into Donny's backyard, and almost falls over a swing set, which was not there at the time of his last visit. Donny's landlord lived on the first floor. Carl Winslow is a Boston fireman in his thirties married to a pretty woman named Millie. They have two kids under five, and a third child on the way.

He looks for lights in the first-floor windows and sees none. Carl's pickup truck isn't in the driveway, but he works shifts at a firehouse on

Columbus Ave., so it is most likely he is at the station and Millie's in bed.

Grayson creeps up the wooden back steps, opens the hallway door quietly and goes up the carpeted hall stairs the same way. He listens at the back door to the kitchen and can hear television noise. He tries the knob and the door is unlocked. He slips in silently, shuts the door and advances down to the living room. He peers around the doorway and sees a shirtless Donny sitting on the couch with his back to Grayson. He is moaning softly and his arm is moving up and down in the area of his lap. On the loud console TV, Lee Marvin is snarling at Angie Dickinson in some old movie from the 60's.

Grayson ducks back to the kitchen, opens the oven door. Inside, on two separate racks are pistols. He takes Donny's .22 out from on top of the rack and moving one small step at a time he makes it to Donny and sticks the gun in the hollow between tendons where his head and neck met.

"Sandra?" Donny says with a tremor. "Is that you, baby?"

Millie Winslow pops up from Donny's lap, with Donny's hand still on the back of her head, and she looks up, aghast, at Grayson.

"Oh, honestly," Millie says. "It's your cousin." Grayson has dropped the gun hand to his side, hiding the .22, but Donny knows there is a pistol somewhere close and acts accordingly.

Millie stands up, and brushes her hair out of her face and poses, fully pregnant, with one hand on her hip, as if she were modeling the floor length yellow terry cloth robe she wore: Just the thing in loungewear a woman needs to stay comfortable while feeding on the man upstairs.

She ignores Grayson and looks down and around.

"Don, reach under the couch for my thong, will you?" she says, and holds up a single pink flip-flop. "I only see the one."

Donny reaches to the floor and picks up the other flip-flop and hands it to her. She's about as embarrassed as she'd be if she was discovered watering the geraniums.

"You better keep your mouth shut, Grayson," Millie says, without looking at him.

"Right back at you, Mrs. Winslow," Grayson says.

"Unless you want to be a home wrecker," she says.

"I'll do my part," Grayson says.

"Goodnight, Millie," Donny says.

She walks out to the hall and then pokes her head back in.

"Who is Sandra?" she asks.

"Go home, Millie," Donny says.

Now Grayson has the gun pointed at the side of his cousin's head.

"Eliminating witnesses, are you?" Grayson says.

"Me?" Donny says. "You're the one with the gun at *my* head. Put it away, will you?"

"You, too," Grayson says. "Before I puke."

"I don't have—Oh, yeah." He reaches down to the floor, then lifts his butt off the couch and pulls up his boxers.

"You saw the news?" Grayson says. "And decided to team up with bikers to winnow down the people who could turn you in."

"What? What news?"

"The state cop, Hawthorne, the cop that fucking Bird shot, he died this afternoon." Grayson says.

"Jesus, no. Oh, no." He jumps up. "I was up at the Highlife. But I didn't see the news. I was talking to Scotty outside. Nobody said anything when I went in, they were talking Red Sox, so I figured there was nothing new. He's dead? Hell, no."

Grayson grimaces. "You had to made things worse."

"What? How? What did I make worse?" Donny asks.

"Chucking him off the bridge," Grayson says.

"Are you drunk?" Donny says. "What are you talking about?"

"You knew the cop died, you made peace with bikers and went to war against us. How could you do it? Do you know how many other people could have gotten killed? What the fuck is wrong with you?"

Grayson grabs an ashtray off an end table and scales it at Donny, who blocks it with his forearm.

"Ouch! What are you doing?"

"Who was driving the van?"

Donny furrows his brow. "I don't know. What van?"

"You know what van. The van that just dropped you off."

Donny grows visibly angry. "You're cracking up."

"I suppose you and someone else didn't go to Oliver's in a van tonight?"

"What? When?"

"Don't give me that shit. You know when."

"When!"

"You weren't there about eleven thirty or so?"

"That's correct," Donny says. "I wasn't. I told you I was up at the Highlife with about forty witnesses, including Scotty Walsh, who I was with most of the time."

Scotty Walsh was an old friend of Grayson's from ten years of catechism classes.

"Will Scotty say you were there around eleven thirty?"

"Yes. Because we got into a Watergate argument outside. He thinks Nixon should resign."

"Yeah? So? You do, too."

Donny shook his head. "Yeah, but I don't like Scotty. I wanted to piss him off."

Grayson knows that's true and it makes the rest of the story credible.

Donny says "What's going on? What happened with this van?"

Grayson says, "We went to Oliver's to get Charlie's check. He needs money to leave town. Listen, I'm sorry about the ashtray. Can I get you some ice?"

"No, that's okay. Just hand me my .22 so I can put a pill right between your eyes, you son of a bitch. I'd bounce you around but good, if it didn't wake up Millie's kids."

Donny stands and puts a tee shirt on and tucks it into the elastic waist band of his baggy boxers with the lions on them.

"Yeah, yeah, yeah," Grayson says. "Don't you want to know what happened?"

"What?" He gets his pants and puts them on.

"Somebody who is very big and strong got out of an old white van and threw Charlie off the Brookline Avenue Bridge tonight."

Donny stops zipping his fly and looks up.

"What?" he says. "Wow. Oh, man. Oh, God. Poor Charlie." He sits down on the couch and covers his face with his big mitts. "He was a good friend."

"I thought it was you," Grayson says.

"No way. I wish I was that cold." Donny shakes his head. "He get hit by a bunch of cars?"

"No. He landed on the side with the railroad tracks. He's not dead. He ran away."

Donny makes a shocked face. "Fucking Charlie, man. That's impressive. He's quite a guy."

"Plus," Grayson says, "I think someone is following you in a van."

"An older chick with short, gray hair?"

Grayson shakes his head. "What? No. The bikers. They may be following all of us, off and on."

"Tomorrow," Donny says. "We go after the bastards who threw him over."

"What?" Grayson says. "Who?"

"Stan and his gang. Who else could it be?"

Grayson expels a relieved breath. It wasn't Donny, and Donny didn't think it was Hugh. Grayson is happy it was the rampaging bikers off on a killing spree, rather than his family members.

"Charlie wouldn't have shown up there if he had any brains," Grayson says.

"That's right," Donny says. "So, why did you both go?"

"I figured he'd be safe with me," Grayson says.

CHAPTER
TWENTY-SEVEN

Grayson wakes up the next morning with his heart in full gallop. He sits on the side of the bed, takes some deep cleansing breaths and then smokes a cigarette. He'd dreamt that a sparrow in flight had crashed into his chest and knocked itself out. As he looked down at the bird on the ground, it revived, hopped to its feet and cheeped at him. He bent down to it and held his open hand out, and the bird hopped on. He lifted the bird to his face, and could see the bird was hurt and it began cheeping insistently. He put it down and walked away but it followed him. In the dream Grayson shouted, 'I'm sick of this,' and, as hard as he could, threw the bird at the ground, where it squawked horribly and then died.

Where do dreams come from, and why do they make no sense? What would a shrink say? The young cop is the sparrow? Or is Bird the sparrow? Is he the bird and God is sick of him being a fuck up and cast him down because he is through with him? He'd heard the term soul-sick somewhere and he knew this was it.

The young cop, Hawthorne, is dead. A young man lost his life due to the greed and stupidity of others, and one of the others is Michael Grayson.

In the bathroom, despite misgivings, he looks in the mirror. He'd never borne a morning after sickness like this one, and it is not from drinking. It surprises him that he didn't drive his head through the mirror; it is an idea that holds great appeal.

He quick-showers, and finds himself brushing his teeth without any paste, a simple slip of the mind that fills him with dread.

He calls his brother's place and gets no answer.

He calls Donny: No answer.

Grayson calls the house.

"Hey, Dad."

"Where have you been?"

"What's the matter?" Grayson says.

"Your mother's not so good. She's semi-conscious. We have an ambulance coming to take her to the Carney. Are you coming over? The girls are here."

Grayson is sure he isn't tough enough to deal with this. The idea alone, of watching her being loaded into an ambulance, feels like being crushed.

"Is Hugh there?"

"No one has seen either of you," his father says.

"I'll find him," Grayson says. "We'll meet you at the hospital."

"Did you go to a meeting?"

Grayson says, "I'll talk to you later," and hung up.

He didn't want to give his father the satisfaction of answering him in the affirmative. He didn't want The Old Man to know he'd won, but at the same time, Grayson was filled with self-loathing for denying his father the comfort of what he'd see as some good news. He could have given his father a good moment during a bad time. Why had he not?

Downstairs, Grayson fires up the GTO and begins to pull out from the curb, but held back, to let an old Bonneville go by. The Bonneville rolls to a stop so the nose of the GTO is pointing at the Bonny's broadside. The driver has him pinned down. He expects tommy guns to appear in the windows and open fire on him. Instead he sees John M. piloting the boxy monster and smiling at him.

The power window on the passenger side of John M.'s car zizzes down and Grayson rolls his own open.

"Did you get all better?" John M. says. "That would be a new record."

Grayson beyond frustrated, could only ask himself, man, what does this old buzzard want?

"I can't see it, not for me," Grayson says. "I said I'd give it a try and I did."

"You don't think fifteen minutes is a fair trial, do you? Give it a chance."

Grayson doesn't want a confrontation; he wants to get away from all of it.

"Yeah, well, maybe later. Right now, there's a lot going on," Grayson says.

"I know," John M. says. "None of it good. That's why you should...."

Grayson's brain locks out the rest of what John M is saying. It's fixed on what this guy means by, 'none of it good.' What does he know? How does he know it? Grayson zones out, for what seems like a long time, but is only a few seconds, the time it takes to sharply draw, and then release, a breath. As he exhales, he knows sure as shooting that if he asks John M. what he's talking about, and if this nosy bastard says he was talking about the baby, or the cop, or Bird, Grayson will surely launch himself through the two car windows and choke him into eternal silence. But Grayson doesn't ask, because he is afraid of the answer, and right now he'd rather be tortured by anxiety than driven to action.

"Hey, John, let me ask *you* a question, for a change. What's in this for you, huh? Why are you following me around, and don't hand me the AA bullshit, okay."

John M. doesn't say anything for a few moments, while he runs the palm of his hand around the circumference of the steering wheel, and focuses on it as if the answer could be read on the wheel. "Because I believe a life is worth fighting for. And if I didn't, mine wouldn't be. It's how God made us."

Grayson clenches his teeth to hold in a snarl. Who does this fucker think he is?

"Your father told me last night that your mother is slipping," John M. says. "I'm sure it's doing a number on you, and I can see how you'd think you're too busy for a meeting, but if you don't want to drink, the program can help you through a tough time."

"I know," he says. "But I can't right now."

CHAPTER
TWENTY-EIGHT

Grayson stops at Catherine's house a little after nine that morning. He has to drive by her door on his way to Hugh's place, and more than anything he needs to see her, to hear her voice. He needs to talk to his best friend even if she hates him. He'd settle for pity now: at least she would look at him, and if she saw him, he'd feel better. He rings the doorbell and searches for a smile in his shit pile, standing on the stoop by himself. The stupe on the stoop.

Grayson wonders how much real sleep he'd gotten in the last 72 hours.

Mrs. Chrisolm answers the bell. Smiling, she says, "She's not home, sweetheart."

Her smile fades, and the light in her eyes dims as she shifts to worry.

She says, "Oh, honey. Is it your mother? Come in."

He came in, stood in the entry way, and she folds her arms. He tells her a little of what is on his mind.

"Oh, my. Oh, God help us." She reaches out and gives him a hug. "I'm sure it has to hurt awfully bad. How is your father doing? And the girls?"

"Okay. I thought I'd tell Catherine. She likes my mother."

"She went to New York yesterday. She'll be back in a few days."

He feels his knees start to buckle. New York? New York is where pregnant Boston girls go for abortions.

"Oh, don't worry, sweetheart," Mrs. Chrisolm says. "She didn't go with a boy. She just went to visit Maura. She and John Webster are expecting again."

Grayson nods, certain Catherine would never tell her mother if she was going off to have an abortion. She likely went to New York because they had more experience in these matters, in New York, and she wouldn't see anyone she might know. Did

317

girls still have to go to New York? Wasn't it legal everywhere now?

"Yeah, I heard. That's great," Grayson says. He is lightheaded.

"Oh, did Catherine tell you?"

"Tell me what?" He wants to turn and run.

Mrs. Chrisolm chuckles. "That Maura and John Webster are having another baby."

"No. You told me, the other day," Grayson says. He is sure that if he dared look down, he'd see he's standing at the edge of a bottomless pit.

"Oh, that's right. God loves the babies, but none of them get the parents they deserve."

Grayson is taken aback. "You mean Maura and John Webster?"

"No, not specifically. I mean everyone ever born in the whole world. We're never as good as our kids deserve, we all fall so short, so short, but, when we try really hard, we can be good enough."

Grayson's disorientation has peaked and is resolving; feeling is seeping back into his body, and the fog fuddling his mind is being exhausted, as if by a vented fan.

"Do you want to tell her about your mother when she gets back? Or do you want me to tell her?"

"No. You tell her."

CHAPTER TWENTY-NINE

Grayson arrives at the Carney Hospital about thirty minutes later. He pulls into the parking garage and drives up to the roof level. As he waits for the elevator to reach the third level, he looks out to Dorchester Ave and in the distance sees a shitty white van pull into a space in front of the bench at the bus stop. It looks like the van that was parked outside the Dark Lords shack, the van that was on the bridge and also went by Donny's house. Are they following him? If it's the same van, he's going down and deliver himself, then see if they like what they get. In his present state of mind, he is certain he can make short work of two slobs from the Dark Lords. Unless they have guns. He kept looking over there, and as he watches, an elderly black woman toting a big handbag got out and sat down on the bench and the van drove away. The elevator came and Grayson got on.

Mary Grayson is still in the ER, medicated and semi-conscious, waiting to be admitted and moved to a room upstairs. The three sisters, Emma, Jen and Susan are there along with The Old Man, Aunt Betty, and Donny.

"Where's Hugh," his father says.

"Not home," Grayson says.

A middle-aged doctor is approaching the Old Man, and everyone else converges on him at the same time.

The doctor nods at the assemblage. "We're going to keep her a few days in order to stabilize her. She's on her way upstairs right now. She's dehydrated, so we have her on intravenous. We gave her something for pain, and something to help her sleep, which she needs. I suggest you leave her alone for now. She needs to rest. When she's ready to be released, I'll write her a stronger pain medication and put 'as needed' in the instructions. Just keep her comfortable. There's no need to worry about her becoming addicted."

"What about her doctor?" Emma says. "Did you talk to him?"

"I did. He'll get in touch this afternoon to discuss things, Mr. Grayson."

"About her prognosis?" The Old Man says.

The doctor didn't say anything as he writes on her chart. He looks up. "Yes, among other things. It's time to make some difficult decisions. You may want to have the family available to discuss what you think is best for her in the days to come. But, in the meantime, we'll keep her nourished and pain free."

"We have an older brother in Florida," Aunt Betty says, "who wants to spend some time with her. But he's not in such great shape himself. He recently fell face first down a whole flight of marble stairs. What should I tell him?"

"If he wants to spend time with her, I'd suggest he get up here as soon as he is able. She is very ill. I'm sorry I don't have better news."

The doctor nods once more, turns and walks away.

Aunt Betty gathers the three girls into a group hug, and the four of them put their teary faces in and touched foreheads. Donny looks down at The Old Man and puts his arm across The Old Man's shoulders. Grayson looks away.

Together they leave the ER and walk over to the parking garage where they pack themselves into the elevator car.

Aunt Betty says, "Daniel, I'll make dinner for everyone at your house tonight. I'll expect you all to be there. You girls bring your families." She looks at Donny. "You, too, will be there. Make sure you help your cousins today. Do you hear me?"

"Yup, yup," Donny says, nodding with vigor. "Yup."

They watch as the girls drive off in Emma's station wagon with Daniel and Betty in the back seat with Jen. Grayson has never seen his father in the back seat of a car, in fact, has never seen him riding anywhere in any vehicle. He is always behind the wheel of whatever vehicle he was in. Seeing him in the back like that gives Grayson a chill.

CHAPTER THIRTY

At noon Grayson is leaning against the trunk of his car in The Tradewinds parking lot when Hugh pulls in. Donny is just behind him in his station wagon. Grayson's eyes well up with relief. While they park, he sweeps a forearm across his eyes.

Hugh comes over and says, "What's that look."

"What look? Where have you been? Ma's in the hospital."

"I know. I talked to Dad."

"You told us you had some wild cards going in," Grayson says. "You better tell us everything. Now."

"I don't think I know everything yet," Hugh says.

"What's going on with Stan Belzer?" Grayson asks.

"I don't know," Hugh says. "I still haven't met him. He wants to meet me to discuss where we go from here. In any case, I want to tell him we're cool, no need to worry about us shooting our mouths off, right? What's going on with Charlie? He called about 5AM talking a mile a minute, saying he was already on his way to somewhere far, far away and he'll never talk to anyone about anything in his whole life. Then he just hung up."

"He had a rough night," Grayson says. He tells Hugh about Charlie and the Bridge.

"That's unbelievable," Hugh says. "It's good he took off. He was our weakest link. Now it's Amy I'm most worried about. I haven't seen her since I gave her the bag, to give to Stan."

Donny says, "She has the money? I thought they were just getting the drugs?"

"That equation went out the window when Bird did. She hasn't answered her door since and her car is here. I don't know if the bikers took her or what."

"She could be dead or hurt," Grayson says. "Would they come here?"

"I don't know," Hugh says. "I'll try again, and if she doesn't answer, we'll jimmy the door and search her place."

Upstairs, Hugh knocks a couple of times on Amy 's door and gets no answer. He pulls a credit card from his wallet and slips the lock on the door, and Grayson and Donny follow him inside.

They find Amy on the couch. She is giving a foot massage to a man who is sitting sideways with his bare feet in her lap.

She says, "I was going to answer the door. You're awfully impatient." She continues to knead the man's feet.

"Gentlemen," the man says. His leathery face has the burnt red coloring of one who spends a lot of time outside in the wind. "We were just talking about you."

The man is not introduced. He looks like the senior elf in Satan's Workshop. He's got a vivid black Van Dyke beard that tapers to a sharp point well below his chin. His brow seems harvested from a Neanderthal and transplanted. His eyes, which look like he'd stolen them off a snow man, are shiny, cold and dead as coal.

"Oh, yeah?" Hugh says.

"I'm deciding your fate," the man says.

"You're Stan, I presume," Hugh says.

The man gives a perfunctory salute.

"Indeed, I am. I'd stand up, but my dogs are killing me." He looks at Amy with affection. "Don't stop, dear." He speaks in a rich, relaxed voice, sounding like Mel Torme on The Old Man's records.

The way he is positioned on the couch makes it difficult to estimate his size. He has long hair combed back, parted in the middle and falling over his stick out ears.

He is attended by a foul odor, like burning hair. It is a smell that makes you want to run and hide.

"Give me another minute here," Stan says. He flashes a quick, toothy smile. "It's in your best interests that my feet don't hurt when I decide your fate. Pain is a thing that loves to be shared. So, be patient." He looks over at Grayson, and rocks back slightly, as if in mild surprise.

"You look like you have something to say," he says.

"I do," Grayson says. "Fuck you. Mister President. Decide our fate, my ass."

"I like this kid," Stan says, holding his gaze on Grayson. "He's got spunk. I'm going to call you Spunky from now on, kid. Okay Spunky?"

"Sure, and I'll call you Stinky," Grayson says.

"Stop it, man," Donny says. "Let's hear him out."

Grayson forgot Donny is with them. He'd gone silent and motionless on arrival. Grayson looks at his cousin, afraid that Donny has gone still in hopes of not catching the eye of a predator nonpareil. But happily, he sees that Donny has his eyes locked on Amy, and is ignoring Stan. This is the first time Donny has seen her, and, by golly, she is fun to look at. Amy is Manson-Girl crazy, but she has a figure which could stop traffic at the Indianapolis 500. She is dressed in a conservative blue suit and white blouse, and looks like the woman in the shaving cream commercial who shakes her hair out and drapes herself on the guy who is scraping off the product, and, it's implicit, going to get his ashes hauled. Moreover, Donny doesn't even require a woman be good looking, necessarily; if his glands are firing, he would kick Popeye's ass to woo Olive Oyl.

Stan squints his eyes and runs his fingers through his chin hair as if considering the proposed name Stinky. "I don't think so." He shakes his head, definite now. "In fact, if you call me Stinky once, I'll drill a hole in the top of your head and suck your brains out through a straw. Which shouldn't take long."

"That's grisly, but amusingly grisly," Grayson says.

"Get to it, Stan," Hugh says.

"Here's the deal, chaps," Stan says. "I've wondered how to square things with you in regard to your murder of my best buddy. My first inclination was to kill you in a way that my friends would remember fondly. You know, your heads mounted on our clubhouse wall, stirring fond memories of good, old what's his name."

"Bird," Donny says.

"That, you have to admit, is kind of ironic," Stan says. "I gave him that name when we were kids. Spooky." Stan looks at Amy. "That big one is a good-looking specimen. Do you want to tag team him? He's certainly big enough for two." Amy smiles, as Stan turns to look at Donny. "Do you dig guys, too? I could show you some jailhouse lovin', you'd never go back to girls."

Startled, Donny glares at Stan. "You're pretty funny, man."

"Okay," Hugh says. "Look. We're sorry Bird got hurt, but it was an accident."

"Hurt? He's way past hurt. He's dead, isn't he?" Stan withdraws his feet from Amy 's lap and stands up. He is lanky, of average height, but with very long arms. He wears a bright white long sleeve T-shirt under an unbuttoned, black leather vest. He's tied the ensemble together with a tan, fabric Boy Scout belt, with a gold buckle and dungarees with a sharp crease in the legs. Around his neck, he has a taut gold chain, which has some kind of medallion attached, but the medallion itself is hidden by the T-shirt.

"An accident? No, I'm afraid not," Stan says. He points at Grayson. "I have it on good authority that this man deliberately pushed him out the window." Stan flashes a two second smile. "Many of my brother Lords are howling for his death." He smiles for one second. "Some want to cut his heart out and feed it to the dogs." Again, with the incongruous smile. "Many others want to kill the whole lot of you. You, your family, friends, pets, maybe even your high school mascot." Another smile flashes, almost subliminally. "In any case, Amy, sweetheart that she is, suggested we put our heads together and find a way for you all to redeem yourselves, if you're interested. I kind of hope you're not. I love a blood bath."

Grayson says, "All this trouble is because Bird shot a guy. Why?"

Amy says, "Let me take this one, Stan." She gets up and begins to pace back and forth, rubbing her hands together as if washing them, deep in thought. It is a nice bit of theater, but her physical assets, which are many and distracting, have Donny nearly hyperventilating. "Of course, no one could have known there was a pig undercover in there. The shooting was... unfortunate. Our theory is that Bird, who had been busted numerous times, recognized the undercover pig, and, it's quite likely, the pig recognized Bird. Bird was, in fact, out on bail waiting for a court date. But, that's conjecture, we will never know, since he's--"

"Kaput," Stan says.

They are silent and rueful for a few moments. When that moment had its due, Hugh says, "How would we redeem ourselves?"

Stan says, "By hijacking a trailer load of those M-16s your company is picking up at Colt.

CHAPTER THIRTY-ONE

Back in Hugh's apartment Grayson is on the couch in front of the droning TV trying to fathom how these things have come to pass. Hugh has gone out to "Get something from work."

Donny went into the bathroom for a while, and when he comes back, he finds an apple in the refrigerator and is rubbing it with both hands, like it is a new baseball.

"That Amy is hot," Donny says. "Hugh said you weren't interested. Because I damn sure am." He takes a big bite out of the apple, which sounds like the moment a large tree cracks and falls in a blizzard.

"Be my guest," Grayson says. "Good luck."

A few minutes later there's a rap on the door. Donny reaches behind his back and produces a pistol.

"Who's that?" he says, looking at Grayson.

"How the hell do I know," Grayson says. He gets up to answer it while Donny backs up to the wall and holds the gun out, pointed at the doorway.

"Hello, hello," Amy says, sing song. She comes in and Grayson closes the door, as Donny hurries to put his gun back in his pants.

"How are you guys, after that meeting? " She comes over to kiss Grayson, but he turns away from her.

She acts like it didn't happen. "Stan is intense, no?

"You can almost hear the bees buzzing around in his head," Grayson says.

"We need to talk. Where's Hugh?" she says.

"He'll be back in a jiffy," Donny says.

"You and Stan are pretty cozy," Grayson says. "You rubbing his smelly feet, him asking if you want to make a Donny sandwich with him."

"There's something about him," she says. "You just want to do what he asks. He's charismatic, don't you think? And very sexy."

"Oh, yes, he's sooo dreamy," Grayson says.

"Jealousy is sooo bourgeois," she says.

"He's a switch hitter?" Donny says. "That seems strange for a biker. And, an elected official, no less."

Amy says, "I think he was trying to topple your worldview. Challenge you to keep an open mind, see things differently. He's a type of revolutionary, too. Aligned with my cadre, but different. We share the same goal, to smash the system, by any means necessary. He's gone by the way."

"Oh? Off to play some tennis?" Grayson says. "We're not hijacking a load of guns, is that clear?"

She says, "Think long and hard about that. You don't want The Dark Lords as an adversary."

"How did he know that my company was going to be trucking the guns?"

"I was searching for a way to keep you guys alive," she says, "and up popped this idea. It's elegant. It takes care of all our needs. You should thank me."

"What are our needs?" Donny says.

"To go on living?" she says. "Let's show him some initiative, draw up a plan and take it to him. Think about it, please. We rip off the guns, and The Lords forgive and forget."

"What 'we' are you talking about?" Grayson says.

"I'm in this right along with you. I brought you guys to him, and you killed his top lieutenant. He's upset with me, too."

Grayson says, "He didn't look it. Smiling like a cat on your couch."

"That will always be *our* couch to me." She giggles, which is, for her, unbecoming.

Donny intuits immediately what she is refer-ring to, and deflates promptly. As always, when thwarted, he lashes out.

Donny says, pointing outside, to the world at large, "And make sure he knows we keep the drugs and money we got from the apartment."

She says, "I agree. That's eminently fair. If he gets the rifles."

"I'm not doing it," Grayson says. "That's final."

CHAPTER THIRTY-TWO

Grayson goes up to the corner to get an afternoon newspaper, but since the South Shore paper hasn't come out yet, he grabs a mid-day tabloid. At his apartment he sits on the front stairs in the cold with a copy of the Record American. He opens the newspaper and braces himself. The reporters at the *Record* could make a trip to the store for skim milk sound lurid.

"Hawthorne's widow Amanda told reporters her husband was motivated to become a crime fighter because of a deep, personal tragedy... He hailed from the tony suburb of Cohasset and a family of extraordinary wealth and prestige."

"I never even heard of them," Grayson says.

"*…..the family manse on the ocean…. He could have done anything, or nothing, but he chose public service… a senior at Harvard when his sister Sophia, who was a freshman in college, died from a drug overdose… He left Harvard without graduating, and within days was enrolled at the State Police academy.*"

He reads each story and every sidebar in the paper. There are pictures of William James Hawthorne, as a trooper, as a boy, with his sister and his parents, pictures of his two brothers, grimly facing a mob of reporters, the house in Cohasset, the apartment building on Peterborough St., and cops milling around outside the apartment building on the day of the shooting. The "Jimmy" that Bird shot had long hair and a scruffy beard, but it was easy to recognize "Jimmy" in the picture of the clean-cut young man in the State Police graduation photo. The wake is being held tomorrow and the next day, visiting hours two to four, and seven to nine.

He closes the paper, not wanting to read anymore. He has to move, to get away. He folds the paper and tucks it in between the step and the bottom of the railing. He digs his car keys out of his pocket and jumps in the car and drives away.

If he could just sit still, he'd be okay, but he has to keep moving because each time he stops his mind catches up with him.

He has to keep moving, and not stop, not at a bar or a liquor store. He wheels out of Quincy, and down Rte. 3A, towards Hull and Paragon Park, an old amusement park where he'd often taken Catherine to ride the rollercoaster and drive the bumper cars. When he got to the traffic circle, he realizes he wants to find the house in Cohasset that William James Hawthorne had lived in. He continues on 3A until he sees a sign for Cohasset Center. From there he kept going east, toward the ocean, and soon finds himself on a coast road.

On both sides of the road are big houses on big lots that cost big money. The Atlantic Ocean here looks different than the Atlantic Ocean in cramped Quincy Bay. Quincy Bay has boundaries, and you could only see so far. Here there appears to be no boundaries, although there has to be. Maybe the boundary out there is the west coast of the Iberian Peninsula, but there are boundaries to everything in this world.

As he pilots the GTO along, the road unwinds in front of him and could well have been the model for the roller coaster over at Paragon Park. Jerusalem Rd. fell away, reappears, turns ninety degrees, rose up, disappeared, turns this way and turned that way and turned the other way, but always there is the ocean. There are sections of the road that are without houses and serve only to connect one collection of rock outcrop to another, but after a sharp swerve more monuments to mammon would rise up to overwhelm the eye. These shingle-style 8,000 square foot 'cottages' were often erected during the so-called Progressive Era, sometime between the 1890's and the Depression.

At one point, Jerusalem Road crawls through an S-turn under a low canopy of old growth oak trees, and at the end, the road emerges onto a bridge. On the right side of the bridge is what appears to be another pond, but this is actually salt water and is called Little Harbor. It is fed and drained by the ocean tides through a boulder walled channel that runs under the bridge. An incoming tide pushes a strong current from the ocean into Little Harbor and is made visible by its course over rocks, some of which can be seen and others which are just below the surface. Grayson stops on the bridge and looks. He saw that the tide is rising and the great rocks that had come to rest here some ten thousand years ago during the latest, but certainly not the last, Ice Age, are all marked at the same height by smeared algae and barnacles. He sees by the same sort of signs that the water would expand into a much wider basin before it rose. When the tide goes out, the level of the salt pond would drop and the flow would be out to the ocean on his left.

He continues over the bridge and sees a Massachusetts State Police car at the top of a long half circle driveway filled with cars. The huge driveway curved in front of a spectacular old house set way back from the street. On the porch in the distance he could see a number of people, mostly men, standing around smoking and talking. There is a State cop sitting in a State cop car reading the newspaper. He folds the top of the newspaper down and glances at Grayson as he drives by in the GTO. The cop goes back to reading the paper before Grayson has fully passed.

Here, just beyond the house, a slew of TV news vans, both local and network, clog the roadsides, each with their splashed logos in cartoon colors painted on the sides, all representing the rearguard of the Bad News Carnival. Near the Channel Four van veteran newsman Walt Sanders is standing on the grass at the side of the street with a microphone in his hand, talking into a camera that is perched on the shoulder of a guy in droopy dungarees and an untucked white shirt.

Grayson lifts his foot off the gas pedal, not wanting to make any noise on the news. He pretends to be gawking at the newshawks, but he is actually checking out the house behind Walt Sanders.

The house is like something you'd see in the movies. It stands alone on a bank of rocks with a great expanse of grass in the back that runs down to the water's edge. It is big, very big, but also just right. There is even a wraparound porch. It is a great house, and unlike many homes of the very rich, this one doesn't invite a sneer. It is beautiful, and he feels a brief pang of lust in the pit of his stomach. But, he can only imagine what a grand old house like this would cost. His parents paid $5,700 for their house in 1954, and today it was said to be worth $25,000. So, this ocean front mansion, with a huge yard, backed up to the ocean would probably go for some insane price, like three hundred thousand, or more, a price not easy to wrap your mind around.

Grayson wheels a U-turn and goes by the big house again, looking but not staring at the house and the cop, the news crews and the neighbors shooing them away. He drives away, anxious and depressed.

Driving, he tries to think. People are always telling him to think, but the truth is he is fairly certain he really doesn't know how. Impulses, images, ideas, the odd curse word, rehashed arguments, imaginary arguments, a funny line from a TV show, song lyrics, all popped into his head unbidden. Sometimes he reacted to these "thoughts" and other times he'd shoo them away, shaking them off like a willful pitcher in baseball. Is that thinking? In high school, when an exasperated teacher would come to his seat and yell at him to 'Think!' he'd knit his brow as he'd seen other people do, but when he did that, the only thing on his mind was, 'I can keep my brow knitted longer than you can stand there.' He knew eventually the teacher would tire of looking at his knitted brow and move on so he could go back to reading whatever paperback book he had hidden under his text book. If it wasn't for smuggled paperbacks, like *Catch-22, The Godfather, On the Road, One Flew Over the Cuckoo's Nest, The Moviegoer, Slaughterhouse 5,* he'd have never been able to sit through high school. Why aren't there books on the process of thinking? Thinking can't be just having shit pop up in your head, could it?

Thinking, perhaps, causes him to remember the family is gathering at the house to eat dinner.

When he gets there the rest of the tribe are all sitting down to eat a smoked shoulder dinner, with all the fixings. There are about twenty of them, including the grandkids, who cry, laugh, and argue, slightly more than the adults. The kids refuse to eat any smoked shoulder at all. The kids are big into spaghetti, which they shoveled down while sitting on metal folding chairs at a long folding table in the living room. Grayson's three brothers-in-law sat in there with them, quelling skirmishes and eating when they could.

"I didn't know the little ones didn't like smoked shoulder," Aunt Betty says. "My boys did. They only thing they didn't eat was something that could still run away from them."

They drank coffee and tea while waiting for the doctor to call.

"I'm still not used to cooking meat on Friday," Betty says.

"Is Benny on the way up from Florida?" Daniel asks. "I didn't know he fell down the stairs."

"When did Uncle Ben fall down the stairs?" Susan asks. She bounces baby Doris on her knee.

Betty nods, purses her lips, and raises her eyebrows, pleased to be the carrier of a bit of news.

"He fell face first down a long, long set of marble stairs and broke his glasses, his nose and his clavicle," Betty says.

"Ma, I didn't know Uncle Ben played the clavicle," Donny says. They all laugh, grateful for the opportunity.

After dinner the kids go outside to play in the street, and the others broke up into usual groups, along gender lines. Grayson goes in the front room with his brothers-in-law and his father. Hugh went upstairs and Donny went out to the garage to check on his stored motorcycle and make sure it was ready to go.

His mind drifts in and out, as he listens to them talk about the advent of cable television.

"That's what they're saying," Matt says. "It sounds pretty good."

"That would be pretty good," The Old Man says. "A hundred channels, no more commercials, for five bucks a month. I'll believe it when I see it."

Grayson goes outside to the porch and watches the kids play tag on the street. He sits on the glider and looks at the world through the slatted glass windows.

The Patriot Ledger delivery boy, a tall fourteen-year old, walks heavily up to the top step and opens the porch door.

"How you doing, Mike?" the pale, plump paperboy asks.

Grayson goes over to get the paper from the kid.

"Good, Arthur. How're you?" He looks at the headline as he goes back to his seat. To his surprise, he hears Arthur answer his question.

"Not good. I'm late delivering because I just buried my dog Bruno. It's really hard when they die."

Grayson is tempted to say something like, *'It's harder to bury them when they're still alive, the fuckers keep jumping out,'* but the young doofus lives on this street and is known to be emotionally fragile and subject to tantrums.

"Yeah," Grayson says, but what he wants to say is *'Fuck you and your dog.'* "Bruno was old, right?"

"Fifteen," the kid says. "Older than me."

"Well," Grayson says. He has nothing to offer someone moaning about an old fucking dog; not today. He has a dead baby, a dying mother, and a murdered cop on his hands. Not to mention fucking Bird. To hell with Arthur and his dog.

As the kid stands there, though, Grayson can almost see the waves of pain pulsating from him, as if Arthur is the sketch in a medical pamphlet, a line drawing of a suffering boy. But Arthur is not the illustration of a boy with a toothache, Arthur is a real kid, a kid innocent of the truth. The truth is that the crust of the earth is crammed with the dead, and if you love one of them, you mourn them, and soon enough join them. It is the way of this world; sooner or later Mother Earth eats her young. All Grayson knows about pain is to run from it, like it is a killer. The ache that young Arthur is brave enough to suffer today would be surpassed in the future, but that didn't diminish what the kid is feeling right now. Grayson admires Arthur's courage, standing there and feeling it. This, too, is pain from Mad Mark's knife, the knife that opens you up.

Grayson stands again and offers his hand.

"Hey, man, I'm sorry about Bruno. He was a great dog. He came around a lot, and my mother would give him cheese. We were always happy to see him, looking in from the top step."

"Bruno loved cheese," Arthur says. He chuckles as he shakes Grayson's hand. "That's for sure."

344

He looks serious for a moment. "But he would've come here anyway, he really liked your mother, and the rest of the family, too. Besides the cheese, I mean." After protecting Bruno's reputation, he smiles again. "He also loved squirrels. They were always surprised by how fast he was when he caught 'em."

"He was a heck of a dog," Grayson says. "He'll be missed."

Arthur's eyes fill with tears and he turns and goes down the stairs. Grayson watches him trudge away with the strap of the ink stained canvas newspaper sack slung over his shoulder and the back, heavy with papers, bumping against his hip.

Grayson opens the Ledger to see an above-the-fold picture of Trooper Hawthorne in his State Police uniform, smiling gamely. Grayson drops on to the middle cushion of the glider and stares at the paper.

The Ledger covers the area south of Boston so the shooting death of a Cohasset resident, and a member of a rich family is really big news. Grayson can't bring himself to read the story, but he looks at the photos. There is yet another picture of the big house with State Police cars in front, and another all the TV news vans along the street. There is also a sidebar about all the media covering the story. The news reporters are covering the news reporters who have traveled in from across the country. This seems something new to Grayson; the media covering a story about the media covering a story. There'd likely be a day when the media covered the media covering the media covering the story. He sticks the paper in between the glider cushions, angry that he'd been mentally attacking a silly target like the news media. He knows things are going to get worse, but, with a little luck, his mother would die and not have to see it. How fucked up is that kind of thinking?

He hears the phone ring inside, and goes back to the kitchen, arriving in time to see The Old Man walk out of the kitchen into the living room holding the phone to his side as Emma tries to untangle the knots in the extra-long phone cord. He can only get so far, and they hear his end of the conversation.

"Yes, Doctor. I was hoping to come over to talk to you. Did you have a chance to see her yet? Okay, then. What time this evening? Okay, I'll be right along. Thank you."

The Old Man tells them he is going back to the hospital to talk to the doctor alone, and then he is going to talk to his wife alone. He asks them to wait an hour before going over there and encourages them to hang together.

Daniel leaves. Grayson goes upstairs and into the girl's room, where Hugh is sitting on the couch looking at the blank TV screen.

"Amy came by after you left."

Hugh looks up at him but says nothing.

"She says Stan wants a meeting tomorrow at your place at noon. She says if we don't hijack the load, there will be severe consequences."

"I'm working on something but I'm not ready to disclose it." Hugh pulls his keys out, and wiggles two off the ring. "Here. Lobby door, apartment door."

"What do I need those for?"

"Don't worry about it. I have another set in the car."

"I'm not worried about it. But why are you giving them to me?"

"I may, emphasize may, not make it home right at noon tomorrow. You and Donny can get in this way to keep her and Stan entertained."

"That's swell. I'll see you at the hospital."

"Donny didn't leave yet, did he?" Hugh asks.

"Why does everyone keep asking me about things I don't know?"

Downstairs, Grayson hugs each of sisters and his Aunt Betty and goes out to the street.

He says good-bye to the kids. They are playing tag between the telephone poles. On the opposite sidewalk, too, are a couple of neighbor kids, little boys, around three years old, who run up and back as if they are playing, too. They are not actually part of the older kid's game, but don't seem to know it. So, the little guys run between their invisible poles undistracted by who is *It,* or any other conditions, rules, other players, not even the game itself. The small boys alternately run and hop, too excited to control their limbs. Grayson's nieces and nephews laugh and occasionally shout good-natured cheers, urging the little boys on, while they stick to their own game.

Grayson pulls away, keeping an increasingly paranoid eye on the rear-view mirror for cops, bikers or both. But he sees no one, nothing behind him or waiting at the end of the road.

CHAPTER
THIRTY-THREE

Grayson drives over to the Carney Hospital, parks in the small lot at the front of the hospital, and smokes while he waits to go inside.

After thirty minutes straight of high intensity chain smoking, he takes his queasy self inside. He gets his mother's hospital room number from an elderly woman behind a desk in the lobby. The woman is friendly and cheerful and wearing a festive hospital jacket that is the color of orange sherbet.

He gets lost mentally in the elevator and might have gone right by his floor if he didn't see The Old Man sitting in the waiting area alone, smoking and apparently in deep thought.

"Oh," he says. "Hi Mike." He puts the cigarette on the lip of an ashtray, stands and shakes hands.

Daniel Grayson looks five years older than he did an hour ago.

"Dad," Grayson says. "What did Dr. Levine say?"

Daniel thinks for a moment.

"One thing he said was that within fifteen years, all cancer will be a thing of the past, like polio or the measles. By 1988 there will be a cancer vaccine. But that doesn't do us any good right now."

He shakes his head, pull his Luckies from his shirt pocket, and lights one, without regard for the one still burning in the ashtray next to him.

"What did he say about Ma?" Grayson asks.

"Sit down. Let me think," Daniel Grayson says. "I just called the girls and Betty at the house."

The Old Man takes a deep breath. "Levine says un-medicated she would experience a lot of pain, and that the pain will sap her strength. The cancer has spread from her lymph nodes to her liver, stomach, bones and now it has moved into her brain. It's traveling quickly. As it spreads in her brain, at some point, it will shut her down. The only way to deal with the pain is by increasing the morphine, which will eventually put her out. We talked to her, and he told her there wasn't much he could do for her but keep her comfortable. She thanked him for everything, and asked if she could go home."

"What did he say," Grayson says, just above a whisper.

"If we get twenty-four-hour nurses. Which I can get through the service we have now. It shouldn't take any time to arrange. I do need some help. She says she won't go home to die in that hospital bed."

"Anything," Grayson says.

"Tomorrow you and your brother take down the hospital bed in our room, and take our bed from your room and put it together back in our room."

"We'll do it in the morning," Grayson says. "Can I see her now?"

"Go ahead in. We talked about dying. She's okay with it. Maybe even good. I'll wait here. They're all on the way," Daniel says.

In the hospital room, the bed has been raised and Ma is sitting up and looks pretty good, all things considered. He kisses her on the forehead.

"Is Hugh with you?" she says.

"No. I think he's on the way."

"I haven't much time, honey. I'll be with Paul soon from what Dr. Levine says. Is Levine still here? I wanted to talk to him without your father around."

"No, I think he's gone," Grayson says. "Why? What do you need? Can I get it?"

"No. I feel too numb or something. I can't keep my eyes open. A little pain won't kill me. I can't even feel my lips move."

"I'll tell the nurse," Grayson says.

"No, don't run off. Stay," she says. "What's new with you? Anything good?"

"Not really," he says.

"How's Catherine? Did you talk to her?"

He hesitates. "About what?"

"About the baby," she says.

Grayson is shocked. "She told you?"

"Not in words. But I've been around the block a few times, mister." She holds up her hand and he takes it. "I had six of my own. Plus, with friends and family, I've been through about a hundred pregnancies. They're a miracle but not a mystery."

"How did you know?" he says, with a small, nervous laugh.

"From the way she talked, but mostly the look in her eye. You be the man I know you can be. Everything will be fine."

"I don't know, Ma. I'm really screwed up. I don't know."

"You do know," she says to Grayson. "Get Catherine back. On this topic, don't ever take no for an answer from her. Get married, grow up, and take care of your family."

"She says she hoped I'd grow up before we got married."

"It doesn't work that way, unfortunately. Did you see John Whatchacallit?"

"Minihan. I did. Twice."

"And?" she says. "Did you follow his advice?"

"I will."

"Now is the time, not in the future."

"Okay."

"Let me finish," she says. "Before I go, I want to know you're going to be okay."

"You can't go until *I'm* okay," he says.

"Honey, I can't. Promise me you'll do it."

"I promise."

"You have to keep your promises to your dying mother," she says, smiling.

"Great," he says. "Trick me, why don't you."

She is laughing quietly, gently, when The Old Man comes in, and he smiles to see it. Daniel announces that there is a gaggle of kin down the hall who want to see her.

"Are you up to it?" he asks his wife.

"Send them in two at a time," she says.

Daniel smiles. "Like The Ark?"

She nods her head. "Before they come in, tell the girls I don't have the energy anymore to pretend I'm not dying, and I'm not strong enough to console them, at this point. Tell them we should be happy that I'm here, right now."

Daniel points at her, and says, "You got it." He goes off to make it happen, as jaunty as if she'd merely challenged him to get her a cheeseburger.

"God love him, your father. Putting on a big act for me. He's such a baby."

Grayson kisses her good-bye and she hugs him weakly, but he feels it strongly.

"Remember," she says.

He nods.

Sitting in the waiting area, are the girls and Aunt Betty, and a couple of the older grandkids along with Donny. They listen as The Old Man, serious now, instructs them in the way it has to be, and then Grayson signals his cousin with a nod and they go to the far side of the room.

"Where's Hugh?" Grayson asks.

Donny shrugs. "He said he had to meet someone. Then he's coming here."

CHAPTER
THIRTY-FOUR

Grayson feels that he needs to withdraw from the rat race for just a little while. He doesn't want to drink but he needs to, but instead he drives out to the old Squantum Naval Air Station, now defunct, passing the old airplane hangars where once broken Navy planes came in one door, got fixed and went out the other door, back when this acreage was an active military airport defending the Massachusetts coast. The air station had been abandoned sometime in the 1950's, partly because the runways here aligned with the runways at Logan and with the ever-increasing commercial air traffic it became a safety concern.

He drives out to the spot where they drank as kids, at the end of one of the old runways. The once perfect cement pad now buckled and split in places by little green shoots, proof of life having its way. At the end of the runway, just short of the water, where the mouth of the river met Dorchester Bay, he stops the car. Hidden by a thick growth of bulrushes on either side, he shuts down the engine and rolls up his window. He looks over at the city, and when the big commercial jets come in over his head on a flight path to Logan, the noise is enough to shake the car. He is out there alone, but still, he uses the scream of the jets to cover the sound of his anguish.

Finished screaming, Grayson looks in the rear-view mirror and wonders how long it takes puffy, red crybaby eyes to go away. His eyes give him away. He doesn't want to see anyone just now, so he sits and smokes in his car at the end of the runway. The last time he cried, it had led to a pregnancy and when he thinks of the loss of that, he starts crying again. He gets out of the car and walks down the incline to the shore. He bends to pick up a rock and throws it out into the water, just as far as he can. He throws rocks at the water until his arm aches.

CHAPTER THIRTY-FIVE

Grayson sits on the couch in Hugh's place.

Hugh's black leather briefcase is open on the coffee table and Grayson looks at it for a minute and realizes it wasn't there yesterday. He ignores it until, out of boredom more than anything, he looks in it. On top of whatever else is in there is this security booklet with the Colt logo. Paging through, he figures out these are the security instructions and underneath the report is a handgun of some kind. Grayson drops the security booklet on the couch and grabs the gun. He knows little about guns, except that he doesn't like them. He handles it carefully, always keeping the barrel pointed away. He puts it back in the briefcase. He picks up the booklet again and is starting to look through it when he hears the buzzer sound. He wonders who it is, then he remembered he has Hugh's keys. He shot up and puts the booklet back in the briefcase, and closes the case but doesn't lock it. He thinks for a second, then slides it under the couch. He looks at the intercom and realizes it would be quicker to go to the lobby than figure out how to speak to someone and buzz him in.

In the lobby Donny is staring at the panel of buttons, holding the handle on the door and muttering to himself. He is startled when Grayson knocks on the glass door and pushes it open.

"Is Hugh here?" Donny asks.

"No, and his bed hasn't been slept in. He may have had an early morning meeting somewhere and grabbed a hotel nearby. But I don't think so."

Donny shakes his head. "He never showed at the hospital."

Back in the apartment Donny paces while Grayson smokes.

The telephone rings and Donny, closest to it, picks it up.

"Hello." His eyes focus, lose focus, narrow and then close.

"My father?" Grayson asks. "Hugh?"

Donny shakes his head. Still holding the phone to his ear but not speaking, he reaches around to the small of his back, lifts his shirt and takes out a pistol.

"Who is it?"

"Stan," Donny says. "He's across the hall."

"Tell him to come over."

"He wants us to go there."

"Bullshit," Grayson says.

Donny says, "You come here," and hung up.

Almost at the same instant, there was a knock at the door: *Shave and a Haircut, Two Bits.*

Grayson opens the door, while Donny backs to the wall, and holds the pistol so the end of the barrel will be about two feet away from the head of whoever comes in.

Stan swaggers in and sees Donny pointing a gun at him.

"Why so tense, fellas?" he says.

Stan lamps an innocent grin, but it is overshadowed by the blood in his eye.

Grayson pushes the door as far closed as he can, but Stan stood in the way of shutting it.

"Excuse me?" Grayson says.

"Why?" Stan asks.

"I mean," Grayson says, "Get the fuck out of the way."

"Oh. That's what you should have said," Stan says. He shifts out of the doorway, and Donny moves over to pat him down.

"Settle down, guys," he says. "We're on the same team. We just need to coordinate a few things here."

"What do you want?" Grayson says.

Stan says, "I come to offer you a choice deal. Like Monty Hall. Door number one, hijack the guns, and we part as friends, or, door number two, we turn you in for killing Bird and the cop during the course of a strong-arm robbery, and you'll be sentenced life at Walpole. I don't know, maybe you'll dig spending your days scooting around, like wormy dogs, dragging your ass along the floor, trying to keep the Butt Bandits away."

"Yeah," Donny says. "Like that's going to happen."

"Are you saying you'll welcome their romantic overtures?" Stan says. "A brawny, fine looking boy like you?"

Grayson says, "Why would we steal a truck load of guns for you?"

"Because if you don't, it will get messy? Is that a good answer?"

"Here," Grayson says. He picks up the security booklet, and tosses it to Stan. "The security booklet. Take the load yourself."

"Why would I, when I can get you to do it?" Stan says.

"We have leverage on you, too," Donny says.

"Think about this, handsome," Stan says. "The Dark Lords have chapters all over this continent, so I can disappear down a rabbit hole, in Mexico, or wherever, and enjoy all the creature comforts imaginable. Right after I drop a dime on you. Or, you can do this for me and we can be pals. Maybe have a picnic every five years to reminisce about the good old days. Laugh about Bird, and so forth."

"What are you going to do with the guns?" Donny asks.

"Me?" Stan asks. "Keep a few, sell the rest to the highest bidder. Amy's half, I don't know. Probably the Mideast, maybe Germany."

"Amy's getting half the load?" Grayson says. "Since when?"

"Oops," says Stan. "A slip of the tongue. But, yeah, that's the plan. You know she came up with the plan to take the guns, right?"

"Why should we believe you," Grayson says.

"You absolutely should not, not a thing I say, except this. You will hijack that load or you will regret it. You have 24 hours to give me your answer. The load moves in a few days."

Grayson says, "I've noticed, in all this back and forth, you've never asked us where Hugh is."

"Well, he told you he might be late, right?"

"How do you know that?" Grayson asks.

Stan shrugs. "How do I know anything? I listen, I ask, I overhear, I think. Maybe he went to the hospital? That's where your mother is, right?"

Grayson is thrown by his response. For once, Stan almost seems something like a human being. His answer seems genuine, informed and unaffected, and besides, Grayson wants to believe Hugh is at the hospital.

"You guys sure have a lot on your plate. How are you doing with everything?" Stan asks, with sincerity.

Grayson now knows it's an act. "Fuck you, man."

Stan appears wounded. "I'm serious. I want to know. I imagine Bird was your first, right?"

Grayson doesn't answer him, but he knows what he meant.

"That can be a tough one, your first. A lot of people aren't emotionally equipped to handle killing. I hope you're not a big symbolism guy. Are you?"

No answer.

"Because," Stan says, "In cultures around the world, certain birds are symbolic of the soul. So, I'm worried about you. A sensitive guy might say," and here Stan laid his forearm on his forehead, put on an agonized, old movie persona, and spoke in a high, mocking voice, "'Oh, no, oh, no, I killed Bird, and thereby I killed my own soul.' That seem familiar?"

He looks at Grayson and laughs.

"I'm just teasing you. Look, your brother won't be visiting your Momma anytime soon. We've had him in lockdown since last night. He's our insurance until you grab that load for us. I dropped his briefcase here this morning, so you can peruse the security info. Listen carefully. I'm not fucking around now. You're going to take that load. You're going to deliver it where I say. You're going to do it by any means necessary. You're going to do it without our help. We planned to help you but you don't want to play nice. Fuck it. Do it yourself. If you don't, we're going to kill your brother, then your baby mama, and by default, your baby. Although now, as I understand it, that isn't even a crime. I think that's what I read."

Grayson and Donny start toward Stan, but he holds out his hand in a stop signal. "Hold it. I have six heavily armed guys in the parking lot out back. They will storm this place and kill you both if I'm not back by a certain time. Don't get any stupid ideas. Any more stupid ideas."

Stan smiles at them for a moment, says, "Good boys." He salutes and grabs the door knob..

Donny turns to Grayson. "Baby mama?"

"Oh, oh," Stan says. He lets go of the door. "You didn't tell your best friend?"

"I didn't tell anybody. She might not be. It's uncertain."

"So, she visited the baby doctor in Wollaston, and got a vitamin prescription from him, and she might not be? Weird."

"Don't get too far ahead of yourself, Stanley. I don't think it's mine."

CHAPTER THIRTY-SIX

Grayson wonders if Stan was lying when he said he had Hugh. He tells Donny to go by Corinne's and see if he's there, and if not, go to the Dragon and ask if they've seen him.

At a variety store he picks up a fresh copy of the newspaper and reads about William Hawthorne's wake and the upcoming funeral. Cops are coming in from all over the country to pay their respects.

The District Attorney says they are still trying to confirm the identity of the man who'd shot Trooper Hawthorne, and then fallen, jumped or was pushed out the window. Thus far, they have found no next of kin for the shooter, so they are reluctant to give his name to the media.

The wake is being held in Scituate today from 2PM to 4PM and tonight 7PM to 9PM. According to the story the crowds are expected to line the sidewalk outside the funeral parlor. Grayson wonders why Hawthorne isn't being waked in his hometown, but figures the Cohasset funeral home, if there is one in Cohasset, isn't large enough to accommodate the anticipated crowd. Or maybe there isn't a funeral home in Cohasset because the rich don't like being reminded that they, too, will die.

Grayson was a participant in the murder of a police officer, as well as the killer of that goofy bastard Bird, so it seems like a good idea to stay as far away from the funeral home as he could. Scituate would be teeming with cops and only a fool would go there. Still, curiosity, cats, and so on.

He motors over to Route 3A south, and takes it to Scituate. The funeral home is on First Parish Rd. which is the main drag that goes from 3A down to Scituate Harbor.

He turns left off of 3A and almost immediately he is at the end of a line of slow-moving traffic. Even though it is an hour before the starting time for the wake, at the end of a long slow bend in the road there were two Scituate cops directing traffic.

Five minutes later he is near the front of the funeral home where there is a bunch of motorcycle cops in State Police uniform, that get up that looks like it was designed by someone who hated cops and wanted to make them look silly. The uniform has the weird pants which balloon out sideways on the upper leg, like the pants worn by ritzy polo players. The cops also are walking around wearing the Smokey the Bear hats, with the chin strap hanging down the back of their heads. They can't help but look ridiculous.

The cars going by the funeral home slow to a crawl, mainly to gawk. Grayson gawks as well, since there are so many other gawkers it won't attract attention. Meanwhile the Scituate cops wave their arms and gesture at the long slow lines of traffic from both directions. Periodically, they throw up a stop gesture as some car signals a turn into the funeral home lot from the opposite lane.

Right when he gets to the front of the funeral home a cop steps in front of the GTO and holds up his hand. Grayson feels his hair stand on end, which he thought, until now, was just a saying. But, the cop just turned and waved at the traffic coming the other way. Cars from the other side of the road crossed in front of him and make their way into the crowded parking lot, which is now jammed. Two State cops on motorcycles are halfway in the lot and behind them is a black Cadillac limousine with darkened windows. The limo is perpendicular to Grayson's car, and the rear window is about twenty feet from his windshield. Hawthorne's family is no doubt sitting behind the smoked glass, the widow with her life shattered by nitwits, one of whom is close at hand. He wants to crawl under a rock, or jump out and confess, or jump from his car and run away on foot. He wants to kill Bird again, this time with his bare hands.

After a time, the limo pulls in the parking lot and up to the front of the funeral home, but the other cars are still lined up crossing the street, blocking his way forward. Despite himself, Grayson watches as a state cop wearing long white gloves, opens the back door of the limo. A woman in a black dress and a widow's veil gets out and says something to the cop. The cop smiles sadly, and she sweeps him up in a gentle hug. Mrs. Hawthorne turns and looks out to the street, and her gaze falls squarely on the GTO's windshield, as Grayson's involuntary nervous system sucks in all the air it could fit into his lungs--the first step in activating the fight or flight response.

The Widow Hawthorne lifts her veil and pats it down on the top of her head. Then she looks right at Grayson and gives him a sad smile.

Amanda Hawthorne and Amy Nihill are one and the same.

CHAPTER
THIRTY-SEVEN

Grayson's skin is burning up as he sits in the traffic. His whole head is a bad toothache. The traffic is still stopped, as Amy, or Amanda, is ushered slowly into the funeral home. When he finally breaks free, he speeds back toward North Quincy. He crosses the Fore River Bridge (No Jumping!) and pulls into the Dairy Queen lot at a payphone and calls Hugh's place again. Just because Stan said he was holding Hugh captive it doesn't mean it's true. In fact, Stan told them not to believe anything he said. So, Grayson calls Hugh and relief sweeps over him when the phone is picked up. But the relief didn't last.

"Hello, Grayson residence," Stan says.

Grayson almost swallows his own tongue.

"Let me talk to Hugh," Grayson says.

"He's not conscious at present. Can I take a message?" Stan says.

"Where is he?"

"Guess," Stan says.

"What the fuck are you doing there," Grayson says.

"Looking for his toothbrush," Stan says "He's got one tooth left, so I advised him to take good care of it."

"Where is he?"

"Indisposed. But he will be disposed soon, unless…."

Grayson is silent.

"I said, 'Unless.'" Stan says. "Now you're supposed to say---"

"Fuck you, Stan?"

"No. You say, 'Okay, I'll hijack the truck.'"

"I'm going to need Hugh's help."

"We have the security booklet, and in it is the schedule, so we already know when the loads move, the route they're required to take and how they plan to protect them. What else do we need, guy?"

"There are a lot of unanswered questions. Where, when, how are we---"

"So. Are you in?" Stan asks.

"Yes."

"Welcome aboard," Stan says. "This should be fun. Although, I have to say I was looking forward to dishing out some punishment. You may not know it from my tone, but I don't like you."

"Ouch," Grayson says.

"Where is your cousin," Stan says.

"I'm the only one around," Grayson says.

"You and your pregnant girlfriend," Stan says.

Grayson is tongue tied, but only for a second. Then he laughs.

"Yeah, don't remind me," Grayson says. "You know how many little bastards I already have crawling around out there? I don't. One more, or one less, either way, no big deal."

Stan says, "I ain't buying that bullshit. Listen to me: In all my years, I have never kicked a pregnant woman in the stomach. Many of my friends have, so I feel a powerful urge to get that notch on my belt."

"I bet you'd love it. But, look, Stan, you cockroach, I will cooperate. I'll drive, but we have to plan."

"All right," Stan says, in a comically disappointed way. "Come over here. I have the security info, and a map already. Could be fun. Bring some snacks, we'll make a time of it."

"No. A public place. Meet me at the beach."

"Wollaston Beach?"

"Yes."

"Why?" Stan asks.

"So you can't kidnap me, too. Look, do you want to meet and reach an agreement or do you want to argue? Because I'm in no mood--"

"All right," Stan snaps. "Wollaston Beach. You're worse than a woman. Where?"

"At the wall, diagonally across from Billings St. I'll be there any time after five but don't make me hang around. You can tell Amy I'm in, but I want to talk about our strategy. Will she be there?"

"She's got the wake tonight, too," Stan says. "From seven to nine."

Shocked silence rushes over the line from Grayson's end of the phone. Had Stan let that slip? Or, had he spoken to Amy?

"What wake?" Grayson asks.

"Stop it," Stan laughs. "Don't be coy. You'll make me suspicious, and we're just starting to be friends."

"No. What are you--"

Stan says, "Do you think I don't know what you're doing?"

"What am I doing? I have no idea, so, how could you?"

"Ah, playing Mickey the Dunce again, your favorite role, I'm told."

"Now that I know the story, I want money. From her. Tell her I want twenty grand for hijacking the truck. It's a fair wage, and she's all for the working class being well compensated, right? Or is that her act?"

Stan says, "We all have to play our parts. I'll tell her, twenty grand. She's going through a difficult time and could probably use a good laugh."

"Five o'clock, tomorrow, Wollaston Beach. Are you going to see her later tonight?"

"I sure hope so," Stan says. "She promised to wear her widow's veil while I fuck her in the master bedroom."

"Be sure to pull the shades, so the five hundred people out front don't see you."

Stan says, "Good advice."

"So, are you just going to drive up on your bike? With the cops?"

Stan says, "I'll use my Benz. Cops? So what? I clean up nicely. Navy blazer, with brass buttons."

"What are you going to tell the cops?"

"They know me already. I'm her brother."

CHAPTER
THIRTY-EIGHT

Grayson opens the door to the apartment on Newbury Ave to find Ron Kerr and his latest hostage sitting in front of the TV in the living room. Kerr is howling with laughter watching a *Dean Martin Roast*.

Grayson sticks his head in to say hello.

"Grayson, you know Nancy Anne, right?" Curly says.

"Yes, we've met a few times. Hello again, Miss Cianci," Grayson says. He nodded toward Curly. "Mr. Kerr."

Grayson starts down the hall to his bedroom.

Seeing him go, Kerr shouts, "No! Come in here. You've got to see this."

On TV, Don Rickles is at the podium calling Flip Wilson a hockey puck. Seated at the dais, beside Norm Crosby, Dean Martin has the burning tip of cigarette butt smoldering between his fingers. Grayson expects Dino to jump up cursing, and douse his charred fingers in Joey Bishop's cocktail. Phyllis Diller, Peter Lawton and the rest of the gang are doing that exaggerated flopping around in their seats, a signal to the post production crew to turn up the canned laughter because, *this is hilarious.*

"Isn't that racist?" Nancy Anne says. "Calling Flip Wilson a hockey puck?"

"Maybe," Curly says. "But it is funny."

"He calls everyone a hockey puck," Grayson says. "That's why he is the court jester to the Rat Pack. And we all know how cool they are."

"What's the Rat Pack?" Nancy Anne asks.

"You know, the Rat Pack?" Curly says. "Frank Sinatra, Sammy Davis Junior, those guys. And, of course, Dino."

"Dino?" Nancy Anne says. "The dog on the Flintstones?"

"No, the guy on here," Kerr says, pointing at the TV. "Dean Martin."

Then Curly starts talking about his favorite Flintstones episodes, and how crazy were the clothes that cavemen wore in the old days and how he read somewhere that Fred and Barney were fictional people based on the real Ralph Kramden and Ed Norton. At that point, Grayson realizes that Kerr and Nancy Anne had ingested something from Kerr's cache of hallucinogenics and it has kicked in hard. Few things are as unpleasant as being around the seriously fucked up when you're straight. Grayson went to the bathroom, brushed his teeth and went to bed.

He can't sleep, so he tries to read but can't focus, and finds himself rereading the same paragraph over and over again. He's given up and is trying to will himself to sleep when he hears moaning and groaning, punctuated now and again by the occasional yip. It's coming from Kerr's room across the hall. Grayson puts on his pants, goes out on the third-floor porch to smoke a cigarette and wait for Nancy Anne's ordeal to be over.

Grayson sits on the porch in a lawn chair, smoking, shivering and looking at the sky. He takes a final drag, and steps to the edge of the porch to flip the butt off. Going by on the street below, he sees a LeMans, and when it passes under the streetlight it is identifiable by the good-sized dent in the roof, the result of an Idaho baking potato chucked by a lovesick sous chef. As the car goes by, Grayson almost calls out. He fantasizes for a moment that she's driven this route to catch sight of her beloved, and seeing him she'd slam on the brakes and beg him to take her back. But, the fact is, if she is just getting back from New York, this is the street she would use to get home.

He thinks about following her, but lacks the will to move from that spot. He's afraid if he tries to turn around to go in the house, he'd topple backward off the porch. Is that a fear or a wish?

And, if he followed her, again, what would he say? Things are way different now that she'd gone to New York. What can she say? He didn't want to face her and find out just how much more she hates him now.

He hears a familiar, blat and rumble of a blown muffler. A white van scuttles through the lamplight on the street below, and Grayson might have jumped down thirty feet from the porch to get more quickly to his car had he not realized his keys were on the table in the kitchen.

He races in, running heavily down the wooden hallway floor, bounces off a wall in the kitchen, grabs his keys and storms back down the hall and fumbles with the knob on the door. Behind him he hears shouts and questioning of some kind from Curly, but by the time he realizes it, he is at the stairs. He grabs the railing and vaults down to the landing where the stairs turn, between the second and third floor. From there he vaults down to the second-floor landing, turns, jumps to next landing, and so on until he's on the sidewalk, then running to his car. He jumps in the car, got the key in, lit it up and roars away from the curb and down Newbury Ave.

Moments later he comes around the corner of Catherine's street on skidding wheels, he drops a gear, the engine bellows and pushes on. Just ahead, he can see her LeMans at the curb, and down at the far end of the street a pair of red tail-lights are glaring back at him. The van is signaling a left onto East Squantum St. Grayson speeds up, assuming that some Dark Lords have grabbed Catherine and thrown her into the van, but as he passes her house, he sees Catherine standing in the light from the fixture over the front door. She turns to the street to identify the source of the ruckus. He jumps on the brake pedal, the tires screech, loud as hell at midnight, and the car slides sideways between the cars parked on both sides of the street and all together they form the letter *H*.

Grayson jumps out, starts toward Catherine, stops, looks down to where the van is turning, then sees her coming over to him, carrying a horrified look on her face. She has her pocketbook strap over her shoulder and she's holding a bulky paperback book in her right hand.

"What," Catherine says, "are you doing! Are you insane!"

Behind her, the front door to her house opens, and Mrs. Chrisolm appears in the doorway, her hair in rollers, clutching her bathrobe at the neck.

Catherine is in her waitress uniform, and she stands with one hand on her hip, the other holding the book.

"You were at The Harvest?" he says. "I thought you were in New York?"

"Is that supposed to explain why you're racing around out here like Evel Knievel?" she says. "Look at me. I'm shaking. You scared me. You idiot."

She swings the book at his elbow, giving it a sound whack, and the book falls on the street.

"Catherine!" Mrs. Chrisolm yells in a lady-like whispery voice. "Stop squabbling in the streets! Come in, you two. I'll make cocoa."

Grayson bends down to pick up the book and realizes he is barefoot and wearing only a tee shirt and pants.

"Mum, I'll be right in," Catherine says. She waves her mother inside without looking away from Grayson. "Have you been drinking? I thought you were going to quit?"

"No. I haven't."

"What the hell are you doing?" she asks.

He looks down at the book in his hand. *Doctor Spock's Book of Baby and Childcare.*

"What's this?" he says.

She has to refocus. She looks at the book.

"Suzanne Darwin gave it to me."

"What for?" he says.

"Take a wild guess."

"I thought you were in New York?"

"So? I got back this afternoon. I had to go to work." Her face softens, and she touches his forearm. "I'm sorry I wasn't here when you came over. When my mother told me, I called you. I guess you were at work, so I went over to see your father--"

"What, did you just go see your sister in New York?" he says.

"Yes, I ---"

"Then you went to work?"

"Are you going to let me---"

"Sorry," he says.

"---Answer? I wanted to see your mother. Did you tell her yet?"

"What do you mean?" he says.

"What do you mean, what do you mean?"

"What do I tell her?" he says.

She blinks, then closes her eyes a few seconds.

She says, "Well, even if we don't get married, we still have a baby to tell her about. And we should tell her soon, don't you think?"

Grayson pounces. "Yes," he says, nodding. "Yes, let's tell her in the morning."

Now Catherine sighs. "Oh, I can't tomorrow morning. I'm leaving at 6AM. For a couple of days, probably. I told my Uncle Greg I'd drive the equipment van up to Vermont for their high school hockey tournament. Chaperone the kids. If they get eliminated I'll be back sooner."

"With Sully?"

"No, behind him. He's driving the player bus, and I'll follow him. I'll be back the next night. We can tell her then."

Her repeated use of the two-letter word "we" land on him like a soaking rain on a parched field. Something has changed, her attitude has shifted, favorably it seems, but he doesn't want to press her for fear of finding out he is wrong. The bleeding has stopped, the wound has been bandaged, and to tear it off too soon was to beg for trouble.

"What happened at your sister's?" he asks.

"What? Oh." Now she looks pissed off again. "I went because I thought New York might be a good place to live after the baby comes. Close enough but far away enough, too."

"I don't want to live in New York."

"Yeah, well, that *was* the idea. Did you know John Webster has been sober in AA? I didn't. He hasn't had a drink in over a year. Maura says he is like a new man. She gave me hope. I might never forgive her for it, but she did. So, maybe it does work. Sometimes. For some people."

At the top of the street, a white Chevy van passes by slowly, and then comes to a stop. Catherine has her back to the van, but he sees it clearly. Indeed, from this perspective and distance, it looks almost like the van had driven through her head. Grayson takes an involuntary step toward the van, brushing Catherine to the side, and positioning himself so that he was between her and the van, and the van rolls away.

Catherine pushes back, and says, "What the heck are you doing? Why are you shoving me around?" She looks at him like he's nuts.

"Well, okay, then," Grayson says. He stretches his arms over his head, and groans, a fake full body yawn. "Oh, boy, I'm tired. Good night."

"What?"

His nerves are shot, and now he gets mad. "Never mind asking me what. Just go in the house. It's dark out and you're pregnant."

He bent to kiss her, and as he leaned in, she broke up the attempt and pushes him away. "Not yet, Buster."

"Just go in," he says.

He jumps in the car, wriggles it out of the tight spot, then backs all the way up the street, then onto Newbury Ave, turning every so often to watch her go into her house. He guns it after the van. He cannot screw around anymore, can't take the chance that things might work out okay, not now.

He has to wrap this up, he has to make sure nothing happens to Catherine and the baby. Or his brother, if he's not dead already.

He isn't cracking up. They are being followed by Stan and his confederates and flunkies. He has to meet with Stan and put an end to this for good.

CHAPTER THIRTY-NINE

Still barefoot, and in his tee shirt, without cigarettes or money, Grayson drives to Port Norfolk looking for the shitty house. He remembers driving by it before, but Charlie gave the directions, so Grayson hadn't been paying attention. But he doubts there'd be more than one with motorcycles parked outside, or maybe even inside. The house would have to be shitty if the bikers had been living there longer than ten minutes. They converted good things to shitty things like fire converted wood to ash.

He rounds a corner, heading toward the river and hears a rumble in the distance. Further down the street, some sort of chopped hog zips away into the dark. Grayson takes his foot from the gas and rolls down to the area the motorcycle came from.

More hogs lean on kickstands which dig into a bald lawn, and in the driveway is the van he's just seen go by Catherine's house. This is the same van that was on the bridge when Charlie had been launched into the night sky. It certainly looks like the same one, anyway. It has to be it. He comes closer to it, rolling alongside the high curb, clutch depressed, and the engine murmuring. The back doors of the van are open and a big guy is looking into the cargo space. He doesn't turn as the GTO goes by, probably because he didn't hear it, since many bikers are almost deaf from years of riding.

There are large shadows moving around on the porch of the house, and loud, incoherent shouting that seems to be coming from inside. Grayson keeps rolling, not touching the accelerator until he is well by.

Most motorcycle clubs had vans that followed behind the procession on road trips. The vans carried tools, replacement parts, gas and sundry items like firearms and bail money that would be needed in the event of a breakdown or other mishap.

Grayson kicks the GTO up and shot over to Tenean Beach, pulls into the double wide entry way to the beach parking lot, makes a U-turn, drives up to the sidewalk, so that he faces the street and is hidden by one of the two large bushes that flank the entry way. He kills the lights. Now what? He has to do something. He sits for a few minutes; no fidgeting, no smokes, no radio. Not really thinking, but imagining what could be done. He needs a gun and knows where to find one.

Charlie had stuck Donny's .22 down the back seat of the GTO, which Grayson had forgotten, until right now. Grayson jumps out, then into the back seat. He fishes his hand around in the seam between the seat and the seat back. He pulls up a pistol but it is not the .22 he had jammed in Donny's neck, the gun that Donny later gave to Charlie.

This is a short-nosed revolver, a .38, if he had to guess. It looks much like the gun Bird used to shoot William Hawthorne. Or, is he, or Charlie, mistaken about the gun Donny handed over? Grayson had been driving, so he didn't see what Donny had handed Charlie. Did Charlie say when he was getting out the car, 'I hid the gun,' or did he say 'the .22,' and if he did, did he know a .38 from a .22 or a Tommy gun, for that matter. Grayson sticks his hand back down there and gropes around some more. He feels another gun barrel in his hand and when he retrieves it, he recognizes the .22. What the hell?

Okay, so now the question is who planted the .38 in his car?

He leaves the car unlocked in his own neighborhood, like most people do. Maybe he'll have to start locking it up, because the times, they are a' changing.

He sits and after a while, the white van bounces by on shot springs with two large figures in the front. Grayson isn't able to see if Stan is one of the entities in the van. Most importantly, the van is headed away from North Quincy.

CHAPTER FORTY

At 6 A.M. Grayson is still awake and slumped down in the front passenger seat of the car, parked behind a big Grand Prix but with a sight line that took in Catherine's front door. His view of her place is fuzzy and clouded since it has to pass through his windshield, and the rear window and windshield of a Grand Prix. All that rounded glass at different angles is bad for clarity. He wants to go down there, ring her bell and tell her to stay in the house and be safe, but he couldn't tell her why, or that would be the end of the flickering "we" she'd floated last night. Something changed and the possibility of a joint future now teases him. He didn't want to screw it up. It would really aggravate her no end if he told her that her life was in danger. That would lead to a series of questions, and the answers to those would cast him in an unflattering light, and he'd have a whole big thing on his hands. At their easiest, women are tough to please; tell one you're doing your best to keep her from getting kidnapped by a motorcycle gang, and you *still* end up in hot water. He smiles to himself. No wonder guys drink.

A yellow school bus appears in the side view mirror with her uncle, Greg Sullivan, at the wheel. The half-sized bus rolls by the GTO and up to the curb at Catherine's duplex. The bus, marked with the name of the Catholic high school where Greg coached hockey, is called the midget bus by the kids. Inside the bus, the high school team slept with the abandon of teenage athletes. The kids seated beside the windows had their faces smeared against the cold, fogged glass. Catherine came out and got on, and the bus drove away. They'd stop at the school to drop her at the equipment van. She'd be safe driving in tandem with a hockey team.

Grayson drives back to his apartment. He is on the sidewalk when Kerr came out and passes by him, on the way to his job at the Mug and Muffin. Kerr did not appear surprised to see Grayson coming down the street barefoot and in a tee shirt.

"Morning," Kerr says, as he passes.

"Yeah, finally," Grayson says.

CHAPTER FORTY-ONE

Grayson sits on the Wollaston Beach seawall in the adequate light of the five o'clock sun, and watches the traffic pass by thirty feet away. If Stan shows up in the van, that would mean bad news for Grayson. They'd kidnap him, like they kidnapped Hugh.

Around 5:30, Stan pulls his motorcycle into a parking space at the beach, close to where Grayson sits on the wall. Stan undid the chin strap on his helmet, designed to look like a military pot, swings his leg over the bike and walks up to the wall about ten feet on the other side of Grayson. Stan puts a hand on the wall and leans over to look at the beach, probably checking for an ambush.

He walks over, close to Grayson, raises a foot and puts it on the wall and rests his forearm on his thigh. There he stood, like General Washington crossing the Delaware, except Stan looked demonic, not heroic. He's smirking as he takes off the helmet, and shakes his head and fluffs his hair, like The Breck Girl.

"First, where's my brother?" Grayson says.

Stan says, with a smile. "The already dead one? Or the soon-to-be-dead one, if you don't cooperate."

Grayson pats the wall beside him with his left hand.

"Come on, sit," Grayson says. "I said I'll drive the hijack, but first, I need you to answer my question. Where is Hugh?"

He pats the wall to his left again. Stan looks at him, and then sits on the other side, the right side of Grayson.

"I'm having some trouble figuring you out right now," Stan says.

"Is my brother okay?" Grayson asks.

"Do the hijack, and you'll see him soon after," Stan says.

"Okay. I don't like that answer. Is my brother all right?"

Stan laughs. "You know what you have to do to find out."

"Well, yes, but I'd rather not."

"Rather not what?" Stan asks. "Drive the hijack?"

"Go to the cops."

Stan shakes his head. "Listen to me, youngster, if you expect you and yours to get out of this unscathed......" Stan had seen something that took his attention.

Grayson turns his head to see what has alarmed Stan.

"Yeah," Grayson says. "A police cruiser rolls by about every ten minutes. I can always stop them."

"I wouldn't if I were you."

"Come on. Let's close this out. Tell me where Hugh is or I stop the cops and let the chips fall where they may. The clock is officially ticking."

He nods toward the Metropolitan District Commission prowl car rolling along the main drag in their direction. Grayson stands as if to hail the cops, but the police car stops about a quarter mile away, when five pre-adolescent boys run over and flag it down. The kids went to the window of the cruiser and are telling the cops something that requires the kids to point at each other.

"Tell me where my brother is or else," Grayson says.

"Are you that stupid?" Stan asks. "No, you're not that stupid. You deliver us the load of guns, and you'll see him again. If you don't, he's gone, your little honey is gone, along with your spawn, and then we go after your father."

Stan is trying to play it cool, but Grayson detects some rapid eye blinks.

Stan continues to blink and looks away. "It's simple. You do your part, and we'll do ours."

"You mean you'd shoot me? Like you shot Amy's husband?"

"First off, if you think I'm carrying while driving my bike, you're stupider than I thought. The cops are prejudiced against us, they stop me at least once a week."

"What I heard is what you're not saying," Grayson says.

"Man, you talk gibberish," Stan says.

"You didn't deny it. The whole plan was about killing her husband."

"I wasn't there. You were." Stan grins. "You're the one the kids can identify, not me."

"Okay," Grayson says. "Bird was going to kill the other kids, too."

Stan motionless, says nothing.

"And then, once we were away from there, we would have been killed, too. Me, Hugh, Donny, Charlie."

Stan says, "Why? We need you for the hijack."

"Yeah, that's right. You would have let us live until we hijacked the guns."

Stan shook his head. "'Look, let's start fresh. You have your complaints about us and vice versa. I say let bygones---"

The cop car starts rolling and Grayson stands back up and waves it down.

"Hey! Over here!"

Stan, excited and nervous, jumps up next to Grayson and grabs him by the arm and pulls him close. He speaks into Grayson's ear as if the cops in the approaching vehicle can hear him.

"Good work," Stan says. "The gun that killed Billy Hawthorne is in your car. And, if you say one word to them about anything, I'm gonna enjoy telling them where it is." It was only then that Stan notices the GTO is nowhere to be seen. "Shit! Where's your car?"

While Stan's attention is otherwise engaged, Grayson lifts the .38 from his right jacket pocket, and slips it into the left-hand pocket of Stan's Army jacket. He pushes Stan away and at the same time removes the paper towel he has around the gun. Between the push, the jostling and the excitement of the approaching squad car, Stan didn't notice the gun has been dropped on him. Meanwhile Stan's head swivels between scanning the beach parking lot for the GTO and the oncoming police car.

Grayson smiles and looked at Stan. "You're not quite so smug now. Let's see what happens."

Grayson waves again and pulls away from Stan. The cops didn't seem to notice them, until Grayson waves and hollers some more at the police cruiser.

Stan says, "You're going to be sorry, you and your family. If I get arrested, you'll have to deal directly with the big boss. Much worse for you and yours."

The cop car slows and pulls into the lot, and backs up. Grayson steps toward the car and points at Stan.

"This guy here has a gun," Grayson says. "He just drove up on his bike and threatened to shoot me, if I didn't give him my money."

The cops look at Grayson and at Stan as they get out of the cruiser.

Stan shrugs and displays a friendly smile. "This man is insane. I don't have a gun." He slaps around his torso, and when he gets to the area of his jacket pockets, a sharp look of consternation lodges in his eyes.

Grayson shouts, "It's in his jacket pocket. He showed it to me when he demanded my money."

"Not so," Stan yells. "He planted it in my pocket. It's the gun he used to kill Billy Hawthorne."

"Who?" Grayson says.

Now they had the cop's full attention, as is made clear by their drawn weapons.

"All right," one cop says. "Everybody freeze. Nobody move."

Stan fidgets and continues to shout.

Stan says, "He's a liar. He's the devil."

"All right," one cop demands. He has his fire-arm up and at the ready. "Both of you, down on your knees, now. Hands on top of your head. Now!"

Grayson kneels down on the asphalt, and puts his hands on the top of his head. But Stan must have seen he was in a bad situation, and came to a quick decision: He's going to make it way worse. What is two more dead cops in Stan's world?

Stan turns toward the water, puts a hand on the wall and vaults over to the other side, onto the sand. In a nifty show of athleticism, he removes the gun from his pocket in mid-flight and lands facing the street. He is, however, clearly dismayed at how low the wall is; it only came up to his chest. Stan drops out of sight behind the wall. One cop hollers, 'Halt,' while the other screams 'Stop.' As they advance toward the wall they spread out, and then the gun barrel appears on top of the wall about five feet from where Stan had disappeared. Stubborn Stan stuck his head up behind the gun barrel and a mere half a second later a burst of po-lice gunfire opens up. The first shot takes an ear off Stan, and the next one peels back his haircut, and with it, a good-sized chunk of his head. Stan is propelled backward and out of sight so fast he's gone before Grayson can duck.

"Drop your weapon or I'll shoot!" one of the cops' yells.

Grayson remains kneeling with his hands atop his head. "I don't have one!"

"Not you," the other cop says.

CHAPTER FORTY-TWO

Roughly two hours later there still are a score of cops at the scene, and after a time, one came up to Grayson and says he is making a coffee run to Dunkin Donuts and asks Grayson what he wants.

Now Grayson is sitting in an unmarked police car on the edge of the back seat with his feet outside on the ground, and his elbows on his knees. He's draped a blanket over the top of his head and shoulders like a prize fighter. Stan is dead, and Grayson still didn't know where Hugh is, but by now he's figured he has to be in the biker's flop house.

The scene, with its yellow tape and whirling blue lights and armed men, is a natural for television. For Grayson it's too close to home. He hopes the blanket wrap is sufficient to hide his identity. Across the street the crack newsmen from the three network stations in Boston are on the sidewalk fussing with their hair.

A senior level cop who walks like a pigeon came over with two coffees and gives one to Grayson. Then the old cop opens the front door of the car and wedges his ass-less behind on the edge of the front seat. He puts his elbows on his knees, mirroring Grayson, and begins talking to him. The cop is as loud as if he were standing across the road with the newshounds. He's past retirement age, judging by his old Irishman's white hair, puffed and rounded into drifts, and fat cheeks the color of cranberry juice. He could have made a nice buck playing Santa at Jordan's, if it wasn't for the growl that is his voice.

"Thanks for your patience, son," the senior cop says. "My two officers are very upset. Very upset. You know, their first thought was for your safety. They thought that the asshole was going to shoot you. It's only on the TV that the police fire warning shots, and tell people reach for the sky and all that sort of thing. We don't have that luxury. It's never a good feeling when some maladjusted son of a gun makes you shoot him. It is especially bad when his gee-dee weapon isn't even loaded. We call it 'suicide by cop.' He got what he wanted, whoever he was. He wanted to get his skull ventilated with your tax dollars and that's just what he got. We found a leather vest with gang insignia in the saddlebag on his bike, so we suspect he's in a biker gang. Maybe robbing someone is the initiation or something, who the hell knows. But better that this fellow gets killed, rather than an innocent man or one of my men. That's how I see it. I'm hoping you will agree. How about it?"

"I'm with you one hundred and ten percent," Grayson says. "That guy seemed like a frigging nut."

"I'm not a shrink, so I'm reluctant to diagnose," the old cop says. "But, if he wasn't a frigging nut, he'll do until one comes along."

"And how," Grayson says.

"When you're debriefed, make sure you explain that you felt in mortal peril, meaning you were in fear for your life."

"Damn right," Grayson says.

A couple of hours later, Grayson walks out of the MDC police station at Carson Beach and got into the front passenger seat of an idling, unmarked Ford. The man at the wheel is in his late thirties, wore a bristle haircut, a white shirt with a badge on the pocket, dungarees and a gun.

"I'm Detective Tom Bernardo. Thanks for your help in there. I understand you told the investigators that the guy had his weapon up and pointed at our men when he was shot."

Bernardo took off at top speed, heading back to Wollaston Beach.

Grayson says, "That's right. He was going to shoot. How were they supposed to know the gun wasn't loaded? If I knew the gun had no bullets in it, I would have punched him right in the chops when he demanded my money, instead of flagging your guys down. That bastard was crazy."

"Did you hear him say it was the gun used to kill Trooper Hawthorne?" Bernardo says.

"I was pretty shook up, at that point in time. But he was yelling something about somebody named Hawthorne. Is that the state cop who was killed? Oh, jeez, do you think that guy did it?"

"No, the guy who did it is dead, but that might be the gun. We're going to run a ballistics test on the weapon, but it smells as if it's recently been fired. We also printed him, see if we can find out who this guy was. He had no I.D. on him at all."

The unmarked cruiser pulls into the beach lot.

"Which car is yours?" Bernardo asks.

"That one over there. The Chrysler."

He points to a ten-year old Newport.

"We'll be in touch. Thanks for your help. We appreciate it," Bernardo says.

"I'm just grateful to be alive, Detective. I would appreciate it if you could hold off on naming me to the news. That guy has a biker gang and they may come after me for being involved in this."

"No problem. Go home and kiss your wife and kids, Mr. O'Brien," the detective says.

CHAPTER FORTY-THREE

Grayson pulls the Chrysler Newport into the lot beside the hangar sized taxicab garage. He locks the car up and goes through the front door of the garage. He trots over to the office in the corner, which is nothing more than an enormous crate with a big window and a single flimsy door.

The latest manifestation in the endless string of new night dispatchers slides a plastic window to the side.

"Need a taxi?" the man asks.

"No, I need to see Johno for a minute," Grayson says.

"He's in the shop."

402

There is always another new night dispatcher. According to Johno, in his first weekend shift this poor bastard would field a minimum of three hundred phone calls, with maybe half of them coming from the same dozen or so of drunks, each one of them ordering him to send a cab to get them, despite the fact most of them knew not where they were. Some of those who actually did know where they were would have, while waiting, another idea leap into what is left of their brains. They'd forget they called a cab and wander off. Besides, half of the time the drivers wouldn't go where the night dispatcher told them to go anyway. Within two weeks the new night dispatcher would be threatening to kill himself every time the phone rang. Then, very soon, there would be a new night dispatcher.

"Are you his brother?" the poor bastard in the enormous crate says.

"No," Grayson says. "We're cousins."

"You two look alike," the sad sack says.

"We heard that a lot when we were kids and hung out together," Grayson says. He pointed out to the shop. "I know the way."

In the shop, he hands Johno a wallet with a license in it and the Chrysler keys, and Johno hands Grayson's wallet and keys back to him.

"How'd things go?" Johno asks.

"Better than I could have hoped."

"You okay?" Johno says. "You look beat, kid. I know Aunt Mary's doing lousy. My father went to see her. I'll try to get over in the next few days."

"She'd like that. There's a couple of hundred dollars in the wallet," Grayson says. "Thanks again. Don't ever change the address on that license."

"I've moved five times since that East Broadway address in Southie. It comes in handy to have a license with an old address, a bad social security number and a name like John O'Brien. They say these computers they're all getting will put a stop to phony ID's and shit, but I doubt it."

"Hey, how is the scholar thing going? When're you done at Northeastern?"

"One more semester," Johno says. "Then, look out world."

"You got a wife, two kids, and pretty soon a college degree, all by the age of twenty-four, man. You're like an adult or something."

Johno says, "Next thing is get a real job, a day job, one that's clean and indoors, then buy a house. Get some slippers and a recliner and in forty years I'll be just like Grampa Spike! Only without all the girlfriends on the side. I tell you, man, there's hope for anyone with the love of a good woman. Having a family is powerful stuff, if it can even straighten out a fuckwad like me."

"Johno, one more favor. I need some gas and a gas can. Do you have one I can keep?"

"Yeah. You want a one gallon can? Or a five gallon? What do you need it for?" Johno asks.

"I'm going to burn down a house."

"You'll need the five, then," Johno says, and goes to get it.

CHAPTER FORTY-FOUR

Grayson parks the GTO under the low, full branch of an old elm on Walnut St. He took a walk over to the biker squat, and stopped where he could see in and yet be obscured, standing under yet another old tree.

The first floor of the biker house is well lit and the outside walls seemed to throb and bow outward to the beatless racket of Deep Purple. *Smoke on the Water* was the song to which the average tin eared doper invariably played air guitar. That one song was enough to make Grayson wish he'd lived before the discovery of electricity.

Underneath the amplified noise, a creature is screeching. It sounded like bacon was being stripped from a live pig. The door to the front landing burst open and a human body flew out to the street, and from the trajectory seemed about to turn a cartwheel, but instead crumpled to earth, and skidded. Four men in biker duds came out the same door and strolled over to the prone man. They tattooed him with a few desultory kicks, and then hopped on their bikes, strapped on their helmets and headed off leaving behind echoes and gasoline fumes. Grayson trotted over to the guy and saw he was out cold. Grabbing the guy under his arms, he dragged him, the only sound that of the man's boot heels scraping the sidewalk. He laid him down under a dying tree and looked at him. He was breathing, and Grayson poked him under the ribs. The guy squirms and winces. Grayson tries to rouse the guy, but can't.

Leaving him there, Grayson gets low, runs to the house and peers in a window. There are still a few life forms inside but they seem pretty well out of it. One is on the floor snoring, another is face down on the couch, and a third sits in a corner licking his forearm. He'd lick it, look at it, and lick it again. Then he looks around the room, does a long slow blink, gives the arm another lick, blinks again, and follows that with another look around the room, as if he is waiting for someone to bring in a saucer of milk.

The bikers must have learned that Stan is dead, and they are in mourning. It didn't seem much different than the way his uncles mourned; booze, brawl, then sink into a coma.

Grayson ran back to the car, pulls the .22 from the glove box, lit the engine and drives up to the house. He pulls the gas can and a rag from the trunk. Five gallons of gas, plus a sturdy metal can weighs about fifty pounds. Also, the sloshing around in the unwieldy can makes it very awkward to run with, and it stinks. He stops to catch his breath, and takes the rag out of his pocket and tears it in half. When he gets to the back porch in the back, he sets down the gas can and tries the back door. It is unlocked, of course. Who would be stupid enough to break and enter into a biker gang's crash pad?

He steps quietly around looking in the rooms at the back of the house, holding the loaded .22 down by his side. He peeks his head into the living room and finds the arm licking guy has joined his pals in dreamland. Grayson makes his way quietly upstairs, to look for his brother while checking for other Dark Lords. He looks in closets, under blanket piles, cots, in the bathtub, and every place large enough to hide a big man. Still moving at a whisper level, he heads down into the basement.

Down there is a wide, old dirt floor cellar. He pulls a shoelace strung from a bare bulb light and is surprised how bright was the light that came from it. There seems to be nothing in the cellar but stacks of old newspapers bundled and lined against the far wall. He goes over to investigate, but that's all they are, stacks of old newspapers. On the side wall he sees a wide wooden bin. It looked like a horse stall for the back half of a horse, but it was where, in times gone by, coal was stored after it was delivered down a chute put through the cellar window above it. Grayson, filled with fear, is sure he's going to find his brother on the floor of the coal bin. He goes right to it and looks over the wooden side and straight down. All he sees is the bumpy dirt floor blackened by years of coal dust.

Upstairs and out to the back porch and sloshes a quantity of gas on it. Then he walks all around the house, splashing the foundation and, as the can got lighter, on the old pine shingles above the foundation. He lights the rag with his Zippo and tossed it on the gas on the back porch. The resulting fire was a disappointment; it looks merely merry. He sets the can on the back porch, trots around to the front and goes inside. When he could see the flames out the window, he begins to yell.

"Fire! Fire!"

No one moves. He tries to rouse the arm licker. No dice. He then tries in vain to wake the other two. He runs in place, stomping his feet, thinking the vibrations might reach them, and he yells "Fire" several more times. Nothing.

The fire is getting serious quickly so one by one he drags the inert shitheads outside Not one stirs, even as they bump down the front steps. If they do wake up, Grayson is prepared to pose as a passer-by, valiantly rushing in to rescue the inhabitants of a house on fire.

"You boys know how to get fucked up," Grayson says.

Across the street, a man is standing on his porch, with his arms folded, watching.

Grayson runs across to the sidewalk, panting, acting the distraught passerby.

"Call the fire department!" Grayson yells.

"No fucking way," the middle-aged man says. "I wish you had left them to burn after you set the fire."

The man watches the sparks fly up into the night sky.

"I'll tell the cops, if they even come, their guys started the fire, then took off."

Back in the car, Grayson guns it in reverse to an intersection, and turns around. He shoots over to the Pony Room and parks, lights out. In under a minute he hears the fire trucks coming from the station a half mile away, up on Neponset St. When the fire trucks and cops were fully by, he flies across the bridge and back to North Quincy.

CHAPTER FORTY-FIVE

Grayson arrives at Hugh's apartment, fresh from burning down the Dark Lord's hive.

Grayson doesn't know what to believe. Stan is, was, a liar, so is Amy/Amanda. Hugh might not have been grabbed by them at all. If that were true, then where is he? Hugh would never run away. He checks around the apartment but sees no sign his brother had been there. In the bedroom, on the dresser, was a picture of Hugh in his football uniform, during his freshman year at Syracuse, standing with the varsity head coach, Ben Schwartzwalder. The picture causes Grayson to wince, the pain is like an abscessed tooth under the pick of a clumsy dentist.

Grayson, at that time a senior in high school, had been throwing passes to some grade school kids out on the street in front of the house. Hugh was home from Syracuse the week prior to the start of spring football and wanted to put a game together with the kids. It would be Hugh against his brother, each of them with three neighborhood kids. Grayson's team had the ball and his three kids all went out for long passes. Because they were kids, they all wound up clumped together, jumping up and down in the same spot yelling for the ball.

"No, fellas, spread out," Grayson yelled.

Hugh tried to stay in the middle of the street, ready to go in any direction to make a play on the ball. Grayson faked a pass to the right side and Hugh stepped with it, but instead Grayson lofted the ball in the other direction, way, way too high for any of the kids to catch, but Hugh turned and went after the ball, intent on an interception. Michael Grayson's football career ended when Hugh's car was T-boned by a crazy guy trying to kill himself and his wife. Hugh didn't see the guy coming because he was fiddling with the radio when he should have been paying attention. Grayson was in the passenger seat and as a result was near death for several days and in the hospital for two months. As a junior in high school Grayson was an All-Scholastic quarterback and celebrated for his ability to zip a tight, thirty-yard spiral to a precise spot. The precise spot he aimed for now was about eight feet up on the telephone pole. He let go of the ball and watched Hugh turn and run full tilt toward the pole, looking over his shoulder at the ball. Hugh running full tilt meant that two hundred and twenty pounds of highly trained college athlete was going to cover ten yards in less than two seconds. In the same instant the ball left his hand, Grayson wanted it back.

He screamed a warning, "No!"

Hugh and the football hit the pole at the same time. Like all defensive players, Hugh longed to touch the football, and like all injured players Grayson hated the guys who were still playing. When he heard his brother's bones cracking on the pole, he was sickened. Hugh made no cry. He was out, sprawled on the asphalt, as still and silent as the dead.

Hugh was right. Grayson did owe him. He is going to square it with him, no matter what it takes.

He slept like a baby in his brother's bed.

CHAPTER FORTY-SIX

A little after 9AM he drives up the hill on West Squantum St. and is making his way to Donny's apartment. He has the .22, but it only had five rounds in it so he needed more ammunition, due to the fact he'd never shot a gun. It is very likely he'd need to shoot off a lot of bullets before he hit something.

He pulls up in front of Donny's place, and shuts off the GTO. Inside the fence Carl Winslow, the cuckolded landlord, is pushing a mower. He is wearing a tee-shirt with **BFD** printed across the chest. Carl is the older brother of a guy that Paul Grayson had played baseball with in Pony League.

"Hey, Grayson," Carl says. He stops mowing. "How's Don?"

Grayson got out of the car. "Hi Carl. I haven't seen him yet."

Grayson looks up at the house and sees the concerned mien of Millie Winslow in the first-floor window. The front door opens and she trundles out and stands on the porch.

"Is he okay?" she says.

"I'm....What's going on? Did something happen?"

"Oh," Carl says. "You don't know? Don got shot last night, right here. That's his blood right over there." He points just up the sidewalk to a brown stain the size of a Volkswagen. "He was alive but unconscious when the ambulance took him away. To the Carney."

Grayson is speechless for a brief time.

"Who shot him? Did anyone see?"

"No. Like I said, he was out cold."

"Carl, come inside, I made French toast," Millie says.

"I'll be right in," Carl says.

She says, "Hurry up. The kids are at the table already. Yours will be gone."

"Millie, I'll be right in, I said."

Millie waddles into the house.

Carl says, "She's worried you're going to tell me something I already know."

Grayson jumps in his car. He thought it was quicker to go the Carney than to start calling a bunch of people who weren't home because they were at the Carney.

He asks for the room number at Information and runs up the stairs and down to Donny's room.

He pulls the privacy curtain open. His cousin is sitting up, sipping soup and listening to the radio news. His right arm is in a cast that runs from his wrist to his shoulder.

"Fuck happened?" Grayson asks.

"I got shot. Right outside my place."

"You're by yourself here?"

"My mother and your sisters just left. My mother has been here since I was brought in."

"Was it the bikers?"

Donny shook his head. "No. Uh, uh."

"Who was it?"

"I'd prefer to keep it under wraps. For personal privacy reasons."

"Who was it?'

Donny makes a face. "Sandra. Okay. Sandra. I told the cops I didn't know who did it, so don't say anything."

"Sandra? Who's Sandra?"

"You don't know her."

"Where were you hit?"

"She was aiming at my business, but I turned around and tried to run. I grabbed the fence, and I was trying to hop over it. She fired and hit me in the side of my thigh and I fell on the sidewalk and shattered my elbow. She came over with the gun, and I thought, oh, oh. Curtains. But she saw how much I was bleeding, started crying, really bad, and just said, sorry, and ran away to call an ambulance. I think the poor thing feels awful. She knows she messed up."

Grayson falls into a chair by the bed.

"Cripes," he says. "Who is she? You never mentioned her."

"It's kind of awkward. She's an older lady. She's 44. People won't know what to make of that. She wants to get married."

"To you? What the fuck?"

"Yeah. I think I might do it."

"What, you like her shooting you?"

"I love her passion," Donny says. "She's got it bad for me."

"Hey listen, I'm going to your place and grab your guns and so forth."

"Yes. Good idea. Thanks," Donny says. "That's stuff I might get in trouble for. In case the cops decide to search, who knows what they do when a person gets shot."

"Well, I need it, too."

"Right, no, I get it. Thanks."

But he didn't get it and it didn't matter, as long as Grayson had been straight with him.

Back at Donny's apartment, he tries the door and it opens. He goes in, does a fast look around the place, then hustles back into the kitchen and pulls open the oven door and sees the .38 in there. He pulls it out and heads to the bedroom.

In the bedroom closet he's moving giant shirts from side to side looking for anything behind the shirts, on the shelf, in the corners. In the corner of the closet there is a length of round black aluminum tube with a rubber handle. On the other end of are two metal pins. Grayson looks at it, then throws it on the bed.

The dresser drawers are full of clean socks, tee shirts and skivvies. The bottom drawer contains a paper bag which itself contains a box of rounds for a .38. He put the gun on the bed while he looks at the black tube with the electrodes at one end. He picks it up, read the logo, *HotShot*, and then figured out what it was.

"Jesus! A cattle prod?"

Grayson could only wonder what sort of sales pitch was used to induce Donny to purchase this item. He operated in zip codes that were entirely cattle-free.

Grayson sits on the chair in the corner, and looks at the revolver. He had never carried a firearm of any kind. The first time he'd used a gun for anything was when he held the .22 to Donny's head.

Grayson takes the guns, the cattle prod and bag of ammunition down the stairs and almost crashes into Millie on the porch.

She raises a section of her top lip in a sneer and looks like she is going to say something. Grayson raises a finger to his own lips in a 'shh' gesture.

"Don't speak," he says. "Not one word."

CHAPTER FORTY-SEVEN

"Please God, don't let me shoot myself in the nuts. Amen."

Grayson tucks the .38 into his belt, taking care to point the barrel away from the interior of his pants. He zips his jacket to cover it, grabs the cattle prod from the back seat and heads toward Gumby's place of business. He knows that Gumby and his brother operate their late father's printing business in the industrial area not far from Brewer's Corner. The business's main purpose is to act as a front for Gumby's real business, crime of all kinds. Anyone asking for a quote on a printing job, would be shocked to get back a price like you'd see on a new Cadillac. Consequently, the presses were usually idle and the taxable revenue stream was a trickle, at most.

On the only part of the building that faced the street is a faded sign that reads, *Gummer and Sons Printing.* The area where there once was a front door is bricked up. Grayson walks along the side of the building, out to the back. There are a number of parking spots and the new front door is now located beside a high, wide and closed garage door. He notes one could easily back a 48' trailer in there and close the garage door. The unlocked front door inserts you into a lobby so small there is only room for an old vinyl armchair, one person and a door to somewhere else. There is a doorbell beside the door to somewhere else, and above it, written with shaky hand and a black marker, a sign reads, *No solicitations! Ever!* The only other thing in the lobby is an 8x10 publicity picture of Shemp Howard tacked to the wall, above which, also written in a shaky hand is, *Our Founder, Franz (Gummy) Gummer 1890-1967.*

Grayson reaches toward the bell when the door flies open and he is grabbed at the neck of his zipped jacket and yanked into the somewhere else. He's sprawled on his stomach and when he turns over he's looking at the scary end of a sawed-off shotgun, wielded by homeliest guy he's ever seen.

"Can I help you?" the guy says. His voice is muffled by the rubber Halloween mask he's wearing.

"Hi. I'm looking for Gumby. Is he in today?"

"I'll have to check. Whom shall I say is calling?"

"Mike Grayson, Hugh's brother."

"What's this in reference to?"

"My cousin Donny bought this cattle prod here and I wanted to see if I could return it."

From behind, he hears, "What? You think I'm Sears Roebucks Junior?"

Grayson allows a small chuckle, unsure if this other guy is attempting humor.

Grayson assumes this is Gumby himself standing above and behind him, looking down at his face.

"Get up from the floor, come on," Gumby says. "It's making me dizzy, looking at your upside-down face."

Grayson gets to his feet, still hanging onto the cattle prod. Before him stands Gumby, legendary, but largely unseen. He is tall and lean, and has a high forehead and a long jaw, with a fearsome unibrow bisecting it all. He's wearing a pair of striped bell bottom pants that end high above his ankles and a long-sleeved thermal undershirt.

"Are you Hugh's brother?"

"Exactly."

He's standing with Gumby to his left and the masked man to his right. He grips the *HotShot* at the top, and holds it out to Gumby.

"I'm not taking it back," Gumby says. "I don't care what you do with it. How did you get it, anyhow? I sold it to Big Donny What's-his-name, that big lunatic from up Norfolk Downs."

"He's my cousin. He's worried the cops are going to search his apartment. He told me to get rid of it. I thought maybe I could give it back, rather than throw it out on the street where kids might find it. Start shocking the shit out of each other."

"Sounds like good, clean fun to me," Gumby says. "If you don't want it, throw it in the ocean."

"Won't it shock the fish?" the masked man asks.

Gumby ignores his henchman. "You're really here looking for your degenerate gambler brother Hugh. Am I right? I'm right aren't I? Come on admit it."

"No. Why? Is he here? He's not here," Grayson says. "He's too smart to get caught."

"He's right down in the room in back, asshole," the masked henchman says, gesturing with the shotgun up toward the street side of the building. That's when Grayson, backhand, whips the prod around and clouts him on the side of the head with the metal shaft. The guy lands so hard he drops the shotgun and it skitters away.

"Oh, no!" Gumby shouts and starts going for the sawed off. He's bent over, scrambling, and is almost to it, when Grayson presses the tip of the cattle prod into Gumby's kidney area. Gumby falls over onto his back and screams, "Ow, mother---" and Grayson gives him another, longer jolt, just below his chest.

"Stay down," Grayson says. He gives Gumby another jolt for good luck.

"Ach, ach," Gumby says, as his eyes flutter. He's panting up a storm. "I can't get my breath," he says, between the gasps. "I can't catch my breath." He's in obvious distress and Grayson kneels beside him and gets him to a seated position.

"What can I do?" Grayson says.

"Call an ambulance, you stupid fuck," Gumby says between gasps. "I have cardiac issues, all my life. Since I'm a boy." In between shallow, rapid breaths, he continues, "When I get back on my feet, I'm going to fucking kill you, and your brother." Then, seeing the tactical flaws in his announcement, he gasps, "I'm just kidding."

Grayson thinks about it. It takes him less than half a minute to decide he has to call an ambulance, then another 15 seconds to conclude he must be an idiot. Meanwhile, Gumby's panting has grown irregular and he starts to fall backward from his seated position. Grayson grabs him, and puts an arm behind Gumby's back to stop his fall.

Gumby says, "Shit." His eyes roll back and he relaxes totally, then begins to shake and then really relaxes and stops shaking. It seems that Gumby is dead.

Meanwhile, a key is inserted into the lock on the lobby door, and Gumby's ghost enters. He came back, quickly, having only changed his clothes. Grayson's blood is chilled until he realizes it's got to be Gumby's brother, and that they're twins. Gumby Two halts in his tracks when he sees his brother lying in another man's arms.

Two says, "What the fuck? What are you guys doing?"

"It's your brother. I think he had a heart attack. I think he's dead."

Two grabs Gumby from Grayson and shakes him like a rag doll. "Willard! Wake up! Willard!"

Grayson says, "I'll call an ambulance. Where's there a phone?"

"What happened here. Why is Jean Claude wearing a mask? And lying on the floor with blood coming out of his ear?"

"Let me call an ambulance first."

"Yes. The office down front, there's a phone in there."

Grayson runs to the front, and finds the door marked office. He finds the phone and dials zero then hangs up when he remembers you're supposed to call 9-1-1 now. After the call, he tries to open a few doors which are locked, then he comes across a door marked Break Room, which is open. Inside, Hugh is strapped to a straight-backed kitchen chair with a gag in his mouth.

Grayson strips the gag out, and undoes the strapping. Hugh tries to stand but falls back. His face is badly bruised and one eye is closed up from the swelling. His lips are swollen to about four times their regular size.

"There's at least two of them here now," Hugh says. Grayson has to recast the sounds in his mind before he figures out what's being said. "Gumby and Jean Claude."

"Gumby's dead. Jean Claude may be, too."

"We're in for it now," Hugh says.

"Maybe not. I've got a story to tell Gumby's brother, whatever his name is. I didn't know they were twins."

"Gumbo."

"Figures. Look, don't talk anymore, it must hurt, and you sound so funny, I'm afraid I'm going to laugh."

Hugh says, "Asshole."

"We're not going to escape, per se, I want him to let us go."

"How?"

"I'm going to tell Gumbo I rang the bell, Gumby opened the door and let me in, then this guy appeared out of nowhere, with a mask and a shotgun. He levelled the gun on Gumby, who collapsed in a heap, when the masked guy took aim at Gumby, I took the opportunity to brain him with the cattle prod. Now, if the guy wakes up, and has

426

amnesia, we're golden. If not, I hope I can come up with a Plan B. But this should get us out of here, anyway. So, stay in here for now."

Grayson runs back to Gumbo and tells him the ambulance is on the way. Gumbo asks for help carrying his dead twin out to the parking lot.

Gumbo says, "I don't want the cops and ambulance guys looking around inside the building. We got stuff that's none of their business."

"Should we carry the other guy out, too."

"No, that turncoat bastard. That low IQ swine. I'll get rid of him." He pauses and looks pained. "I was going to say I'll have my brother take care of him."

Grayson worries Gumbo is going to cry and then get mad at Grayson for seeing it.

Grayson goes back inside to confirm the existential status of Jean Claude. He lifts the mask a little to see Jean Claude's blank eyes. He listens for breathing and hears none. He looks at the side of his head where Grayson had whipped him with the length of the prod. He'd hit him just above his ear, and Grayson wonders if he'd hit and snapped a major blood vessel of some kind. He stands up and says aloud, "Jean Claude est morte."

Grayson almost falls to pieces when he realizes he's killed three men in just the last week or so. It's no consolation that they were all bad news, and in all cases their deaths were accidental. He came on this job to keep Donny and Hugh, his family, plus Charlie, from screwing things up. Now look. Four men are dead, when Hawthorne is included.

He says a Hail Mary for Jean Claude and Gumby, then adds himself onto the list. As he goes back up front to check on Hugh, he looks around at the hundreds of pallets of razor blades, power tools, French wine and premium grass seed that the Gummer brothers had acquired. No wonder Gumbo didn't want anyone in here looking around.

After discussing things with Gumbo, and twisting everything around to fit his story, Gumbo tells him that he and Hugh are free to go. But, Gumbo warns, he's going to need the loan repaid.

"It's a way for me to honor my brother," Gumbo says. "We can work out terms."

"How about a hundred a month? That work?"

"How much does he owe?"

"Three thousand? I think that's what he said."

"Okay. In any event, get your brother out of here, before I change my mind. I was told we were essentially storing him for those bikers. By the way, they roughed your guy up pretty good before they brought him. I'd take him straight to the hospital if I were you."

"Will do. Thanks."

"This business is just nasty, loan sharking, fencing hot goods, beat ups, hit manning, I never liked any of it. It's ugly. We don't need to do it. We have a first-rate print shop, and all the tools to make money right here, right now."

"All the best to you, man. I'll be rooting for you."

"I never wanted to be in this dirty business, anyway," Gumbo says. "I was just trying to protect my brother from himself. Now, I've got to tend to getting my brother buried, and that damned Jean Claude, too, although he'll be getting buried at sea. Then, I will immediately get to work to extract myself from this slimy operation, selling the hot goods and so on. Who needs it? I can make good money in the printing business."

"Oh, I bet," Grayson says.

"And, it's great fun, printing counterfeit money!"

CHAPTER FORTY-EIGHT

Hugh looks terrible and sounds worse. He's down to his T-shirt and boxers and is covered in ugly bruises everywhere that can be seen. He's moaning in the front seat of the car, and every time they hit the slightest bump in the road, he moans a little softer.

"Hang in," Grayson says. "We're almost there."

"She asked if I wanted to go get a coffee with her, we could talk about what had to be done."

"Save your strength."

"Instead she drove behind the Mr. Donut, where they were waiting. They yanked me out and beat the piss out of me. I was in and out a bunch of times and had no idea where I was, what day it was or the time. Then they said Stan was dead and

430

they were dumping me at Gumby's. Which meant I was dead."

"Yeah, but now, you'll be fine, and Gumby's dead."

"Did Gumbo say anything about collecting the debt?"

"Yes. He wants a hundred a month in an installment plan. I told him you owe three grand."

"How did you know?"

"Donny told me Gumby wouldn't lend more than three grand to the Queen of England."

"How come you were there?" Hugh says.

"I checked on the biker's place. No dice. I thought maybe Gumby grabbed you. I have the .38 Donny bought so I had protection. If they asked what I wanted I was going to pretend I wanted to sell them back the cattle prod."

"Cattle prod?"

"Don't ask."

"I appreciate you coming to look for me. That was ballsy."

"I was scared as hell."

"Makes you even braver." Hugh says.

"You're my brother."

"Did Amy go into hiding?" Hugh says.

"Let me tell you about Amy."

CHAPTER FORTY-NINE

Grayson is in Hugh's apartment getting some clothes for Hugh's release tomorrow from the hospital. He'd told his father Hugh had been in a car accident yesterday and they were keeping him until tomorrow.

Before he gets out the door, the phone rings, he's startled by it and considers not answering.

"So, Little Mikey Grayson," Amy says. "Did all your snooping around make you feel better?"

"Who's this? Amy Nihill? Or Amanda Hawthorne?"

"Both," she laughs. "Or maybe neither. Hey, have you seen Stan?"

"Not in what a day or so. I saw him down the beach. He might be there still, some tiny, little bits of skull and hair, anyway. But hurry, once the seagulls get on the job---"

"That's funny," she says.

"No, it's true," Grayson says.

"I know. The top cop on the State Police told me this afternoon that they had a lead in my husband's case. A gunman was killed last night in a shoot-out with MDC police, and the dead gunman had a weapon that ballistic tests revealed to be the gun that killed poor Billy. They expect to get the name of the dead man through fingerprints. He also had a tattoo that marked him as a member of The Dark Lord's motorcycle club. Last night they set fire to their own clubhouse and police now theorize that the fire was an attempt to destroy evidence in the case. Four men are in custody and the other members are being sought. They are presumed to be armed and dangerous. The Commandant of the State Police assured me that cop killers rarely make it to jail alive."

"Poor old Stan," Grayson says. "You don't seem too broken up about your brother getting killed."

"He said that?" She laughs. "He did love to shock people."

"So, he's not your brother?"

"No comment," she says. "That's two of our guys you've taken out. I'm impressed with how you pulled all that together at the beach. That was a nice piece of work. Very tidy. I really wish you would join our movement."

"Bird was an accident, and Stan got ventilated because he chose to point his gun at the cops, a poor choice, but one he made, not me."

"Oh, please," she says. "Be a man about it. Look what you did to your own brother, I heard about you running him into a telephone pole. You're like one of those sorority girls in the 50's, pulling her skirt up, while saying to her boyfriend, 'Please. Don't. Stop.' You love it but can't admit that because you don't want to face the truth about yourself."

Grayson chuckles, but finds nothing funny about what she said. Instead, it made him angry and almost sick. Is she right?

"My guess is you're not actually a revolutionary," Grayson says.

"I am so. It's just that I have another life, too. Plus, I like my efforts to yield benefits on many levels."

"Also, you don't like cops," he says.

She hesitates. "Wrong again. I do like them. I find them admirable adversaries in many ways. They have so many sterling qualities. They just happen to be on the other team."

"You like and admire them so you bomb a police station?" he says.

"Ah, I see. 'Do I contradict myself? Very well then, I contradict myself. I am legion.' Guess who said that? His initials are WW."

"Woody Woodpecker?" he says.

"No, wait a second. I don't think legion is the right word in that quotation." She pauses. "In any case, Billy was at a meeting with the drug cops in the station that day. Too bad it failed."

"You must have really hated him," he says.

"His death was an act of mercy. He was a tortured soul. Do you know who got the drugs his sister OD'd on? Him. That's how I met him. His sister was at Brandeis-"

"More bullshit."

"He dropped off some smack for her, and that's when I met him. He was rich and handsome, and tall, and rich, and funny, and rich. That weekend she used the dope and wound up dead. Maybe from a hot shot? Who can say? Billy didn't understand, since he and his hoity-toity Harvard pals used dope from the same stash. I was able to comfort him, poor baby. I was there for him. He loved me. I didn't hate him, not at all. I liked him enough that I hated to see him suffer from the guilt of providing heroin to his sister, which killed her. He's at peace now."

Grayson says, "You're a fucking monster."

"A very rich, beautiful, newly single monster. You think it's a big deal because Billy died, and his sister. Everyone dies. Ev-ery-one. It's just a matter of timing. You were born, in what, 1949 or 50? You did not even exist for 15 billion years, and you'll be dead for eternity, so what difference does sixty or seventy years make, one way or another? You're a one second spark from a fire, a fire that lasts ten million years. You're nothing."

"You did all of this to get rich?"

"*Rich-er.* I was rich the minute he married me. I still intend to redistribute it. Some of it, at any rate." She pauses. "It's funny. You think a hundred million is a lot of money when someone else has it. When it's yours, it doesn't seem like as much. Do you know what I mean?"

"Not really. So, I guess the gun hijack is off the table, huh? Now that your flying monkeys are on the run."

"You think so? No, sadly for you, it's on, very much so. My buyers are more excited, now that the Lords are out of the deal. Twice as many guns for them. Theirs is a wonderful cause, so I'm happy to help."

"Who are they? Maybe I'm partial to their struggle, too."

"Baader Meinhof," she says. "Let's just say they make Stan's crew look like Eagle Scouts. We, my small band and I, are hoping to go from affiliate status to full-fledged members."

"I wouldn't order new business cards, just yet. I found Hugh. He's safe."

"You did? That's interesting. Where did you find him."

436

"You know where he was. At Gumby's. What you don't know is Gumby's dead."

Silence on her end for a good half a minute.

"Hello, hello?" Grayson says.

"Who killed him? You?"

"And now I turn my attention to you."

She quickly says, "We know an awful lot about you, probably more than you know about yourself. And that little cutie who is preggers, we know all about her, too. Although, the last I heard they were trying to figure out why she's in a Vermont hotel with an entire hockey team. Is she that high spirited?"

He lets his silence do the talking for him.

"Listen,' she says. "We're done fooling around. You get on board or dust off your funeral suit. I'll meet you at Hugh's place tonight, after the funeral. Billy's brothers don't like me so they'll go back to their big jobs at H&H Capital in New York. I'll be surprised if a bomb doesn't go off in their office sometime soon. I'll ask the police to leave. I'll choke out a sob and tell them it is too sad to see uniformed policemen, and I need to be alone. You know I can act. Now that we've tested each other's mettle, maybe we can arrive at an accommodation. I want to point out a few things and see what you think then."

She hangs up.

Grayson is rattled by the facts: Amy and her thugs know Catherine is in Vermont. Amy made her point; she had people who could follow Catherine anywhere, and get to her any time they wanted. But not tonight. Tonight, Catherine was safe.

Grayson has to take the fight to Amy. He couldn't wait for her to come to him. He always believed the best defense was a good offense, except for when he believed the best offense was a good defense. Like The Old Man's "Hang On" and "Let Go" AA sayings, you just had to know when to do one or the other.

CHAPTER FIFTY

Grayson drove The Goat hard, muscling his way through the gears, once more flying by the *"No Jumping"* sign, and over the Fore River Bridge. The thought came that he is on the road to Hull with bad intentions. When he got to the Cohasset turn off at the rotary, he took it, his mind going faster than the car, but in due course, he stops well short of the Hawthorne house.

Back down the street, high on a hill behind him, on the opposite side, is the skeleton of a huge house under construction. He drives back to check it out. The house is roughed out, the framing work done, the bones fully exposed. He pulls on to the lot, where there are a couple of dumpsters and a construction office trailer. The tires slip and grab as he rolls up the muddy incline. The driveway is a series of ruts and mounds. He parks in between the dumpsters. Getting out of the car he makes sure of his footing, because the recent rain and ongoing thaw makes the muddy, bare ground very slippery. He zips his Baracuta Jacket against the wind, and snaps the pockets closed.

By the light of the nearly full moon, he spots a plank leaning against the foundation in the rough cut where the front door will be hung. He walks the plank up into the framework, and ahead sees the stringers for a staircase that opened wider and curved as it descended to the first-floor landing. It stood out amidst all the other raw wood banged into angles. If he can't see Amy's house from the first level, he'll have to get up to the second, but the stringers have no treads. He picks his way across the floor. There is just enough ambient light to think you can see where you're going. He steps carefully among the piles of lumber, stacks of plywood, and bundles of roofing shingles, kicking into the odd take-out coffee cup. He walks the bouncy floor over to the wide hole where a picture window has been boxed out. He can almost see all of the front and one side of the Hawthorne house from here, but he can't see it all the time because of the trees waving back and forth in the wind.

There were several cars in the circular drive, but not Amy's Corvette. It must be behind one of three doors in the free-standing garage.

He has no firm idea what he is going to do but he has a clear eye on what he wants the result to be. He wants Catherine and the baby to be safe, and he wants his brother left alone.

In any event, he can't do anything now because the post-funeral get together seems to be still hanging on. He smokes and watches her house and the driveway. As time passes, people get in their cars and drive away in Mercedes, Caddies, and Volvos. There are no Harleys at this gathering. Off and on, Amy, would walk her guests to their car, hugging herself against the cold March wind which carries the smell of rain. The wind is strong enough to push around the pines and bushes, here and across the street.

When the last car pulls out of the driveway, a light rain begins to fall as she walks slowly back inside, alone, arms folded across her chest, like the brave widow in a 40's war movie.

His eyes had adjusted all they're going to, so the movement he believes he sees in the deeper darkness beside Amy's house came with a disclaimer. He doesn't know if the movement is animal or vegetable; it may have only been the wind slapping a hedge around.

Twenty or so minutes pass, when door number three on Amy's garage rolls up, and the Corvette backs out, turns and zips to the top of the driveway and sits with the turn signal blinking. Then she turns the car toward Quincy.

Grayson runs heedlessly across the cluttered floor, tight-rope walks down the bouncy plank until he reaches a height safe for jumping, and leaps in the direction of his car, pitching forward on impact, so that he ends up on all fours. He stands and tries to wipe the mud stains from his hands onto his pants before he reaches in his pocket for the keys. His view of his hands improves immeasurably when the Corvette pulls onto the lot, too, and lit him up with headlights on high beam. She gets out of the car holding a gun.

"Don't move or I'll shoot," she says, followed by a peal of laughter. "Doesn't that sound so fun."

She's changed out of her widow wear to dungarees and sneakers.

Grayson says, "How do you like this neighborhood? I'm thinking of buying this place."

"You couldn't afford the taxes, never mind the house. Not even if you stopped smoking. I spotted the glowing tip, looked out poor Billy's telescope and saw you lurking in the shadows."

"Listen, I thought I'd meet you here, save you driving up to Quincy, your eyes all full of tears."

"I have new orders. I'm going to kill you. You're not going to hijack the truck, you're lying and stalling for time and without an inside man, we're out of business. We were looking forward to getting a trailer load of guns. But, there will be other ways on other days to acquire weapons. You're too much trouble."

"Sorry. I hope you're not in any trouble with corporate."

"No, but I do want to tell them I killed your chick and her baby and your brother in revenge," she says. "And then you, but only after I let you live long enough to suffer through it, knowing it's your fault they're all dead."

A heavier rain moves in and washes her hair over her eyes. She pushes it back with the same hand holding the gun, giving him time to duck between the dumpster and his car. He unsnaps the jacket pocket and takes out the .38 he'd gotten from Donny's oven. When he pops his head out, she fires, shattering his passenger side headlight. She turns and slips and slides back to her car. Grayson starts toward her but the bumpy, slick ground got the drop on him. His feet flew out from beneath him and he wound up flat on his back sliding toward her car. He decides to stay sitting on the ground where he is, about ten feet away from her. He holds his ground and trains the .38 on her.

"Don't move," he says. She looks at him and the gun and then rolls her window down.

"I said, don't move. I will shoot you."

He means it. He can't take a chance that she will get away, he believes her now when she says she'll go after Catherine and the baby. He has to make sure she doesn't get away. He's going to have to turn her and himself in and tell the entire story to the cops or the Feds or whoever.

She says, "Where did you get a gun? I thought you were against them, Mr. Limp Dick, stick-in-the mud."

"This is the gun Bird sold Donny. Ironic, huh?"

"I'm leaving." She smiles. "Go ahead, Killer, shoot me."

"Don't move or I will."

"I don't think so. I'm off to coordinate the kid-nappings. I mean, of little Cathy and her tadpole, plus Hugh. I shouldn't have said tadpole. The fact that you'll suffer so greatly when it's dead, proves it's a baby."

He gets up and moves toward her but stops when she unleashes a loud, almost glass shattering scream.

She says, "I'm sure the neighbors heard that. How long before the cops come? Who are they going to believe? Me? I live here on Jerusalem Road and I'm the widow of a heroic slain policeman. Or you, a would-be rapist from Whitetrashville?"

She puts up her window and locks the door, smiling all the while.

He shuffles forward, careful not to fall on his ass again, and stands near the window, pointing the gun at her.

"I will shoot you," he says. "Stay there."

She shakes her head and starts the car. He holds the gun out, and cocks it.

She rolls the window down slightly. "See? You'd love to kill me. Come on, admit it." She smiles and puts the transmission into reverse.

"Final warning," he says.

She says, "Bye-bye, tell your little girl I'll see her soon."

He extends his arm, aims and squeezes the trigger, again and again. The car rolls backwards out to the road, and Grayson looks at the .38 in his hand.

Out on the street, she runs the window down. "You fired right at me. Lucky thing Bird took out the firing pin before he gave it to your handsome, but stupid, cousin. Ironic, huh?"

She puts it in gear and takes off.

He makes his way up the hill and jumps in the GTO, rolls out to the street and turns after her. He reaches into the glove box and pulls out Donny's .22, and puts it in his jacket pocket.

Grayson hits the gas and speeds through the turns along the hilly road. He sees her taillights ahead and he turns off his headlights. He closes in on her and runs his front end up close to the tail of the yellow Vette, pulls his lights back on, steps on his brakes and flashes his high beams, dropping back quickly. She slams on her brakes and comes almost to a full stop. He veers to the other side of the road, planning to run up in front of her to box her in, but she figures it out and rockets off. He jumps on the gas and they slalom along in tandem on the unlit road. They fly up and over the hills and down again and skid into the turns on Jerusalem Road, but they are going too fast when they head into the lazy S turn close to her house. Before they reach the low bridge over the channel that linked Little Harbor to the ocean, Amy jumps on the brake and then speeds up again, but this time Grayson doesn't slow down. He pulls the GTO to the left of the Corvette and races up on the other side of the road, pulling even with Amy. He blows his horn and veers toward her, pulling back before the cars make contact, but she doesn't pull over and stop. Instead, she flinches and snaps the steering wheel away from him and the Corvette launches off the road, flies between two trees, turns driver's side down and bounces over a few smaller boulders before landing upright in the water of Little Harbor. He jams on the brake, backs up and looks out at the car. The window and windshield are in place but shattered. The car door is badly damaged. There's no movement in the car that he can see.

Grayson rolls onto the bridge and stops. He jumps out and runs to the railing on the Little Harbor side. He sees the yellow Corvette sitting in water up to the bottom of the window. The water is too shallow here to swallow it whole, but deep enough to carry much of the weight, and the Corvette body is made of fiberglass, just like a Boston Whaler.

He spends a couple of seconds trying to see through the dark to find the quickest way to get down the rocks to the car. The spring tide and full moon has filled the harbor past its usual measure but now the tide is going out which means the flow of salt water through the channel to the ocean is greater than usual, too. The Corvette shudders as the great suck of the outgoing tide grabs it and pulls it from the rocky bank and toward the roll of the water which sluices underneath the bridge, passing some eight feet below. He can see Amy's silhouette through the windshield, she's slumped over the steering wheel, not moving. The partially submerged yellow car floats along to the rushing water and slams into the rocks on the passenger side of the car. With both doors crumpled it's unlikely he'll be able to get them open.

Should he stand here and watch her drown? That will solve the problem, certainly. But, she could also float along, under the bridge and out to the bay, and maybe find her way out of the car and swim back to some place along the shore. No, he can't chance it.

He runs up to the GTO and opens the trunk. He's looking for a tire iron, or anything to pry out the shattered windshield and get her out. The tire iron is under the spare, and the spare is bolted to the trunk floor. By the time he could get it all unfastened she'd either be sunk or halfway to Truro. He spots his utility knife and knows he can cut through the canvas convertible roof and pull her out that way. He sticks the knife in the jacket pocket holding the .22. He goes back to the bridge railing on the Little Harbor side. The water underneath the Vette is picking up speed. He can't jump in on this side, too many rocks and the car is bouncing along helter-skelter. The car could easily push him into the rocks ahead of it.

He crosses the bridge and climbs over the railing on the ocean side and finds there is almost no footing. He turns around, puts his heels on the lower bar of the bridge rail, leans his back against the railing to face the sea, arms extended to the side, holding tight to the top rail, waiting for the Corvette to pass by in the channel underneath.

If he jumps feet first onto the convertible top he would likely bounce off like some goofball on a trampoline, so when the time seems right, he lets go, falls forward and lands a belly flop on the canvas roof. He bangs his chin off the top of the windshield, and sees stars, but he shakes it off and manages to hang on by clutching to the roof on both sides of the car. The vehicle is picking up speed as the banks of the channel narrow and the flow of water quickens. The forward motion of his landing gives the Vette some extra momentum but his weight causes slightly more submersion. They are still going out with the tide. He inches forward and looks through the fragmented windshield to see Amy's face registering confusion. Perhaps wondering about the thump of two hundred pounds of Grayson landing on the canvas roof. Then she sees him peering in, his face upside down.

"You!," she screams, above the sound of the rushing water. "You did this to me." Grayson is an old hand at waking up in surprising circumstances, so he can't help feeling some sympathy. Worse for Amy is she has to deal with the added complication of Grayson on the roof, and he can tell she doesn't much care for the prospect.

"No, no, no." She sounds like a bitching blue jay.

"I'm going to cut the roof and get you out," he bawls.

He gets up to his knees, grabs the box cutter from his pocket, slides the blade out and presses it into the convertible roof, cutting a two-foot slice.

The car is almost out beyond the mouth of the creek and starting to sink further down. He again slices the roof, this time perpendicular to the first cut and peels back a good-sized piece.

"Give me your hand so I can pull you out."

She reaches up and he grabs her hand and begins to pull, but she's stuck.

He looks down at her. "You have a seatbelt on? Who the fuck wears a seat belt? Unlatch it." She tries to unbuckle the belt but the rising water is causing panic and she starts screaming. She finally gets the belt unlocked and she's moving up toward the hole on her own.

"My bag," she shouts. He sees her leather handbag on the dash in front of her, where it has wedged, probably after being thrown about in the crash. He's dumbfounded: Her bag! But, it becomes clear why the bag is important when she reaches into it and pulls out the revolver and points it at him.

"Get me out," she yells.

"I'm trying. Just give me your hand."

He sticks his arm in, grabs her left arm above the elbow and begins to pull. He's making progress, she's standing on the driver's seat, as he starts to push himself up to his knees.

"You're not turning me in," she says.

"Of course not. Hurry up!"

"Of course not!" she says. "Sap!"

Hearing that, he lunges to the side as she pulls the trigger, firing point blank into his upper chest. The shock is like being hit with a lead pipe swung by a gorilla. He falls forward onto the cut canvas and then through it, his weight driving her back down into the seat where he finds himself on top of her. He passes out from the shock of the bullet slamming into him. When he comes to, he sees his body has her pinned down. Unfortunately, his arm and shoulder and her torso are wedged in the space between the bottom of the steering wheel and front part of the driver's seat. When he tries to pull his arm out, the grinding pain in his upper chest is like nothing he's ever felt before. It has him panting. Underneath him, Amy's wriggling and gasping are getting more frantic.

He lifts his face off the side of Amy's head, she comes up for a gulp of air just before the rising water covers her head again. The water is coming in faster and the added weight of that water is coupled with his added weight, so it's getting worse by the second. Her head is now completely under water and she's struggling. Like a yellow submarine, the car continues to move forward while sinking.

He's trying to push himself off her but with each move he's hit with blistering pain. His right arm is useless, and between the bleeding, panicky exertion and heavy breathing, his oxygen supply is going fast. With each movement he tries to make, his whole upper body is jolted with pain, pain that takes his breath away. He fights through the pain and finally gets his arm free, but the struggle exacts a great price and as the water keeps rising he's all the way under it now and between the pain and not being able to breathe, he falls into the void.

CHAPTER FIFTY-ONE

A few hours later Catherine is standing at the window taking small sips from a glass of water, trying to quell a bout of sudden onset morning sickness. Ron Kerr pulls up out front and comes up the walk with an envelope in his hand. She hears him open the screen door just as she reaches to open the inside door.

"Hey, Catherine," he says. "Grayson gave me this to get a stamp and mail it, maybe yesterday or the day before and I kinda forgot to do it. I just found it in my car. I saw it was for you so rather than mail it, I thought, it'd be quicker if I drop it off on my way to work."

"Oh. Thanks, Ron."

"Do me a favor, and don't tell him I forgot. He's been in a wicked bad mood."

Kerr lets the door go and turns back to his car. She sees her name on the envelope, written in Michael's hand. She sits down and looks at it for a time before she opens it. Tucked in the envelope is a check wrapped in a handwritten note. Her name is on the check in raised letters and red ink. Printed under her name are raised numbers in blue. It looked formal, final, and it made her anxious.

C, - This is a bank check which means I don't have the money anymore, meaning I already gave it to the bank. If you rip this up the bank will keep the $15,000 and not me. This amounts to the money I saved for us to get married. If you throw this check away you will only make the New England Merchants Bank very happy, which I don't get why you'd want to do that. I've been thinking about when we took the train to NYC the June we graduated. When we went into that weird little restaurant and I ordered clam chowder and the hippie waiter brought me vegetable soup with celery, tomatoes and other stuff in it. I said I didn't order vegetable soup and the hippie asked if I was from Boston and then he said, "Man, you are a stranger in a strange land. Maybe it's not what you wanted, but you got what you asked for. And I'm sorry but that is your problem if those are two different things."

I don't know what I can say to make things better, so far it seems like what I've said in trying to make things right has just made you mad. So, I'm going to say what I want. I love you more than anything. I can't imagine living without you, although I wouldn't kill myself or anything like that, so don't worry. I say that because it looks like you decided you've had enough of me and my bull. For a long time I thought I loved to drink. When I realized love had nothing to do with it, I thought about quitting but I couldn't see how I could manage myself without it. I felt like it kept me sane. If I had to live without drinking, I'd murder someone (Donny, Hugh) or have a nervous breakdown. For at least a year now I haven't wanted to drink and tried to quit many times but I'd end up drinking anyway. It's very hard to admit that. I couldn't stop for long. I can't explain what happens to me. But now something inside me has changed and I don't know when it did exactly. Or what is different. When you said you were going to have a baby, I made up my mind in that moment that I was through drinking for good. And I really meant it. But I didn't even get out the front door when I knew I was on my way to the liquor store. It was like I was trying to fight off a tornado with my fists. I talked to this guy who helps my father with the AA stuff. He's kind of a jerk but he says he's willing to help me, too. I'm going to go there and try again because the guy says I don't have to drink anymore and it was weird but I kind of believed him. I hope I can talk to him while not drinking and without trying to strangle him. I see now that I have to do this for myself, and not you, and not my mother or father. I'm worried that you will think to yourself, "Oh sure, now that he doesn't have to worry about supporting a wife and a baby he can get squared away." If there was any way we could go back in time to when you still loved me, I guarantee I would be different. I know that's no consolation and may even make you feel worse. If so, I'm sorry. I'm really sorry about everything that happened to you because of me being who I am, or what I am, is a better way to say it. Maybe one day we can talk. But if I could see you happy with a happy baby that was ours, I would never need anything more in my life again. I have to do it mostly because of the memory of the baby that we lost because of me. If I don't do it our baby's little short life would be even more of a terrible ache and I am not tough enough to live with that. I'd much rather be dead.

EPILOGUE

About forty-five years after my father, Michael Grayson, wrote that letter to my mother Catherine, I tried to smooth the letter flat on the dining room table, but when I took my hand away the parched paper folded itself along the old seams that were as much a part of the whole now as the ink. I re-sealed it in the plastic freezer bag, cloudy with age, and put it back in the fireproof box that I'd found among my mother's things.

I stood up to put the box in the corner with the other stuff going in the car, rather than the moving van.

I looked out to the backyard, where Daniel, my ten-year old, was playing ball in the same yard I played in at his age. I thought about how our lives, my sisters and brothers and I, would have been very different if the local police hadn't been called to the area after various neighbors reported a woman screaming, cars racing around, and a crash. The first cop that got there saw my father jump off the bridge. The cop stopped his car and got out. He saw my father cut the roof and stick his arm in through the roof. The cop then went back to his car to get a flashlight. When he looked again, the car had wedged itself between a large rock in the water and the great rocks on the bank. Now, only my father's lower legs were visible. The cop ran over, slid down the rocks to the water, and soon was joined by a second cop, and together they yanked my father out through the roof of the Corvette. They got him breathing again, and went back to the car but by the time they got Amanda Hawthorne out, she was beyond saving. The Cohasset police called my father a hero for trying to rescue her. Why she'd shot a guy trying to save her remained a mystery, although the consensus opinion was that she was knocked out in the accident, and woke up to a nightmare, in her terror became irrational and may have thought my father was trying to kill her.

In the back of our house my son Daniel trotted into view, coming from a section of the yard I couldn't see. He passed by the old umbrella pine tree, threw a feint at an invisible defender, cut a sharp right turn and put on a burst of speed, arms pumping, elbows tucked, racing toward the house. He looked back, reached up, and as I watched, a football fell softly out of the sky and into his hands.

Made in the USA
Middletown, DE
03 April 2020